LuLu Books by Pam Garlick

At the Pineapple Inn

*Into the Flames

* Everyday Heros Series

INTO THE FLAMES

by

Pam Garlick

Pam Garlick

Pam Garlick admits to writing her first short story when she was 12 years old, though she won't admit how long ago that was. She remembers her struggles as a single-mom juggling the raising two lively sons and a job, and still trying to find time to write. She'd find herself typing on her old portable typewriter late at night, recycling any papers she could get her hands on for her manuscripts.

Then twenty years ago she received a computer as a birthday gift and her life changed. In 1988 she sold her first article and short stories soon followed. Today she's been published in a variety of media.

Pam lives with her husband and two dogs in southeastern Pennsylvania where they are actively involved with their church. Much of what she writes is driven by her faith.

As much as she enjoys writing, she treasures her time away from her computer when she can be with their five children and four grandchildren.

Published by:
www.lulu.com

ISBN 987-1-4203-2645-8

DEDICATED TO:

Those who save the lives and those who support them; but, most of all, those who have the vision of a better way.

ACKNOWLEDGMENTS:

To all my special friends -- you know who you are -- my sincere thanks for believing anything is possible. And, to my husband, who has been patient while I chase my dreams. But most of all, to the Lord my Savior, because without His unending love, I'd be lost in a dark world.

He comforts us in our troubles so that we can comfort others. When others are troubled, we will be able to give them the same comfort god has given us.

2 Corinthians 1: 4 NLT

PROLOGUE

The ringing of her alarm clock disturbed Lacy's dreams. She reached instinctively for the button to silence the shrill beeping sound even before her eyes opened and registered the total darkness. No wonder she was so tired: it was the middle of the night.

Then the beeping changed to a scratchy voice and she was immediately alert, listening as the dispatcher's voice came across the airwaves, giving the type and location of the emergency. Lacy felt the bed give and the sounds of her husband, Mike, quickly slipping into the clothing he kept close beside their bed.

"Eleven Eighty Cindy Lane, a structure fire," the dispatcher's voice stated, as Lacy flicked on the bedside lamp, squinting as her eyes adjusted to the light. She, too, rolled from the warmth of their bed, as quickly as her eight month pregnant body would allow.

"People still inside," the disembodied voice continued. As adrenaline started to flow more swiftly through Lacy's veins, she said a silent prayer that whoever was still inside the structure would be okay. She grabbed her maternity jeans and slipped them beneath her cotton nightgown.

"What do you think you're doing?" Mike said gruffly as he slipped socks onto his bare feet, followed swiftly by his *Nike* sneakers. These were the only times Mike wore socks with his sneakers. Many years ago, he had learned that blisters and open sores were a firefighter's reward for slipping bare feet into heavy rubber bunker boots.

"I'm coming, too," Lacy replied simply. "It's a sure thing I won't be able to go back to sleep."

"Lacy, you know you're out-of-service till after the baby's born," Mike stated harshly.

"I'm not going in-service," she spat as she hurriedly slipped her gown over her head. "I'll just watch."

"That'll be the day," Mike replied sarcastically as he rushed toward the door, with Lacy following, still buttoning her blouse. "Even 'God' says the paramedics can manage without you till after the baby comes."

Lacy bit back her retort, knowing there wasn't time, now, to fight over the nickname "God" many of the firefighters, including her husband, gave to the chief of the city's rescue crew.

It wasn't that she totally blamed any of them. She knew, as well as anyone, that Brody Langford wore his authority like a general wears his

1

clusters. But the fact was, putting his conceit aside, Brody had every reason to be that way. Aside from the fact he was Rescue Chief, Brody also was the best paramedic in Schuylkill Valley – in Montgomery County, for that matter.

Truth was, she admired Brody's skill, if not his disposition. She'd probably trust him nearly as much as Doctor Kelly to deliver her baby, more if she were to deliver in an emergency. She didn't know anyone who kept their cool more than Brody.

Of course, she didn't admit any of this to Mike. He already had enough resentment toward the other man. Mike blamed Brody because she had chosen to become a paramedic. At the time, she had thought Mike would be happy she had given up firefighting. Instead, if anything, he grew more bitter.

Knowing how he felt, she sometimes wondered how he had ever managed to fall in love with her. She never wondered about her own reasons for falling in love with Mike. She had admired him for so many years as they worked side-by-side fighting fires. Next to her father, he was the best firefighter she knew.

"I'll stay out of the way," she promised Mike as he raced toward the door. "I'll probably see if I can help the Ladies Auxiliary. I'm sure they'll be out for this one."

To that, her husband only laughed. That was another of his pet peeves. As far as he was concerned, the Ladies Auxiliary was worthless and had outlived their usefulness.

Lacy knew, in part, that was true. But not because the women didn't care or want to help the firefighters; more because they no longer had enough members to do the job. The days were gone when every spouse of a firefighter had joined the auxiliary. Active membership was lower every year. The members they had were either older and could no longer handle getting up at all hours of the night, or had small children at home so they couldn't come out. Those in between, like her mother, had drifted away to careers and other interests.

Lacy knew many of the firefighters felt the same as Mike. If nothing else, they were an opinionated lot. But then firefighters, were always known for that.

"Just be careful," Mike said more softly as he turned to face her before going out the door. "Wouldn't want anything to happen to our future firefighter, would you?"

"Hey, with four weeks to go, what can go wrong?" She laughed in return, then watched as he gave her his familiar wink, then raced out the door.

Lacy returned to the task of getting dressed, hating the way being pregnant made her feel awkward, slowing her down. She had always prided

2

herself on her swift actions and fast thinking. Now she struggled just to put on her shoes.

"At least you haven't slowed the brain," she joked, lovingly stroking her protruding stomach. She smiled when she received a strong kick in response. "Oh, I see the future firefighter is raring to go, too."

It was while she was undergoing her paramedic training that Lacy had found out she was pregnant. She had been anxious to begin working in the field, and was fortunate to have been actually able to respond with the unit for a brief time before her pregnancy became too advanced.

Now she was anxious to return to the work she had begun to enjoy almost as much as she had loved firefighting. The best part was that there were paid positions for paramedics in their city, while almost all the firefighters were volunteers. . . Yet another fact that didn't sit well with some of the firefighters.

But she didn't care. Once the baby was born, she'd be able to do the job she enjoyed and get paid for it. That was, if she could prove she had enough ability to get hired for the next paid opening. And even though Brody was not the Chief of Ambulance, he still carried a lot of influence among the Emergency Medical Units. In the end, he was the person she'd have to prove herself to. He'd be tough, but fair.

Part of Lacy's reason for becoming a paramedic had been because of her desire to have a child. She knew once she was able to apply for a full-time, paid position she'd have more time to spend with a child. As a volunteer, she knew she'd always feel like she had to chose between them.

The other part of her reason, she knew, was better off forgotten. But it wasn't easy. There was a competitive part of her nature she couldn't deny. Competitiveness was second nature to so many of the members of the department.

She knew competition could be healthy, or it could be destructive. She chose to give up firefighting completely rather than find out which hers would be. But it didn't stop her from wondering.

She and Mike had risen through the ranks of the fire department through their years as members. She had joined at sixteen as a junior firefighter. Mike joined right after graduating high school. They had started out as competitors, at a time when women were still thought to be unable to do the job. Being one of the first woman to join, she tried hard to prove them wrong.

At the time that hadn't sat well with Mike. But eventually he grew to respect her and the competition practically disappeared. They eventually fell in love and got married.

But then a little over a year ago, they were both nominated to run for Assistant Chief of their fire company. It would be an election of their peers and she knew she stood as good a chance as her husband of winning that position. But the competition, she feared, would have been destructive to their relationship.

So, rather than take the chance and pay the price of a ruined marriage, she decided to enter a totally new line within the department. Paramedics were always in demand. As their community grew, medical emergencies were increasing, far outnumbering any other type of emergency call. She knew once she met the training requirement she'd be able to respond with the paramedics as a volunteer, prove herself, then eventually be able to get hired for a paid position when one opened.

She knew that would provide a solution to other problems as well. She had been miserable at her job as a secretary. She was used to the excitement and hectic activity involved with the emergency service. Sitting behind a desk had grown staid and without challenge, with every day the same as the one before it.

But she also knew she had to keep working if they were ever going to make the payments on their house. It was the house she had wanted. The house she hoped to someday fill with children.

Mike had been perfectly content in the apartment where they had previously lived. At least they knew they could afford it. The mortgage on their home made it a necessity that she continue working.

Lacy always believed anyone could have anything they wanted if they were willing to work for it. She also believed there was nothing wrong with working at something you enjoyed.

"If you use your head, you can have your cake and eat it too," she often joked. Becoming a paramedic was going to be just that.

She left the house and drove straight to the scene of the fire. From her portable two-way radio, she heard that one victim had already been brought out of the house. As she got out of her car, an ambulance was just pulling away.

There was another ambulance there, waiting for another victim to be brought outside. And, she heard on her radio, that yet another ambulance was on its way to take the place of the others in the event another medical emergency would strike, as it often did in this type of situation.

Lacy felt only a twinge of guilt as she walked toward the second ambulance, knowing she had told Mike she'd be helping the ladies auxiliary that night. She knew the ladies were probably back at the fire station making coffee for the personnel at the fire. It was a cold night and coffee would not only provide warmth, but the caffeine would take over when the adrenaline flowing through their veins started to fail.

Maybe when the ladies started making sandwiches for the crew she'd go back to the station and help. From the looks of the dark, billowing smoke coming from the windows and the bright flames shooting out from the back exposure of the two-story townhouse, she was certain they were going to be there for a long night.

"How many are left inside?" she asked the paramedic standing by the back door of the ambulance. She had to practically yell over the din from sirens of incoming emergency vehicles, voices over loud speakers giving orders, and the shouts of the firefighters as they did their job.

She recognized Rich Marlowe as he turned to her with a frown. "One more," he replied grimly.

She recognized that look and turned to stare at the heavy smoke conditions in the building. She knew it would take a miracle for someone to survive after being surrounded by so much smoke: smoke that contained poisonous gasses, the very reason firefighters never entered a building to fight a fire without donning the self-contained breathing apparatus, they called their SCBA's.

She was all too familiar with those dangers. She had been one of the firefighter who went inside the burning building on search and rescue. She knew the firefighters inside that house were up against nearly zero visibility as they made their way through the endless black, searching with their hands, not their eyes for the second victim.

She knew they were also up against intense heat. Heat that could melt the masks covering their faces if they stood. But they didn't stand they crawled, staying low where both the heat and the smoke were the least intense.

Still their progress would be slow. Probably too slow for the victim still inside. But that wouldn't stop them. She knew they would continue their search until forced out by either an order from their chief, or by the hostile conditions inside the building.

Dear Lord, I know the chances aren't good for the one left inside, but, with You anything is possible. Lacy said a silent prayer.

She glanced around the scene and spotted the Borough Fire Chief, her father, Carl MacDonald. She could hear his voice across the speakers as he issued orders to the men on the roof who were ventilating the building, cutting a hole at just the right spot to allow some of the smoke and heat to escape.

She looked again at the burning structure, the acrid smoke burning her nose even at that distance. The fire hissed and crackled as firefighters from outside sprayed water in an attempt to stop its onslaught.

Judging by the intensity of the fire and smoke, she knew that at any moment, her father would order the men inside the building to give up the search and get back outside. She knew he would not risk his men any longer.

5

He was a firm believer in what firefighters were taught: You are number one, your partner is number two, the victim is number three.

The sad reality was that no victim could be alive within that building without the aid of some kind of breathing device. And if her father did not order the men out soon, even SCBA's wouldn't help the firefighters still inside.

She glanced around, silently noting who was where, by the names on the backs of their bunker coats. She suspected Mike was one of the men inside conducting the search. He had always been an "inside man", even after making assistant chief.

Almost simultaneously, as she heard her father's voice calling off the search and rescue, she spotted a tall figure stumbling from the building. She couldn't tell if it was her husband, but as lights were directed on him, she could see he was carrying a tiny lifeless form.

Rich and another medical technician grabbed their bag and hurried in that direction. She followed instinctively, watching the scene as they took the tiny child from the firefighter's arms and immediately started administering first aid.

Lacy saw that the man had his face mask in his hand and had obviously broken every rule of firefighting by taking it off to give air to the child. She also saw it was not her husband standing there, but another man, a member she had met only a few times. She wasn't even certain of his name.

She noted the frightened, concerned expression on his soot-covered face as he stared at the crew working on the tiny child. He turned slightly, focusing on her, as if for the first time taking notice she was standing right in front of him. She wanted to say something to comfort him, knowing how he must feel.

The harsh reality was that it was rare, with the high toxicity of today's fires, that they could find a victim alive. She had been in his shoes only once, and had done exactly as he had done: removed her mask to give air to the victim of that fire. Hers had been a happy ending, just as she prayed his would be. It would help when it came to the reaming she knew he would receive from her father for taking off his mask. Just before he patted him on the back, saying, "I can't condone what you did. But you did a good job."

"Let's get a trach tube in her now!" Rich's firm orders pierced her thoughts, making her aware just how serious the little girl's condition was. The medical team would be cutting a small hole in the girl's trachea and inserting a tube, the only way they could get oxygen to her tiny lungs. Lacy knew the girl had suffered severe smoke inhalation, and because of that, her throat had swollen to the point that they could not get a breathing tube down her throat to administer oxygen.

It was only seconds, but seemed longer, till the ambulance pulled away, its high-pitched siren filling the air. She looked up at her companion, seeing his gaze following the departing vehicle. He looked so distraught. She knew how he felt.

Before she could speak words to comfort him another sound came through the air. It took only a moment to recognize the shrill sound of a LifeGuard®, the warning device that signaled a firefighter was down. Her head jerked toward the burning structure.

The man standing in front of Lacy touched his own LifeGuard®, yet they both knew the sound was coming from someone still inside the burning building.

"Mike?" she raised her eyes to meet the eyes of the man standing before her. "Is it Mike?"

"He was right behind me," the man almost groaned, turning to look back at the building.

"No!" Lacy felt a scream coming from her throat as she started toward the building. She felt the intense heat burning her face. Heavy smoke burned her eyes, choking her. She covered her mouth, still running forward, till suddenly, strong arms were pulling her back.

She could hear her father's voice across the P.A. issuing swift orders, one of which was that no one was to go back inside.

"No!" she shouted again, struggling to be free of the man's restraining hold. "We gotta get him out."

"Stop it!" the man shouted back at her as she struggled. "I can't go if I've gotta hold you back!"

She stopped, allowing his words to register. She looked up into his soot-smudged face, and realized he meant what he was saying. He was going to go against orders and reenter the building.

She felt his hold relax and watched numbly as he put his mask back over his face and started toward the inferno. Part of her knew it was a crazy move. She didn't doubt that he knew it, too.

He was going back inside to try to save his partner. But more than that he was going back inside to try and save her husband. She was certain that had been the deciding factor. She had seen it in his eyes.

The trained firefighter in her knew with certainty he was wrong. The building was near the point of flashover, the point where it would be totally engulfed in flames. If he entered now, he'd be entering his tomb.

She couldn't let him do that. "Don't go!" she called, flinging herself after the departing figure.

"Hold it!" she felt another set of strong arms grab her from behind. She turned to look up into Brody Langford's face. "Where do you think you're going?"

"We gotta stop him," she shouted, struggling within the circle of his arms as he pulled her out of harm's way.

"You don't gotta do anything!" Brody stated firmly. "Except calm down. Now tell me what's going on!"

"He's going back inside," she quickly explained, her words rushing out through trembling lips. "For Mike. Mike's the man down."

She watched Brody's hard expression soften ever so slightly as he looked down into her face. Then he looked again toward the burning building, frowning.

As he did, there was a thunderous roar as the building became engulfed in an explosion of heat and dark smoke, followed by bright orange and yellow flames eating everything in their way.

Lacy turned too, her eyes wide with horror. Then to make matters worse, she felt a sharp cramp-like pain pass through her middle. She gasped.

No, not now, Lord. Please, let it be the excitement causing the baby to stir.

Another pain followed, this one more intense.

"Come on," Brody ordered as he started pulling her back out of the way as the firefighters switched from a defensive mode of fighting the fire to an offensive mode. When she didn't move quickly enough, he lifted her and carried her like a baby in the cradle of his arms.

She leaned her head against his shoulder, feeling hollow and empty. She had enough years of firefighting experience to understand what was happening, to have known what was going on. It didn't make any of it easier. She had seen death. Still, this was different.

Yet, in a way everything seemed unreal. At least until another pain stabbed her abdomen.

Then suddenly, the reality of all that had happened and what was about to happen hit her, and tears slowly streamed down onto Brody's shoulder.

"Brody," she hiccuped. "I hope you have your OB kit handy."

"What?" he looked down into her face. "Oh, no! Are you sure?"

She winced in reply as another pain shot through her.

It wasn't supposed to be like this. She thought. *Not this way at all.*

CHAPTER ONE

Lacy laid against the pillow, drained, both physically and emotionally, her face practically colorless except for the purplish rings beneath her closed eyes. Her honey-gold curls hung long and loose, spilling out across her pillow.

She wasn't really asleep, but wanted to be. Then everything that had happened the night before, could actually have been a nightmare. Maybe if she never opened her eyes again, maybe then everything would be all right.

But even as the thought passed through her mind, she knew it wasn't true. Just the opposite. Nothing would ever be right again. Mike had died. Killed in the raging fire from the night before. Mike, and how many others she thought, trying to remember, yet not really wanting to.

Was there another wife out there feeling just as she did right now? The wife of the firefighter who had gone back inside to try and save her husband, his partner?

She felt another tear dampening the edge of her dark lash and knew if she gave in to the urge to cry again, it would result in another uncontrollable torrent of tears. She couldn't allow herself that weakness. Not now when she had to be strong. Strong for her baby son.

Carl, she thought. That was what she and Mike had agreed to name their son once they learned they were going to have a boy. Funny how modern technology had allowed them that advance knowledge. Yet modern technology could not prevent the tragedy of last night's events.

God could have prevented it, she thought, then in frustration tried to dismiss that thought. *But why didn't you, God?* She sighed, forcing her thoughts back to her child. Her son.

Considering all that happened, she wondered if she should name their son, Michael, after his father. It would be all the little boy would ever have of the man who had missed his birth by only a few hours. The man who would have been there coaching her through the delivery, had fate not taken him away.

Both eyes were feeling moist now, and she angrily rubbed away the dampness with the heels of her hands. She couldn't, no she wouldn't, give in to the tears.

"Lacy, Dear, are you awake?" She opened her eyes to her mother's soft, caressing voice.

"Mom." Her own voice was a hoarse whisper. Turning her head, she watched as her mother got up from a chair by the bed and stood beside her, reaching out and gently stroking her hair. "Did you see the baby?"

9

"Yes, he's beautiful." Her mother's own blue eyes were glowing with tears, and her voice husky, belying the crying that had filled her night.

"Is he really okay?" She asked, afraid fate could be cruel enough to have dealt her another blow.

"He was just a little too anxious to come into the world," her mother assured her. "Probably all the excitement. . ."

Her mother bit her lip, then squeezed Lacy's hand as though to receive strength rather than to give. But then that had always been the case with Lois MacDonald, the traditional wife and mother. She had never been able to understand her only child's desire to become a firefighter. . . to face the inevitable horrors that went with that job. She had been relieved when Lacy had left firefighting to become a paramedic. But only slightly. Her daughter would still be too closely involved with life and death. It wasn't the life that bothered her. It was the death. Lois had wanted to protect her daughter from that, as she wanted to protect her now.

"So he's okay?"

"Yes, dear." Lois made a valiant effort to keep the worry from her voice. "He's in an incubator, but that's just a precaution because he's premature. Doctor Kelly says he's doing fine."

Lacy allowed a long sigh to escape her lips. She was relieved to know her child was safe. It would be up to her to keep him that way. And she would have to do that alone, without Mike.

Once again, that reality charged in and threatened to overcome her. Lacy turned her moist blue eyes away from her mother, looking toward the window. Funny, the sun was shining brightly. Somehow it didn't seem right. The day should be cloudy. There should be rain. It should be the same outside as it was in her heart. . . as she knew it was in the hearts of all the other members of her department. She had lost a husband. They had lost a brother. Two, in fact.

She looked back at her mother again. "Who was the other firefighter that was killed? Was he married? Is there another woman feeling like I do right now? Maybe even other children left without a father."

Her mother's eyes narrowed in puzzlement. "What other firefighter, Dear?"

"The one who went back in to try and save Mike. It was my fault he went back, you know. He wouldn't have done it if it hadn't have been for me."

"Stubborn fool would have anyway," the brusque, deep voice of her father came from the doorway where he had just entered the room in time to hear Lacy's words. "Any man who would take off his mask inside a smoke-filled room, even to save a child's life, would also go back inside that building to try and save his partner."

"Is that any way to talk about one of your men who was killed?" Lois snapped, turning her angry blue gaze at her husband's tall, burly frame.

He gave her a grim smile as he approached the bed. "Would be if he were dead. But the fool never made it back inside. Though just about."

Lacy was used to her father's gruff, tell-it-like-it-is manner. But she knew that even after over twenty-seven years of marriage, her mother wasn't. She never would get used to it. She was of a far gentler nature. That was why she had never understood her daughter's choice to become a firefighter.

Not for the first time, Lacy wondered how her parents, so different from one another, had managed to stay together for so long. She and Mike had differences, too, of another kind, but differences no less. She wondered if their love would have withstood the years of trials. But now she would never know.

"Lacy, how are you doing, Sweetheart?" her father asked more gently as he leaned forward and pressed a kiss against her cheek.

She shrugged, trying to swallow the lump in her throat. "I could use some water."

Her mother quickly obliged, pouring her a glass from the pitcher beside her bed. "Oh, the ice is melted. Let me get you some more."

"It's okay, Mom," Lacy said, hoping her mother was not going to start waiting on her hand and foot like she was an invalid. "Even warm water will do right now."

She took a sip from the glass her mother would have held to her lips, if she hadn't taken it from her before she could. It felt good going down her dry throat. Felt good against her parched lips. Now at least she could swallow again, despite the lump that refused to go down.

"You said the man didn't make it back inside," Lacy continued, feeling less guilty knowing the man had survived.

"No, he was banged up pretty bad. No burns, though. His gear protected him," her father explained. "Lucky man. Any closer and the concussion could have killed him if the fire didn't first."

Lacy knew that was true. She knew that when flashover occurred, it was like a bomb going off. The heat and smoke containing deadly gases filled up inside the building to the point where it exploded into flames, totally engulfing everything.

"What about the victims?"

"I just checked before I came back here. First one is doing fairly well," her father explained, his frown deepening. "The second one's in pretty bad shape. But she's alive."

She didn't doubt that child would be dead if not for the firefighter taking the chance and giving her some of his air.

11

"Are you going to give him your standard lecture?" she looked up into her father's brown eyes, seeing how exhausted he looked, and strained. She realized what he, too, must be going through. He was the Borough Fire Chief, the one in charge of the emergency. One of his men was dead, another one injured. Then to top it off, his first grandchild picks that same night to make his entrance into the world.

"No lecture this time," his father replied grimly. "Besides, I doubt it would work. This one's got a mind and a crusade all his own."

Lacy wondered what her father meant. But she was too tired to ask any more questions. All she wanted to do now was sleep. And to see her baby. Not necessarily in that order. But when she suggested the latter, her mother insisted she still wasn't allowed out of bed.

"The baby will be brought to you at feeding time. Till then he needs his rest, too."

"Well, if you're going to rest, I've got another patient to see," her father said as he touched her cheek with a calloused hand. There was a gentleness about him she hadn't seen since she was a little girl. The side, she was certain, was what made her mother fall in love with him.

"Thought you said you just checked on the kids."

"I did. But there's a young man on the sixth floor who's probably giving those nurses a hard time trying to find out about them, too. I figured I'd fill him in."

"I thought you said he was okay."

"He is, but the doctor insisted on keeping him for observation. Best they do it here. He doesn't have anyone at home to look after him."

That answered Lacy's other question about the mysterious firefighter. There was no one to mourn him had he died. The only one mourning today was her. She supposed that was both unfortunate and fortunate. But at the moment, she was too tired to decide.

#

When she awoke she looked through the window and was greeted by darkness outside. She had no idea how long she had slept. Nights came early during these late winter months. She supposed it was still fairly early, since no one had wakened her for her dinner tray, as they had at lunch.

Though the only light was coming from the hallway, she knew someone else was in the room with her. It took only a moment to recognize the barrel-chested figure in the dim light. Still, had it been total darkness she'd have known it was her father by the sound of his sleeping.

12

She smiled as she heard the familiar long snort as he inhaled, followed by a wheezing sound as he allowed that breath to exhale again. Her father's snore had always reminded her of scenes from the Three Stooges.

Then, just as quickly, her momentary humor dissolved as she remembered where she was and why. She listened to the clang of carts containing dinner trays being pushed somewhere down the hallway. She had no appetite at lunch, forcing down only a little, because the nurse told her she needed nourishment if she wanted to nurse her baby as she had planned.

She remembered the moments sometime earlier that afternoon when the nurses brought her son for his feeding and how they had patiently told her how to clean her breasts before she fed him. All the while her mother was hovering in the background, adding bits of helpful information along the way.

Then, when they placed the tiny bundle wrapped in blue into her arms, how her mother had cried. How she, too, very nearly cried, but managed to hold back her tears until they had taken little Mikie back to the nursery and everyone had gone. She had been told a baby can pick up on their mother's emotions, and she wanted so much to keep her emotions in check while her infant was in her arms.

Then once he was gone, and her flood of tears subsided, she lay thinking about the responsibility she would now have for that tiny little boy and wondering if she would be able to go it alone. At the same time knowing she would, because she had to.

She felt the rumbling of her stomach, nearly as loud as her father's snore and knew she was hungry, though still lacking an appetite. She would eat because she had to. She wondered, before this ordeal was over, how many more things she would do because she had to?

Or would it ever be over?

"Mrs. Boyce, are you awake?" a nurse said from the doorway. "It's time for dinner. Shall I get your light?"

Her father grunted, sitting up, immediately awake. That was a trait he had, of being able to awaken swiftly at the sound of a voice calling, the alarm clock, or the pager signaling another emergency call. He always said it was a trait that came naturally after years of firefighting, and she knew it was true. She knew she possessed it. Mike did, too.

Mike *had* possessed it, she corrected her thoughts, knowing the sooner she accepted he was gone, the sooner she'd be able to get on with her life. Another thing she would do because she had to.

"I'll get the light, Nurse," her father said as he stood and reached for the long cord beside the bed. Giving it a tug, the reading light cast a warm glow over Lacy as she laid with her head pressed against the pillow.

13

"Did you finally talk Mom into going home?" She asked, pushing herself up on one elbow, then turned and slipped her feet over the side of the bed. "You should have gone, too."

"You know very well your mother won't leave until visiting hours are over." Her father's voice held a hint of humor as he spoke. Lacy saw the dark stubble on his face and knew he probably hadn't been home for more than a quick shower after the fire.

"What about you? You're just as stubborn. You look ready to drop."

"That bad, huh?" He sighed, running a hand over the stubble. "Your mother only agreed to go downstairs to get something to eat when I promised to stay right here by your side."

"Thanks, Dad. She skipped lunch. Probably breakfast, too."

He nodded his agreement. "And right now she's probably hovering somewhere right outside this room, letting us think she's gone."

Lacy laughed, for a moment forgetting her sorrow. But only for a moment. She suddenly remembered the only reason her mother was worried was because of everything that had happened last night.

A woman entered carrying her dinner tray. She was dressed in the uniform signifying all kitchen personnel. A navy-blue pants uniform covered by an apron in a brightly colored flowered pattern, with a matching cap that didn't allow a bit of hair to peep out from under it.

"Please put it by the chair," Lacy said. "I'm tired of being in bed."

She thanked the woman then waited till she had gone before sliding out of bed. The moment her feet made contact with the floor, she felt her knees turn to Jell-o.

"Whoa, Girl," her father said as he put one hand beneath each of her arms and lifted her back onto the bed as easily as if she were a rag doll. "Better not over do it."

"I'm certainly not going to stay in bed forever, Dad!" she snapped, and immediately regretted it as she saw her father flinch. None of his men would ever have dared talk to him like that. She would never have talked to him like that. It was a matter of respect. She didn't know what had gotten into her.

Then to make matters worse, she felt tears welling in her eyes. "I've got too much to do to stay in bed," she said with a whispered sob.

"Nothing that can't wait," her father said with uncommon softness. "At least until you get back your strength."

"But what about. . .Don't we have arrangements to make. . . A funeral. . . a viewing. . ." Again brutal reality stabbed her moment of peace and she leaned back and sobbed into her pillow. "Oh, God, Daddy. . .Mike's. . . Mike's body. . ."

"That's enough, Honey," her father soothed, stroking her long, golden hair. "Shhh, tomorrow's soon enough to worry about any arrangements."

She turned and allowed her father to gather her into his strong arms as he had done when she was a small child. She leaned her head against his wide, solid chest and cried. He rocked her as she cried like she had not allowed herself to cry before.

From her haven, she could feel her father's own body trembling as he attempted to suppress his emotions. He was a strong man, one who had withstood so many things. But this must have been his most difficult trial. It was because of him that she pooled all her strength and taking a deep breath, pushed away from his comfort.

"I'll be okay," she said, looking up at him through red-rimmed, glistening blue eyes. She saw his own eyes were watery as he looked down at her with concern, swallowing hard and taking a deep breath to regain his composure.

"I know you will, Honey. It'll just take some time."

She nodded then looked away, noting the food tray still sitting by the chair. She looked back at her father again. "Maybe if you help me this time, I can get up and make it to the chair."

"If you really must."

She forced a grim smile. "I must. Women who have a baby don't remain in bed this long anymore, Dad. They're up and around right away. Almost like the days when they worked in the field, went inside had a baby, and went back outside again to the fields."

"I'd say that's highly exaggerated," her father commented as he helped her from the bed. "But I know better than to argue with you. You're as stubborn as your mother."

"What's that?" Lois said from the doorway.

"Ooops!" Carl MacDonald stood looking at his wife, then back to his daughter before making a face.

"He just said I'm just as strong as my mother," Lacy lied, winking conspiratorially to her father. "That's why I'm going to make it through this."

"Well, we'll be right here to help you," Lois said, rushing over to take Lacy's other side as they guided her to the chair.

Lacy didn't doubt that for a moment. She'd probably get more help than she needed, just as she was getting far more than she needed just to get into the chair. But for now it was easier to accept it than to argue about it. Especially when she wasn't certain she could have made it there alone.

Lacy was awakened once in the middle of the night to feed her infant son. She hadn't been sleeping well anyway, but refused to request any medication for fear it would affect her production of milk and, in turn, be bad for her son. She wasn't even certain they would allow her to take anything for that very reason.

Doctor Kelly had offered her a mild sedative shortly after she had given birth. But she had adamantly refused. The graying doctor simply smiled a grim smile in reply and said he hadn't expected her to take the easy way out.

"But even tough gals like you need a helping hand from time to time," he had said as he squeezed her hand. "Don't be afraid to accept that hand. We all care about you, Lacy."

Yes, she could see how everyone cared, she mused. Too much so.

"There's people worse off than me," she said softly as she looked down into her son's round little face, trying hard to see the face of her dead husband. "You, for instance. . ." she continued. "You have a long road ahead of you without a father. But you'll make it. We'll make it."

She felt the sting of tears in her eyes again and she forced them away, reminding herself her baby would sense her unease and it would not be good for him. She inhaled a long calming breath, taking his tiny hand in her's, gently rubbing her thumb over each finger and stopping on his thumb, so small by comparison.

"Someday these hands will grow to do so many things, including fight fires," she whispered, remembering Mike saying the very same thing so many times.

"How's our future firefighter today," he'd say when he came home from work each day. He had even bought a tiny tee shirt with a picture of a fire engine and the words *Future Firefighter* on it.

She frowned, looking down at her child. He had practically stopped sucking at her breast, his eyes closed in sleep. "It may be in your blood, little guy, but if you decide you don't want to fight fires, I'll understand. I mean, who knows, you may want to be a neurosurgeon. I've never heard of any type of surgeon being a volunteer firefighter. Probably isn't good for their hands."

She lifted his fingers and pressed them against her lips. "Or, maybe you'll be President. Now, I know the President doesn't have time to run around chasing fires."

Suddenly, she laughed, realizing she must be sounding like so many other new mothers as they thought about what their new offspring may someday become. Her laughter made the baby start, his blue eyes opened wide as he pulled away from her breast and started to cry.

"Hush, it's okay," she quickly soothed. "Mama's sorry. She just got carried away thinking about the future. How I'm going to make it up to you for not having a daddy. Shhhh. . ."

The baby calmed again, his eyes slowly closing.

#

The tall dark-haired man stood just outside the door, out of sight of the room's single occupant propped up in her bed. No, there were two, he realized as he saw that the blanket in her arms was wrapped around her newborn baby. A son, he remembered Carl telling him.

The dim light from the overhead reading light cast a halo around her blonde head, creating a Madonna like picture of mother with child, he mused. He could remember a time when he stood in a similar corridor, watching another woman holding her newborn child, a daughter. His daughter. But that was a more pleasant time. Before . . .

He stepped closer, taking the chance the woman may see him, but unable to resist becoming an interloper on this special moment between mother and child. He needed to share this moment, no matter what memories it brought back to him. No matter how wonderful. No matter how sad. No matter how painful.

He listened to the woman talking about the tiny child's future. He heard her say something about being a firefighter. Probably like his father or grandfather. Or, like his mother had once been, he reminded himself. He had seen her at the station often, yet hadn't really ever worked with her. He knew she had fought fires and handled every other duty. In fact, if he remembered correctly, he'd heard she had been nominated for assistant chief shortly after he joined. But that was before she turned to another line. Paramedic. Yes, he had seen her assisting at an accident once a few months ago. Handled herself well for a novice. But now, that seemed like a very long time ago.

He watched as the young mother laughed, then suddenly there was a faint cry from the child in her arms. He supposed he should get out of there before one of the nurses heard and came to check if something was wrong. It probably wouldn't be good for them to find him wondering around on this floor. But somehow he had just ended up here. He couldn't sleep and had been too restless to remain in his own room.

He knew he had to return there soon before it was discovered that he had decided to go for an unescorted walk around the facility. He didn't doubt it was against some sort of rule. But he had learned a long time ago, you miss out on a lot if you don't break a rule once in awhile.

One last look at mother and child assured him she was doing far better than she had been the last time he'd seen her. Then he was on his way. Just one more, quick stop before he returned to his own room.

#

Lacy relaxed as her child returned to sleep. She leaned her head back against her pillow and sighed, content in this special moment she was sharing with her son.

She turned to glance at the door and realized they hadn't been alone. A tall, dark-haired man had just turned and was walking away from the door. Or was she just imagining him?

No, she was certain of it. But there wouldn't be any men wandering around the maternity ward at this hour of the morning. Not unless he was a doctor, or male nurse, or someone else affiliated to the hospital. He was dressed in what looked like white, or near-white. Yet, it hadn't looked like a uniform he was wearing. In fact, it looked very much like the horrible gowns they made you wear when hospitalized. Yes, she had been thankful to be rid of hers when her mother brought her something from home.

Could it be . . .?

By the time the nurse arrived to return her son to his incubator in the nursery, her curiosity had been peaked. If she guessed correctly, the hospital-garbed man who had been at her door was probably the firefighter who had been Mike's partner at the fire the night before. The one who had been about to return to the building to attempt to save Mike. And if it was, she wanted to thank him.

Now. Not later. She knew things would be crazy later. She might not get the chance to catch him alone. And she wanted it to be that way. Just in case she broke down and started crying again. She didn't want to do that in front of everyone.

As soon as the nurse was gone, she silently went to the closet for her burgundy terry-cloth robe and matching slippers. She stood at the doorway, tying the belt at her waist as she peeped around the corner to make certain there was no one in the corridor to catch her as she made the short dash down the hall to the stairs.

The door was rigged with an alarm, so that eliminated the possibility that he had entered that way. She looked around, trying to remember the layout of the hospital. There were two sets of huge double doors, one leading to elevators that went down to the lobby. Those were the ones the visitors used. And there was a door leading to the stairs beside them. But you had to pass the nurse's station to get to them.

No, if the man had come from another floor, he had most likely taken the entrance leading to the hospital's private elevators. She'd used those elevators to pick up patients who needed an ambulance transport. She knew there were stairs opening beside the private elevators, too. It was unlikely they were rigged with an alarm.

She made her way to the first set of double doors, listening for sounds at the nurse's station. There was a faint ringing sound from somewhere on the opposite hall. Someone had called for the nurse. Perfect timing. She pressed the button that would open the double doors and hurried through, hoping there wasn't anyone else close by that would hear her.

Once inside the stairway, she realized she had several flights ahead if she intended to make it to the firefighter's floor. Her father had said it was the sixth. She was in good physical condition, she could make it.

She started up the stairs and made it two flights to the fourth floor before realizing her folly. She was feeling quite weak, and her legs seemed to be filled with lead – molten lead. At this point, she wasn't certain if she could go up or down on her own. Maybe if she sat on the landing for a moment before going on.

Having a baby must take a lot out of you! I've worn full bunker gear, with a fifty pound SCBA on my back, in the middle of a raging fire and gone up more stairs than this.

She heard the door behind her open and jumped up, her face red from the embarrassment of being caught in the act of sneaking around the hospital when she was supposed to be asleep in her room. She was about to make an excuse when she realized she was face to face with someone who was equally guilty.

"What are you doing up here?" he asked in the same tone of voice she remembered him using at the fire.

"Looking for you," she replied, adding the same question of him. "What were you doing outside my room?"

"I couldn't sleep." He turned his tired, green gaze away from her.

"Do you make it a habit of wandering around hospital corridors whenever you suffer from insomnia?"

"I don't make a habit of being in hospitals."

She supposed that was true, but wondered if that meant he often suffered from insomnia. She decided it didn't matter if he did. She hadn't been looking for him to find out his sleeping habits.

He was watching her closely, his expression showing his concern. "So, now that I answered your question, why don't I see you back to your room?"

"I wanted to talk to you. I was on my way to your room. . ." Then as if just realizing it she turned and looked at the large number four painted beside the door. "Which isn't on this floor. My father said you were on the sixth."

The man nodded, not offering an explanation.

Lacy left out an exasperated breath. "This is the children's ward." Her blue eyes shown bright as she suddenly understood. "How is she?"

He shrugged. "It's difficult to say. You can't exactly get close to the Pediatrics Intensive Care Unit. I probably should have known that."

"We could ask a nurse or a doctor."

"And risk getting caught out of our rooms." He smiled down at her. "We should be getting back to them. There seems to be a draft funneling up these stairs."

For a moment, as Lacy looked at this man dressed in hospital garb, she forgot her reason for being there, and had to suppress a note of humor at seeing his distress. She didn't doubt he was feeling less than comfortable dressed this way. Hospital gowns always had a way of humiliating a person. Not that she'd worn them often. Only twice before. Once when she was ten and had her tonsils removed and again about two years ago when she had been kept for observation after suffering smoke inhalation.

She suddenly remembered her reason for seeking him out. "I hope you're feeling better." He certainly looked that way, except for his obvious discomfort from the draft. The way he was fidgeting one would have thought he was a small child who had to go to the bathroom.

"I was going to say the same to you if you were awake, but I decided not to interrupt."

Her face flushed as she realized he had been watching her nursing her son. Of course, that was an act of nature and she had nothing to be embarrassed about. Unknowingly, her chin jutted out.

She watched him change his position once again, this time crossing his right leg in front of the left.

"Do you have to go to the bathroom or something?" she blurted.

"No! I told you, there's a draft."

She smiled, but felt her face burn as she realized his problem. "Why didn't someone bring you something else to wear?"

"I didn't want to bother anyone. Though I'm sure any of the guys would have stopped by my apartment, had I asked." His green eyes looked grim.

She remembered her father had said something about him not having anyone to look after him at home. She wondered about this man who had been so willing to risk his own life to save her husband. Even though he must have realized, as she had realized, the danger was too intense for him to have made it. Was there no one that he cared enough about that he would take such a risk? She knew they took risks at every emergency call. But not like that one. That one would have been stupid. It would have been suicide.

"Why were you going to go back inside?" For some reason she had to know.

"I'm a firefighter. That's my job."

"Don't give me that. Even a novice knew it was too late," she felt the lump rising in her throat again, and her lower lip began to tremble. "You did it because of me. You could have been killed, too." *Oh, no. I'm going to cry again.*

"Come on, let's get you back to your room," the man who was really a stranger, yet had put his life on the line because of her, put his arm around her and started leading her down the stairs. Yes, he had done it for her. He hadn't denied that.

His arms felt strong, and she was more tired than she had realized. She allowed herself this momentary weakness and leaned closer against him.

Suddenly she felt him stiffen and an audible gasp came from his mouth. She pulled away and looked up in time to see a flash of pain cross his green eyes.

"Maybe I should be the one helping you," she said, stopping at the next landing. "Dad did say you were banged up pretty bad."

"Just a cracked rib, and a few bruises."

"Then what are you doing wandering around?" She scolded.

"I believe this is where we started." He smiled down at her.

"Yes, and this is where we end it! I can manage the rest of the way to my room alone. I suggest you go right back up to your room." She looked up between the concrete stairs and made a face. "You've got pretty far. Maybe you should attempt the elevators."

"What? And get caught? The elevator will ding its arrival and signal the nurses. What's the punishment for escaping your hospital room in the middle of the night?"

"Probably an hour session with the hospital shrink."

"Then I'll see you there, too," he retorted.

"Not if we don't get caught. By the time they realize the elevator's stopped on their floor, you'll be long gone. But just in case, I'll go check how many nurses are at the station. I'll signal if it's clear and keep them busy till you're safely on the elevator."

"And if we're caught, give them only our name, rank and serial number."

"You fool," she suddenly felt a bubble of laughter in her throat as they started down the last flight of stairs to her floor.

When they got to the door, she stopped and stared up into his sober green eyes. "Thanks. For a moment, you helped me forget."

He touched her cheek and smiled a weary smile. "Thank you. For the same reason."

CHAPTER TWO

Lacy had been to the funerals of other firefighters killed in the line of duty. She had admired the strength of the widows and children of her fallen comrades as, one by one, they accepted condolences from hundreds of sympathizers.

Today she admired them even more. How did they manage to make it through the long tedious day? She didn't know if she could. She had wondered that ever since arriving at the funeral home for the services. That was when it had all hit her. The hard truth. The reality. Up until that time, it had seemed more like a bad dream. None of it had seemed real.

That morning she had risen early from a sleepless night. It was just like any other morning, except she was sleeping in her old bed, in her old room, in her parents' house. It was her first morning after being released from the hospital. It had seemed almost like stepping back in time. And, in a way, she had wished that was what she had done. Except. . .

She had felt tears stinging her eyes as she thought of her infant son still in the hospital. Funny how quickly she had developed an attachment to her newborn child. There had been times during her pregnancy that she wondered if she would adapt to motherhood. Certainly she wasn't cut from the same mold as other mothers, especially those like her mother.

What kind of a mother would she be? She had wondered, as she showered and went to her closet. There she stopped, remembering her clothing was all at her home. She glanced around the bright room once again, noting the lace-trimmed pink and white gingham curtains, and matching spread still folded and placed carefully on the bench at the foot of her bed, which was painted white, to match the rest of the furniture in the room. She felt the warmth of plush pale blue carpets beneath her bare feet, only a shade darker than the baby blue painted walls.

Not at all like the bedroom in her home. Her room was far less frilly and feminine. The curtains and bedspread were navy, green and white in a geometric design, dark in contrast to the mint green walls. And the heavy dark pine furniture sat on highly polished wood floors.

She had chosen the decor for that room, as her mother had chosen the one for the room where she now stood. She had carefully chosen every detail, wanting it to be favored by her husband, hoping it would make him enjoy his new home as much as she knew she was going to enjoy it.

And now she wasn't there. She was back in her childhood room, designed specifically for the little girl her mother had always hoped she'd be. Tears still stung her eyes as she thought of what a disappointment she had been to her mother. Never quite able to fit the image Lois had chosen for her.

She swallowed those thoughts as she opened the closet, seeing a single black dress hanging there, its price tag still attached from a string on the sleeve. Somehow her mother had found time to purchase the dress. She couldn't imagine when, for it seemed she had spent every waking hour at the hospital. Still, she had gone out and purchased this dress; the proper attire for a mourning widow. Lacy wished her mother hadn't.

Her breathing quickened as she thought of what lay ahead that day. It was the funeral of a fallen firefighter, a member of the emergency service. And she was just as much a member of that service as she was that man's wife. As she thought of that fact, a note of rebellion sparked inside her. A rebellion she hadn't felt in years.

By the silence of the house, she could tell everyone was still sleeping. She could leave a note so they wouldn't worry, telling them she'd meet them at the funeral home at the appointed time. By then it would be too late for anyone to try and make her change her mind, or more adequately for her mother to try and change her mind. Her mother never could understand her dedication toward the fire service. She had viewed it as a distasteful phase Lacy was going through. Only, to her dismay, that phase had lasted far longer than she had hoped.

Lacy slipped into the clothing she had worn to come home from the hospital and tiptoed down the stairs into the kitchen where she placed a note by the coffee pot: the first place her parents would look when they got up. Then she opened the drawer by the sink where she knew she'd find the spare keys to her father's truck and started out the door.

There was plenty of time for what she had in mind. First going home, to her own house, and dressing in the formal dress uniform worn by members of the fire service when attending the funeral of one of their own.

She was too determined with what she was doing to think of what lay ahead. She slipped into the white uniform shirt and navy pants, with the half-inch wide blue stripe going down the side, then stood before the mirror as she made certain her tie and her badge were straight. She reached into a tiny accessory drawer for the small, black, elastic band that slipped over the badge, to signify the mourning of a fallen comrade.

She picked up her navy blue eight-point hat and a matching uniform jacket, the last parts of her uniform, and started back into the hall, stopping suddenly as she faced the door just across from her room. She opened it slowly and looked at the nursery she had planned for her son. The white walls she had painted herself, with stenciled paintings of every cartoon character imaginable riding inside some type of emergency vehicle.

Her mother had frowned distastefully the first time she had shown her the room, but then she had expected no different. Lois MacDonald had never been able to understand her daughter's feelings toward the fire service. It was like being part of a special family, sharing good times and bad. And with that thought tears filled her eyes. Today was going to be one of the bad.

It was still another hour before Lacy was expected at the funeral home. Long enough time for her to make one more stop, at the hospital, where she could visit her son. She had wanted him to come home with her so she could care for him, and nurse him when he was hungry, but the doctor said he should spend at least two or three more days in the hospital. So she had gone there late the previous night and nursed him before he went to sleep. And now, if she had timed it right, she could again share those intimate moments with her child; if not to feed him, then to just hold him for a little while before she went on with the rest of what she knew would be a long day.

And it had been a long day already, with still more ahead. Lacy was exhausted, emotionally drained, too numb to realize more than a blur of faces as the long line of people passed by the closed casket, then by her, her father and mother. At least she was thankful they were there beside her.

She looked again at her father's weary face, lined with a combination of worry and exhaustion. She knew this was all taking its toll on him, too. He had lost not only a son-in-law, but one of his men, and she knew he felt a great deal of responsibility toward all his personnel. Add to that, his worry about her.

Instinctively, she reached for his hand and gave it a squeeze, reassuring him, wishing her mother understood what it was he was feeling now. Lois MacDonald's face was a mask, void of emotions except the grief she felt at the loss of her son-in-law.

Lacy knew the real feelings behind her mother's mask: her resentment of the fire service that consumed so much, of not only her husband's, but also her daughter's, time. Yet, more than resentment, there was the fear. Fear that what had happened to Mike, might someday happen to her husband or daughter.

Lacy felt a moment of guilt as she thought about her mother, and how difficult it must have been for her. She had often said the thing she feared most was that phone call, or visit from someone telling her that Carl or Lacy had been killed in the line of duty.

Unlike many spouses, when there was an emergency call, she had adamantly refused to listen to the scanner which picked up all the radio transmissions from the scene. If something went wrong she didn't want to know about it until she had to know. Lacy knew the silence of the scanner never stopped her mother from worrying.

It seemed strange to Lacy that her parents, having so little in common, had ever managed to find each other, much less fall in love. But they had, she had no doubts about that fact. Despite their dissimilarity, their love was strong. Through the years, through all the differences – and there were many – they had somehow withstood all.

Lacy remembered her parents often bickering, most often over something to do with the fire department. She glanced at her mother, smiling to herself as she thought of the most common taunt her mother had used, when she reminded her husband that he hadn't even seen fit to be there when his daughter was born, rather he had been off somewhere fighting a fire.

"Ah, my love, is it my fault that Lacy decided she wanted to see what all the excitement was about?" he chided his wife. "And isn't it true that as soon as my sister got word to me, I came to the hospital to be by your side?"

"Smelling of smoke and sweat," she chided.

"At least I was there."

"Yes, but she was already born by the time you got there," her mother would say, shaking her blonde head. "You had missed the most wonderful part."

To that, Carl would wink and give her a rakish grin. "Wrong. I was there for the most wonderful part, and had I missed that, we wouldn't have such a lovely daughter now, would we?"

Then her mother would blush. Even after all their years of marriage, though Lacy knew her mother had to have grown used to her father's teasing banter, she still had the ability to look shocked by his words.

Yes, in spite of their differences, her parents loved each other very much. She sighed, wondering what it would be like for her twenty-five years from now. She absently ran her left thumb over her wedding band, a nervous habit she had when she daydreamed. Would she and . . .? She stopped, biting her lip as she glanced again at the casket beside her, feeling suddenly unsteady.

"Lacy, are you okay?" she heard the familiar voice of her aunt and felt her hand grasped between two comforting ones.

Lacy broke out of her daze and wondered how many people that she hadn't even noticed through her zombie-like trance had passed by and taken her hand. Now, thankfully, when reality chose to surface, it was Aunt Rainy standing in front of her. Aunt Rainy always had a way of brightening the day.

She met the other woman's concerned brown eyes, then noted the lines on her face.

"Okay? No," Lacy replied softly, forcing a weak grin. "Surviving? Yes. I have to." She felt her hand trembling, her resolve crumbling. She quickly pulled her hand away, as though hiding her threatening emotions would keep them at bay.

Her aunt's face blurred, then passed as her hand was taken by another one. A strong, firm grasp, belonging to a tall, dark-haired man. As her vision cleared, she recognized the familiar glittering, green gaze concentrating on her face.

Ryan Simon looked quite different in his uniform from the last two times she had seen him, first in bunker gear then in a hospital gown and robe. But his eyes still held the same expression. More than compassion, it was shared pain. Somehow she knew this man understood what she was going through.

What was it her father had said about him? That he had a mind and a crusade all his own. At the time she thought his comment strange, now looking into Ryan's gaze she knew he, too, had experienced grief. That was why he said nothing as he finally released her hand and broke from her gaze. There were no words that could ease her pain, nor phrases that would somehow make everything right again. Ryan knew that because he had gone through similar grief.

But he was walking testimony that somehow you do survive. She watched him as he passed by her father and then her mother. Yes, you do survive, no matter how difficult it may seem, and she had no doubt that for Ryan Simon, it had been a very difficult survival.

The fact that members of their own fire station were now coming through the long line of sympathizers was a signal that the procession was finally near an end. Six of these men – her husband's closest companions – would carry the casket out to the waiting pumper, where others would help raise it to the top, carefully setting it on the hose bed.

This was the most traditional of farewells to fallen firefighters, fitting that the apparatus they rode in when alive, should be that which carried them on their last ride. The truck carrying her husband's flag-draped casket led the procession, with Lacy and her parents in the chief's vehicle next in line, followed closely by emergency apparatus from nearly two hundred fire departments. Pumpers, tankers, ladder trucks, snorkels, cascade units and ambulances, every array of apparatus imaginable, in just as many different colors, prepared for the slow procession to the mausoleum which was set aside specifically for emergency personnel killed in the line of duty.

Lacy had seen all this before, too many times, when other firefighters had been killed. Yet, then it had been different. They had been strangers, though still brothers in the emergency service.

They drove in silence down the main street of town, which had been temporarily closed during their procession. Police officers and fire police were holding up the traffic at the intersections, standing at attention, saluting as their vehicles passed by, showing their respect for the man who had died.

Lacy could no longer fight the lump rising in her throat as they progressed toward the traditional arch across the street, created by two aerial ladders raised and meeting in the center high above the street. As the vehicle ahead slowly drove beneath the arch, her tears finally spilled. Silent tears, but no less painful than if sobs would have raked her body.

They turned into the cemetery and headed down the winding lane toward the Memorial Mausoleum. She dried her eyes before getting out of the back seat of the car, again forcing herself to continue with what needed to be done.

"I told you this was too much," she heard her mother whisper her concern to her father.

"Please, Mom," Lacy pleaded through shaking lips, not wanting her mother to launch into a disapproving declaration about the traditions of the fire service. "This is the proper farewell for Mike. I wanted no less."

"I'm just worried about you, Dear." Her mother stepped up her pace to catch up with her, placing her arm across her shoulder and guiding her on as though she were a little girl.

Lacy knew her mother needed to give her comfort as much as she needed it to be given, and for that reason she accepted the gesture. She glanced from her mother's worried expression, to the weary lines of defeat on her father's face. She knew he, too, could use some support, for his own grief had to be a personal hell.

As though her very thoughts had conjured him up, Ryan Simon appeared at her father's side, nodding once silently, then remaining by the older man's side and walking toward the mausoleum for the brief service.

As chief, Lacy knew her father would be expected to express some words, some type of eulogy to honor Mike. She suspected he had spent a great deal of time preparing for it, trying to find just the right words. This was not going to be easy for him, she worried. Neither would it be easy for her.

Carl MacDonald had always been a man of few words, this being no exception. He chose his words well, hailing Mike as a firefighter, a leader, a friend and a son-in-law. His deep voice quaked slightly as he gave a final note:

"From today forward, how Michael Boyce lived, not how he died, should be our memory, his legacy being in how those he leaves behind will live in his absence," her father said. "As anyone of us in the emergency service knows, perhaps more than any other breed of person knows, life and death both go on. For that very reason, we must go on, continuing to do our job and our duty. We owe it to those who have gone before us. We owe it to Mike."

Only Lacy heard the tiny gasp that came from her mother's lips because she did not agree with what her husband had said. But Lacy couldn't deny that, for once, she agreed with her mother. The stakes were high in their line of business. Maybe too high. Too high for the ones who were left behind.

Ryan listened intently as Carl MacDonald spoke, respecting the Borough Fire Chief more than ever for his words. Words he knew were not easy for the older man to express under the circumstances. But words he knew Carl believed. Words he, too, believed, because he had learned the hard way just how true they really were.

For a moment, he felt the all too familiar stab of pain as he remembered how quickly he had learned that truth. Life and death do go on, he thought. And there is only a fine line between the two. Only a matter of seconds.

He closed his eyes to the growing pain in his head. Was it still the effects of his injury, or was it caused from the memories that kept forcing their way into his mind? He couldn't forget. He didn't know if he wanted to.

"We must go on, continuing to do our job and our duty. We owe it to those who have gone before us." He heard Carl's final words, knowing that was exactly what he was doing. Going on. But in his case, it was a new job, a new duty, self-imposed because of events over which he had no control that had taken place in his life. He had felt that for once he was in control, but the other night had proven that to be a misconception. A reminder, of the One who was supposed to be in control. It was something he was careful to never again forget, as he once had done.

If only he had realized Mike had not been behind him as he left that burning building. If only he had been swifter in going back inside. If only. . .

His lips pressed together as he forced back his thoughts. As always, there were too many *if onlys*. Those were the words that always came too late. He had to remember the importance of dealing with now. With the present. And in trusting there was a Greater Power who knew the reasons why things happened as they did.

Taking a deep calming breath, he opened his eyes again, allowing his green gaze to look around him, seeing the present, absorbing all that was real around him.

His eyes stopped on the tall, willowy widow, her honey-blonde curls, released from the hat she had worn earlier, now blowing in the light breeze. He noted her proud stance, her chin held high. He noted the uniform she had chosen to wear, rather than the traditional black, that in some spheres was considered the proper attire for a recently widowed woman. But there wasn't anything traditional about Lacy Boyce, other than the traditional pain he knew she was feeling. That wouldn't change no matter what her manner of dress.

He looked beyond Lacy to the woman beside her: her mother, he had no doubt. She looked too much like an older version of Lacy to be anyone else. But if rumors were true, that was where the similarities stopped. Mrs. MacDonald did not share the rest of her family's dedication to the fire service. She had never fully accepted her daughter's interest swaying in the direction of her father's.

But then, Ryan reminded himself, he had always hated listening to rumors. He preferred to observe things first-hand before coming to a conclusion.

What he observed now was a look of unhappiness on the older woman's face. That, he knew would be normal for a mother whose daughter had become a widow and a mother within hours of each other. It would be normal that she'd be concerned for Lacy. But he also detected a look of distaste, barely visible, but there just the same. He guessed it had to do with the manner of the events taking place rather than the events themselves.

They were both very strong women, Ryan thought, as he continued to watch mother and daughter standing side by side, one in a black dress, the other in her fire department's uniform. Yes, equally strong. Lacy for doing what she wanted, though it may not have been the fashionable thing.

Just as it had not been the fashionable thing for a woman to join the fire department. He had heard she was the first woman to join, and he had no doubt she had been up against some strong opposition. She had had a lot to prove, both to the other men, and to herself. She wasn't a woman who joined just because she could, because a fire department was not allowed to discriminate, rather because of her dedication. He had sensed that about her the first time he saw her. He respected her for that.

But her mother was equally strong in her convictions. It would have been easy for her to get involved with the fire department as a way of being closer to the rest of her family. Easier to join and be a part of what they loved, rather than an outsider, the only member of the family who was not actively involved. But she chose to remain aloof, while accepting the choice of the rest of her family. He guessed she didn't like it, but she had to accept it, or her family would be destroyed.

That was something else he had learned quickly after joining the fire service. He had already seen several marriages break up because of one spouse's involvement in the fire department. It was a demanding job, and a spouse had to be supportive of those demands. In fact, more and more spouses took the attitude of "If you can't beat 'em, join 'em".

On that thought, his eyes darted to another member of the MacDonald family, Lorraine Shelby, Carl's younger sister. Everyone knew "Rainy", but not only as the sister of the local fire chief. She was a name in her own right.

Like Lacy, Rainy grew up with the fire department, hung around the station as a girl, but didn't join until later years. In fact, it was a few years after Lacy joined. Women weren't allowed to join when Rainy was growing up, and by the time they could, she was married with young children to raise.

Rainy must have been the ideal firefighter's wife. She understood the demands of the job. The meals delayed because of a fire. The holidays and family get-togethers interrupted because there was some type of an emergency. The many nights of sleep disturbed because of tones going off.

Though she wasn't a regular member, Rainy had always taken an avid interest in the fire department. It came as no surprise that when her boys were old enough to be left unattended, Rainy also joined the department. The only thing surprising them was when it wasn't as a firefighter, like other MacDonalds before her. Rather Rainy joined the fire police, like her husband, Mark, who had quit active firefighting several years before.

"Hey, we're closer than ever!" Ryan had heard Rainy teasing one night after they had been out on a call. "Now if we're in the middle of a discussion and we're interrupted by the tones, we can finish it on the way to the call."

And then, her usually quiet husband had rolled his eyes toward the sky saying, "Yes, God, give me strength. Now there's no escaping her, even during an emergency."

Ryan smiled at that memory, knowing he had admired the couple. Though they joked and teased each other a lot, it seemed they shared something very special.

Yes, Rainy Shelby, fit the description "If you can't beat 'em, join 'em."

Then others, like Lois MacDonald took the attitude if you can't join 'em, accept 'em.

His eyes returned to the woman, suspecting today was one day she was having a very difficult time accepting.

He watched as Carl returned to his daughter's side. Suddenly realized the service was over and that most of the people around him were leaving. Only the family would remain to say their last farewell.

He knew he should leave. Not only because he felt like an interloper on their private moment, but because of the painful memories these moments evoked. Yet he couldn't seem to leave.

There were short siren blasts as the fire trucks began leaving, saying their good-byes to their fallen comrade. Still, Ryan stood frozen in his place, watching as three people stood beside the casket.

31

"Just the man I wanted to see," Ryan's attention was averted suddenly to the red-haired woman taking purposeful steps in his direction, and the stout, frowning man following patiently behind. "I'm glad you're okay," Rainy added more softly as she stopped directly in front of him.

"Thanks," Ryan hesitated slightly, noting a determined look in the older woman's brown eyes. He had heard she was a stubborn woman who liked getting her way. And he suspected she wanted something now. "They only kept me in the hospital overnight for observation. I was the lucky one." He glanced back toward the mausoleum.

"Yeah, you were." Rainy nodded. "So were those little girls. Thanks to you."

He shrugged, not feeling like a hero, and hoping that wasn't what she was about to make him out to be.

"You do realize though, that you would have been more help to those kids if you were working with me."

This was it; he realized what was coming. Rainy was in charge of all the fire safety education programs conducted in the community. He had heard she was having problems getting help from the rest of the volunteers. So now she was recruiting. Smart move, coming to him now, he thought, then smiled.

"When do I start?"

She gave him a warm smile of satisfaction. "Depends on how fast you learn to do things my way."

"The right way," he added, already remembering hearing that she was particular about the quality of the programs her people presented.

"The only way," Mark Shelby said from beside his wife, giving her a half-grin that took the bite out of his sarcasm. "I keep telling her she'd get more help if she'd let some of the men do it their way."

"Oh sure, back to the days of letting the kids climb over a fire truck and call it fire prevention." She made a face. "My pet peeve," she continued, turning back to Ryan. "But this isn't the time nor the place. I just thought it was the place to corner you."

"You should have asked me sooner," Ryan heard himself saying, as if the thought had occurred to him before, though it hadn't. He had been too determined to be a firefighter. Too determined to run inside burning buildings to attempt daring rescues, to have even considered another way of saving lives.

"I was hoping you'd wise up and come to me." She replied sternly, then more softly, "If what my brother said about you is true, I figured it was only a matter of time before you'd realize there is another way."

He saw the compassion in her brown eyes and knew coming to him this way hadn't been easy. For all her brusk mannerism, she was a very caring

32

person. He had heard she put her heart and soul into her fire safety programs. Someone had once said she pushed too hard, as though trying to make up for lost time, for the years when she wasn't a member of the fire department. They complained that she expected everyone else to adhere to the pace she set for herself.

Well, he could admire that. Besides, he realized, there had to be a better way. "So when do you want to start teaching me to do things your way?"

"Is tomorrow too soon? It's a Saturday," she added. "But, we have a couple school programs to do before the term ends and I want to get you trained so you can help with them."

As they slowly left the cemetery they agreed on a time. From there, they would all be heading back to the fire station where the Ladies Auxiliary would be serving dinner to anyone who had attended the funeral. It was the culmination of a long day for everyone, but as Ryan well knew, there were still many more long days to come for the young widow and her family.

#

Lacy was glad to finally be able to sit, though she didn't have much of an appetite for the food provided for the guests. What she really wanted to do was leave so she could go to the hospital and visit her son. She missed him as though he had been a part of her life for many years. She longed to hold him for just a little while. Besides that, she felt the pressure of the milk in her breasts and knew it was well past his feeding time.

She'd be happy when she could take him home and they could get on to a normal schedule. A normal schedule, she almost laughed, realizing her life hadn't possessed a normal schedule in years. Few people in the volunteer emergency service could maintain one for long.

No, now that she had her son, she'd give all that up. After all, hadn't that been her reason for becoming a paramedic? She had to remind herself it wasn't, but when she learned she was pregnant, it had seemed a good alternative. If she had to work, she'd be able to work in the emergency service she loved.

Now she wondered if things would be so easy. She knew she wouldn't get hired for a job as paramedic until she proved herself. She and Brody, the department's rescue chief, got along well, but she didn't want any exceptions made because she was his friend, or because of anyone's sympathy over what had happened.

Still, she had little Mikie to think about. How could she provide for him and have the spare time to put into proving she could do the job?

33

Maybe she shouldn't even be considering it. *Mike, I wish you were here to help me decide?* But then she remembered, Mike hadn't been keen on her decision to become a paramedic. He had wanted her to quit everything, but, she had stubbornly refused.

Was I being too stubborn? Maybe I'm being a fool.

Lacy wasn't aware of her pain-filled expression as these thoughts crossed her mind. But Ryan was. He knew she was probably trying to think ahead. To make decisions about tomorrow, next week, next year, maybe even years ahead. It was normal. But it was wrong.

He thought of going to her and sharing some of his learned wisdom. The simple wisdom of taking it a day at a time. One step, then another. Solving first one small problem, before going on to another larger one.

But even as he thought about it, he saw someone joining her. He recognized the tall uniformed man as the chief of the town's rescue unit, Brody Langford. He didn't really know the man, but he knew of him. If what he'd heard was right, Brody would have a lot of good advice, and no problem sharing it with her. He was known as a take-charge sort of guy. But would he have the compassion and understanding to know exactly what would be helpful to her right now? Would he know that right now, she needed nothing more than time, and that rushing into anything could be a mistake?

Well, it really wasn't his business, was it? he reminded himself. But what was? Saving lives was, he answered his own question. But too few were really saved, and those that were still had to endure so much suffering. There had to be a better way. Maybe tomorrow Rainy would teach him that way. At least it would be a start. Then maybe . . .

His thoughts returned to a little girl he couldn't save. Then on to one he had, though she still lay suffering in the hospital. He wondered how she was doing.

"I'm sorry I couldn't make it for the service," Brody said as he joined Lacy. "We've had a busy morning."

"It's okay, Brody," Lacy smiled grimly at her friend. "We can't all be out of service at the same time. Emergencies don't stop just because we want them to. Someone has to be available in case there is one."

"I just wanted you to know, if there's anything I can do. . ." Brody gently cupped her cheek with the palm of his hand, then just as quickly pulled away again. "Just call me."

"For the moment, you can get yourself something to eat and come sit with us," Lacy invited. "Mom went to the ladies' room and Dad is thanking the others for coming."

"I can't guarantee how long I'll be able to sit. . ." Brody nodded, tapping the pager attached to his belt. "You know how it is."

34

"Oh, I know." She replied, remembering how often other affairs had been interrupted by emergencies.

She smiled suddenly reminded of another funeral. Her grandfather's. Her father's father. He had died at home of a heart attack, rather than in the line of duty, so the service had been small. Afterward they congregated here at the station so all the members of the fire company who had served with him could join them. In the middle of their meal the siren sounded, alerting them to a fire downtown.

She was only twelve at the time, but she still remembered the look of indecision that crossed her father's face before he got up from the table and responded to the call. Nor would she forget the look of distaste on her mother's face as she watched him leave.

Later when he returned, Carl had told them he knew it was what his father would have wanted him to do. His father had been a firefighter and a fire chief for too many years himself to have wanted it any other way. In fact, if he could have, he would have been responding himself.

Young as she was, Lacy had imagined her grandfather somewhere in heaven watching his men as they responded to that call, and every call afterward. He was looking out for them, helping to keep them safe as best he could.

Now Lacy wondered if Mike was somewhere with her grandfather, looking down on them.

She shook away her thoughts as her mother returned to the table. It would do her no good to share such a fantasy with her mother. Just the opposite. Lacy also remembered a few years later, after she, too, had joined the fire department, when her mother's father had passed away. That funeral had been a different matter indeed. Both she and her father were warned that their pagers were to be kept at home and that under no circumstances would anyone respond to an emergency any time that day. Neither she nor her father doubted they would be in serious trouble if either one of them disobeyed her order. It was the only time she had made her objections quite so adamantly known.

"Lacy, are you okay?" her mother said. "Is something wrong?"

Lacy felt her face growing red, thankful her mother could not read her thoughts. She had no doubts her mother would not be pleased with her dredging up those unpleasant memories. This day had held enough of its own.

"I was just thinking about Little Mikie," Lacy said, knowing it was half true, since she had been thinking about her son before her thoughts began to stray. "I'd like to stop at the hospital on my way home."

"Certainly, Dear, we can . . ."

"Mom, I can go alone in Dad's truck like I came."

"You don't have to be alone . . ." her mother started, but stopped as Brody came back to the table carrying a plate of food.

"Right over here, Brody," Lacy said, motioning to the seat on her right. She was relieved he arrived before she had to hurt her mother by telling her she wanted to be alone. She preferred to be alone. At least for a little while. So she could think, and plan.

#

An hour later, the crowd in the room was thinning. Lacy felt certain no one would blame her if she slipped away. Her mother had finally left her side long enough to join her father to thank the members who had come out and helped that day. At that moment, they were in the kitchen giving a special thanks to the members of the ladies' auxiliary who had prepared and served all the food.

Brody had gotten called out on another emergency before finishing his meal. Aunt Rainy and Uncle Mark had sat with their fire police unit to eat, then had come to her table for a little while before going home. Her cousin Kevin had been with them, in uniform too, since he had just joined as a junior firefighter. And his fourteen-year-old brother, Brad, looking so uncomfortable in his suit and tie, still not old enough to become a junior member.

Some of the men had already begun putting away tables and chairs. There was so much activity going on, no one noticed as she slipped outside into the damp afternoon air. She felt a chill and slipped into the jacket she had worn earlier.

CHAPTER THREE

Lacy looked down at her newborn son as he slept, knowing he represented all that had been good in her life. *Will I be able to give him all that he deserves?* she wondered. Without a father it wouldn't be easy. Yet, that was the way it would be.

She sighed, leaning her head back against the brightly-colored cushion on the old wooden rocker, closing her eyes. *What will tomorrow hold?*

Her mother was already under the assumption that they would move back home with her parents. Lacy knew they would do everything to help her. Perhaps that in itself was the problem. She wanted to stand on her own two feet. To make it on her own.

She thought of all the other single mothers. Whether through choice or fate, they did everyday, what she was going to be doing all of her tomorrows – raising a child alone. If they could do it, why couldn't she?

A gray-haired nurse quietly stepped back into the room, tapping her on the shoulder. Lacy smiled to the kindly woman who had seemed more like a grandmother than someone she'd just met. "You really should go home and get some rest," the older woman whispered, compassion filling her glistening pale-blue eyes. "It's been a long day."

Lacy suspected the woman knew about her situation. The hospital grapevine must be every bit as swift as the one in the fire department, Lacy thought. Of course it would be. How could it not be? There had been five victims of that common tragedy admitted to this hospital. Three were still here.

She placed her son back into the incubator, knowing if all went well he'd be out of it soon. The doctor was only being cautious. Her son was doing quite well under the circumstances. Far better than the fire's other victims.

She thought of the two sisters upstairs on the fourth floor. Luckily neither had sustained burns. The culprit had been the thick, black smoke. Had they not been rescued they would have been dead before the fire ever reached them. Still, she knew one child was in critical condition. Ryan had mentioned she was in the pediatric intensive care unit.

If she hurried, she could still stop by and check on them before visiting hours were over. She wondered how they were. She knew she wouldn't be allowed to see the one in ICU, but she could at least ask the nurses about her. She suspected Ryan would be interested in hearing about the child.

As the elevator doors opened on the fourth floor, she caught a glimpse of the familiar tall figure with wavy dark hair as he passed by, heading for the stairs. His steps were hurried, his head bent, as though in deep thought.

She was about to call out to him, but he had already passed through the stairway doors. Curious, she followed, looking through the door's small, rectangular pane of glass before opening it. Ryan was standing at the foot of the stairs, his shoulders hunched.

"You have a habit of sneaking around in stairwells," she said, trying to sound cheerful as she opened the door. Immediately, she sensed something was wrong.

Ryan raised his dark head and squared his shoulders. She heard his sharp intake of breath before he turned to face her. His green eyes glistened with tears as he tried to swallow away his pain.

He looked at the woman before him, forcing himself to regain control. The last thing he wanted to do was worry her. And judging the lines of worry around her deep, blue eyes, she was indeed worried. She had been through enough in the last few days.

"Lacy, don't sneak up on a man like that. Especially when he's sanding at the top of the stairs." He could see his false humor didn't fool her. She stepped forward, her hand outstretched.

Her touch was gentle on his arm. He was in awe of her. After everything this astonishing woman had been through, she was going to try to comfort him.

"Did the . . . the little girl. . . did she. . .?" Lacy started.

"Thank God, no." He quickly released a long sigh of relief. "I just saw her. She was still in the ICU, but her condition has been upgraded to stable."

"That's wonderful!" Lacy said, understanding now that his emotions were happiness. Or, were they? She looked up into his eyes, reading the pain in them. Once again she was certain this man had deep pain. And it went beyond this emergency call. In fact, she'd bet the circumstances of this call had merely rekindled it.

"The other girl's doing great. I didn't stay long. Her parents were with her, of course," he said, forcing a smile. "They were kind of emotional when they realized who I was. I have to admit, it got to me."

You don't fool me, Ryan Simon, it was more than that.

"I know what you mean. I've seen it before," Lacy said instead, searching for something to change the subject. "We're heroes and everyone is ready to praise us and put us up on pedestals − too bad they don't realize the whole thing is such a waste. Half the time − no. . ." she corrected, her frustrations rising to the surface. "more than half the time − the whole situation could have been prevented. We only react to that situation. Come in and do what we can after it starts. The heros are people like Aunt Rainy who are out there before it happens, trying to prevent tragedies from happening in the first place. It's such a waste."

Ryan watched with concern as Lacy finished her statement, getting it out of her system. When she was through, he gave her a grim smile. "Proactive rather than reactive."

"What?" Lacy looked up.

"I was recruited by your aunt this morning," he explained. "So I stopped by her station on the way home and picked up a few articles on the subject of fire safety education."

Lacy nodded, now realizing what he meant. The two were common words to fire safety educators. She had heard her Aunt using them often. Proactive: education before the emergency to prevent it from happening in the first place; versus Reactive: fighting the fire and all the emotions involved after the fact. The "if onlys".

"Reactive comes just a little too late." Her words were a near-whisper. She knew this time it had been too late to save her husband. The irony of the situation, she knew, was that Mike had not been supportive of her aunt's work.

"I take it you're on your aunt's committee," Ryan said.

"Team," she corrected. "Aunt Rainy has a fire safety education team."

"Same difference, isn't it?"

Lacy laughed and was happy for the moment's release from her grief. "Not to her. She thought referring to team would represent team work, a team effort. That sort of thing."

"And I gather it hasn't worked that way?"

Lacy frowned. "Not always. But for now, for awhile at least, she'll have more help."

"Reactive," Ryan repeated the word.

Lacy's honey-gold curls bounced as she nodded her response.

"So, are you?"

"What?"

"On the team?"

She nodded again. "I was to some extent. It got a little difficult to keep up."

"Being pregnant can do that."

She smiled again. "Hey, that only prevented me from demonstrating "Stop, Drop and Roll". No, I was pretty busy with my paramedic training."

They heard the announcement over the public address system that visiting hours in the children's ward were over.

"I guess that's my signal to leave," Lacy said.

"I take it you were heading the same place I had been."

"I thought I'd check on the girls' conditions. I'm glad I ran into you first," she admitted. "I don't think I'd have been up to facing the family yet."

"Bitter?" Ryan said softly, knowing the investigation had proved the fire had started by a cigarette in the trash can, simple negligence.

"No, not bitter. Not yet, at least. I feel more. . . defeated. It's all such a waste." She sighed, the deep blue of her sapphire eyes suddenly glazed with tears. "My son has to grow up without a father because someone just didn't think. One second of carelessness cost a lifetime, and very nearly cost several of them." She swallowed hard. "I couldn't handle their apologies right now."

"Look, I better get back to my parent's place. Mom's probably ready to send out a search team." She started down the stairs, but Ryan grabbed her arm.

"Hold on there," he said without debate. "I doubt stairs are the prescribed mode of descent for new mothers. Let's take the elevator."

Lacy instinctively wanted to rebel, but gave it a second thought as she looked down the stairs. They looked suddenly longer. She allowed him to guide her to the elevator, rode down with her, then walked with her through the lobby toward the doors.

"Thanks a lot, Ryan," she said. "I think you're probably one of the few people who understands how I feel right now."

He didn't reply, wondering if somehow she knew of his past. Of the events that led to his becoming a firefighter. His being reactive rather than proactive.

"Is that all you're wearing?" he asked, changing the subject as he glanced down at her light blue uniform shirt. "It's too cold to be out without a jacket. Here, take mine." He slipped out of his navy blue jacket with the fire company patch on its sleeve and placed it across her shoulders.

"Are you always this bossy?" she asked, but didn't refuse his offer. It was cool, and the last thing she needed now was to catch a cold. Besides, she suspected he'd only persist.

"Only when I have to be."

"Keep it up and you'll start sounding like a line officer," she said sarcastically. "Or a mother hen."

He threw back his head and laughed. "And I suspect you know about both."

"Do I ever." She glanced at the clock on the wall. "And if I don't get going now I'll have more to worry about from the mother hen than the line officer." She started out the door, glancing back over her shoulder. "I'll see that you get your jacket back soon."

As Lacy pulled into the driveway she saw a beat up Chevy Blazer parked next to her father's Chief's car. Even without the red emergency lights on top of the tan vehicle, to signify a Chief Officer, she'd have recognized the vehicle as belonging to Arlen Maxwell, Chief of Vigilance Engine Company Number One, the company where she and Mike had belonged as firefighters. They were called Vigilantes for short, the nickname their company members had acquired through the years.

She suspected she knew why he was there, as any of the Chiefs from one of the Borough's five fire stations would be under similar circumstances. Not to offer condolences to the member who had lost a husband, nor the Borough Fire Chief who had lost a son-in-law. He had done that already earlier that day.

No, it was time to return the status quo. Time to chose a predecessor for Mike who had been the company's Second Assistant Chief. It was the chain-of-command. The order of things in the fire service, and as soon as they filled the vacancy they could return to that order and things could function normally.

At least for them, Lacy thought, with no animosity. She knew and understood that was the way it was. Life must go on, especially for them. The need for their services didn't stop just because they did. It was their duty. And they had to be prepared to answer the call to duty. People were depending on them.

"Evening, Lacy." The chief slipped off his navy-blue cap with the scrambled eggs on the brim as she stepped up onto the porch. His thinning, gray hair made him look older than his forty years.

"Good evening, Chief," she replied automatically. "I want to thank you, since I didn't earlier, for everything you and the rest of the crew did today." She swallowed her tears, standing tall as she faced the man who had once been her fire chief. Still was, since she was technically still a member of his company.

"The baby okay?" her father asked from his perch on the porch rail, his manner far more relaxed than that of his companion. She suspected it was because the chief wasn't certain how to approach her. How to act around her. Nor what to say. She had seen that often in the past few days.

"He's doin' fine." Her chin raised as she forced a weary smile. "They say he may be able to come home soon."

Carl nodded. "Your mother'll be happy to hear that."

"I suppose you're here to talk about who should fill Second Assistant till the next election," she acknowledged.

"Yeah. I thought maybe Carl could help me decide." The Chief nervously ran a hand over his balding scalp, looking at the larger man still leaning causally against the porch rail. "Not that long ago he was in my shoes. I figured he still knows most the members well enough to offer some advice."

41

"Like I said before Lacy got here," Carl replied. "It's not good policy for the Borough Chief to stick his nose into any of the Borough five fire companies' business, unless the business is creating a problem with us doing our job."

Chief Maxwell nodded, turning to her as he replaced his cap. "To be honest, my first thought would have been you, Lacy. But I suppose that's out of the question."

"Yes, Arlen, that's definitely out of the question," she replied. "Wouldn't you normally offer it to the person who ran in the last election for that position?"

"They'd have the experience all right. At least, should of, to have run." The Chief frowned. "But in this case, I'm not too keen on that solution. You know how it is sometimes. Woody Brown wasn't too happy when he lost the election. We haven't seen much of him since then. He's been more active with Friendship."

Friendship Hook and Ladder was one of the Borough's other companies. If the grapevine was accurate, Lacy had heard that Woodrow Brown, Woody as he was better known, was making himself indispensable there. She had no doubt if that were true, maybe after the next election, or possibly even the following one, he'd become one their assistant chiefs.

The difference there being he wouldn't have to win by popular vote, as was the case at the Vigilantes. At Friendship, only the chief was elected and he appointed his assistants. Each company, though part of the department as a whole, set up their own by-laws and guidelines of operation.

If Woody didn't become an assistant within a year or two, she had not doubt he'd next try East End Station, the Borough's third company. He had already been a member of the bordering township company. After losing his bid for election there, he'd joined the Vigilantes.

Yes, Woody wanted a position of power and he wouldn't give up till he had one. She'd seen others like him before. She thought little of any of them, but perhaps even less of Woody. But then she had good reason, she mused, remembering that reason all too well.

#

It had been a particularly grueling day. Bitter cold against the heat of flames that engulfed a restaurant, a community landmark, at that. Every station in the Borough had been there. They'd even had needed to call mutual aid from three bordering townships. They had managed to save the foundation. But then, you have those days. When everything you do isn't enough. Still, you never learn to accept them.

They were all tired. There was a lot of tension in the air when they got back to the station. It had been the last straw for Dick McKinney, the First Assistant Chief.

For Dick, it had been a long five years since he'd won the position of first assistant, filling the vacancy left by Arlen Maxwell when he was voted in as Chief. That had been a year of changes, starting with Carl's appointment to the Borough Fire Chief's position.

That had also left an opening for second assistant, the one previously filled by Dick. Barry Carlisle, Mike's best friend, had surprised everyone by running for that spot. There had been speculation that Mike might run. But at the time, he had been too busy courting Lacy. Because of that, Barry ran unopposed.

For Dick, second assistant had been bad enough, the change to first had been even more of a struggle. Everyone knew his wife had never been fond of his involvement in the fire service. Not that he admitted it. It was just something you could sense. In their case if you didn't sense it, you had the hide of a crocodile.

A meeting night never went by without the interruption of a phone call from Christiania McKinney, wanting to speak to her husband. Tuesday and Thursday nights, work and training nights respectively, were no exception. She would inevitably call, and shortly after, he'd leave for home.

During the last few months, Dick had been at the station less and less. Some of the members were growing bitter that he hadn't been doing his fair share of the work. But no one actually said anything to him. They all knew he was under enough pressure at home.

Finally, on the night of the restaurant fire, he had informed everyone present this was his last year as assistant chief.

"Hey, we all feel that way after a big one," Mike had said. "Especially after one we lose."

"No, it's not just that," the older man shook his head. "You need someone in here who has more time. I've been so busy lately I don't know whether I'm coming or going."

Lacy suspected that was only partly true. She was certain his wife had more than likely given him the ultimatum, if he was coming to the station, he was going from their marriage.

After his announcement there was a lot of speculation about who would run in the next election. It was pretty obvious Barry would run for Dick's position. It was only normal he'd want to take the step up from second assistant to first.

"Lacy's made a good training officer, and has as much experience as any of us," Jack Mulholland stated with good humor. "Puts some of us macho men to shame." Jack had always been supportive of women in the fire service. He had even coaxed his wife into giving it a try. Though she didn't work out as a firefighter, she had turned out to be an excellent treasurer of the company. Their financial records had never looked so good. Even Jack's daughter, Paula, was getting into the action, having recently joined as a junior firefighter.

But not every man in the company shared his feelings. Many clung to the old belief that women belonged in the kitchen, not at the fire.

"What about you, Mike?" suggested Barry as he slapped his best friend on the back, his red-rimmed gaze darkening as he turned to Lacy.

He had made little secret he thought Mike had been overshadowed by Lacy and that he thought it was because of her ties to the Borough Chief. Many times Lacy had to pray for the ability to bite her tongue to prevent herself from telling Barry what she thought of him and his opinions. But she had been afraid that would, in turn, give the impression she didn't think her husband was as good at the job as she was.

That had always been a sore point between them. Even before they were married. In fact, it had come as a surprise to everyone when they started dating. There had been such competitiveness between them. More on Mike's part than hers.

Truth was, she thought he was just as good as she was. She had just been there longer. Since she was a junior member. She was a far more experienced firefighter.

"He'd have my vote," Lacy said with a smile.

There was a little good-natured ribbing and insinuations about the possibility she was trying to butter up her husband.

"Butter up for what?" she teased in return.

"Don't play dumb with us, you know what we mean, Lacy," one man joked.

"As if either of us would have any energy left after spending the whole day fighting that fire."

"Speak for yourself," Mike retorted, placing his hand suggestively on her backside. "I'm never too tired for that." Though she hated when he did that at the station, Lacy forced a smile.

"Save it till you get home," one man groaned, throwing a dirty, rolled up sock at them.

"I'll try," Mike teased as he practically dragged Lacy toward the door.

"What would be the difference which of them got assistant?" Woody Brown made the sarcastic comment before Lacy and Mike were out of the room. She felt Mike tense, and knew he'd heard.

She reached for the door to open it, but not before they heard the rest of Woody's comment.

"Everyone knows which one of them calls the shots. She'll run the show whether she has the title or not. I'd say she's got him tied to her apron string, but I doubt she ever has time to cook she's at the station so often."

"Come on," Lacy pleaded, her dark blue eyes wide as she saw Mike was about to turn back to the group of men. "He's just baiting you."

"I'd like to. . ." Mike ground the threat through gritted teeth.

"You do and you'll never make rank," she snapped. "The first thing a line officer has to do is set an example for his men."

She was relieved when Mike followed her through the door, but she knew he was furious. Woody had managed to target Mike's biggest sore point. She knew she had to do something to prevent that situation from every happening again.

So it was, when they were both nominated for second assistant chief, she declined the nomination. That was when she told everyone she had decided it was time to move on to something new, "Another challenge," she had said, hoping that would give the impression she wasn't doing it for the sake of her husband.

She had joined the emergency medical unit and spoken to their officers about starting paramedic training as soon as the next class started. Thankfully, everyone seemed to accept her reason. Especially her husband, but he wasn't necessarily happy with that decision either.

It came as no surprise to anyone when Woody Brown was nominated to run for assistant chief against Mike. He had been campaigning ever since Dick had announced he wasn't going to run for the position. His campaign platform, if that's what you'd call it, could have been, "Vote for a man who has a mind of his own. Not one ruled by his woman."

For Lacy, he was easy to ignore. She had long since risen above the prejudice over women in the fire service. But for Mike, it had been a painful reminder that everything he did, his wife had done before him.

Accept become a line officer. Lacy was more than thankful – she was relieved – when he had won the election.

In reality, Woody had few friends. True, they voiced themselves loudly. But there were so few of them that when it came to counting the votes, Mike won by a landslide.

#

No, Woody would be the last person Lacy would want to see as the next assistant chief. The position needed someone with not only experience, but a willingness to accept change and an openness to new ideas. Someone with determination to do a job well, while still being compassionate enough to understand another's mistakes, and willing to take the time to help correct those mistakes.

A person who would live by the rules, unless he felt there was a very good reason not to. One person came to mind.

A person who broke the cardinal rule of removing a face mask in a hostile environment in order to save another person's life. A person who would have returned to a building, against orders, to save his partner's life, knowing there was only a slim chance he would survive.

"Ryan Simon," she spoke her thoughts aloud. "I think you should consider him."

"He's a good man. But he hasn't been with us very long," Arlen stated. "Could tick-off a few others who may think they should have the job."

"Bottom line is who's best for the job." Carl stated.

"Or who's got the most experience," the company chief stated.

"Sometimes experience is a two-edged sword," Lacy's heard her father saying as she let herself into the house. "Experience, as in qualified to do the job. Or, experience, as in years on the job."

Whatever was decided, it would be up to them, she thought. Right now she really didn't care. She was too tired to care. No, she was exhausted, both emotionally and physically. All she wanted was to go to bed. To escape to the security of her old room, the way she had escaped there as a child every time she'd had a problem. It had been her haven. A place for quiet solitude and prayer. It was that again, now, and she knew it could be habit forming. She couldn't let that happen. She was no longer a child. She was an adult, responsible for a child of her own.

"Honey, you're finally home," Lois MacDonald said, jumping up from her chair as soon as Lacy entered the room. "I was so worried about you."

"I told you I was going to the hospital."

"All this time?" her mother said, the lines around her bright, blue eyes so prominent, Lacy felt guilty for making her worry. "The baby's okay, isn't he?"

"He's doing fine, Mom. Sound asleep when I left him."

Her mother sighed in relief. "I can't wait until we bring him home. Did they say when that would be? I thought we'd move all the nursery things here tomorrow or the next day."

"Mom, his nursery things are fine where they are," Lacy said, forcing a smile to take the bite out of her words. "I'll be back home before he's discharged. Staying here has been wonderful, considering everything. But it's only a temporary situation."

Lois bit her lip, worrying, as she always worried. "I think you should give some serious consideration to everything before you make a final decision, Honey. You've been through a lot. Taking care of a newborn won't be easy."

"Mom, other women have done it before me."

"But they have husbands to help them. I'm sorry, Honey, but it's not going to be easy alone."

Lacy was too weary to argue. "We'll talk more about it tomorrow, okay? Right now, all I want to do is sleep." Without another word, she trudged up the stairs.

But sleep didn't come just because she wanted it to. She had too much on her mind. Too many decisions to make. And she wanted to be sure she made the right ones.

Dear Lord, please help me do the right thing. Help me make the right choices for my baby.

#

Lacy tossed and turned for hours, her mind not letting her rest. Still she had come to no decisions when exhaustion finally overcame her and she fell into a deep sleep. By the time she awoke, the sun was shining brightly through her window from high in the sky. Still, she wasn't ready to leave the comfort of her soft haven. There were still all those decisions to face.

She was about to pull her covers over her head to prolong her blessed escape just a little bit longer, when something else drew her attention. She twitched her nose then inhaled deeply, enjoying the familiar scents. Her mother was baking.

Lacy savored the scent, remembering her mother's ritual of baking early every Saturday morning. She always said it was the only day she could get her husband to sit down long enough to eat a decent breakfast.

Blueberry muffins. Lacy smiled, remembering her father's favorite. It was what her mother always made him. Not that muffins were the only thing she baked on Saturday morning. There would be Shoo-fly pies, rich, gooey molasses, covered with crumbs and baked in a pie crust; or AP Cake, those tasty brown sugar breakfast cakes, both Pennsylvania Dutch recipes handed down from generation to generation. Both were her father's favorites.

Yes, she remembered her father often sampling a slice and eating half a cake himself. He'd insist it wasn't his fault, but rather blame it on their ancestors. Both his and his wife's.

"The Irish love eating." He'd laugh. "And the Pennsylvania Dutch enjoy cooking. So we do what we've been born to do." Then he'd wink. "But together we're a match made in heaven."

Then her mother would chide him for making a pig of himself. "If the Irish among us don't slow down on their eating, we Pennsylvania Dutch may just stop cooking so much."

Lacy smiled at the memory, knowing her mother still hadn't followed through on her threat.

As she rolled to the other side of the bed, Lacy spotted a small tray on her night stand holding a napkin covered basket and an insulated cup.

Her stomach growled its request that she give in to the temptation. She had lacked an appetite since the night of the fire, eating more out of necessity than desire. Now, to her surprise, the thought of her mother's blueberry muffins was actually making her hungry.

Sitting up she stretched her weary bones then reached first for the insulated cup. "Coffee, the sustenance of life," she said as she lifted the lid to find white instead of black, cold instead of hot. "Milk." She wrinkled up her nose remembering she had given up caffeine while she was pregnant and she knew it wasn't good to drink coffee while she was nursing.

Still, she had grown so tired of drinking milk, insisting the only way she could bear it was to dunk some kind of cake or pastry into it, then when finished eating it, she'd use a spoon to scoop up the rest of the milk-soaked crumbs from the bottom of the glass.

"Oh, no." Mike would groan, wrinkling his nose distastefully whenever she did. "Do you have to do that?"

"I've done it ever since I was a girl. Just be thankful I don't do it in public."

"That's so gross. A person could lose their appetite watching you."

"Then don't watch," she'd retort, flashing him a bright smile.

She forced herself to take a sip from the insulated cup before reaching into the basket for a blueberry muffin. Breaking it in half, preparing to butter it, she saw that it wasn't a blueberry muffin after all.

"Thought I heard you moving around in here," her father said from the doorway. "How are you this morning?"

She shrugged. "Tired."

"Your Mom thought you might be. She figured you'd want to stay in bed so she brought the tray up for you."

"It's not that kind of tired," Lacy said with a sigh. "But I appreciate it anyway."

"Takes time, Honey," Carl said with a concerned look on his face as he watched his daughter concentrating on the muffin in her hand.

Her father's unaccustomed sentimentality caused tears to sting Lacy's eyes. She didn't want to cry. She wanted to be strong. She had to be strong.

48

"Where's the butter?" Lacy said, hoping the change of subject would help end her lapse into weakness.

"The little plastic container," Carl said, hiding a smile. "It sprinkles on."

Lacy picked it up and read the label. She had heard of the popular butter substitute, but she had never tried it. She couldn't believe her father would even taste the powdered flavoring, much less use it on a regular basis.

"It's not too bad when the food's hot enough to melt the stuff."

"Think I'll pass," she said, pressing a finger against one half of her muffin. "Mine have cooled."

"I can take them down and nuke'em for you," her father offered, using his nickname for using the microwave to cook foods. "Or I can offer you a little of this." He pulled a stick of margarine from behind his back."

Her smile returned as she reached for the stick. "Is this from your private stash? Or does Mom know about it?"

"It's for special occasions," he replied. "But she made sure she bought the brand with the lowest amount of cholesterol."

"Since when has she been so health conscious?"

"Since my last check up," he replied gruffly.

"You never told me there was anything wrong with you?" Lacy was immediately concerned for her father. "What is it?"

"Nothing. My cholesterol was about 220 so the doctor said I should start watching what I eat. Your Mom is just making sure I do. You know how she is."

"And I know how you are." Lacy laughed. "It must be a real picnic around here."

"Don't say that word!" her father said with pretend fright.

"What word?"

"Picnic. It reminds me of food. Good food. Cooked the way it ought to be."

"Oh, come on. It can't be that bad."

Golden sparks of light seemed to radiate from his brown eyes. "Not all of it. She's actually come up with some pretty good food. And she's been experimenting with some of her favorite recipes, trying to make them as cholesterol-free as possible."

"That explains the muffins," Lacy said. "I didn't think it was your favorite kind."

"Oat bran," Carl stated. "A lot better than the regular bran muffins she made a couple of times. They were like chewing moist sawdust. Thank goodness someone decided oat bran was good for lowering cholesterol."

"So I suppose that means no more trips to the Golden Arches."

Her father ignored the statement. "I'll let you finish eating, then you can go back to bed if you want."

"I haven't been out of bed yet, and stop changing the subject, Dad. You're not following your diet when you're away from home?"

"I'm cutting down on fast food," he said. "I take fruit to the office and eat enough carrot and celery sticks that I feel like a rabbit."

"You set a find example for the men in the Department," Lacy scolded. "You know it's inevitable: fitness requirements will someday be mandated. If you flunk your physical, you'll be out the door."

"I use brains not brawn," he replied. "But you're right. And I have been doing better. I've even started going for walks with your mother at night."

Lacy was surprised. Though she never doubted her parents love for each other, she had never seen them do that much alone together. Perhaps her moving away from home had brought them closer together.

"You know, Dad, I've been thinking I should go home," she said.

"Don't rush yourself. You always have a place here."

"No, I think it's best that I do it sooner, rather than later. It's going to be hardest at first. You know, getting used to the fact that Mike isn't there. . ." She took a breath. "I thought I should get that over with before I bring the baby home. I thought I should move back today."

Carl nodded. "I see you've given it a lot of thought."

"When you can't sleep, you have a lot of time to think."

"Your mother isn't going to like your decision." He made a face. "You know she thought you might want to move in here indefinitely."

"I know, Dad. But I can't. I've got to make it on my own."

"Just as long as you realize that sometimes there is no harm in accepting a helping hand when you need it. Don't be so stubborn you forget that."

"I at least have to try," she said. "Will you support me on this? I know Mom's going to be determined to change my mind."

Carl raised his eyes to the ceiling. "Suppose you let me break it to her for you. Sort of pave the way."

"I take it this is one of those times I should accept a helping hand," she said with a smile.

"Definitely," he replied with a sigh, raising his eyes to the ceiling as though seeking help from above. "And I guess I better go down and start paving."

CHAPTER FOUR

Ryan placed his hands over his face then dropped to his knees, rolling back and forth on the floor in front of the russet-haired fire safety team leader. Lorraine Shelby stood above him, her head cocked to the side as she carefully watched his actions. She was a hard taskmaster indeed, he thought, wondering how many times she would make him do this, the most basic of all fire safety lessons, before she was satisfied he'd gotten it right.

He heard unstifled laughter coming from just beyond the doorway and knew they had drawn an audience.

"Would a few of you like to come in and show us how it should be done?" Though her words were cheerful, her smile was forced. "We can always use more help."

There was some mumbling in reply. Ryan stopped rolling, propped himself on one elbow, and looked toward the doorway to see the group of observers thinning.

"I already put in my time," said one man, Ryan recognized as an ambulance driver. "I was with you at Saint Joe's Pre-School."

"Yes, and you did a great job," the red-head said, turning back to Ryan. "Jack works real well with the kids."

Ryan saw that her teeth were gritted as she spoke and sensed she would have liked to have added something more.

"You just give me a call any time you need me again," the man said before disappearing from the doorway with the last of the observers quick on his heel.

No doubt their hurry was to avoid being asked to participate, Ryan suspected.

Rainy's smile relaxed, easing some of the tension from her lightly freckled face. "And when I call, he'll be busy," she said skeptically.

"Ye of little faith," Ryan mocked as he got up from the floor, bending to pick up the piece of red felt that had been laid on his clothing to represent an actual flame.

"Faith, no. Experience, yes," she said grimly. "I've gained a lot of that through the years. But. . . I better shut my mouth and stop complaining. It doesn't help the cause. Word spreads too quickly around here. I don't need to create any more hard feelings. I've already lost too many helpers for our fire safety programs."

"And you're gaining a new one," Ryan reminded her. "If you'd like to keep this helper, you won't insinuate he'll run back and tell the others everything you say."

He saw the red-head's face grow nearly as bright as her hair, but in her brown eyes he saw something else. Could it have been a glimmer of hope? Respect, maybe. Somehow he liked that thought. He suspected gaining this woman's respect was something special. And definitely not easily accomplished.

"Mark always warns me my big mouth will get me in trouble."

"Too much cynicism will, too," Ryan said, reaching out to pat her on the arm. But when he removed his hand he left the red flame on her blouse, hoping it would lighten the mood.

"Turning the tables, are we?" She laughed.

"Every second the flame is on your clothing it doubles in size," Ryan reminded her. "Are you going to stand there until you're consumed?"

Rainy immediately dropped to her knees, though carefully, then laid on the floor doing a repeat of the Stop, Drop and Roll Ryan had done only moments earlier.

"What they say about paybacks is true." Her voice vibrated with laughter as she stopped rolling, raising herself on hands and knees before attempting to rise.

Ryan watched her slow, careful movements, seeing the signs of strain on her face. Judging by the amount of difficulty she was having getting to her feet, he felt guilty for putting her through the ordeal. He stepped forward and placed a helping hand under her arm for support as she rose.

"I've gotta do some serious dieting," she said in a voice that was breathless from her exertion. "Especially if I'm going to have someone around who believes in tit-for-tat."

Ryan suspected that her problem was more than being overweight. Her actions weren't just exertion. He had observed pain dulling her brown eyes.

"The arthritis doesn't help either," she admitted, confirming his suspicions. "You know, good days and bad days. Today is a bad one."

"Yesterday's dampness," he stated, remembering what it was like for his mother. He wondered how she was today. It had been over a month since he'd seen her, though he called several times a week. He'd have to call her tonight. He'd neglected calling her since the fire. Not that it usually mattered to her. She had good days and bad days, too. And not just from arthritis.

"Ryan, are you still with me?"

"I'm sorry." He turned back to her, forcing the unhappy thoughts from his mind. "What were you saying?"

"For a moment you were miles away."

52

He shrugged his broad shoulders. "Yes, I certainly was." And that was the truth. His mother was still in New York, in a nursing home on Long Island. She had been there for years. Three years to be exact.

#

After his father died of a heart attack, he and his wife, Norma, had brought his mother to their home to live. At the time her illness hadn't been quite so progressed. The bouts of forgetfulness were not so severe that they couldn't handle them.

Ryan had been a CPA with a successful firm in the city. But as the Alzheimer's disease progressed, he decided it was only fair that he be home more to help with his mother. His wife was busy enough with their baby daughter, Michele.

He decided to go into business for himself, converting the attic of their garage into an office, with an intercom to communicate between the office and house. That way he could be called quickly if there was a problem.

For the first year, they often worried whether his decision had been a smart one. Business was slow. They had to dip into their savings to survive.

Fortunately, after that first frightening year, business picked up. By tax time the following year, he had a booming business. Often he'd work till late at night. Sometimes Norma helped too, when she could, working from the house so she could be close to Michele and his mother.

By that time, Ruth Simon had a tendency to wander away, going for a walk, as she put it. Too often forgetting her way home. The doctors had warned him the disease would progress that way, if indeed Alzheimer's disease was what she had. No one would know for sure, since there was no way to diagnose the disease. It was more a matter of ruling out everything else.

She would remember things from her past longer than those which happened in more recent years. More than once when she'd disappear, Ryan would find her back at the apartment where she and his father had lived all their married lives. Sometimes she'd even be arguing with the new tenants, insisting it was they who did not belong there.

He had been thankful for their patience and understanding. After the first incident, they invited her into the house, then called him to come and get her. They even gave her the freedom of their home, allowing her to think it was still her home and they the guests, until Ryan arrived to take her home again. She'd always seem so lost, so frustrated and confused.

He had known how difficult the situation was on his wife, having a mother-in-law living with her who barely remembered who she was, much less what she was doing there. There had been many frightening, sometimes even hostile confrontations between them, when Ryan would have to patiently reintroduce his wife and daughter to his mother.

Yet, whenever he suggested putting his mother into a nursing home, it was Norma who'd disagree.

"The time will come when she'll have to go into a home," she said. "Till that time we'll do everything we can to make her comfortable and happy."

Ryan looked upon his wife as a saint. She had not only opened the doors of her home to his mother, but she had also taken the time to learn as much about the disease as possible. She had even insisted they join a caregiver's support group and attended their meetings whenever they could find someone to stay with Ruth and Michele.

Perhaps Norma's insistence stemmed from losing her own parents at a young age. She had been barely out of high school when they were killed in a car accident. It was her older sister who had insisted she come to live with her in New York. And subsequently helped her get a job as a model, like herself, in the city.

Yet, Norma hadn't been happy as a model. It was a faster life than the one she'd grown up knowing. Because of her deep faith and Christian upbringing, it was difficult to relate to some of the other models who changed relationships almost as often as they changed their outfits.

But her modeling days had not been for long. Once Ryan and she met at a church function, it was love at first sight. Within a year they had been married. Making plans for a long, happy future. Making plans for a dream home, with many children to fill the house with love.

That dream burst one evening in the midst of income tax season. As usual for that time of year, Ryan was working late. It had been over an hour since Norma had come outside to say good-night, assuring him both his daughter and his mother were sound asleep.

She had insisted it was time for him to take a break, drawing the heavy curtains on the window that over-looked the back of the house. She then joined him behind his desk, on the large over-stuffed executive chair, climbing onto his lap, cuddling close, her arms around his neck, her body pressed close.

He couldn't resist the invitation, but knew they couldn't risk both being away from the house that long. And he knew it would be long. For some reason that night he felt like he could go on holding her forever. He'd seen her so little during that busy time of year.

Instead he lifted her into his arms and carried her out of the office, down the stairs, and into the house. Norma protested that she could walk, then giggled loudly when he said she was no heavier than the first time he'd carried her, on their wedding night, when he carried her over the threshold.

A long time later Ryan laid awake, propped up so he could stare down at his sleeping wife. Her silky blonde hair spread out around her pillow. He inhaled the gentle flowery scent of her perfume. He adored her more with every passing year.

Finally, remembering the mountain of work he still had to do in his office, he forced himself to return to his office.

The rest of the evening was somewhat of a blur. He hadn't been aware how much time had passed before he looked up from his work to see a strange light through the curtains of his office. Curious he got up and pulled them aside for a closer look.

"God! No!" he yelled as his eyes grew wide at the sight. He watched in horror as the flames seemed to burst from the windows of the kitchen, shattering it, before licking up the side of the house. He raced to the office door and as soon as he opened it he was assaulted with the sickening scent of heavy smoke.

As he approached the house he could feel the extreme heat, the smoke so dense it was choking. He knew he couldn't get inside from the kitchen. The open door had heavy smoke and flames roaring outside.

He raced around the house to the other door, not even aware he was still shouting, "No! God, please, no!" It was a horrified plea that what seemed to be happening wasn't real.

He tried the door, but it was locked. Norma always locked the doors at night. He insisted on it, even when he was working so close. He could hear the sound of smoke detectors going off inside his house. More than one, so he knew the deadly smoke was spreading fast.

His breathing was rapid as he reached into his pocket for his keys, fumbling with them in the darkness as he tried to locate the one for the front door. He cursed himself for not replacing the bulb that had blown just a few days before on the outside light.

Giving up his quest for a key he decided to try a window. He was so intent on getting into the house to save his family he didn't hear the sounds of sirens blending with the shrill pitched sound of the smoke detectors.

Of course, all windows were locked. Their usual caution for security extended to every possible entrance.

He had to get inside. He had to! In desperation he used his fist to punch the window, shattering the glass, cutting deep gashes into his hand and arm.

"Hold on there!" a voice shouted, and he felt himself grabbed from behind as he was about to climb inside. There was already smoke spewing from the entrance he had made. "You can't go in there."

"I have to!" Ryan stated frantically, trying to pull free. "My family is inside."

"You can't help them like this," the man stated, pulling him further back from the building. "You wouldn't last two minutes. My men are dressed to go inside. They have gear and air packs."

Ryan realized for the first time the man pulling him out of harms way was a firefighter. His white hat said "Fire Chief". Thankfully someone must have called the local fire company, a volunteer company with members throughout the community.

"What rooms will your family be in?" the Chief asked, then repeated the information Ryan gave him over his radio. Ryan heard the words over a loud speaker. Someone hearing the location would go in there and save the people he loved – they had to.

Another person came up behind him and took his arm. "Come with me, Sir." It was a feminine voice, but when he turned he saw she wasn't going to take no for an answer. There was a determined look on her face, that overrode her small stature. And there was something more. Compassion. Genuine concern. He went willingly, knowing it was the best thing he could do at the time. He'd only be in the way of the firefighters doing their job.

At the ambulance he saw two other uniformed people busy working. As he drew up close one of them moved and he saw that their victim was his mother.

"Mom, are you okay?" he asked, rushing toward her.

"Make them go away," she cried. "Michael help me!"

He knew she was mixing him up with his father. She did that often lately. Another side effect of her disease.

"Sir, a neighbor found her wondering out front. They saw her burned hands, then realized there was a fire," the young paramedic said.

He looked at his mother's bandaged hands, and knew one of his biggest fears had become a reality. She had gotten up in the middle of the night before and decided to cook something for herself to eat, then forgotten all about it. He had been going to place an alarm on her door to warn them. Norma had insisted that was far more humane than locking her inside the room.

Norma.

He turned again to look back at the house, waiting what seemed like an eternity till the firefighters inside came back out with his wife and daughter. When the first ones did, he held his breath, watching the scene taking place, as the paramedics raced to meet them with their equipment. The firefighters laid his wife's lifeless body on the stretcher. The paramedics went immediately to work.

The second firefighters followed shortly with Michele. The crew of the ambulance who had been tending his mother rushed to meet them.

56

He watched the scene as though it was in slow motion, finally gasping as he took in a breath of the acrid smelling air. He watched them load his wife into the second ambulance just as another arrived. His daughter was loaded onto that one.

He tried to follow, but the feisty young paramedic who had first escorted him was back again, blocking his way. There were tears in her eyes. "Come with us. We'll need your help with your mother," she said, but her eyes told him again what her words failed to say. He would be no help to his wife or daughter. Perhaps no one would.

They hadn't really needed him with his mother. They had given her something and she had drifted into oblivion. He vaguely remembered them asking him if she had any allergies or if she was on any medication. They had radioed that information to some unseen being who gave them orders of what treatment to use on his mother.

At the moment, he honestly didn't care. She was alive. That was all that mattered. They said she would be okay. Whatever that would be in her case. They couldn't know it had been a long time since she'd really been okay. He could barely remember that time himself.

But at the moment, what concerned him were the other two victims of the fire. His wife and daughter.

He was forced to wait in the emergency waiting room. He knew everyone he loved was just beyond the double set of doors. If only he could get past. He already knew he couldn't. So, he did what he knew was the most important thing he could do right then. He prayed.

Moments later he looked at the young paramedic who had become his constant companion almost since this nightmare began. Her own head was bowed. As thought sensing his scrutiny she looked up.

"Someone will be out soon," she assured him, reaching for his hand. He didn't doubt her kindness was above the call of duty. Weren't these people a breed above all others? Weren't they hardened to the horrors they faced day in and day out?

The pain in the woman's pale gray eyes showed that to be a misconception. Unless she was unlike all the others. But at that moment several of her fellow crew members passed through the double doors. He glimpsed his answer. Though they quickly masked their emotions when first coming through the doors, their faces told of their shared pain.

Ryan jumped to his feet, and the women quickly came to stand beside him. "How are they?"

"The doctors are working on them now," one of the uniformed men said. "Someone will be out soon."

"I'll be out after a bit," his companion said to the others, who only nodded in reply.

Ryan caught the look that passed between them. There had to have been a hidden message and he prayed it wasn't what he feared.

Minutes later a nurse came through the door. Her grim expression told the story. "We did all that we could for your wife," she said.

"Nooo! Please say it isn't so," he groaned as tears rolled down his cheeks. The paramedic put her arms around him, so small beside him, not even able to reach his shoulders, yet still comforting. "What about my daughter?"

"They're still trying to revive her," the nurse said. Just then the doors opened again and a doctor stepped through, his balding head glowing beneath the lights as he bowed it between hunched shoulders. He looked up at the nurse in defeat, shaking his head. "Is this the father?"

"Yes, Doctor," the nurse replied, then quickly stepped away, allowing him the unhappy task of giving the next message.

"Sir, we did all . . ."

"That you could," Ryan interrupted, using the same words as the nurse. *Is this your pat speech for survivors? Something you learned in their medical training?* Almost immediately his bitterness dissolved as he saw the pained looks on the faces around him. They cared. They didn't even know him, yet they shared his pain.

"Everyone did all that they could," he continued, knowing that to be true. He had seen a lot that night. From those first horrifying moments as everyone worked together. Team work. Highly trained and skilled to help others.

But it hadn't been enough. – Not this time.

"Patty, we've got another call," one of the paramedics said as he raced into the waiting room, calling the woman beside Ryan.

She hesitated a moment, looking up into Ryan's face. "I can't stay any longer. We're short of help right now. I gotta go."

"Thank you," he whispered, understanding. He had heard similar statements all evening. First when the Fire Chief had called for additional fire companies. Then for more manpower. They were making every effort to save his home. As they had made every effort to save his family.

#

"My mother has arthritis," he told Rainy, pushing the past back into that private part of his mind. "So I guess I understand a little of what you're going through."

"Does she live near here?"

He shook his head. "No, she's still in New York."

58

"I thought I detected a slight accent."

Ryan laughed. "Thought I left that. . ." *and a lot of other things*, "back there."

"So, does your mother ever come to visit?"

He frowned. "No. She's in a nursing home on the Island."

Rainy pulled a face. "Her arthritis that bad?"

"No, Alzheimer's Disease," he replied sadly. "She's been in there quite some time." Since he no longer had a home for her. Or for himself. Since he'd realized she needed more care than he could give her. If for no other reason than her own safety.

"Oh, bad news," Rainy acknowledged, shaking her head. "I've gotten familiar with a few families affected by the disease."

He thought her words strange, but accurate. Most people only included the actual person having the disease as being a victim of the disease, when in reality it affected the entire family.

"Of course, I've come in contact with a lot of people with disabilities since starting our program," she continued. "Certainly made me see that the little arthritis I have, is nothing compared to the problems of others."

"What program?

"A program to teach fire safety to people with disabilities and other special needs."

"I haven't heard about it?"

"Do you have a couple hours? I'll explain it all." She laughed.

He looked at his watch. "Well, I'd like to hear about it, but I'm afraid my chief called this morning and asked me to meet him at the station around one."

"I'll summarize for you over lunch," she said. "You can come back to the house and eat with us."

Ryan saw that she again left no room for debate. Not that he would. For some reason he was curious about the program she was talking about.

"But for now," she continued. "Let's see how well you can demonstrate crawling under smoke. Kids need to visualize, so when we don't have the real thing we have to create a picture for them. Using this." She held up an battered, old, dark blanket.

By the time they were ready to break for lunch, Ryan had not only learned how to demonstrate Stop, Drop and Roll and to crawl under smoke, he also could explain how a person could develop an escape plan and how to practice that plan.

He had a crash course on smoke detectors and plenty of reading material to study about residential sprinklers.

"Next week I might even teach you how to do our new baby bag program," she said, turning her freckled face toward his with a smile. "Of course, it won't be ready to go public till I manage to get all the props."

"Your what?"

She laughed. "Baby bag. You'll have to see it to understand it. How's your sense of humor?"

She went so fast his head spun. What did a sense of humor have to do with any of this? He certainly didn't think there was anything funny about fires.

"I laugh at jokes," he replied drily.

"I see I'll have my work cut out for me."

Ryan decided he'd just have to wait and find out about this program also. His mind was filled with enough information for one day. Well, almost enough. He still wanted to find out more about the safety program for people with disabilities.

Over cold turkey on wheat toast, Rainy explained the details of that program.

"You see, the first step is finding the people in our community who have disabilities," she told him. "That's not always easy. Many are frightened. They feel vulnerable."

"It's understandable." He remembered how secretive his father had wanted to be about his mother's illness. He had been afraid people wouldn't understand, or they'd take advantage of her.

"The next thing we do is ask them to share information about their condition with us. – That can be as difficult as finding them. Though we do promise to keep the information confidential. For emergency use only."

She explained that the information helped fire company officers better plan for an emergency involving that person. The information about them could be transmitted to them so they'd know what to expect once the arrived at their home.

"Of course, that requires a little training," she continued. "We're developing a course that goes along with the fire safety program to train firefighters what to expect, and how to safely evacuate people with special needs."

"I thought it was a prevention course. Now I see it's a lot more."

"It sure is," Rainy said with pride. "We've been working on it for years. It started out with a request for some fire prevention literature for people with disabilities. And ended up with a multi-faceted program.

"It goes like this: first we find the people, and try to teach them as much fire safety based on their own needs and abilities. Usually we only have to modify the usual stuff a little. Safety is safety. The basic rules are the same. But when we do it, we learn what the people can and can't do for themselves.

"That's where the form comes in handy," she continued. "Sort of a back-up plan, for when fire safety isn't enough."

Ryan thought of another time when fire safety wouldn't have been enough. His mother wouldn't have understood.

"Then last, we train our own emergency personnel."

"What can you actually train them to do differently?" Ryan asked, his interest growing.

She shrugged. "Mostly to use a little more care. Time permitting, that is. Knowing what to expect when you arrive on the scene is a definite time saver."

"Seconds count." Ryan nodded.

"If you move a person who already has a spine injury wrong, you'd more than likely kill them," she said, frowning. "Mary Ann, the woman who helped us start this program had a spinal injury. I remember thinking at first, that her spine couldn't be as fragile as she made it out to be. I figured she moved herself fairly well. But then I did research. Spoke to doctors and specialists. I learned, if anything, Mary Ann had under-estimated the care needed to move her in an emergency."

Rainy took a breath, frowning. "Imagine a piece of thread you might use to sew on a button. Wrap an end around each finger, tug and see how much it takes to tear it. It takes even less to tear an already damaged spinal cord."

Ryan whistled. "Whatever happened to that woman? You speak in past tense."

"The whole program was emotionally draining. She had to drop out because of the stress." Rainy frowned. "Working with the fire service hasn't always been easy. There have been those who've been against the program from the start."

"But you wouldn't give in," Ryan said, smiling affectionately at the woman. He had no doubt her husband had not exaggerated when he said his wife was stubborn. It must be a family trait. He thought of her niece and suspected she was stubborn too. She'd need to be. The next few weeks, even months, would be difficult ones.

"Anyway, before Mary Ann left the group, she made me promise not to let those people stand in our way," Rainy continued, bringing Ryan's thoughts back to the subject at hand. "So, I decided to forget them and did what had to be done. I found the best people in the fire service I could find and got them to work with us. If it weren't for them I doubt I'd have been able to keep the promise."

"Somehow I think you'd still have managed."

Rainy laughed. "I was determined. But, one person couldn't do it alone. Thank God, I had a family who stood by me. As it was it took too long. Part of it my fault. I ended up in the hospital and needed surgery. What a setback! I was climbing the walls till I could get back to things. By the time I got back on my feet, some of my committee had found other projects. It was like going back to square one.

"Look at the time!" she changed the subject so quickly it was dizzying. Something he realized happened often with Rainy. "Didn't you say you had a meeting with your Chief at one? It's quarter to."

"Well, Rainy, it's been quite a morning. I've learned a lot," he said, as he got up from the table, lifting his plate. "Thanks for lunch."

"Leave that and get going," she ordered. "You should know you never keep a white hat waiting. They think their time is the only time that's precious, you know. Of course, don't tell my brother that one. He may decide to get even and not show up the next time I'm in a pinch for help."

Ryan laughed, feeling great after a morning spent with this energetic woman. Being around her had been infectious.

#

"You want me to be Second Assistant," Ryan repeated the Fire Chief's words.

Arlen Maxwel nodded. "Till the next election. Then, if things have worked out, I can't see any reason why you shouldn't run for the position."

"What did Barry Carlisle think about it?" Ryan asked. He knew the company's first assistant had been good friends with Mike Boyce. He wondered how would he feel about him as the man's replacement?

Arlen spread his hands out in front of him and shrugged. "He seemed concerned about how some of the older members would take it since you've only been with us a couple years, compared to others who've been here a long time."

"I can understand his concern there," Ryan stated, doing a mental click of the other members and who would have been qualified to be an assistant chief.

He pictured Lacy, and remembered there had been some strong support for her in the last election. Just before she announced she was going to start running with the ambulance squad.

"But after discussing it," the Fire Chief continued. "We decided, the decision should be based on who's best for the job."

"And who is that?" Ryan smiled.

"Okay," the older man smiled, shaking his head as he changed his wording. "The person best for the job, who can, or will, take it." He placed his hand on Ryan's shoulder. "That leaves you, young man."

"Thanks for being honest." Ryan nodded, thinking. "When do you need to know?"

"Before the rest of the crew starts nagging at me to pick someone."

"Give me the night to sleep on it."

"Fair enough," the older man said as he extended his right hand, firmly grasping Ryan's. "You've come highly recommended, so I hope you'll say yes."

Ryan was about to ask who had recommended him when the tones went off and they were called to a dumpster fire. He raced for his gear as the Chief wrote the address on the black board so when the next units arrived at the station, they'd know exactly where to go.

CHAPTER FIVE

Lacy unlocked the door to her home, stepping slowly inside. She looked around, amazed that everything still looked exactly the same as when she had left it. Yet, why wouldn't it? There had been no one there to change anything. It was more a feeling that nothing should be the same.

She sighed, knowing it wasn't. Her husband was dead. And nothing would ever be the same again.

Mike was gone.

He would not be there to share in the excitement of bringing their son home from the hospital. He would not be there to watch him take his first steps, nor to hear his first words. He wouldn't be able to share in their son's excitement on his first day of school. Nor would he be there for Mikie's later years, to help him with his homework.

Mike wouldn't see his son grow into a fine young man. He'd never be able to teach him how to drive, nor help him pick out his first car.

He wouldn't watch him go down the isle wearing his cap and gown on graduation day. Help him pick a college. Kiss his bride. Hold his first grandchild. . .

Lacy dropped the small suit case she was holding and raised her hands to cover her face, her long honey-gold curls cascading around her down-turned face. She had to stop thinking like this. It was going to drive her mad.

She had to be in better control. Accept things that were beyond her ability to change. Change the things she is capable of changing. And know the difference between the two.

The Serenity Prayer says the same thing, she remembered, combing the fingers of both hands through her long hair as she raised her head skyward. The Serenity Prayer had always been her favorite. She'd silently think the words during times of stress. Those times when she'd felt unable to cope.

She wondered why she hadn't even thought of it since Mike's death. Why it suddenly came to her now.

God, grant me the serenity to accept the things I cannot change, courage to change things I can, and wisdom to know the difference.

She closed her eyes, waiting for the peace she usually felt after remembering that verse. There was something – something nagging at her thoughts. Just beyond her memory's reach.

Aloud she repeated, "God, grant me the serenity to accept the things I cannot change, courage to change things I can, and wisdom to know the difference."

She waited. Still, no peace. No acceptance.

"God, grant me the serenity to accept the things I cannot change." Her voice rose more loudly this time, almost demanding. "The courage to change things I can, and wisdom to know the difference."

Again she waited, her breathing growing rapid. Her frustration led to near rage. Then suddenly she realized the truth. Her eyes fluttered open.

There was no invisible cloak going to suddenly surround her. There was no bolt of lightening going to come down from the heavens and hit her on the head, so that when she awoke everything would be back like it was. There was no miracle going to happen that was going to make everything go back the way it was. If that's what she was waiting for, she had been wrong.

She had lost the whole meaning of her favorite prayer. But now she remembered. The serenity, the strength and the wisdom were going to come from within herself. God would give her the power. But she would have to make things better.

Yet, a distant memory still nagged at her. Something important she was missing.

Well, she had more to do than stand around musing about her future. It was time for action.

Mike had put off doing so many things in the nursery, saying he'd have plenty of time. But he had been wrong.

Her mother had wanted to come home with her and do the work for her, but she wouldn't hear of it. It was going to be her job now that Mike had died.

She headed straight to the nursery and opened the door. The boxes in the middle of the room still contained the crib, matching dresser and changing table she had chosen so carefully. There were shutters leaning against the wall waiting to be hung. She remembered the care she had taken in painting them, red around the outside, then alternating red, white and blue on each of the shutter's tiny slats.

There were clean sheets and blankets in the cedar chest in her bedroom. Along with all the stuffed animals, toys and clothing that she'd been given at two surprise baby showers. One by her mother for family, the other by Aunt Rainy for all her fire company friends.

Funny, her life had always seemed divided that way. She wished it were different. With a sigh, she knew this was not the time to worry about that problem. It had gone on so long already. A few more days, weeks, or even months wouldn't make much difference.

She started to tackle the boxes in the middle of the room, finding them more difficult to open than she'd thought. She left them to search for a sharp knife, then returned to cut through the cardboard of the largest box, careful not to damage the mattress she knew was inside.

Once she had the crib's box opened she spread all the parts on the floor in front of her, and picked up the single sheet of instructions. She was usually very good with her hands, but the instructions may as well have been written in Greek. She started out by counting all the parts to make sure they were there. That would be the easy part. Putting them together would be the challenge.

"A drink, that's what I need," she said aloud as she got up from the floor. "Something loaded with caffeine." Then she made a face, remembering she had sworn off caffeine.

She went to the refrigerator and took out a plastic half gallon container of milk. She opened it and a took a sniff, wrinkling her nose before pouring it down the drain.

"So much for that," she said, poking her head further into the refrigerator. "Oh no, it gets worse!"

It took her only a moment to decide it was time to clean out the refrigerator. She started pulling out the first containers of a green, fur-covered substances, that left no resemblance at all to food. Yet they had to be food, since she knew she hadn't been intentionally growing any scientific specimens in there.

She smiled pushing a stray curl back around her ear, pleased that for a second she had actually regained her sense of humor. Pulling out a paper plate covered with torn aluminum foil. She opened it and her smile faded. The dehydrated piece of yellow cake with mold-spotted frosting was what was left of Mike's birthday cake from a party they had a month ago.

She felt tears stinging her eyes as she threw it into the trash with the other containers. Closing the door to the refrigerator, she lost interest in the task. She'd even forgotten she was thirsty.

Returning to the bedroom she took one look at the crib on the floor and knew she'd need a few more tools to do the job right. She headed toward the attached garage and found Mike's tool box. She carried it back to the nursery.

The shiny tools inside had been her gift to him the previous Christmas, soon after they'd put a deposit on their new home. She remembered telling him he'd have plenty of uses for tools once they started adding the little touches that would make the house their home.

She started tearing the labels off the tools she was going to need, wondering if she should save the crib for last, and start on the chest of drawers. Perhaps they would be easier.

She cut open this box and began to pull out the unassembled pieces of heavy maple boards. "At least their pre-finished," she said as she laid them aside and searched the bottom of the box for the instructions.

This set of instructions was no easier to read than the ones for the crib. She threw them down in frustration, sighing as she got up from the floor. Hands on her hips, she looked at the mess surrounding her.

"The only thing on the instruction sheet I understood, was where it said do-it-yourself!" She kicked the pile of boards, then winced, hurting herself. "Ouch!"

She hobbled toward the door. "I'm thirsty, I have a headache," she fumed. "Then to top it off, I probably broke my toe!"

Limping back to the kitchen she took a glass from the cabinet and turned on the spigot to let the water get cold. She spotted a bottle of aspirins on the counter and was about to reach for it, then remembered that along with her resolution to give up caffeine she had given up all medications.

She took a drink of plain water, then rubbed her temples. She remembered the doctor telling her to take things easy for a few days. The past days had been unavoidably hectic ones. Maybe she should rest a little now.

Slowly she made her way down the hallway toward her bedroom, relieved that at least the throbbing in her big toe had lessened. Her day hadn't gotten off to a good start.

No, she corrected her train of thought – it had started fine. She smiled, remembering the breakfast left by her mother beside her bed. And the mischievous way her father had sneaked her some margarine for her muffins.

Then came the moment of truth, when she had gone downstairs and confronted her mother. Her father may have paved the way, but it hadn't made things any easier. Her mother had thought of so many reasons why she shouldn't go home. She could think of only one reason why she should. It was *her* home.

She laid on the bed, unaccustomed to resting during daylight hours. Yet, it didn't take lone for fatigue to overcome her. It was a restless sleep. A sleep filled with nightmares reliving the night of the fire.

The tones went off and she and Mike jumped out of bed. "Just be careful," Mike had said. "You wouldn't want anything to happen to our future firefighter, would you?"

"What could go wrong?" she had replied, the last words she'd ever said to her husband.

She thrashed from side to side, awakening at the point when the heat and smoke inside the building built to such proportion that it exploded into all-consuming flames, turning the home into a death-chamber for her husband.

Realizing it had been only a nightmare, she wiped her damp brow and laid limply back against her pillow. She wanted to lay on her left side, the one she favored, but hat meant she'd have to face the empty space beside her. But it was empty no matter how she laid, she reasoned, forcing herself to turn.

Closing her eyes, she tried to relax, but this time sleep refused to come. She remained un-moving for several moments longer.

Suddenly the tones went off. Lacy instinctively jumped up from the bed. She paused. It was that nightmare again.

Then the voice came across the pager still inside the charger beside the bed. "Structure fire, 365 Chestnut Street," the dispatcher said.

She sat back down on the bed, realizing this time it was not a nightmare. There really was a fire.

She tried to rub the tension from the back of her neck. Then left her head hang, slowly moving it from side to side. It was hopeless. The tension was there to stay.

She listened again to the pager. It was the second fire call her company had responded to that day. The first had been a dumpster, and hadn't taken them very long to extinguish that. This call sounded like a different story. Police on the scene were reporting that heavy smoke was showing at the exterior of the house.

Lacy's exhaustion was replaced by a sudden burst of energy. It was the adrenaline rush most emergency workers experienced when they responded to a call. Like an addictive drug, once you experienced the feeling, you wanted more.

It was the feeling that separated the good from the bad firefighters.

Thankfully most knew the high they experienced when responding to, and working at an emergency, was caused by a hormonal change, when chemicals are released into the body to help it function during times of extreme stress. They accepted it as just that.

Then there were those few who could not function for long without that feeling. Those were the people who took the unnecessary chances. The ones who lived for the next emergency. And sadly, the ones who went to the extreme, even setting fires so they could enjoy the excitement of putting them out again.

Fortunately those were few, but that was all it took. It was just like the saying about bad apples.

Lacy thought about driving downtown to the scene of the fire, then felt like kicking herself. That old feeling. That desire was still there. Becoming a widow and a mother hadn't changed it. She wondered if that made her bad, crazy, or stupid. Maybe all three.

She'd just have to resist the urge.

She had intended to stop at the hospital and visit her son. Looking at the clock, she saw it was nearly his feeding time. Yes, she'd go take care of her son.

She smiled, thinking about how cute he looked as she nursed him. His little lips sucking as though he had been starved. Then when satiated, his sucking would slow as his tiny blue eyes closed, his lips releasing their hold on her nipple as he drifted into a peaceful sleep.

All thoughts of the fire were forgotten as she hurried to the bathroom to freshen up for her visit with her son.

#

She felt a strange anticipation as she left the hospital later that night. The doctor had been in to see Mikie earlier and said he could be discharged the following day. It was something she'd been looking forward to since the day he was born, yet at the same time she was afraid.

What if I do something wrong? What if I'm not a good mother? What if I don't possess those mothering instincts every woman was supposed to have? Perhaps Mom was right, and I've been around the men too long. Maybe I've lost that nesting instinct normal women are supposed to have.

She forced her doubts aside, knowing once she set her mind to it she could do nearly anything. Hadn't she proven that before?

As she crossed the parking lot she looked into the sky and saw a faint glow high above the trees and buildings. It looked like it was coming from the general direction of the fire her company had been dispatched to just before she came to visit her son.

She had purposely avoided looking in that direction on her way there, not wanting to put temptation in the path of her resolve to do anything but properly care for her son. Now she wondered if going to the fire could work just the opposite. Perhaps she could go there and somehow purge all desire to fight fires. Maybe then she could be a good mother.

The decision made, she got in her car and drove to the scene. It had been a serious fire, destroying one double house and spreading to another close beside it. Part of that one was still burning, though they had finally contained it to one general area.

It wouldn't have been an easy fire to fight. She knew that from experience. Most of the homes in this area were old and of frame construction, built before the community adopted stricter fire codes. A few were doubles, and all were close together. Too many were fire traps.

Landlords in this area claimed they tried to adhere to the codes, but the truth of the matter was, most of them did only what they had to do, and then it was often because an inspection of the building resulted in a fine.

For years landlords claimed as soon as they installed smoke detectors tenants removed their batteries for other uses. That had been why her father had fought to get a borough code that required permanently hard-wired smoke detectors in all borough buildings. All rental properties had to comply, there was no "Grandfather Clause," no exemption as there was for private homeowners whose homes had been there before the code was adopted.

There were also codes requiring that junk, especially combustible items, not be stored around the outside of each house. The problem there, the same landlords insisted, was that tenants didn't care. If they asked tenants to comply and they didn't, they had little recourse than to have them evicted.

Evicting them only meant they'd become a problem for another landlord down the street, and another family would move in and do much the same thing all over again. That was a more difficult problem for her father. One he was constantly working to change. It was part of the reason he'd so readily supported Aunt Rainy's educational approach to fire safety. Because of the work of her committee, people were beginning to learn and practice better fire safety habits.

Lacy allowed her mind to wonder as she stood across the street. How much time passed, she wasn't certain. She saw how exhausted some of the men looked. This, too, was a familiar scene. Those who had been inside doing search and rescue were now sitting on the curb or leaning against the truck, recovering from their task.

Junior firefighters were taking several used air bottles and setting them aside to be refilled when they got back to the station. Others were already rolling hose from the trucks that would soon be released to go home.

She realized that the flames in the attic area were now practically gone. It would now be only a matter of going inside and looking for "hot spots", places where the coals of the fire were still hot enough to rekindle.

A fresh crew from the outlying township must have been called in for relief. It would be the perfect job for them.

She looked among the men, counting white hats. Her father was over by "Command Seven", the new rescue unit that served as a command center when needed. Beside him was Arlen and Colin Smith, the Fire Chief from Friendship Hook and Ladder.

She watched as the Chief from the township company joined them. It was impossible not to recognize his hulking frame. That was why early in his volunteer career he'd been dubbed the "Incredible Hulk". The title stuck, and today there were many people who didn't even know his real name.

70

She saw her father talk to him, pointing him over to where Barry Carlisle stood near their own bright yellow pumper. When he joined Barry, as she suspected, he and his men headed inside. It was a critical point in the fire. Overhaul was when the most accidents occurred. It was when over-worked crews tended to relax, letting their guards down. It was always a good idea to bring in fresh troops, as they had done here.

She looked around for a few more white hats, wondering if they had chosen someone to fill the place left by her husband. She wondered if Arlen had taken her recommendation.

Her eyes stopped when they found the man in question, seeing he was still wearing his regular gear. No white hat. Perhaps Arlen hadn't chosen him.

She watched as he helped the junior firefighters rolling up the hose. Not many officers would do that, she thought.

Then again, she had suspected Ryan was different from so many of the others.

After she had first realized who he was, she had remembered seeing him doing many different jobs at the station. It seemed no job was too menial.

Of course, a white hat has a way of changing things.

She frowned, remembering when Mike had been elected Assistant Chief. She'd heard rumors he'd come down pretty hard on the juniors sometimes. She had asked him about it once, and he told her she was just being defensive since she had once been a Junior. In fact, she had been in charge of the Junior program before she left. He added that if kids wanted to do a *man's* job, they should learn to do it right.

His words had raised her hackles. Yet they hadn't surprised her. He'd often hinted at the way he'd felt. But that time she'd bitten her tongue. She was no longer active with the Vigilantes. A fact her husband was all to willing to remind her.

Now, as she stared at the activity going on in front of her, she tried to look at it with the same sort of detachment she had learned to do then. This was no longer part of her job. She no longer had a right to suggest what she thought they should or shouldn't do.

She supposed Arlen probably had come to the same conclusion and chosen someone else for Assistant Chief. Probably someone more to Barry Carlisle's liking. She quickly looked around again and found Woody Brown, still wearing the bunker coat with "Friendship H. & L." on it's back. At least Arlen didn't pick him, she thought, with some consolation.

What was wrong with her? Why should she care?

She again reminded herself. *I'm a mother now. I've given up firefighting. I no longer belong here.*

She turned to leave, not realizing that someone had been watching her defeated expression. The way her shoulders slumped, her long honey-gold hair hung loosely hiding her face as she looked toward the ground. Her entire demeanor giving a look of total dejection.

#

Lacy returned home planning to finish the work in the nursery. Tomorrow her son would be released from the hospital and she didn't even have a place for him to sleep, not to mention any of the other things that still needed to be done.

She again though about calling her father, but he had still been at the fire when she'd left. He'd, without a doubt, be there long after the last firefighters went home. He'd want to begin a preliminary investigation into the cause of the fire.

By the time he'd be through, she knew he'd be exhausted. And he still had to get up for work the next day.

"No, I'll get it done," she said with renewed determination, heading toward the kitchen. "A cup of strong . . ." She sighed again, remembering she no longer drank coffee. Instead she put some water on to heat for herbal tea, then searched in the cabinet for a box that's label didn't say anything about soothing or relaxing.

She decided on apricot flavored. As the tea bag steeped she rested her elbows on the table, holding her head in her hands, wondering how she could feel so tired, and never less like sleeping. She must have dozed, for the next thing he knew she awoke with her head cradled in her arms, still hunched over the table.

She heard a light knock and wondered if that was what had wakened her. She got up and went into the living room, realizing the sound was coming from the door. She opened it in time to see the tall shadowy presence of someone heading down her front steps.

She quickly flipped the light switch on. "Can I help you?" she called, unconcerned that she was alone and it was awfully late for visitors. When the figure turned she was surprised to see it was Ryan.

"Do you always stand with a door wide open for strangers?" he asked as he started back up the steps toward her.

"You're not a stranger?"

"And you knew that before you turned on the light," he stated as he reached the doorway.

"I'm not in the mood for a lecture," she snapped. "I wasn't thinking, okay?"

He slowly scrutinized her face, taking in the dark rings beneath dull blue eyes. She looked worse close up than she had when he'd seen her earlier watching the fire.

"You look too tired to think," he replied softly. "I saw all the lights turned on so I thought you might still be awake. I'm sorry if I woke you."

"Don't be. You did me a favor. Actually, I had only dozed off. I was in the kitchen. . ." She frowned. "Waiting for my tea to cool enough to drink. I suppose it's plenty cool now. Care to join me?"

"Tea?" he thought of the tea someone else used to make. He hadn't had any in a long time. "Sure, why not."

Lacy led the way into the kitchen and turned on the heat beneath the pot of water. She pointed to a chair, then quickly got a second cup from the cabinet. "Do you like apricot tea? Or would you rather something else. I have several flavors."

"I'll try the apricot," he replied, watching as she pulled a tea bag from a box on the counter and put it in the cup. The water didn't take long to boil. She poured some over the tea bag then set it in front of him.

She sat down and checked her own cup. As she suspected the dark liquid had cooled. She pulled the bag out and squeezed it into her spoon. "Least it's strong," she said, making a face as she looked at her cup. "I'll pretend it's coffee."

Ryan laughed. "A prerequisite for being a firefighter."

"I'm not a firefighter. . ." she snapped, then frowned before she finished more softly. "anymore. – And I'm sorry I'm so irritable."

He shrugged, removing his own tea bag before his drink got too strong. "I saw you tonight."

"I had nose trouble, that's all," she replied as she dumped a spoon full of sugar into her cup. "I thought maybe being there would exorcize my desire to . . . to be there." She sought for words to explain, wondering if she was explaining to him or still trying to explain it to herself.

She put another spoon of sugar into her cup and stirred. "Want some sugar?"

"Straight is fine." Ryan waited, suspecting she had more to say.

She lifted her cup to her lips and took a sip, making a face. She reached for the sugar and put two more spoons of white granules in her cup, then stirred the now syrupy liquid. "It'll either make it taste better or give me some energy. Either way I'll be happy."

"Maybe you'd be better off getting some rest," Ryan suggested as tactfully as he could.

"I'll have plenty of time for that later," she said. "Tonight I have a lot of work to do. They're letting my son come home tomorrow."

Ryan thought she had that a bit backward, but decided that was something she'd have to find out for herself. He didn't want to dishearten her again. Speaking about her son coming home had managed to return a smile to her too-pale face.

"Is it the kind of work that could use a second set of hands?"

She frowned, looking away, thinking it should have had a second set of hands. Mike should be there with her to prepare for their son together.

Ryan wished he could kick himself for saying the wrong thing. "I'm sorry, Lacy. I came here tonight to see if you were okay, and you probably were better off before I got here."

She thought he looked like a regretful child. "People can't walk on egg shells around me – afraid to say anything that may remind me about what happened – as if I could forget." She put her hands together on the table, nervously twisting her wedding band.

Ryan nodded, watching her nervous actions. "So, could you use some help with whatever you have to do?"

"I'll manage," she replied, thinking of all the work still left to do in the nursery. "As soon as I finish this for energy." She lifted the cup and took a few more sips, again making a face.

Ryan reached across the table and took the cup from her hand. "Hasn't anyone ever told you, no man is an island? Or, woman, in this case."

Lacy immediately remembered the words. She looked up into Ryan's penetrating green eyes and smiled. They were the words that kept eluding her earlier that day when she'd prayed for the strength to make it on her own. It had been the thought that had been nagging at her, like a distant memory.

"No man is an island. No man walks alone," she whispered, feeling the moisture of her tears running down her cheeks. She closed her eyes, trying to stop the flood, but it was impossible.

She heard Ryan groan, then the sound of his chair as he slid away from the table. She felt his strong hands under her arms, pulling her up, against him, where she suddenly felt safe and warm.

She could no longer hold back the torrent of tears as all her pain, her doubts and her fears came crashing in on her. She leaned against his comforting form, feeling his arms around her, hearing his soothing words.

When the flood of emotion began to cease to mere sobs, she pulled back slightly, seeing the damp markings of her tears on Ryan's shirt. Suddenly she felt her cheeks flame. "I don't know what got into me."

"I do," Ryan whispered, raising her chin with his fingertips. "You're acting perfectly normal under the circumstances. Lacy, you shouldn't try and face everything alone. Let your family and friends help you."

74

She took a ragged breath, trembling as she released it. "To be honest, tonight, I could use some help."

"That's why I'm here," Ryan replied. "And if I can't help you, I know at least a dozen others who would be here in a second if you called."

"No need to keep everyone out of bed." She forced herself to laugh. "Especially since you so graciously volunteered your services."

"Okay, where do I start?"

"How are you at reading instructions?"

"Are they in English?" he teased.

Lacy shook her head, feeling better already. "I've already decided they're in Greek."

Ryan's green eyes flashed with humor as he made a face. "In that case, I'll probably need you to read them to me."

She led the way to the nursery, stopping at the door as she saw the mess she had made earlier. "It's worse than I remembered." She turned, seeing her companion's sober expression as he took in the room. Misunderstanding his look, she added, "You can still bow out if you'd like."

Ryan remembered another time he had put together furniture for a nursery.

Honey, we've got four months till the baby comes. He could still hear Norma's voice as she stood in the doorway of the room that would be their nursery. *Honest, you can come to bed. We won't be needing all this tomorrow.*

"So you see, I have a lot to do till tomorrow."

Ryan smiled, returning to the present. "We have a lot to do," he corrected. "But for now, I'd say I'll be needing something a little stronger than apricot tea."

"Like coffee?"

"Black."

She laughed. "Can you manage without me reading the instructions till I get back?"

"I'll muddle through." He looked at the scattered piles of parts and sighed. *Though, muddle, may be an understatement.* He wondered how Mike had managed to put off getting these things done.

He had to remind himself that she had delivered their baby prematurely. The man had probably thought he'd have plenty of time. They both probably thought they had plenty of time.

Time, he thought. Whoever knows?

It was near dawn when Ryan finished the final task in the nursery. He closed the shutters that were letting in the first rays of morning sun. Too bright for my weary eyes, he thought.

He turned to look at the woman sleeping in the corner of the room and smiled. She had managed to stay with him, trying to help. They had finished the crib together, then while she put on the fresh sheets, he'd gone for his third cup of strong coffee.

When he returned she had herself propped up in the corner, insisting she was just resting her eyes until he returned. He suggested she stay there while he started the chest of drawers, promising to let her know if there was anything he needed.

As quietly as possible he worked, noting that within minutes she was sound asleep. He'd been tempted to carry her into her bed, but suspected she'd awaken easily, as most firefighters do. No, he decided, she'd get more rest if he left her alone.

When the dresser was finished, he started work on the changing table, then the final job of installing the shutters.

He walked to the corner and decided it was time to wake Sleeping Beauty. He would go home and she could go to bed and get some proper rest, or so he thought.

Once she opened her eyes, her blue gaze sparkled like sapphires, nearly taking his breath away. She practically jumped up from the floor, smiling at the finished room. Then she turned back to him looking contrite. "Why didn't you wake me?"

"I just did."

"You know what I mean. To help."

"I left the best part for you," he replied. "You get to fill the drawers. You have a lot to get ready till this afternoon when you bring that little guy home."

She glanced at the rays of light slipping through the slats in the shutters. "You worked all night."

"Hey, once I get started on something like this, you can't get me away from it till I'm finished."

"But, all night," she stammered. "You'll be exhausted at work." She frowned realizing she knew so little about this man who had been so good to her.

"I don't start that early," he replied. "Besides, I have a very understanding boss."

"Lucky, mine never understood if I was five minutes late." She frowned. "It didn't make her any happier when she found out she couldn't fire me for being late because of an emergency call. And since that was the only time I was ever late, she was stuck."

"Your boss mustn't have been a member of the fire company."

"And your boss is?"

Ryan nodded, his grin growing wider. "Karla Mulholland is in charge of my department."

"Then you work at Lawton's," Lacy acknowledged one of the largest industries in Schuylkill Valley. "I knew you and the Mulhollands were friends, I didn't realize you worked with Karla."

Ryan nodded. "She helped me get the job shortly after I moved to Schuylkill Valley."

"Karla's great." Lacy had always liked the older woman. She had been the second woman to join the fire company, though it was several years after Lacy. "I didn't feel quite so out of place after Karla started coming to meetings."

Ryan showed his surprise. "You never looked like you felt out of place."

Lacy sighed. "Don't ask me to explain, or you'll never make it to work, much less get some rest before you go."

"I'm so full of caffeine, I doubt my eyes will close for at least another twelve to fourteen hours."

"You asked for it."

"I'm not complaining. Just stating a fact."

"So, what do you do at Lawtons?" Lacy asked. "Karla's in accounting."

"Like I said, she's my boss."

"Doesn't it bother you . . ." She didn't know why she wanted to know, but Lacy felt the need to ask. "having a woman boss?"

"I never looked at it as having a woman for a boss. I look at it as having a good boss."

Lacy smiled, softening her features. "I like your attitude."

"Besides, she keeps telling me she's only being nice so I'll take her job. – Not at Lawtons – at the station."

"She's a good treasurer."

"And her job is safe as far as I'm concerned," Ryan said. "Besides, I may have enough to do. . . That is, if I decide to take Chief Maxwell up on his offer." Ryan wondered if he should have brought it up to Lacy considering who's position he'd be filling.

"So, you might accept Second Assistant."

Ryan's dark eyebrows rose a fraction as he looked down into Lacy's curious expression. "You knew about the offer."

She felt her cheeks burn. "I . . .well, I. . .overheard Arlen talking to my Dad about it the other night."

Ryan cocked his head to the side. "Maybe you know why they decided on me?"

"Actually it was Arlen's decision. Dad doesn't like to get involved in company politics."

"And you don't have that problem." He suddenly had a good suspicion of who had recommended him for the position.

Lacy shrugged. "I try to stay out of things since I'm not active anymore. But sometimes. . ." She met his emerald gaze and smiled. "So, are you going to take it?"

"I told the Chief I'd need the night to sleep on it." Ryan teased. "Since I haven't done that yet, I can't say."

"Trying to make me feel guilty?"

"No, trying to say, I'm still not sure."

"Well, Arlen's sure, or he wouldn't have asked you," Lacy said. "We need someone like you."

Ryan noticed the way she said "We", and liked the sound. Her opinion, was one he respected. Perhaps he would accept the position.

CHAPTER SIX

Lacy looked down at her son sleeping so soundly. He looked so tiny in the large crib. There was a much smaller one at her parent's house. The one she had once slept in. Her mother had made her father dig it out yesterday. Right before she told them she was moving back to her home.

She knew her timing had been terrible, but then again, knowing her mother, any time would have been the wrong time. She had been so certain Lacy would agree to continue living with them.

Lacy sighed, regretting the hurt she had seen in her mother's eyes. Felt relief at the memory of the pride that had shown in her father's. *Why was it he always understands, yet Mom doesn't? Maybe because he never had any expectations for me. Nothing I ever felt I had to live up to.* Yet, even as she thought about it, she knew that wasn't entirely true.

"I hope I never make you feel you can't live up to my expectations," she whispered, patting her son gently on his back. Slowly she turned and went out of the room, resisting the urge to leave the door open. She smiled, remembering the literature her aunt had given her at her baby shower. Of course it was about fire safety. Filled with tips for new parents.

At the time, Mike had laughed, saying it was just like Rainy to push her beliefs on others. "She's as bad as your mother," he'd said, setting the information aside, refusing to read it. "They both want to tell you how you should do everything."

"They aren't that bad," she had defended, making Mike laugh harder.

"No, you probably wouldn't see it. You're on the other end of their strings. You'd have to look up to see who's pulling them. And the puppet masters won't let you do that."

Lacy had felt herself growing angry. She had fought hard to be her own person, even when others didn't agree. She thought she was being receptive to the advice she received from others, making her own decision as to what advice was good for her to follow, what not.

"If the two of them ever really lock horns against each other, it should be an interesting sight," he continued sarcastically. "It would be the proverbial irresistible force meeting the immovable object."

"You're not being fair," Lacy snapped, defensively. "They both think they're helping."

He rolled his eyes in reply. "If you'd only listen to me half as well as you listen to them."

She knew that summed up the situation entirely. Mike had his own expectations of what she should be like, and often argued that since they were married, she should do what he wanted. She had tried to live up to his expectations, but she knew she had failed.

"Now it's too late," she whispered, feeling defeat, then with renewed determination she thought of her son. "I will not fail with you."

She went to her room and got the portable intercom that her aunt had given her as a shower gift. It was with this package she had found the fire safety literature. Aunt Rainy said that new parents thought they were doing right by leaving the bedroom door open so they could better hear their child if it cried. They often left the door to their own room open too. In the end, if there was a fire, the deadly smoke could spread to those rooms all the more quickly.

So, she had given her the intercom and in a package marked from her sons, there was also the cutest little smoke detector designed as a red-helmeted dalmatian holding a hose. She had mounted that right between the nursery and her own bedroom.

She had tested the smoke detector earlier that day before bringing Mikie home. Now she took the intercom into the kitchen as she made herself some apricot tea. She thought of the cup she hadn't been able to finish the night before, thinking it did taste much better when it was made correctly.

She strained her ears listening for sounds of her son. Hearing none, not even his breathing, she wondered if the transmitter in his room was close enough to his crib. She went to the nursery and took the intercom from the chest of drawers and put it at the foot of the crib.

Back in the kitchen she listened again, wondering if the batteries were still good. Her aunt had sent two with the set, in separate unopened packages. The kind where the package had a built in tester. The tester showed they were good.

Still she wondered. She went to the drawer where she kept her spare batteries and pulled out an extra pair. She wasn't certain when she had bought them and since they had no tester build into the package, she had no way of knowing for sure.

This brand had always stayed fresh for a long time before. Yet, then, she didn't have a baby to protect. Her body tensed as she tried to decide if she should leave the ones that were in, or replace them with the ones in her hand.

Then suddenly she heard a sound coming from the intercom receiver. The soft murmuring sound of her son. She relaxed, smiling at the sounds, knowing the devices were working fine. She had just been worrying needlessly.

Still, she went to the grocery list she kept attached to the refrigerator and marked down batteries. She'd buy fresh ones for the smoke detectors while she was at it. Just to be on the safe side.

The sound coming over the intercom grew louder, changing from a soft murmur to a definite cry. Mikie was awake and something was wrong. She hurried to his room.

She immediately picked him up and held him close, whispering soft, soothing words. She decided to check his diaper, which wasn't wet. Then she sat in the rocking chair she had lugged from her bedroom to the nursery earlier that day.

She had just fed him before putting him down, so she doubted he could be hungry again. She doubted she'd have that much milk if he was hungry. Then she worried that maybe there was something wrong with her milk and it wasn't satisfying him. Maybe they had been supplementing her feedings with something else at the hospital.

They hadn't told her that. They would have told her. She was certain. Wasn't she?

"I'm turning into a worry wart." She shook her head, and smiled down at her son, realizing that he was again asleep and all her worrying had been for nothing.

She held him a little longer before putting him back into his crib, covering him slightly with a bright blue receiving blanket, part of the crib set that Paula Mulholland had given her at her shower. The girl and she had always been close but she had seemed particularly interested by Lacy's pregnancy. She also offered to baby-sit whenever Lacy was on duty. Perhaps it was just the interest of a friend. Or perhaps it was a young woman's awakening to the miracles of motherhood.

Lacy thought she'd invite Paula over sometime soon. And of course her mother and father too. But first, Paula alone. She suspected her friend was going through some of the normal curiosities of a teen-aged girl. Though Karla seemed to be a great mother, she supposed there might be things the girl would prefer talking about with someone closer to her own age.

It had been that way with her. She'd often go to her Aunt Rainy to discuss things. She really wasn't that much younger than her mother, but she had always seemed so much more worldly. She remembered going to her aunt when Mike had suddenly started showing an interest in her. When she had been afraid his attention had been just because her father was Chief.

Her Aunt had laughed saying if that were his reasons he'd find out very quickly that Carl played no favorites, as Lacy and she both knew from experience. It would be of no benefit for Mike to date the Fire Chief's daughter.

"If you have any doubts, take things slow," Rainy had advised. "If Mike is really interested he'll wait. He'll be patient."

Lacy smiled, knowing her aunt was talking about sex. She never found the subject embarrassing. At least not when talking with Aunt Rainy. It seemed to be one of her Aunt's favorite subjects. She spoke openly about it. And never sugar-coated it with fancy words for normal physical reactions.

"He's got more experience than you," Rainy reminded her.

Lacy frowned, remembering the rumors she had heard going around the station. Rumors about Mike and Rose Sinclair. But then, there had always been rumors about Rose with nearly everyone. No one knew which ones were true. But since Rose had gotten pregnant those rumors had increased, with the speculation about who the father was.

"Everyone has more experience than me," Lacy replied, forcing the other thoughts from her mind.

"Don't be so anxious," Rainy had replied. "Wait till you're married. I'm not just saying this because I'm a Christian and it's what I'm supposed to say. There's a lot of emotional baggage that goes with being married, even more having an intimate relationship. If you're not ready to be married, you certainly aren't ready for the intimate stuff. It can mess up your head."

Lacy laughed at her aunt's to-the-point explanation. She remembered hearing her mother say that Aunt Rainy had "been around," and if that were so, she should know what she was talking about. Lacy decided to listen.

Of course, everyone else at the station seemed to think there was more going on between her and Mike than there really was at first. Mike didn't seem to mind the rumors as much as she had. He said if they were talking about them, they were leaving someone else alone. Which didn't hold true in the case of Rose. Because as the birth of her child approached, so did the increased speculation about the father.

Herself, if she were to make a guess, she'd have suspected either Barry Carlisle or Woody Brown. Though he was married, Woody had been very edgy since Rose had gotten pregnant. Both men had spent a lot of time with her at the station. Joking. Talking. Sometimes touching. But that was Rose's way. She touched when she talked. Of course, only the men. She didn't relate well to the women. Not that there was any wonder why.

Lacy forced those thoughts from her mind too. Because it only served to remind her that at one time Mike was among that fun-loving group. He'd also spent his share of time joking and talking. And touching.

Lacy frowned as she again closed the door to the nursery, wondering why her thoughts had taken that direction. She'd begun thinking about Paula. Ended up thinking about things that no longer mattered. That never should have mattered in the first place..

What is wrong with me? Since Mike died I should be thinking about all the wonderful times we had shared, instead of dredging up old unhappy memories that were best forgotten.

Smiling she tried to imagine how happy Mike would have been bringing his son home from the hospital. How he would have looked sitting on the floor the night before, hurrying to put the nursery's furniture together so everything would be ready when they brought their child home the following day.

The energetic way he'd absorb himself with the task. The pleasure on his face when he completed the crib and slowly lowered the mattress into place. The gleam in his bright green eyes as he went on to the next project, the chest of drawers.

Lacy squeezed her eyes closed, chiding herself. Even her imagined thoughts were betraying her. Mike's eyes had been brown.

She went to her room and slipped into her night gown. She was just getting comfortable beneath the covers when she remembered she left the intercom receiver in the kitchen. Quickly she got up again, stopping to peep through the nursery door at her son before heading to the kitchen.

Back in her room she placed the receiver on the nightstand next to her side of the bed. She listened carefully, hoping she wouldn't miss any sound that may warn her of a problem with her baby.

She was tired, exhausted actually. She hadn't gone back to bed that morning. Instead she'd spent all her time transferring her baby's clothing from the chest in her room to the one in the nursery. Then she'd gone to the grocery store to pick up some items so she wouldn't need to shop so soon after her son came home.

All in all, she had been exhausted by the time she'd gotten to the hospital. But it took only one look at her child to give her renewed energy. She had felt a rush of excitement as the nurses allowed her to dress him to go home.

Then, she couldn't possibly rest later. Her mother had come over to see if she could help. She had been so busy doing whatever she could, it had made Lacy even more restless. She knew her mother was only being helpful, but every time she wiped away a speck of dust, or took the mop to a floor, it made her feel like it was something she herself should have done.

The last straw had been when her mother had checked the refrigerator and decided there wasn't enough healthy food in there for Lacy to eat. Lacy had been perfectly satisfied with the choices she'd made earlier that day when she'd gone to the grocery store.

But her mother insisted she needed more fresh fruit and vegetables to help increase the vitamins in her breast milk. Lacy didn't want to under-nourish her son, so she bit her tongue while her mother went to the store, silently wishing she had at least done one thing that would have seemed right to her mother.

Finally after Mikie was again napping, she convinced her mother to go home. She promised she'd lay down too, but she hadn't. Instead she made a list of all the cleaning she was going to do every day from then on. She also started a new shopping list, which included fresh fruits and vegetables, and posted it beside the other on the refrigerator.

Now she laid on her pillow, relishing the feel of it's softness beneath her head, compared to the hard wall the night before. Yet, sleep did not come. Her mind wouldn't let her rest.

Lacy looked at the lighted dial on her alarm clock and saw that she had lain an hour without sleeping. Finally she got up and went to the kitchen for a glass of milk. Milk would be good for her. It would be good for her son.

Half an hour later, back in bed again, she felt far more relaxed. She was even drifting off to sleep when the gentle stirring of her son came across the intercom beside the bed. She jumped right up, as is so often the case when awakened abruptly after just starting to doze.

Hurrying to the room, she saw that her son was simply cooing in his sleep. Smiling at herself she knew she was just being an over-protective parent. More like her mother than she thought she'd ever be.

Back in bed she finally slept. Satisfied that she was going to be a good mother.

The tones interrupted her dreams. She jumped out of bed, instinctively rushing to the chair where she kept her cloths. Then she remembered she'd turned off her pager after bringing her son home.

The sound came again. This time she recognized it as crying and she hurried to the source of that sound.

She lifted her son and saw his tiny mouth puckered and making sucking sounds. Smiling she knew he was hungry. Something the nurses had handled during the night since she'd gone home. For the first time she realized they must have been supplementing her feedings. She should have realized that before.

Now she felt the pressure of the milk in her breasts and was thankful she had been drinking more since Mikie came home. She had been afraid she wouldn't produce enough milk for her son, even though the doctor had assured her it was sometimes a case of supply and demand. That once her son got home and onto a regular feeding schedule she'd begin to produce more milk.

She changed his wet diaper first, then settled on the rocking chair to feed him. She relaxed as he sucked on her breast, thinking that being a mother was a pretty good feeling. Being needed. Depended on. Maybe she wouldn't be so bad at it after all.

When he fell back to sleep she waited a few moments before putting him back into his crib. Then she stretched, yawning as she made her way back into her own room, wondering how many more hours she had until morning. To her surprise the lighted dial told her it was only two o'clock. She felt like she'd slept much longer.

Yes, being a mother wasn't going to be so tough after all, she decided.

By four-thirty when the same familiar cries awakened her, she knew it was not her pager. This time she got up less quickly and headed toward the nursery. The energy she'd felt at two had disappeared.

She again changed her son's diaper, then settled down to let him nurse, but he fell back to sleep after only a few gentle pulls on her breast. She sighed, wondering if she may have been better off letting him cry himself back to sleep. She'd read that was sometimes the best thing to do.

So, an hour later that was what she did. Though she did silently slip into the nursery just to make sure Mikie was okay. After a few minutes his crying finally subsided.

At six-thirty that wasn't the case. She felt like she had barely gone back to sleep when she heard her son's cries once again. She waited a few minutes before getting up to be certain it wasn't another false alarm.

When she got into the room she found her son soaking wet, and worse. She wrinkled her nose, wondering if changing messy diapers was something that had to grow on you, or if you never got used to it. As she cleaned her son's bottom she suspected the latter.

Finally after he was changed into a clean diaper and dry pajamas, she tried laying him in his crib while she took care of the deposit he had left in his last diaper, and carefully washed her hand. Since he was more comfortable she hoped he'd fall back to sleep.

But he didn't. Once again he cried. Sobbing between unsatisfied sucks on his tiny hands.

"Hungry little fellow, aren't you?" She laughed as her son greedily took hold of her breast as soon as it was offered.

Leaning back she closed her eyes, again feeling a satisfying peace come over her. She was so relaxed she herself dozed, awakening to the feel of cool air against her exposed breast. Her son was sound asleep in her arms.

As she put him back into his crib she noticed that bright sunshine was peeping through the slats in the shutters, telling her she had slept long enough. There was plenty to do.

Then she stopped smiling. What was there to do that her mother hadn't already done sufficiently the day before? "Thanks Mom," she whispered aloud as she slipped back beneath the covers for just a little more much-needed sleep.

It was eight o'clock when she heard the neighbor's car start as he left for work. Content that the sound was not her son, she lowered her head to return to sleep. Then she heard the sound of brakes, and knew the school bus was making it's eight-thirty stop for the neighborhood's elementary school children.

At this time she'd ordinarily have been leaving for work, she thought, and smiled. That was just another of the things she was going to enjoy as long as she could. Maybe, with any luck, a paramedic position would open up so she could quit her dreaded job as a secretary.

Yawning, she decided it was useless to try and go back to sleep. She'd just take a nap later in the day. Yes, that's what she'd do. That was what she was supposed to do. Get plenty of rest.

But things didn't quite work out that way. It seemed each time she tried to lay down the telephone would ring. She thought of letting the answering machine get the calls, but she didn't want the ringing to awaken her son. So, each time it rang she bolted upright in the bed, and grabbed the receiver.

Two calls were from concerned neighbors offering their condolences – they thought mid-afternoon would be the best time to reach her so as not to bother her. She lied, assuring them they hadn't interrupted anything, then thanked them for their concern.

A third call came from the insurance company of the bank that held their mortgage. After everything that had happened she had forgotten about insurance. They politely offered their sympathies over her loss, and reminded her she'd have to supply them with a death certificate before they could settle the mortgage.

She hung up thinking about the other insurance policies on her husband. Both their own, and those provided by the fire company. She supposed she'd need death certificates for those too. She dreaded the thought of having to get them. She didn't have any idea how to go about it.

No man is an island. She sighed as the words returned to her. She picked up the phone again deciding it wouldn't hurt to ask for help. She dialed her father's number at Borough Hall.

"Sweetheart, how are you today?" he said with his usual warmth. "And how's that little grandson of mine?"

"One's tired, the other is sleeping great," she replied.

"You're not over-doing, are you?"

"No, I'm doing exactly as the doctor ordered. I'm just going to need time to adjust to the baby's schedule."

"Do you think I can visit the little guy tonight?" he asked. "Your mother's been raving about what a lil' darlin' he is. Thought tonight I'd join her for a visit. I figure by then she'll be chomping at the bit to come by. – She hasn't

86

been there yet today, has she? She promised she'd wait till I got home from work. Thought we'd even pick up some dinner on the way."

"You mean she'll allow you some fast food," Lacy teased.

"About as fast as a salad bar can be," he responded good-naturedly. "But, I'll try and convince her that red meat will help you build up your iron."

"Sure, Dad, then I'll slip you some of mine while she's doting on her grandson."

"That's the idea!" He laughed a deep hearty laugh over the phone.

"The reason I called, Dad, is to ask a favor."

"Ask away."

She took a deep breath. "It seems I'm going to need a death certificate for insurance purposes. Maybe more than one if our other policies require them."

"They will, Sweetheart," he said. "As will those the company has. And the state and federal benefits programs."

Her eyes opened wide. She'd forgotten about those.

"At least money won't be a worry for you, for awhile," her father continued. "You'll be able to put that boy through college if he wants to go."

She wouldn't have to worry about how she was going to support her son. At least not right away. She might even be able to stay home with him longer than her maternity leave allowed. If her boss didn't like it she could quit. She could find another job. Better still, she could afford to wait for the next paramedic opening.

Later that evening her father informed her the money she'd receive would be well over two hundred thousand dollars. It was more than she could handle all at once.

"Sweetheart, it sounds like a lot. . ." he started.

"It is a lot!" Lacy was stunned. She had known it was a large sum. But she hadn't thought of it in specific amounts.

"It takes a lot to raise a child," her mother reminded her, looking lovingly down at the child in her arms.

"Listen," her father said more firmly. "You and that boy deserve every penny of that money. Your mother is right. I don't often interfere in your business. But I do think you need to have someone advise you how to invest the money you receive so it will give you and that boy the most benefits."

She looked toward her son's clear blue eyes as her mother held him. Her father was right. He didn't often give advice. But when he did, it was sound advice.

"I'll call Karla Mulholland," she said, thinking of her friend's experience in accounting. "I trust her. She'll be able to recommend someone who knows about investing and that kind of stuff."

Carl reached out and took his daughter's hand between both his own larger ones. "It's going to take some time – these things always do – but you'll get what you deserve. Good people eventually do."

She suddenly felt he was speaking about more than money. But whatever he meant, it didn't matter now. What mattered was, she'd be able to care for her son the way he deserved. She may be a single-parent, but at least she'd be able to provide for her baby.

After a second night almost identical to the previous one, Lacy drug herself around the house, more tired than she thought possible. She was again trying to take an afternoon nap, when the doorbell rang.

She hurried to the front door, opening it to a tall rectangular box with arms and legs. "Oh my," she said, stepping aside so the delivery man could bring the package inside. "Could you put that down over there." She pointed to the middle of the living room.

The man grunted as he put the clumsy box onto the floor. "There's more," the brown uniformed man said gruffly. "I'll need the hand truck for these others. Would you mind if I put them in the garage? An incline is far easier than the steps. They're awfully heavy."

Since she hadn't any idea what they were, she didn't see why he shouldn't. As he went outside again she raced to the kitchen entrance to the breezeway that let to the garage. She pushed the button that signaled the automatic garage door opener.

The man had not been exaggerating. He unloaded several boxes, sitting them just behind where her car was parked in the garage. Judging by the bulge in his upper arm they indeed were heavy. She didn't have the heart to tell him she'd prefer he put them somewhere that didn't block her car. As it was he was breathing heavy by the time he slid the last box off the hand truck.

"You've gotta sign, Mrs. Boyce," he said as he slipped the clip board off the back of the hand truck. "I hope your husband enjoys these more than I did."

She frowned, biting the bitter retort that came swiftly to her lips because of the man's sarcasm. Besides, what did it matter? The man had no way of knowing Mike was dead.

When he left she pushed the button to close the garage door, before inspecting the labels on the boxes. The company sounded familiar, yet she couldn't quite remember where she'd heard the name before.

Just then she thought she heard the faint stirring of her son. She hurried back into the house and to the nursery about the time the stirring became an actual cry.

For the moment the boxes were forgotten while she tended to her son.

It was late evening before she thought about the boxes again. By that time she was too tired to care. She simply moved the long rectangular box from the middle of the living room to the garage with the others.

That night was no better than the two before. Her son, she learned, was a very restless sleeper. She wondered if there was something wrong with him, and decided to call the doctor first thing in the morning.

"He's perfectly normal, Lacy," the doctor said when he returned her call. "More than likely you have more wrong with you. Take time to rest. You've been through a lot recently."

Rest. An illusive commodity. She immediately regretted her resentful thoughts. Other mothers coped. So would she.

"Lacy, I have to warn you, you need to look out for yourself. You're health, both physically and emotionally," the doctor warned. "With the stress you've been under, I'm amazed you're still able to nurse your son. If you hope to continue, you'll have to start taking care."

Lacy wondered if that could be part of her son's problem. "Do you think my milk is bad, or weak, or something? Because of everything that's happened."

The doctor sensed her worry. "Give it time. And try to relax. If you continue to have problems. We'll have to start supplementing your mother's milk."

"I hope that won't happen."

"Just remember what I said. Try to relax. Don't be afraid to ask for help," he added before he hung up.

No man is an island.

She sighed, deciding she'd soon have to give in and let her mother do more. She could imagine how elated her mother would be. Probably delighted that she could remind Lacy how poorly she was doing as a mother. As a human being!

Tears stung Lacy's eyes as she realized her unnatural bitterness. There'd always been tension between her and her mother, but her thoughts now were growing unreasonable. It had to be the exhaustion.

When her mother stopped by to see how she was doing later that afternoon, Lacy thought it was the opportunity to rest. Instead she had lain in bed feeling guilty that she wasn't handling the situation better. In the end, when she got up, she felt worse than ever.

"Did you call Mrs. Mulholland?" her mother asked.

"Call Karla?"

"Yes, about investing that money you'll be getting," her mother replied. "I know your father said it will take time for all the bureaucratic red tape, but it won't hurt to have some idea about what you're going to do."

"I was going to call her today," Lacy lied. Actually she had forgotten about it entirely.

After her mother left, feeling guilty about her lie, she made the call.

"I know a couple people, but most would charge an arm and a leg," Karla replied. "But maybe. . ." she hesitated. "I know of someone who might not charge since he's involved in the fire company too. You probably know him – well actually, I'm sure you do since he was . . .he was injured at the fire where Mike was killed."

"Ryan?" Lacy immediately remembered Ryan telling her he worked for Karla. "But, if he's only in accounting. . ."

Karla laughed. "A displaced C.P.A.. Anyway, he used to be. I have never been able to understand why he gave it up to work here."

"He's from out of state. He's probably not up on Pennsylvania tax laws."

"Who is? The way they keep changing."

"I hate to bug him." Lacy thought about how helpful Ryan had already been.

"Bug him," Karla repeated, sighing. "It would probably do him good to have something to do. I think he keeps too much to himself."

Lacy thought about that too, remembering how lonely he seemed. Yet, he didn't give the impression of someone who preferred being a loner.

No man is an island.

She thought of his words and her decision was made. "I'll give him a call. – You wouldn't have his number handy would you?"

"I'll do one better," Karla said. "I'll put you through to his desk."

"I don't want to interrupt him while he's working. . ."

"His boss won't mind." Karla laughed, then the line switched. She heard the phone ring.

Ryan picked up on the first ring. "Simon here."

"Ryan, this is Lacy Boyce."

"Lacy," his deep voice showed concern. "Is everything all right?" Why would she be calling him? he wondered. "I hope you're not having problems with the furniture."

"No, everything is fine," she replied good-naturedly. "Though I do wish the crib had some kind of magical spell that would make Mikie sleep for more than two hours at a time."

"I thought I should have warned you?"

"What?" Lacy wondered what he meant. It sounded like he was talking from experience.

"It's a well known fact that new parents don't get much sleep," Ryan replied. "Now, what can I do for you?"

Lacy explained the situation and asked if he would be able to offer any advice on how to invest her money. Ryan said he'd look into the current rates of interest on various forms of investment. "Right now, there's a low return on most investments," he said almost absently, as though already mentally calculating her options.

"I suspected as much. That's all the more reason I need to know the smartest things to do."

Ryan promised to get back to her in the next few days.

"No rush," she said. "I don't have any money yet. I just want to know what to do when I do."

With that call made, she felt like she had actually accomplished something. More than she had in days. In fact, she decided it would also be a good time to find out what was in the mysterious boxes in the garage.

Opening first the tall rectangular box that had been in the living room, she found a black, leather-covered, cushioned board. In the next she found numerous lengths of metal tubing, sturdy
metal cable and other pieces she didn't yet recognize.

As soon as she opened the next box she realized what the combined contents of the packages were. A fitness center. Judging by the many parts, it was quite an elaborate set-up. She was surprised Mike hadn't told her he was buying it.

When they had first bought the house he had mentioned something about using the second bedroom as a workout room, but when she got pregnant she'd assumed he changed his mind. Now, she knew he hadn't changed his mind at all. He must have been going to use them in another part of the house.

The basement was the most logical. There was little enough room in the garage as it was. In fact, with the boxes between the door and her car, she'd never be able to get her car out of the garage. She supposed she could use Mike's Bronco. She'd just have to move the infant seat from the back of her car.

It would be far easier than moving the boxes downstairs. Especially since she wasn't even certain she wanted to keep them. Maybe the company would take them back. She rummaged through the boxes and found the packing slip. Her eyes grew wide when she saw the price Mike had paid. He had put it on his credit card.

Credit card. She sighed, knowing that was one more thing she'd have to get changed. All the things that had been Mike's were now her's. She'd have to have everything changed to her name. And she'd probably need more death certificates to do it.

She decided to call her father and tell him she'd need more death certificates than she'd first thought. Though his secretary put her right through she thought her father sounded distracted.

"Am I calling at a bad time?" she asked.

"Bad. Yes," he replied, sighing heavily into the phone. "Suppose we talk later."

"Sure Dad. Call me back when it's a better time."

"I might stop by to see you," he said almost absently. "Yes, that's what I'll do."

She thought her father sounded strange. She hoped he wasn't coming down with something. It was probably all his worry about her catching up to him. She decided, for his sake, she couldn't let on how many problems she'd been having with Mikie sleeping. Or, more accurately, his waking.

It would just take a little time and he'd get on a better sleeping schedule. Till then, she'd manage.

CHAPTER SEVEN

As soon as he hung up the phone after Lacy's call, Ryan started thinking about her request. He was going to have to do some careful research. He knew that currently interest rates were low. Too low to lock in on a long-term investment. Still he knew she wouldn't want to take a chance on anything risky.

He looked up to find Karla watching. He knew it wasn't because he had stopped working. She wasn't that kind of boss. He gave the company a good day's work, and she respected that.

She got up from her desk and walked in his direction. He leaned back on his chair waiting for what he suspected was to come. He remained expressionless.

"So, are you going to help her?" she asked, not bothering to hide her curiosity behind beat-around-the-bush questions.

He nodded. "I came highly recommended."

"Of course." Karla flashed him a wide grin, reaching up to push her unruly, long bangs out from behind her glasses. "I always said you didn't belong here. You've got a lot more to offer than adding up sales and subtracting expenses."

"I think we do a little more than that in here." He cocked his head to the side. "With the aid of my computer I can tell you which products are selling best and where. I can even tell you who's buying them and why."

"That's Marketing's job," Karla grinned, scolding him with a shake of her right index finger. "You've been accessing their files."

"I'll never tell."

"Admit it, this job is boring to you. You were a Certified Public Accountant before you came here. You did more than facts and figures."

"Certainly, I also did people's income tax."

"Those same people trusted your advice."

He shrugged. "Which was usually to send them to a good investment broker when they wanted to earn more on their money."

"That doesn't mean you didn't know which investments were good and which were not."

He smiled. "I had a fair idea."

"Which brings us back to square one," Karla smiled at him with satisfaction. "You're the best person I could think of to help Lacy."

"That remains to be seen," his expression sobered as he focused his green gaze on his auburn-haired office manager. "I'll do what I can. But I don't like taking risks with someone else's money. Especially someone who's going to need that money."

"That's the other reason I recommended you."

Ryan sighed, closing his eyes and shaking his head. He squeezed two fingers to the bridge of his nose, slowly spreading them across his dark brows. He didn't like being put in this position. Yet, he knew he could have refused. He still wasn't certain why he didn't, except that while talking to Lacy it hadn't even crossed his mind. It was immediately after hanging up the phone that the doubts began to nag him.

"You know where I can borrow a computer to access the Internet?" he asked suddenly. "I have my doubts the company would appreciate my using this one for personal business."

Karla grinned. "Since I was about to suggest you come by for dinner tonight – you look like you could use a descent meal – I can offer you use of our computer."

"I'll take you up on both. I'm getting tired of boiling those little pouches. And going out to eat alone never appealed to me." His last experience, when he stopped at the V.I.P. Diner the day after his discharge from the hospital, had not been one of his fondest memories. He hadn't eaten alone that night, though in many ways he wished he had.

Rose Sinclair and her young daughter, Amy, were there for dinner too. She'd stopped by his table to see how he was feeling. Then the next thing he knew they were seated across from him at the opposite side of his booth. Rose was busy showering him with syrupy compliments about what a hero he'd been the night of the fire. Her daughter sat silently listening, her somber dark eyes going from her mother to him and back again, till her eyes grew like saucers and she gaped at him with something akin to hero-worship.

The experience had been more of an embarrassment than a pleasure. He didn't enjoy being treated like someone's teen idol. He hadn't joined the fire company for that. He'd joined because he had to. Because he had to do whatever he could to prevent another tragedy.

He didn't want the glory. Sure, he knew there were others who thrived on it. But not him. Rose had been oblivious to the possibility he was different than those others.

She appeared to be as well versed in turning on the adulation, extolling him for his prowess as a firefighter, and something more. Not so much in words, but in the way she looked at him. The way she stood so close after walking with him to his car.

Worse, after he saw she and Amy were walking, he had offered to give them a ride home. She seemed to take that as a signal of some kind, automatically assuming he'd come in and visit for awhile after they got to her home. Her disappointment was unhidden as he made his excuse and his escape.

"You shouldn't spend so much time alone," Karla chided him.

"What?" His return to the present was swiftly followed by embarrassment when he realized he hadn't been listening.

Karla repeated her words. "I'm sure there's plenty of women out there who would be happy to join you."

He pulled a face, thinking of one. If rumors were true, Rose would be more than willing. But he wasn't looking for that kind of relationship. In truth, he hadn't been looking for any relationship.

"I'll settle for boil-in-the-bag," he stated flatly.

"Man can not live by boil-in-the-bag alone," his manager teased.

Ryan shook his head, his green eyes glowing good-naturedly. "Okay, I'll include an occasional dinner with well-meaning friends."

Karla was about to say more, but Ryan held up his hand to stop her. The corners of his mouth turned down as he shook his head. "Some things are best left alone."

She closed her mouth and nodded, once again brushing her bangs away from her glasses. She had known Ryan for two years, and yet, she felt in many ways she knew him no better today than she did the day she'd first met him.

#

Lacy had just gotten comfortable in the giant blue recliner in her living room when the doorbell rang. Thinking it might already be her father, she jumped up and hurried to the door. She was anxious to find out what had been on her father's mind earlier when she'd called. He'd seemed so distracted.

She put on a falsely bright expression. Hoping to alleviate the worry she had suspected was his main problem.

As she swung open the door, her expression changed to surprise. "Rose?" She eyed the woman standing at the top of her steps, biting her lip as though she were nervous. Rose had never visited her before. In fact, they had never been particularly close. But she supposed she should expect such visits after the death of a husband and the birth of a son.

Not wanting to sound ungracious she asked the other woman inside.

"I. . .I was wondering if. . .if you have a few minutes – to talk," Rose said as soon as she entered the living room.

Lacy eyed Rose, thinking she looked even more nervous than she'd first thought. "Why don't we sit down?" She motioned to the sofa and matching chair. "Coffee?" She offered as soon as her unexpected guest had lowered herself into the chair.

"No, I'm nervous enough," Rose said, confirming Lacy's suspicions.

"I have herbal tea." She realized, that was an offer she'd been making a lot lately. Perhaps she should add some to her shopping list. Apricot tea, she thought, smiling.

"This isn't easy," her guest continued.

Lacy wiped the smile from her face, realizing she should be paying attention to her guest, not day-dreaming about her next visit to the grocery store.

"I didn't know if I should come," Rose explained. "My lawyer said I should leave everything up to him. But, I didn't think it was fair to do it that way. I mean. . ." She stared down at the pale blue carpeting. "I know what people say about me. . .But I'm really not as bad as they make me out." Her dark eyes were sad when they again met Lacy's blue ones. She seemed almost pathetic, as though she were begging for understanding. For a moment Lacy felt sorry for her. At the same time a chill went down her spine.

"Why don't you tell me why you're here, Rose?" she asked with more calm than she was suddenly feeling.

"I'm only doing it because of my daughter, Amy," Rose again bit her lip.

"Doing what? Rose, you have to get to the point if you want me to understand what you're talking about."

Rose sighed. "I never asked for child support. I've never even told anyone who I think Amy's father may be. I did that because I didn't want to make trouble. I knew people thought bad enough of me."

Fine blonde hairs on the back of Lacy's neck seemed to raise of their own accord. Her mouth was suddenly too dry to swallow.

"Rose, why are you saying all this to me. It's past history."

"Because I want you to understand. You see, my attorney went to see Arlen Maxwell this morning. Since he's the one who has to make the request for payment of benefits to the next of kin."

Lacy's blue eyes turned to ice as she stared back at the other woman. "Mike's next of kin?"

Rose nodded. "I only want Amy to get what is rightfully her's. I mean what I think. . .Oh, Lacy, I never bothered anyone before. It's just you'll be getting so much money. . ."

"You want your share," Lacy finished for her.

"No!" Rose stood and started pacing.

"Sit down, Rose!" Lacy ordered, feeling at a disadvantage sitting while the other woman stood. Yet, she didn't feel her legs would support her if she also tried to stand.

Rose quickly took the edge of the seat she had just left. "I don't want any money for me. It's Amy I'm thinking about. Her future. She may want to go to college. And me. . ." She frowned, shrugging her shoulders in defeat. "I hardly earn enough for us to survive."

"Rose, to get any of that money, your daughter would have to be Mike's child," Lacy forced the words from trembling lips.

"I think she is," the other woman replied.

"Think!" Lacy could no longer contain her anger. "That's not something you think is true! It either is or it isn't!" She heard Mikie start to cry and realized her shouting must have frightened him. She sighed, wishing she'd maintained her control.

"Wait here. I'll be right back," she ordered as she got up and forced her rubbery legs to carry her out of the room with as much dignity as she could muster.

By the time she reached the privacy of her son's room she was trembling. She felt angry. Betrayed. Her tiny son left out another wail as he struggled to lift his tiny head.

"It's okay, Baby," she whispered, trying to keep her tumultuous emotions out of her voice. She thought it would be a mistake to pick him up now. He'd sense her tension. But he wouldn't stop crying.

Finally she swallowed, forcing herself to relax. She tried to mask her tension with false cheer as she spoke to her son. She lifted him from his crib and realized his diaper had soaked through to his pajamas. She carried him to the table to change him, still speaking in soft, calming words.

When Mikie was dressed she went to return him to his crib, but he cried again. She didn't care that Rose was in living room. She sat down in the rocking chair and started to nurse her son. It was well past his normal feeding time. In fact, it had been the longest stretch he'd slept since coming home from the hospital.

She sighed, thinking it was unfair for her to expect anything more from her child. The tiny, innocent victim in the horrible nightmare taking place right now.

After long moments she looked up and saw Rose standing in the doorway of the nursery, silently watching. She was tempted to order her out, except for the visible distress on her face. Black trails of tears flowed down her cheeks.

"Tissues are over there." Lacy pointed, reminded there was more than one victim, if what Rose said was true. "I'll be out in a minute. He's settling down again."

She waited till the other woman left the room before putting her son back in his crib. Before he could cry she wound the musical mobile that hung above his crib. The little cartoon characters spun around as the tune "It's a Small World" gently played. She knew he couldn't really see the characters yet, but he seemed to listen intently to the music.

Finally she forced herself to return to the living room and her unwanted guest.

"Rose, what you've been telling me is that you think Mike was your daughter's father," she said. "But you're not really certain are you?"

Rose frowned. "I admit there are other possibilities. – Only two," she quickly added.

Lacy's eyebrows raised. "Only two." She couldn't hide the sarcasm in her voice.

"Look, I've never hurt anyone before," Rose said. "I know what the other women in the Auxiliary say about me. I know some of the men make jokes, too."

"You don't exactly win friends by sleeping with every man who walks into the station."

"I haven't slept with every man," the girl defended.

"No, only those who are willing," Lacy spat, then took a breath, realizing she was getting no where this way. "Look, what you do is your business and the business of those you do it with. As long as it doesn't hurt anyone else. But, don't expect a man's widow to welcome you with open arms, when only a little over a week after he dies, you tell her you were sleeping with him."

"He wasn't your husband then," Rose reminded her. "I don't sleep with married men. – At least not happily married men."

Lacy raised her deep, blue eyes toward the ceiling, almost able to laugh at that statement. If it weren't such a tragic situation she might have.

"I mean, sometimes a man's wife doesn't understand him," Rose started to explain. "She doesn't know how to make him happy."

"And you do, I suppose?"

Rose looked away, having the good grace to blush.

"Rose, I always thought I was the one who was naive," Lacy started softly, almost sympathetically. "But even I know that's an over-used cliche among philanderers."

"Maybe deep down I knew," Rose replied. "I can't explain it. It's all beside the point now. I am what I am. Would you be happier if I put a name to it?"

"No, Rose. Actually I would not. I feel sorry for you. I feel even sorrier for your daughter."

"She doesn't know. I don't run around like I used to. I'm trying hard to settle down. I date nicer men now."

Lacy knew Rose really believed that and wasn't about to burst her bubble with the fact that people just don't forget past indiscretions.

"Rose, you may or may not have been involved with Mike," Lacy returned to the subject. "But certainly you can't expect money to be turned over to you on your word alone. And Mike's hardly able to refute what you're saying."

"I know, I know." The woman's frustration was growing. "My attorney said Amy would have to have a special blood test to prove paternity. We figure there's hospital records that have all the information we need about Mike."

"I see you've thought it all through."

"I've consulted an attorney. He told me everything we have to do." Rose looked troubled again. "That's why I came here. He says he's going to try to get you to agree to settle without all kinds of publicity."

Lacy shook her head, feeling numb, but not too numb to know the attorney was using scare tactics to insure his client win. He was betting Lacy wouldn't want the publicity.

He was right.

"Rose, why did you come here if you have an attorney to do your dirty work?"

Rose visibly flinched. "I told you. I thought it was only fair. I don't want to hurt anyone. But I do want what's best for my daughter. I don't have a lot of money. There's a rumor they're going to close the factory where I work. If that happens I don't know how I'll support Amy." There was desperation in her voice.

Lacy did feel sorry for the other woman. But she couldn't let that cause her to make any rash promises. She'd have to wait and think things through. She'd have to talk to someone. Maybe her father. He said he was coming over later. He had had something on his mind. So did she. Maybe it would help to share it.

After Rose finally left Lacy went back to the nursery to check her son. She smiled when she saw he was awake and totally contented playing with his own fingers. A tiny smile started to break through the ice in her heart.

"No matter what else happened, at least I have you," she whispered. "Money doesn't really matter. I'm a survivor."

But would she survive the pain and the betrayal she felt right now? She tried to tell herself everything Rose said could have been a lie. She and Mike may never have been together.

But if they had been, did he suspect that the baby she carried could have been his?

That opened a Pandora's box of more questions. Was he afraid of what others would say? Was he afraid Rose would use the child to try and trap him into marrying her?

Was that why he started dating Lacy? Suddenly showering her with all his attention after years of acting like she hardly existed.

That had once been the rumor.

Lacy had to remind herself, she had never been one to listen to rumors.

The doorbell brought her out of her confused mix of past and present. This time when she answered she didn't even bother to try and paste a happy expression on her face.

One look at her father and she felt his somber expression must have mirrored her own. He stepped inside giving her a quick kiss on the cheek before heading directly into the living room and looking around.

"How's the baby?" he asked.

"Better than me, I'm afraid."

He turned to look at her again. "Are you sick? I can come back another time."

"No, I just had an unwanted guest."

He frowned, lowering his graying head. "It wasn't a lawyer or anything?" he asked cautiously.

"No, Rose came to do her dirty work on her own." Tears filled her eyes making them sparkle like sapphires.

He exhaled a long breath. "Arlen came to see me today. He told me all about it."

"What should I do?" she pleaded, sobs coming from her lips. "This, on top of everything else. I feel like. . ." She shrugged, refusing to put it into words. She'd already worried her father enough.

"Lacy, I have to ask. . .do you think it's true?"

She shrugged again, keeping her head bowed. She couldn't meet her father's concerned brown eyes. Would he guess that she suspected it could be true? Was she being disloyal to her dead husband's memory? Or was she facing the facts?

What were the facts? What in the world were they?

"I don't know what to think, Dad." She finally looked up into his face. "I just don't know."

He went to the dark blue rocker-recliner and sat down, slowly rocking, silently lost in his own thoughts as he crossed his arms over his barrel chest. Lacy waited, taking a seat on the edge of the same chair where her unwanted guest had sat.

After a while he looked back at his daughter, his expression grim. "Arlen may be right. He's thinking about confronting a few of the other men he suspects. . .well, men he suspects had been with Rose around the time she got pregnant."

"There was a lot of speculation back then. Gossip mostly. You know, 'life at the Vigilantes is in a bed of Rose's.'" She repeated the mocking refrain many of the men had used.

Carl's eyes lit with anger, then regret. "She turned the station into . . ."

"Dad, it takes two." Lacy interrupted, hardly able to believe she was defending the other woman.

"Or three, or four. Who knows in her case?"

"That's just it. Who really does? Did we ever really catch her sleeping with anyone at the station? Were any of them that stupid?"

He thought before he spoke. "None of the men would have enjoyed being the brunt of station gossip. If they were with her they wouldn't have admitted it."

"They may have even taken great pains to hide the fact that they had been." Once again she thought of the way Mike had aggressively courted her during those months, proposing only weeks before Rose's daughter was born.

"Which is the one flaw I find in Arlen's plan. Who's going to admit it willingly?"

"I hate to think what the company will look like if this goes to court." Lacy frowned. "If I agree to share the money, that won't have to happen."

Carl's square jaw jutted out stubbornly. "And if she's lying?"

"Her daughter's future will be secure."

"Ha!" Carl shook his head. "You still like to look for the best in people."

"I learned by example," she said.

"But Sweetheart, there's no guarantee the money will be used for the girl."

"I can agree to settle out of court if she agrees that the money be put in trust for Amy and not be touched till the girl's eighteen."

"You're too generous, Lacy."

"Not generous, Dad."

His frown deepened. "Then you think it could be true."

She nodded, her long honey-gold curls framing her down-turned face. "It could be. I don't know. I just don't know."

"Mike died with that secret," Carl said as he came to stand beside his daughter, putting a comforting arm across her hunched shoulders and giving her a squeeze. "I don't think you should make any decisions till you have more time to think about it. Meanwhile, suppose we let Arlen talk to a few of the men."

"What will it hurt?"

"That's my girl," Carl said proudly. "Now, before I go, how about I sneak a peek at that grandson of mine."

"Sure, he was awake a few minutes ago," Lacy replied. "But you know how it is with newborns. They sleep most the time."

"Except when they're supposed to."

To that Lacy laughed, knowing her father had hit the nail right on the head. But tonight she doubted it would matter. She suspected she'd get little sleep.

#

The following morning Lacy awoke more exhausted than ever, from her restless sleep. She had lain awake for hours thinking about what had happened. Her first thoughts were loyal and loving, ready to defend her husband's memory. Then they were angry and betrayed, certain their marriage had been based on lies.

Back and forth her pendulum of emotions went, preventing her from getting any sleep. Until she finally dozed in the wee hours of morning after getting up only once with her son.

She wondered why on the one night she was unable to sleep, her tiny son had slept his best.

In the morning she awakened from a nightmare, sobbing, her night-gown drenched in perspiration. Then she heard her son cry. He was awake for his morning feeding.

She sat in her damp night gown a long time after changing and feeding her son. She sat holding her tiny blanket-wrapped bundle close to her breast, staring out into empty space. She felt defeated. Her spirit was dying. And she didn't know what to do about it.

It wasn't till she finally realized she was shivering that she got up from the rocking chair, put her son in an infant seat, strapping him carefully in place, then carrying him with her into the bathroom so she could take a hot bath. She sat him carefully on the floor beside the tub.

By the time she had finished she felt more lethargic than ever. She didn't feel up to giving Mikie his morning bath. Yet she knew it was time.

Forcing herself, she managed to fill his tiny plastic tub with luke-warm water and gently placed him inside. He seemed to be getting used to the new sensation of bathing, she thought, as she noticed him looking far less surprised as he felt the water surround him.

She carefully cradled his upper body in one hand while gently washing then rinsing him with the other hand. When finished she lifted him into the fluffy, white towel she kept close at hand and wrapped him so he wouldn't get a chill.

After drying him she placed him back in his blanket and carried him back to his room so she could dress him. She was just finishing the task when she heard her mother calling from the living room.

She sighed, hoping her father hadn't told her about what had happened the day before. She didn't feel up to talking about it just now. She didn't know if she'd ever feel up to it. Perhaps they'd never have to tell her mother. Then she'd never have to talk about it.

"Oh, Lacy, are you okay?" Lois asked with such concern, Lacy knew that her father must have told her the entire sad tale. Trust him not to keep anything from her mother, she thought bitterly.

Lacy could not control the salty tears that started to spill out of her eyes. "Oh, Mom, I don't need a lecture now," she moaned. "I feel bad enough."

Then her son joined in her crying, making her feel even worse for making him cry. So she cried some more.

"Here, give me the baby," her mother said softly as she took Mikie from her arms. "I'll get him settled down then we can talk."

Lacy watched as her mother took her son from the room, feeling helpless to stop her from taking over. She didn't know if she wanted to stop her. She was just so tired. And to top it all off she had a head ache. It had been nagging at her all night, but she was determined not to take any medication while she was nursing.

It was the one thing she was going to do right.

Pressing the heels of her hands to her temples, wishing she could squeeze the throbbing away, she started to cry again. Uncontrollably.

Finally she gave up and went into the kitchen where she kept the Tylenol. Maybe she'd take just one. With some more tea. Apricot tea, she thought.

But when she opened the box she found it was empty. Angry she tossed it onto the floor. She reached for another box. "Camomile," she read the label. "Soothing. Calming." Just what she needed.

She put water on to boil just as her mother came back into the room. "Okay, Lacy. What's wrong?"

"What's wrong?" Lacy turned to her in undisguised anger. "You know very well what's wrong! As though everything else that happened wasn't enough, my surprise visiter yesterday had to destroy what little peace I had left. She had to inform me that my stupid, little, childish dream was just that. A dream!"

"Wait a minute, Honey," her mother said as she came up beside her, putting her arm around her. "I figured you were having normal post-partum depression. But this is more than that. Tell me about it. What's going on?"

"You mean. . .Daddy didn't tell you?"

"Your father came home and locked himself in the basement for several hours. He didn't tell me anything. But I thought there was something wrong."

Lacy's shoulder's slumped. So much for not telling her mother. Now she knew she'd have to tell her the whole sordid story. She'd have to go through it all over again.

In defeat she pulled out a chair and sat down at the kitchen table, allowing her mother to make the tea she no longer wanted. All she wanted now was to hide. Maybe go to bed and never get up.

But that was the cowards way, she reminded herself. She never used to be a coward.

With a deep breath, she started filling her mother in on the events of the previous day.

To her surprise she felt better after talking to her about it. In fact, her mother was more knowledgeable on the subject than she'd known.

"The blood test is a smart idea, Honey," her mother said after several moments of silence. "But, it doesn't really show who the father is. From what I've heard, it eliminates who isn't."

"So what you're saying is the test could be done and we still won't know if Mike is Amy's father."

"On the other hand, you may find out he isn't," her mother reminded her more optimistically.

"But, I'll still never know if he only used me to get out of Rose's clutches."

"Honey, when you calm down, you'll realize he could have done that a lot of other ways. Easier ways. He didn't have to use you." Her mother sounded like the voice of reason. Lacy felt she had never heard her this way. "Listen. Why would he run to the arms of a woman, go to the extreme of marrying that woman, just to get out of paying a little child support?"

"Listening to it put that way, it does seem like a lot to exchange for a little."

Her mother nodded. "He loved you. You just believe that. Keep that thought in your heart."

Lacy smiled, knowing that was exactly what she should do. Now she only hoped that she could.

"Lacy why don't you try and get some rest," her mother suggested. "It looks like everything happening is taking its toll. You look exhausted."

"Since this is my day for spilling my guts, I may as well admit, I feel exhausted too." Lacy gave her mother a grim smile. "It's been awful. I haven't slept well since the night Mike died. And Little Mikie seems to wake up so often during the night. As soon as I do fall to sleep I've got to get up again."

"Honey, I really think you should come home," her mother suggested. "I know you wanted to stay here. But you're under a lot of pressure. No one would blame you for moving back with your parents under the circumstances."

"I would," Lacy replied stubbornly. "I have to make a life for myself and my son. On our own."

"You don't have to do it alone."

"Mom, don't start again!" Lacy said more loudly than she wanted. "You know we'll only argue about it."

Her mother frowned. "Okay. But suppose I come here and spend the night tonight so you can get at least one full night's sleep."

"Mom, I can't expect you to do that."

"Don't you think I had help when I brought you home from the hospital? Don't be so stubborn and independent you end up hurting yourself and your son. There's nothing wrong with accepting a little help."

"I've been doing a lot of that lately." Lacy thought of the help Ryan had given her putting the baby's furniture together.

"We do want to help. We're your family. We love you."

"In spite of everything, I'm a pretty lucky per___," Lacy said softly as she looked at her mother's concerned expres___. ___ ___ up on that tonight. But only one night. Okay?"

Her mother smiled, trying to hide ___ ___ e way her daughter looked she wondered if one ___ ___ be en___. She worried about her. Probably too much, if what ___ ___ was tru___ But a mother just doesn't stop caring because her daughter ___ ___ age. Or because she gets married. No, she's there for the duration. As long as God keeps her on this earth, she'll care. And maybe even after.

That's what mother's are for. Lacy will learn that now that she's a mother too.

CHAPTER EIGHT

Lacy still hadn't slept well even though her mother spent the night. She hated the fact that she was sleeping in a comfortable bed while her mother slept in the living room on the recliner. Sure, she knew it was a comfortable piece of furniture, but she hated the fact that her mother was sleeping on it.

She had lain awake thinking about the unfinished attic, in her Cape Cod-styled house. She had hoped one day it could be converted into two extra bedrooms. There would even have been enough space for an extra bathroom if they'd have built a dormer into the roof.

Mike said they would cross that bridge when they came to it. Now she supposed they never would come to that bridge. They'd never have the large family she had wanted.

She sighed, remembering Mike's doubts whenever she'd told him her secret desire for several children. "Why in the world would you want a lot of kids? Won't they cramp your style? Keep you from being 'All that you can be'," he said, sarcastically using the Marine slogan, as he so often used in reference to her lifestyle. "Well, you can't be it all, Lacy."

As always, she did her best to hide the anger his words stirred inside her, more determined than ever to prove him wrong.

But what had she been trying to prove? Who had she been trying to prove it to?

All night her thoughts had gone round and round, unrelated subjects linking in her mind, making her tense, uneasy, filled with doubts. Doubts she'd had before, but had been able to push to the back of her mind. But in her physical and mental exhaustion she was unable to ignore them. She suffered with them, unable to put them into that safe compartment, while concentrating on more positive things. She couldn't even think of anything positive.

Her son. That was the only positive thing she could find. She tried thinking about him. Of his future. A future without a father. She could make up for that. She could play ball. She could teach him to drive. She could even show him the ropes of firefighting, if that was what he decided to do.

Mike had always called the baby she carried their future firefighter. He'd said he was going to teach him everything he needed to know.

Deep down she knew Mike would have resented her doing that if he were alive. *If he were alive.*

But he wasn't.

He had resented so many things about her, she remembered, wishing she couldn't.

Why now? Why won't my mind let me rest?

She tossed and turned, finally giving up the fight. It would be better to let her torturous thoughts to take their course. Then maybe, she'd finally get some sleep.

But even sleep, when it finally came, was no relief. In her dreams she saw the face of an auburn-haired woman, laughing down at her. The woman was dressed in black. Looking up at her face, she saw it was Rose.

On her right was her dark-eyed daughter, Amy, holding her hand. To Rose's left, another tiny hand was in her's. But she couldn't quite see who it was. She strained her neck, but she couldn't raise her head. She was frozen. Unable to move. She could only see.

She moved her eyes above Rose, and next saw Mike, standing just behind the other woman's left shoulder. He was also looking down. But on his face was a look of anger.

"You were supposed to keep me from this," he said to her, but his lips didn't move. Somehow she was reading his mind.

Then she heard a faint voice from the tiny invisible person she hadn't been able to see. "Mommy, can we go home now?"

Suddenly she knew it was her son. And he was talking to Rose. Her little boy was older now, she saw, as Rose lifted him onto her hip. The image of his father. With the same dark eyes as the little girl who was now taking Mike's hand.

"Yes, Daddy, can we go home?" the little girl said.

"We can all go home now," Rose added, casting a loving look at her three companions, before turning to look down at her again with a sickening smile of satisfaction.

"Thank you Lacy," she said before turning to walk away.

No! No! Lacy tried to jump up and follow. She had to stop them. But she couldn't.

Then suddenly someone was throwing something down on her. It was dirt, and it was covering her face. She could no longer see. No longer breath.

Oh God! They think I'm dead. I'm being buried alive!

"Stop!" she shouted, fighting the blankets that were covering her face. "I'm alive!"

"Lacy! Lacy!" She heard the voice from afar. It was growing nearer. Suddenly she felt cool air on her face. She could breath again.

"Lacy are you all right?" her mother asked.

She gasped for more air. Thankful she could breath. Her eyes were wide open. She could see her mother's face. She reached out to touch her. She could move.

She sighed, relaxing against her pillow again. "It was a nightmare."

She felt her heartbeat returning to normal. Her breathing slowed again. "Are you okay?"

"I'm okay," she lied. *I'm just losing my mind.*

Her mother looked doubtful. Worried. About to say something, but they were interrupted by Mikie's faint cry.

Lacy sat up, throwing back the covers. "I'll take care of him, Mom. Maybe he's hungry."

She looked at the lighted dial of her clock and saw that it was six-thirty. The night was over. Finally over. She breathed a sigh of relief.

#

After the second night Lacy insisted her mother go home. She had slept better, perhaps because her exhaustion had finally taken it's toll. In spite of the same dream, she had for the second night in a row, Lacy felt better in the morning.

She decided that day she'd spend more time with her son. She'd show him around his home. The day before her mother had suggested keeping him in the main part of the house – where it wasn't so quiet – would get him used to his new environment.

"I learned that from my own mother," she had explained. "I didn't know anything about babies when you were born."

Lacy had been surprised by her mother's confession. It made her feel so much better.

Her mother told her that if things were too quiet Mikie would never get used to normal household sounds. He might even be frightened of those sounds if she suddenly sprung them on him later.

"He might even sleep better at night, because the normal activity will keep him from sleeping so much during the day," her mother had added.

"I thought newborns were supposed to sleep all the time."

Her mother had smiled, her blue eyes bright. "They do. And you'll find they'll sleep through all those normal sounds if they're tired enough. But remember, the baby's first knowledge is experienced through sound and touch.

"He's already learning," Lacy said, feeling her spirits brighten.

"Then he'll begin to see more clearly, and he'll be able to see things going on around him," her mother continued. "Slowly he'll stay awake longer and

108

longer, taking in his surroundings. He'll be learning so much in his first few months he'll be tired and ready to sleep at the end of the day."

Lacy's smile grew even wider. She had never thought of it that way. She gave her mother a big hug, then sent her on her way.

"It's time for me to do this mothering thing alone," she said. "Not that I haven't appreciated your help."

"I can still come by during the day. Or, at night if you need me."

"Give me a few days to try in on my own."

Her mother finally agreed, though only after she made Lacy promise to call if she again started having problems. "You've been through a lot. Don't hesitate to ask for help if you need it."

The day turned out to go quite well. Lacy was still plagued by many questions, but she was able to push them from her mind as she focused on her son. She was beginning to feel like her old self. Stronger. It was quite a relief.

It was only while Mikie slept that those worries seemed to haunt her. So it was then she tried to tackle some extra work. Maybe, she'd begin by preparing herself a nice dinner. She hadn't felt like cooking for one person. Oh well, she thought, she could freeze the left-overs.

She went downstairs to the freezer and took out some veal steaks she had bought while on sale. She loved home-made veal parmesan, but rarely made it with real veal steak because of the high price of the meat. That was why she always bought extra whenever it was on sale.

She thawed the meat in the microwave while she mixed her special combination of bread crumbs, parmesan cheese and spices. Then she fried some onions, celery and green peppers and put them aside for the sauce.

She fried the crumb-coated veal steaks until lightly golden brown then placed them in the bottom of a rectangular backing pan. On top she put a sprinkling of shredded mozzarella cheese. She put the onion, celery and pepper mixture back into the frying pan and made her sauce, pouring it over and around the veal steaks.

She put them in the oven to bake, thinking it would have been nice to have had some fresh Italian bread to make garlic bread with the meal. She remembered the doctor's warning that too many spices may effect her breast-milk. Still, some Italian bread would taste great even without the garlic flavor.

Just then the doorbell rang. She went to answer, her smile fading as she hesitated with her hand on the doorknob. It seemed lately, each time she opened the door she was in for some kind of unexpected surprise. Most of them unpleasant.

She mentally prepared herself, taking a deep breath as she slowly opened the door.

Ryan stood on the small landing looking in at her. His green eyes assessing, not missing any detail. Finally he smiled. "You look much better than the last time I saw you."

She grinned, feeling her cheeks burn. Yes, that had been the night she'd completely broken down, crying in his arms. Today she was in better control. And considering everything that had happened, she was relieved.

"I'm feeling much better," she replied, stepping aside so he could enter. "Come on in."

"I just wanted to drop off that information you asked for."

"You didn't have to make a special trip. I did say there wasn't a rush." *Especially now with everything going on with Rose.*

"I was in the area anyway."

She looked doubtful. She suspected Ryan was the type who would make a special trip for anyone, for any reason if they needed his help.

"I really was." He laughed. "That's why I'm in such a good mood." His expression sobered, wondering if his good news would be a reminder of all the unpleasantness she had in the last two weeks.

"So, what news is that? Or, is it personal?"

"I just stopped by the hospital. . . .They discharged the little Miller girl."

Lacy smiled. She had learned the first sister had been discharged the same day as Mikie. She had wondered about the second girl, but with everything that had happened, she hadn't inquired.

"That's great!" she said with sincerity, then sobered slightly, reminded of the seriousness of the girl's condition. "How is she?"

"She's got a long road ahead of her," Ryan replied, sighing. "She has minor respiratory damage."

"Oh no," Lacy groaned, having hoped it wouldn't be, yet knowing from her experience that it didn't take long for the delicate tissues of a child's lungs to be damaged by the heat and smoke of a fire. The very reason firefighters had to wear SCBA's when going into a hostile environment.

"At least the prognosis is good," Ryan continued. "The nurse told me she'll be receiving respiratory therapy. It will take time to know how extensive any other damage may be."

"But she's alive because you broke all the rules," Lacy said softly. "You took off your mask and gave her air."

"I had no way of knowing if it was too late. But I had to try."

Lacy understood and nodded, leaving the rest unspoken. She knew it would be a long road to recovery for that little girl. She thought of the costly medical bills the family would have. She couldn't help wondering if they had insurance. She remembered her father mentioning the family had been hard hit by recent business's folding.

She decided to make a point of finding out more. Perhaps thinking about the other victims of that tragic fire might help take her mind off her own problems.

"Let's go in the kitchen," Lacy suggested. "I was about to clean up my mess. I decided to cook tonight."

Ryan hid his smile as he noticed the disaster area around the stove and sink. But he had to admit, the aroma was certainly a pleasant one.

"I don't want to interrupt."

"Actually, I'm happy for the interruption. It'll help take my mind off the worst part of cooking. Cleaning up after myself." She picked up to empty cans of tomato paste and carried them to the trash can. She stepped on the bottom lever to lift up the lid, and tossed them inside the clean plastic liner.

She turned and looked at the pots and pans on the stove and wrinkled her lightly-freckled nose. "So much for that," she went to the sink and washed her hands. I may as well leave the rest till later. I'll have more to clean up then."

Ryan laughed at her reasoning, happy to see she was in far better spirits than the last time he'd seen her. He only hoped she really was doing as well as she was making out.

"I've got the information you asked for here." He pulled a sheet of paper out of his pocket and slowly unfolded it.

"Why don't we go over that later?" Lacy suggested, not wanting to be reminded of less pleasant things. "After dinner – that is, unless you have plans – I've cooked enough for two." She frowned, knowing she'd be doing that a lot till the double portions in the freezer were gone.

"I don't have plans, Lacy. But what can I do to help?"

"With the food, nothing. . .Well, maybe there is one thing." She remembered the Italian bread she had been thinking about just before he arrived. "You could run to the store for one thing. Or, stay here in case Mikie wakes, while I run."

"Aren't you supposed to be taking things easy?"

She shrugged. "Nervous energy." She bit her tongue, afraid she'd revealed too much about her emotions. Yet, somehow she was certain Ryan already suspected. She'd had that feeling from the first moment she met him.

"Let me know what you want, and I'll run to the store."

"Only Italian bread. I make good garlic bread. It goes with my excellent Veal Parmesan."

"Are you sure that's all?"

Lacy held up her hand, turning to check the grocery list for any items that she could use before she went shopping herself. "Maybe some tea."

"Bread and tea," Ryan repeated, getting up and coming to stand behind her, reading the list over her shoulder. "What about the rest of this stuff?"

111

"I can get it when I shop later in the week." She looked back at him.

"Hey, if I'm going, I may as well pick up a few more things while I'm there," he offered. "Seems silly to go twice."

"There's some . . ." She turned back to the list, blushing. She picked up the pencil attached to a magnet beside the list and crossed off some personal items, resisting the urge to scribble over them until they were unreadable. She knew that would seem adolescent. "You can get the rest." She took the list down from the refrigerator and handed it to him.

Ryan glanced at it, noting the items she had carefully crossed off. He looked away so as not to embarrass her more. "Lacy, if you need them, put down the brands and I'll get them. I don't mind buying them."

Still determined not to look adolescent she took the list from his hand and wrote name brands beside the scribbled out items, then handed the list back to him. "I'll get you some money."

"You can pay me after I come back." Ryan started for the door. "I won't be long."

She watched him leave, thinking it strange that he didn't seem to mind shopping for her personal items. Mike hated shopping to begin with, and he absolutely refused buying feminine products.

Mikie was awake by the time Ryan returned. She was sitting on the recliner nursing him when Ryan knocked and entered carrying two bags. She had a blanket to cover herself, but resisted the urge. Something in the look on Ryan's face, told her it didn't bother him at all.

It was a natural sight, she reminded herself.

She heard him in the kitchen putting the groceries away. A few moments later she saw him standing in the archway between the two rooms. He was smiling as he watched the intimate moment between mother and child.

"I'm sorry if I'm intruding," he said huskily. "It's just you . . .you make a lovely picture." *Madonna with child.*

She smiled, meeting his darkening eyes. "It's not the first time you've eavesdropped. Come in and sit down. I'm not embarrassed." She realized that was true. She didn't feel embarrassed with Ryan. She wondered why. Was it his ability to make her feel comfortable? Or, was it the feeling that he understood?

"Once he's satisfied, I'll put the finishing touches on our dinner."

"No hurry." *I could sit and watch you like this for hours.*

"Would you like to watch something on television? I mean, I don't know what you like to do in the evening after work. You can turn on the radio if you'd like."

"I don't do anything in particular," Ryan replied. "Mostly I read the paper before dinner."

"Then there's Tuesday and Thursday nights at the station," she added, knowing the routine. "Sunday mornings too."

"Yeah, both nights. And after church on Sunday, if there's work to do." Ryan smiled. "Right now there's plenty for me to catch up on. There's a lot I need to know about being a line officer."

"So you accepted Second Assistant." Lacy smiled, happy to hear he had.

He nodded. "I'm already signed up for the next officer's training course at County. And another on leadership."

"Good idea." Lacy knew the Montgomery County Fire Training Academy had some of the best fire service training courses available. "You'll learn a lot from them."

"You've taken those courses already haven't you?"

"I've taken about every course they offer," she replied with no false modesty. "Remember, I've been at it for quite a few years."

"Why didn't you ever decide to become an instructor yourself?" he asked, knowing she had at one time been training officer at the station. One of the biggest parts of her job had been over-seeing the company's junior firefighter program.

"I don't know," she lied. She did know. There had been just too much pressure at home as it was. To advance herself further would have been too much.

"It would seem the natural next step," he spoke his thoughts absently.

She looked away. "I'd rather not talk about it, Ryan," Lacy said, trying not to sound too unkind. She had liked the casual conversation they were having. But she didn't like the direction the conversation was taking.

Ryan sensed he had hit a nerve. He wanted to know more. But he didn't want to pressure her. Besides, he had no right to know more about this woman who fascinated and intrigued him so much.

Rather than spoil the harmony he decided to change the subject. "So, how's the little guy adjusting to life outside the hospital?"

"Today has been the best day yet," Lacy admitted, seeing her son had had his fill. She re-fastened her nursing bra and buttoned her blouse. "Soon it will be our turn."

She lifted her son and started to put him into the infant seat she had beside her chair.

"If you don't mind, I'd like to hold him," Ryan said. "Unless you think that might spoil him."

"It would probably be good for him." She placed her son in her visitor's lap. Ryan cradled her son like an old pro, supporting his tiny head in the crook of his arm while his large, strong hand spread out to support his bottom.

With his other hand he gently touched Mikie's tiny fingers one at a time, as if counting to make sure they were all there.

She watched as he put his index finger into Mikie's tiny palm, allowing the baby's fingers to instinctively curl around it.

She saw the expression on his handsome face, the brightness in his emerald eyes. It was nearly a look of awe.

Tears filled her eyes as she quickly left the two alone while she went into the kitchen to finish preparing their meal. She knew she was just being overly sentimental. But she had been deeply touched by the scene. And yet it wasn't in the way she thought she would be.

When she first laid Mikie in Ryan's arms she'd thought that was what it should have been like the first time Mike held their child. But within moments she sensed the very personal feelings deep inside the man. The expression on Ryan's face was one she'd never seen on Mike's. Yet she was unable to put a label on it.

They ate while Mikie sat in his infant seat across from them, intently listening as they made casual conversation. She could tell her mother was right about his first learned knowledge being from touch and sound. Even as tiny as he was she could still see his facial expressions change as he listened to the variations in their voices as they spoke, or the sounds of their silverware clinging against their plates, his little head turning slightly as though trying to follow each sound.

He cooed along, as though joining in Ryan's deep laughter as she told him the story of the first disastrous time she'd tried her hand at making the veal dish.

"After trying several knives to find one sharp enough to cut his meat, Mike had strongly suggested I try the brand in the supermarket freezer section next time I got hungry for Veal Parmesan," Lacy reminisced.

After laughing at her explanation Ryan cut through his meat with only his fork. "I'd say you've come a long way."

"Sheer stubbornness," she admitted. "Once he said that to me, I was determined to learn how to make it."

"How many tries did it take till you reached this point of culinary excellence."

"Only one," she confessed. "I cheated by going to an expert. Karla Mulholland was Karla Dipetro before she married Jack."

"Ah-ha, that explains how I could manage to have the world's best Veal Parmesan and Lasagna both in one week."

Lacy cocked her head to the side wondering what he meant.

Ryan then told her about having dinner with the Mulholland's three night's earlier.

"She let me use their computer so I could get the latest facts and figures you wanted."

Lacy knew the momentary reprieve was over. It was time to get back down to the hard facts of life. Besides she needed that information to know how best to invest the benefit money, no matter how much of it she received.

Still if it weren't for Mikie and his future, she'd have refused it. In the last few days she'd begun to feel the money was tainted. Like blood money, no good would every come from it.

Ryan helped her clear away the dirty dishes, she scraped them, and he stacked them in the dishwasher. Then, after leaving the rest up to the machine, they sat down to go over his figures.

They were in the middle of a discussion about short term C.D.'s when the telephone rang. Lacy answered it on the extension in the kitchen.

"What have you been up to?" a man's voice stormed over the phone. "I know you've been through a lot. But do you have to destroy everyone else's life?"

"Who is this?" Lacy asked, knowing the slurred male voice sounded familiar, yet she was unsure.

"Who do you think it is, Lacy? The man who's life you're going to ruin. That's who!"

"I don't know what you're talking about. And since you won't tell me who you are, we have nothing to discuss." Without another word she hung up the phone. When she turned, Ryan was watching with concern.

The phone rang again, almost immediately. She picked it up again.

"Don't you dare hang up on me again, Lacy, or I'll come to your house and make a scene."

"Then tell me who you are?"

"It's Woody Brown, who'd you think?" He laughed vehemently. "Oh yeah, you probably couldn't decide if it was me or Carlisle. You're probably trying to ruin him too."

"I don't know what you're talking about," she said angrily, envisioning his bearded face, dark with anger, giving him a devil-like appearance. "And from the sounds of it, you don't either."

"I'm talking about you and your blood money!"

Lacy stiffened, turning toward the wall. She'd been thinking the very thing only moments before.

"What does that have to do with you?" Even as she asked the question she began to realize the answer.

"You know very well Arlen was going to talk to me on your behalf. Says we'll have to have some kind of blood test – just so that you can keep all that blood money – just so you don't have to share it."

"If he spoke to you it was to spare the company any scandal."

Woody's vicious laugh came across the line, burning in her ear. "The company! Ha! You've had him wrapped around your finger so long. . .like all the others. Just cause your PaPa is the big cheese in town."

"Stop it!" she ordered, squeezing the phone, wishing it was his neck.

"Hey, Carlisle is probably ticked off too. But least he doesn't have a wife to worry about. Mary's a pain, but I love her."

"I'd say you should have thought about that before you involved yourself with Rose." Lacy's anger had finally gotten the better of her. She knew if he had nothing to feel guilty about he wouldn't care about having a blood test.

"Lacy, you can't do this!"

"For your information, I'm not doing anything. You better check with your ex-girlfriend about that."

"She wasn't a girlfriend," Woody denied. "She was nothing more than a fun time."

"I don't want to hear the sordid details."

"Well you better hear them. Cause that kid of her's could just as easily be Mike's as mine. Or Carlisle's. We all had a bet to see who could do her the most in one year. Bet our pink slips too. – Mike won, you know. That's how he ended up with enough money for that fancy Bronco of his."

She froze, remembering Mike had bought the Bronco shortly before they started dating. She wanted to hang up. But she couldn't. She felt Ryan's presence behind her. He turned her around, a questioning look in his green eyes. She was trembling as he took the phone from her hand.

"Why drag us all down when you're getting all that cash. All you've gotta do is share some of it. Lacy, why you gotta be so greedy? Carlisle and I both lost our trucks in that stupid bet. We were just dumb kids back then."

"Who is it?" Ryan demanded in a rough voice, as much a question to her, as to the man on the end of the line.

The line went dead.

Ryan hung up the phone and took hold of Lacy's shoulders. He could see she was making a valiant effort not to release the bright tears that had filled her eyes.

"Who was it, Lacy?" he asked more softly.

She swallowed. "It doesn't matter now."

"It certainly does matter," he whispered, his eyes narrowing with anger. "Now either you tell me or I'm going to Carlisle. The caller said something about him. And about losing their trucks."

Lacy hung her head. "It was Woody Brown. I. . .I think he must have been drinking – or maybe desperate."

"Why, Lacy? He mentioned the money. The benefit money, I assume."

116

She took a breath, nodding as she slowly exhaled. "Because it seems either Woody, Barry or Mike is the father of Rose Sinclair's daughter. She's decided to find out which one."

It took a moment for her words to sink in, then a moment for Ryan to contain his fury that Lacy was faced with one more hardship. "Did he just tell you all this?"

She shook her head, pulling out of his grasp and turning away. "Rose told me herself. Only I wasn't certain I should believe her. She said she was only trying to spare me finding out about it another way." She turned again to face Ryan. "And you know . . . in a funny way, I believe her. I don't think Rose is actually a vicious person."

Ryan wondered how Lacy could be so generous to a person who was causing her so much pain. He admired her strength to forgive.

"She picked a bad time to tell you."

"She's a mother doing what's best for her child," Lacy replied. "I understand that now. I'd do the same thing."

Ryan shook his head. Somehow he doubted that.

"In any event, there won't be a scandal," Lacy said, coming to her final decision. "I'm going to make an offer to Rose she'd be crazy to refuse."

"Lacy, think before you do anything rash. Let me talk to Carlisle and find out if all this is true."

She smiled grimly, shaking her head. "It's true."

She didn't tell him how she knew. She didn't tell him how her marriage to Mike had been a lie. It had been her husband's way of keeping the finger from being pointed at him once everyone learned Rose was pregnant. No, she'd settle with Rose. Then no one would have to know. Except her.

"Sounds like any one of them could be the father," Ryan said softly. "You might still prove Mike wasn't the one."

"But I'll never prove that he couldn't have been."

In that moment, Ryan understood. The money didn't matter. Money couldn't help heal the wounds she was suffering. It wouldn't stop the pain. It would only be a constant reminder.

Time was the only thing that would help her now. And the love of her family and friends. More than ever, he hoped that she counted him as one of them.

"I'm going to need your help, Ryan," Lacy said as she turned and walked back to the table. She sat down, then looked up at him through bright sapphire eyes. "If your offer still stands."

Ryan joined her, taking her hand and giving it a squeeze. She had just answered his question. Now he could answer her's.

"What can I do?"

"Come back in a couple of days and I'll let you know."

Ryan knew when he was being dismissed. He hated leaving Lacy in this state. Yet, if he was going to be her friend, he had to respect her decisions.

#

A week later Lacy told him she wanted one third of any benefit money she received put into a trust fund for Amy. A fund that couldn't be touched until the girl was eighteen and then only if it was used for college. If she didn't go to college she'd receive the money when she turned twenty-one.

"She's the real victim of this mess," Lacy said, knowing she had thought that many times during the past days. "But I don't think she should get that kind of cash till she's mature enough to know how to deal with it."

"What if Rose doesn't agree?" Ryan asked.

Lacy smiled, a hint of her spirit showing through. "Then she'll have a fight on her hands. If she cares about her child as much as I do mine, she won't want to put her through that. . .My bet is she'll take the offer."

She had everything written in a letter to the other woman. She had no intention of talking to her face. Right at that moment, she didn't care if she ever saw Rose Sinclair again.

Again Ryan was impressed by Lacy's generosity. More still when she told him what she wanted next.

"I've thought a great deal about this next part," Lacy continued her explanation. "I want a third of the money put into a foundation to benefit fire victims. I want it to be in Mike's name. I feel like there has to be something good come out of his death. Maybe it will help people remember him. Maybe it will just help me."

"Lacy are you sure?" Ryan asked. "Someday down the road you may wish you'd kept the money."

She shook her head, knowing her mind was made up. "No. I think it's the best thing I can do under the circumstances. I know there will have to be some kind of guidelines for a fund like that. I suppose the bank or whomever oversees something like that can help. The only thing I'd like, would be to see the Miller family be the first to receive help. They were the other victims in the fire that started this whole thing."

In the days following her decision, she'd looked further into the Miller family's background and learned they had not had enough insurance. They had put all their money into buying that home. A handy-man's special. Perfect for a carpenter. Not so perfect when a huge decline in new home-construction cost him his job. The family had had to cut corners. Insurance was the first thing to go.

"The last third of the money, goes into a trust for Mikie, exactly like the one set up for Amy," she stated.

"You're being very unselfish, Lacy," Ryan said. "And there's no reason why you shouldn't be. You deserve some of that money too."

She shook her head. "It's blood money, just like Woody said."

Ryan frowned. He had his own opinion of Woody Brown, and it wasn't a high one. The man was lucky to get off so lightly. He wondered if the other man realized that. He knew that Barry Carlisle did. Against Lacy's wishes he'd spoken to him about it.

It was Barry who said he'd take care of Woody Brown, and make certain the man didn't bother Lacy again. They were drinking buddies. Ryan suspected they'd been doing too much of that lately, but he had accepted the man's word that Lacy wouldn't be bothered again.

"Besides, I've sold Mike's Bronco," Lacy said, interrupting Ryan's thoughts. "I've got the money from that."

She didn't add that it had been Barry Carlisle who had come and made the offer. He'd apologized for the problems she was having, and that was all he'd said on the subject. She and Barry had never gotten along, but she respected him for his gesture.

She knew he had to be wondering what she was going to do about the situation with Rose. As First Assistant Chief of the company his position could be affected if he were involved in a scandal. He knew that. And so did she. It was one thing for the members to speculate. It was another for them to know. Worst, it wasn't just the members of their company. Word spread fast in the fire service. Especially anything bad. She could bet that once things heated up, the entire county fire service community would know.

She decided to set his mind to rest, and told him what she was going to do. After a polite thank you, he made the offer to buy Mike's Bronco. She didn't care if the offer was fair or not. She was just happy to be rid of the reminder of what the three men had done.

"I'm also putting the house up for sale," Lacy said. "I know it's not a good time to sell. But I've decided to move home."

Too many sleepless nights were taking their toll. She knew it was unfair to ask her mother to come there and help, though she knew that her mother would. No, it was probably better to throw in the towel and move home.

"Is that what you really want to do?" Ryan asked.

"What I want doesn't matter," she replied wearily, her facade of control crumbling fast. "It's a matter of exhaustion and sanity. Most the time I'm not sleeping well. The rest of the time Mikie isn't, and when he doesn't sleep well I don't. In short, something has to give."

"He's probably picking up on your tension."

"Tell me something I don't know," she snapped, immediately regretting her outburst. "See, it's turning me into a witch."

Ryan smiled, doubting she could ever be that.

"Okay, if you're moving home, it could be temporary. When things settle down you'll have to find another home. It's a buyers market now, not a sellers. You might find it to be the opposite by the time you're ready to be on your own again. You could end up losing a lot of money."

"What are you suggesting I do?"

"Rent the house – to me." He hadn't thought about it, but now that he said the words he liked the idea. He'd hated living in the tiny cramped apartment. Maybe it was time he lived in a home again.

Lacy's blue eyes were wide as she stared back at him. "Rent to you," she repeated. "You're just being nice."

"No, Lacy. Honestly I'm not." He laughed, holding her gaze. "When I tell you what I can afford to pay you, you'll see I'm not being nice." He had expenses and obligations. Things he knew he didn't need to explain. But they left him with very little money for rent each month.

"I'll take it," she responded quickly, knowing she liked the thought of Ryan living in her home. He fit in here. He had from that first night when he sat on the floor putting together the nursery furniture. "Whatever you offer, I know it will be fair."

"And when you're ready to move back, you can just throw me out. We'll put that in the lease."

She laughed for the first time in weeks. If felt good.

"And for the other problem," Ryan started, gently taking her hand and giving it a squeeze.

"What other problem?"

"The stress you're under," he replied softly. "You know it's nothing abnormal. In fact, there are others since the fire, who are showing post traumatic signs."

"What are you saying, Ryan?"

"We're having a special meeting Thursday night. It's for anyone who was involved in the fire. A post-incident stress team is coming in to work with us."

Lacy shook her head. "It's a little different with me. I lost a husband."

"It wasn't different for you at the funeral, Lacy," Ryan said. "Your being a wife didn't stop you from being part of the unit."

She knew he was referring to her wearing her uniform the day of the funeral. And that was true – that was how she had felt. "If it were just the fire, she said. But, in a way, I'm dealing better with that than a lot of other things."

"I'm only asking you to think about it. Keep the option open."

Without another word on the subject they returned to the discussion of Ryan renting her house. He gave her a figure that she suspected was lower than the going rate, but not unfair considering she knew her home would be in good hands. She was satisfied.

CHAPTER NINE

At quarter past seven, Ryan saw Carl enter the station. He frowned when he realized the Borough Chief was alone. He had hoped Lacy would change her mind and attend the post-incident stress session with the rest of the personnel who had been at the fire.

He watched Arlen greet their superior with a firm handshake. Carl returned his old friend's handshake with a grim smile. Ryan knew that night would be just as hard on him as the rest of them. The fire had forever changed the life of his daughter.

Ryan knew that deeply effected the older man. He had seen it written in the weary lines on Carl MacDonald's face when the older man had come to check on him that first night at the hospital. He could see that same distress again now.

The barrel-chested fire chief turned and came his way. He greeted him with a handshake and a nod. "Thanks for trying to talk her into coming," the older man acknowledged.

Ryan suspected there was little the Borough Chief didn't know. Even less failed to get past the father.

"I thought it might help her," Ryan said from experience. "Keeping everything bottled up inside only makes the healing process take that much longer."

Carl put his hand on Ryan's shoulder. "How long did it take you?"

Though he had never told the older man about his past, Ryan wasn't surprised by the Chief's question. He had no way of knowing if Carl had checked up on him, was guessing, or if he just had good intuition. He suspected the latter.

"Too many bottles, then too many miles," Ryan replied simply, knowing there really wasn't anything simple about it.

Carl nodded his graying head, and sighed. "I'm not as worried about the bottles as I am the miles with my daughter."

"Running's not the solution. Not when its away."

"Since Lacy's just moved home I suppose you could say she isn't running away."

Ryan thought a moment, wondering why this man was so interested in his opinion. Because he had been through a similar loss? Maybe.

"At least she's run to people who care."

"That part's true," Carl sighed, with a growing frown "I only wish I was sure coming to us was the solution."

Ryan didn't ask more. He didn't feel he had the right to. But he was curious to know exactly what Carl had meant. He had had the same feeling too. Were they for the same reasons?

Lacy had been through so much in the past weeks, it was understandable that she'd be distraught. But was she running from her problems, or from herself? Ryan mused.

His thoughts were interrupted as Arlen asked everyone to take a seat among the many chairs that circled the room. Ryan knew everyone by now, so the three unfamiliar faces had to be those of the post-incident stress team.

He was right. One man, a counselor, acted as leader of the group, about a third of the way around the room there was a second man, and seated next to Barry Carlisle, was a woman who completed the team. He had been told they were all volunteers in the program, and none were from their area.

The first man introduced himself as John Wilkins, a counselor with a county mental health agency. He started by setting the ground rules. All pagers were to be turned off and no one was to leave the room until they were through. He added that everything discussed that evening was to remain among the group, unless someone later chose to discuss their feelings with others who were not there. What anyone else said, was only that person's business.

He explained that his team was specially trained in post-incident stress related problems. The concept started as a result of the VietNam war when many soldiers experienced similar problems ranging from nightmares and tension to serious alcohol and drug addiction and in some cases even suicide.

"Studies have shown that emergency personnel suffer many similar reactions to the stress of their jobs," the man explained. "The heightened emotions, rise in blood-pressure, acceleration of heartbeats. You've probably all experienced these as part of your job. And each of you have your own way of dealing with it. Usually in a positive way. Only a few end up going over the edge, becoming alcoholics, drug addicts, abusive to their loved ones."

"The thing we've learned in recent years is that all the problems John just mentioned increase after a serious emergency, especially one involving death," added the second man, who introduced himself as an emergency room doctor who works at Children's Hospital in Philadelphia. "The worst problems usually occur after mass casualty, the death of children, or, as in the case here, when a fellow firefighter is killed in the line of duty."

"It's been tagged as post-incident or post-traumatic stress syndrome," the lone woman of the group started. "No one is immune. Some of the sanest people I worked with, as a nurse in VietNam, went over the edge."

"But we have found some people are more susceptible than others," the leader took over once again. "Tonight we have the first step in helping prevent any of the more serious problems from occurring within your ranks. And maybe helping you learn some positive ways of dealing with negative emotions."

He then asked everyone to introduce themselves and give a brief explanation of how they were involved the night of the fire when Mike Boyce had been killed.

Ryan knew that this was an introduction for the stress team, and he suspected more. As each person took their turn he watched their body language, listened to their tone of voice as much as their words.

He saw that Rainy and Mark Shelby were there. They had been on duty as fire police that night. And Brody Langford, who had responded with Rescue Seven, though he ended up helping the ambulance crew when Lacy went into labor.

Ryan's turn came and went. He stated the fact that he had brought out one of the girls. He was tempted not to mention he had been injured when preparing to go back inside again. But he did. He suspected this was a time it was more important to reveal the things one didn't want to reveal.

He watched Barry Carlisle with particular interest. He had his suspicions the man had been drinking heavily since the call that killed his best friend. He saw that Arlen was watching too, and he suspected for much the same reason.

At that point he realized Woody Brown had not come that night. Though he was responding with Friendship Hook and Ladder these days, they had still been at that fire. Mike had once been a good friend of his.

Perhaps he didn't feel he needed this, Ryan thought coolly. Then, giving the man the benefit of a doubt he supposed he could be avoiding the situation, and everyone involved.

Ryan could think of another reason. Woody could be ashamed of the way he treated Lacy, and was afraid to face her in case she was there. Unfortunately, he doubted that was the case.

It was Carl's turn. Ryan listened as the man simply stated he had been in charge the night of the fire. Arlen, who was next in line, stated he was second in command.

The leader asked everyone to take a second turn, but that no one would be put on the spot. If they didn't want to talk about it, they could pass. This time each person was to describe their feelings right after the fire. After realizing a fellow firefighter, a good friend to some, had been killed.

The responses ranged from disbelief, to shock, to anger. Several admitted feeling all three. A few threw in grief, though Ryan wasn't surprised that for many, that didn't set in till later. No one passed.

124

Rainy admitted anger that the fire happened in the first place. There were several soft groans from a few who were probably afraid she was going to launch into a speech about fire prevention. Though her brown eyes narrowed, she said no more.

Ryan had to admit he hadn't immediately realized what had happened since he'd been knocked unconscious when the building exploded into flames. "I was in the hospital when I found out," Ryan stated. "I felt a lot of emotions. Regret was only one of them."

Barry Carlisle spoke of feeling like two people. One wanting to run inside to save his best friend, unable to believe he could be dead. The other, the firefighter, knowing it was hopeless. He spoke of rage because no one had been able to do anything to keep it from happening.

Carl admitted his shock was quickly replaced by concern for his daughter who had been there when it happened. And that his concern turned to worry when they told him she'd gone into labor and had been taken to the hospital.

Ryan saw the lines of tension deepen on the Borough Chief's face when the group leader suggested they take a moment and think about the weeks since that night. When it came each person's turn, this time, they were to explain what they had been feeling since the fire, and how their feelings were affecting them.

This time several people passed.

Rainy willingly repeated nearly the exact words she had spoken the previous time, though she said her anger had changed to regret that the fire hadn't been prevented. Then she quickly eyed the group, as though daring any one of them to mutter a sound against her. When they didn't, she added that she's more determined than ever to see that the people in their community are taught fire safety.

Ryan smiled, openly pleased that she stubbornly refused to let anyone deter her from her goal. He suspected her's was the only real answer to the fire problem. Teach people how not to have a fire and there's no more problem.

When his turn came, he said that very thing. "I feel we can't change what happened that night. There's no way to turn back time," he paused, knowing that was a hard lesson learned from his own experience. Taking a breath, he added. "But we can learn from it. We can do our best to keep it from happening again."

Several people moved uncomfortably as he spoke. He noted Barry Carlisle was one of them. His dark eyes had glanced at Ryan only once, and they had stung like venom.

When the first assistant's turn came he passed, but again he turned his hard gaze briefly toward Ryan.

Ryan could tell the man had hard feelings toward him and was certain the dark expression directed at him was not because of his support of fire safety. He suspected it went much deeper. He only hoped it wouldn't someday become a problem.

Carl again kept his statement brief, saying his feelings were still much the same. As a father, he was concerned for his daughter, and now, for his grandson. As Borough Chief, he knew no one was going to forget the fire, but he hoped everyone would get over it and be able to return to functioning as normal.

The last part of the night was open to anyone who wanted to talk about their feelings. Their concerns. Their fears. Any problems they were having.

As Ryan suspected, few spoke, and those who did were a cross between the ones who always spoke when they had an audience and those who probably needed more serious help than they could get in one evening. Unfortunately he suspected, it might be the ones who weren't speaking who needed the most help. He looked again at the First Assistant Chief and hoped that wasn't his case.

Before the night concluded John Wilkes said he and the two others would remain a while longer in case anyone felt they still wanted to talk. They reminded everyone that the county had a counseling service for those who felt they needed a little more help, or those who felt unable to speak within a group.

"The object of tonight is for all of you to know that whatever you're feeling, you are not alone. By discussing it openly with one another hopefully you've realized you're all experiencing many of the same things – perfectly normal reactions to a tragedy – if you fear your situation is getting out of hand don't be afraid to get help for it."

Ryan sighed, wondering how many would? How many needed it? He hoped that night's session was all that was needed for any of them.

Again he glanced to where Barry Carlisle had been seated, and saw that he had already gone.

Then he thought of Lacy, knowing her adjustments weren't going to be any easier. Her wounds would take a long time to heal, even with the support of her family.

In part he understood what she was going through. And yet, he suspected there was much more going on inside Lacy Boyce. Things she hadn't even begun to share with others.

Friday after work, Ryan went to the bank before stopping at the MacDonald's to give Lacy her first month's rent check. They never decided whether he would move right into the house or wait until the following month when his lease was up, but Ryan found once his decision to move was made he was actually anxious about it.

It had been a long time since he'd lived in a house. After the fire when his own home he had been gutted, he had lived out of a motel room for a short time, then his office above the garage a while longer. Finally it was back to motels as he took to the road searching for something, yet what, he didn't know. Everything he'd loved was back in New York.

It took him a long time to realize he wasn't searching. He was running away. It was with that realization he stopped running away and faced everything that had happened. In time he learned to accept that his wife and daughter were dead, their dreams along with them.

He also had to accept that his mother was beyond any help he could give her himself, and that putting her into a nursing home had been the best thing he could have done, because it was only a matter of time before she, too, would be gone.

He remembered his conversation with Carl the previous night. He hoped Lacy's road wasn't so long before she reached that point.

The point where he was now. Where he could actually begin to think of a future. He could actually begin to look forward to one.

"Ryan," Lacy said from the doorway as she watched their visitor staring into space. "Ryan, are you here or someplace else?"

He laughed, realizing he had been in another world. "I'm here, now," he replied, knowing there was more meaning to those words than she would ever know.

"Come in. Are you here to see Dad, or . . .your new landlord?" She forced the words, trying to make them sound bright.

"You," he replied. "I've got your first month's rent. I thought – if you don't mind – I'd move in over the weekend. Not that I have that much to move."

"No problem, I've got everything I need." She thought of the things she'd left at the house, and pushed it from her mind. That was all behind her now.

"Well, it's all still yours, so anytime you . . ."

"Yes, I know," she interrupted, then forced a smile to take the bite out of her words. "I won't be wanting anything."

He nodded, knowing it was still too soon for her to be sure. The pain was still too fresh. It would take time.

"So, will you be needing any help to move?" she asked. "I mean, Dad does have a pick-up. I don't think you'll get much in your little Toyota."

"I appreciate the offer," Ryan said with a grim smile. "But, like I said, I don't have much to move."

Lacy looked at her companion, silently wondering how a man could live thirty years and not have more to his name than what would fit into a small Toyota coupe. Of course, she knew she was only guessing his age. Sometimes Ryan seemed much older. It was a weary, faraway look he'd get in his green eyes. Like the one he'd had when she first opened the door to him. She realized she'd often seen that troubled look on his face.

This one's got a mind and a crusade all his own.

She thought about her father's words, and knew since getting to know Ryan, she'd felt the same thing about him. Sometimes it's good to be an individual. To have a mind of your own. Other times. . .

"Lacy, why didn't you tell me we had company," her mother scolded cheerfully as she rounded the corner from the kitchen into the hallway. "You're . . . from the fire company aren't you?" Some of the warmth left her voice.

Ryan smiled, holding out his hand. "Yes, Ma'am, Ryan Simon," he introduced himself. "But I'm not here on fire company business."

Her mother's cool blue eyes softened. "You're the young man who's going to rent our daughter's house." Carl had mentioned him. In fact, he'd spoken highly of the young man. He said he was different from most of the men at the station. She remembered because she had teased her husband about that statement.

"And you say I'm the one who puts firefighters all into one category," she'd said.

"And you do. Into one box marked, nuisance," he teased.

"Necessary nuisance," she had corrected good-naturedly.

Carl had given her a look of exaggerated surprise. "Did I hear you actually insinuate that firefighters may be necessary?"

She pulled a sofa cushion from behind her and tossed it at her husband. "Carl, I may never have liked what you do. But I've never said it wasn't necessary."

He winked, hugging the cushion tight against his barrel chest. He knew his wife liked to keep things orderly. It would take only a moment before she'd want to restore it to it's rightful place on the sofa.

"Anyway, you said this man was different. How?"

"Just different," Carl replied. "There are only so many reasons why a person becomes a firefighter. His reason is different than any we've had before. That's all. End of discussion."

Lois had thought about that a moment, knowing her husband would tell her no more. There were some things he shared with her and other things he didn't. When he didn't, it was usually because his job required that he remained silent about them. And she understood that. But she suspected that wasn't the reason this time.

"Here." She reached out her hand. "Give me back the pillow."

"You started it," he said.

"Then throw it back at me."

He grinned, ignoring her.

Her blue eyes narrowed. "You're squashing it all out of shape."

He smoothed it, then wrapped his arms around it again.

"What are you up to Carl?"

"I'm holding it for ransom," he teased, his dark eyes taking on a familiar glow. "Pay the price and you'll get it back."

Lois knew that look and knew she wouldn't get the pillow back until she complied. Slowly she went to her husband's side, leaning over and kissing his cheek. Then he'd given her a mischievous smile.

"Mom," Lacy said, watching her mother's faraway look, and very unusual smile. At least unusual for her. If she didn't know better she'd swear. . . No, not her mother.

"Oh, I'm sorry," Lois's face flushed. "I was remembering Carl telling me about you." At least that part was true. "You haven't been a member very long."

"Long enough to know the ropes," Lacy replied for him. "He's the new Second Assistant."

"So he's taking . . ."

"Mike's place," Lacy completed her mother's sentence. "There's a job to be done. Ryan's the best person to do it."

"At least they . . ."

"Found someone good." Lacy squared her shoulders and locked gazes with her mother. Blue fire met blue fire.

Ryan watched the exchange between the two women. Lacy kept interrupting as though she wanted to keep her mother from saying the wrong thing. Protecting him.

He'd heard rumors the two women didn't see eye to eye. Especially about the fire service. Perhaps protecting him wasn't exactly the right way of putting it. Maybe Lacy was trying to beat her mother to the punch. Preventing her mother from expressing what she thought.

Worst, the two were talking about him as though he wasn't there. It was almost irritating.

"Excuse me," he interrupted watching both women turn to him, with the good grace to look embarrassed.

"I've had a few years experience before that in New York," he said to Lois. Then he turned to Lacy. "I was not necessarily the best person for the job. I was the best person available that everyone else agreed on."

Lacy felt her cheeks burn as he corrected her.

She didn't know what had gotten into her. She'd only been home a few days and she was already getting defensive with her mother. She had no reason. Her mother was merely making casual conversation.

"Ryan, maybe you'd like some coffee. Dad's downstairs, in what's more or less his domain. Maybe you'd like to join him."

"Yes, it may be a bit more comfortable," Carl said from the doorway that opened below the tall stairs that led to the upper floor. Ryan assumed it led to another set of descending stairs.

"Actually I just stopped to give Lacy her first month's rent. I had no intention of staying."

"Nonsense." Carl laughed good-naturedly. "Come on down." Then he sobered. "I've been wanting to get someone else's opinion of how things went last night."

"I'll bring your coffee down," Lois offered. "Some for you, too, Carl?"

"Love some," he replied before disappearing back through the door.

"I thought we weren't supposed to discuss last night?" Ryan commented as he followed the older man.

Carl glanced over his shoulder. "You think we're the only ones who will."

"I see what you mean," Ryan replied, knowing what Carl meant. Since joining the emergency service he'd more than once associated it with being a member of a quilting bee. Yes, as a child he'd had to go with his mother to their church quilting bee. The women there chatted away, sharing bits of gossip, picking on whomever wasn't there that day, just like the men at the station did.

"Besides, that was just an excuse to get you away from them." Carl reached the bottom and turned to Ryan. "I have a feeling I'll be spending a lot of time down here."

"Are they always this . . ." He sought a word that would be most tactful. "tense."

"Used to be worse." Carl motioned to the well worn sofa, then to a torn, black, naugahyde recliner, before going to a second one, that was obviously the one he favored. *Firehouse* magazine laid open on the floor beside the chair. A television remote control on top of it.

Ryan decided to take the second chair, leaning forward, his elbows propped on his knees.

Carl got more comfortable, pulling the foot-rest out.

"So, what did you think?" he asked. "About last night."

"I thought it went well."

"Don't be diplomatic." Carl laughed. "Do you think everyone understood what we were actually trying to do? It's the first time we ever tried something like this. – Hopefully the last."

Ryan sighed. "I'm afraid, like most things, the ones who need it most probably weren't receptive."

"You saw Carlisle. He was Mike's best friend."

"I've heard that."

"They went to school together. Did everything together." Carl's expression clouded, as though he was thinking of one thing they did together that was only recently revealed. "It's hard for me to be objective about him."

Ryan frowned. "I understand."

"You know about that?" Carl's bushy gray eyebrows raised.

"I was at the house with Lacy when Woody Brown called the other week," Ryan stated. "She was pretty upset and ended up telling me all about it."

"Lucky you were there. . ." Carl stopped talking as he heard the upstairs door opening. Soft footsteps threaded down the stairs.

"Here's your coffee," Lois said as she reached the bottom carrying a tray. "I didn't know how you liked it, so I brought milk and sugar."

"Ahh, coffee. I've been waiting for this." Carl winked at Ryan. "I usually don't get a cup before dinner. One at breakfast, and one at dinner. Right dear."

"And whatever you sneak during the day when I'm not there to see you," she said with a twinkle in her blue eyes.

When she smiles like that she looks like her daughter, Ryan thought. He liked it when Lacy smiled, which wasn't often enough since the accident.

"Can't slip anything by you," Carl said. "Never could."

She turned back to Ryan. "Will you stay and join us for dinner? I promise, Lacy and I will be on good behavior. I apologize for the way we acted earlier."

"Certainly he'll join us," Carl answered for him. "I need someone to help act as a buffer in case you two start acting up again."

A pink flush blended with the light sprinkling of freckles on the older woman's cheeks, another trait Ryan found common to her daughter. "It's been an adjustment for Lacy moving home," she said.

"I'm sure it's an adjustment for all of you."

131

"I only want what's best for her," Lois said, then as though she had already said more than she wanted she changed the subject again. "We'll eat in a half hour. If you're not upstairs, you get cold dinner."

"And she means it." Carl laughed. "My wife learned a long time ago, don't try to keep meals warm for a firefighter. Right dear?" He winked at Ryan.

She turned back to her husband. "You're never going to let me forget that are you?"

He laughed then, and Ryan found he couldn't help but join in the laughter.

"Let me escape upstairs before you tell him," the woman said as she rushed toward the stairs.

She was only halfway up when Carl started. "Men!" Ryan heard her grumble. "They think they never do anything stupid."

"Right after we were married, she tried to keep my dinner warm in the oven while I was out at a fire. Turned out to be an all nighter. I came home from one fire and had to put out another, right, Dear?"

In reply they heard the upstairs door slam, and both men started laughing.

After a moment Carl's laughter slowly died. He sobered, looking back at Ryan again, getting back to the original subject.

"Mike was always more out-going than Barry. He did everything first. Made the football team first, joined the fire company first, married first. . . Even died first.

"Barry always seemed to be the follower. Surprised everyone when he became Assistant Chief before Mike. Most of all, I think it surprised Mike. I don't think they were as close after that. But, then again, how many men are, after one of them gets married?"

Ryan waited, suspecting there was more.

"I think Carlisle is headed for problems. I don't think they all started because of Mike's death. That only brought them to a head."

"I've noticed he's a pretty heavy drinker, though it's never seemed to be a problem at the station," Ryan added, not wanting to start trouble.

Carl nodded. "Arlen mentioned that to me. One of the reasons we invited the stress team in."

"You did all you can do then," Ryan said. "The rest is up to Barry himself."

The two men sat staring at each other, both engrossed in their thoughts.

"I think he'll be okay," Ryan said, breaking the silence. "From what Lacy said, he's spoken to her." He wondered how much Lacy had shared with her father. They were so close, he suspected she told him everything. When it was related to the fire company, it was probably more than she told her mother.

"He even apologized to her, which in itself was a big step, when you consider there's been no love lost between him and her. She was the thorn in the side of Mike's and his friendship."

"The one thing Barry didn't do second."

Carl looked up at Ryan as if that thought had just occurred to him. "He even bought Mike's Bronco. But I guess Lacy may have mentioned that when she told you the rest."

"Maybe he wants to mend the fences. They both cared a lot about Mike."

Carl nodded. "It would be nice to see them get along But. . ." he sought the words. "I only hope he's not carrying this second stuff too far. . . I mean. . .he'll be in for a rude awakening if he tries to pick up where Mike left off with my daughter."

Ryan frowned, for the strangest reason not liking that thought. He couldn't imagine Lacy and Barry Carlisle. "They've never gotten along before."

"And that's gone on since way before Mike showed an interest in her. He was part of a group that was totally against women in the fire service."

"And Mike. . .? Was he part of that group?"

Carl frowned. "He joined it first."

"Hey you two. . ." They were interrupted by Lacy's voice. "Mom's got dinner on the table. You want hot food or cold?"

"Hot," Carl called up the stairs. He looked at Ryan, then at his watch. "Only twenty-five minutes. She's probably getting even cause I told you that story."

"You know what they say about pay backs."

"Tell me about it." The older man laughed, lowering the footrest then rising from the chair. "Between her and Lacy, I don't know who is worse. A person doesn't want to cross either one of them."

So, the two women did have something besides their attractive, honey-blonde hair and sapphire eyes in common, he thought. "I'll be careful not to get on their wrong side."

CHAPTER TEN

Lacy yawned, stretching herself awake. She wiggled her nose, smelling the aroma of something baking. It must be Saturday, she thought, frowning as she realized that was the only thing that distinguished one day from another.

Glancing at the clock on her nightstand her frown grew even more. It was almost eight o'clock. Long after the usual time Mikie awoke for his breakfast. Quickly she threw back the covers and jumped from her warm bed, heading bare-footed toward the next room, the one that had once been her mother's sewing room, but now served as a nursery for her son.

As she suspected his crib was empty. "Oh no," she groaned as she returned to her own room to get dressed. Her mother had once again taken over responsibility for her son.

At first it hadn't seemed so bad, letting her mother do little things to help her with Mikie. She had been so exhausted, it was nice to finally be able to sleep through the night.

Then, as her emotions started to settle, Mikie started sleeping better at night, eventually only waking once, and that was for his usual two o'clock feeding. She'd resisted her mother's suggestion she put him on formula so she could help by getting up with him some nights.

"If Mike had lived he'd have shared in the responsibility," her mother had reminded her. But Lacy had doubted that. She had known her husband far too well. A baby would have been her job. Feedings her responsibility. Mike would have thought it was his job to teach his son how to be a man, she thought sarcastically.

Lacy grabbed her robe, knowing she was being unreasonably irritable that morning. But she was growing tired of her mother doing all the things she was supposed to do.

Her mother had been the one who used to say she should try and be more of a lady and do woman's things. Now when she could do the most womanly thing there was, taking care of her son, it seemed her mother was always in the way.

It was worse now that Mikie was eating cereal to supplement her breast-milk. Her mother was constantly beating her into the room in the morning and tending to his needs. It was as though she was waiting with outstretched hands by the nursery door, ready to snatch up her grandson as soon as she heard his first sound.

It didn't matter that Lacy had asked her not to. Had suggested she was spoiling the boy. No, instead her mother insisted it was because Lacy needed her rest.

Rest! That's all she was doing lately, and it was getting on her nerves. She stomped down the stairs, her satin robe billowing behind her as she reached for it's belt, but couldn't find it.

She turned around and saw one end dragging behind, the other about to come out of the robe's loop. Quickly she grabbed it and yanked the whole thing out. The thought of using it as a noose for her mother crossed her mind.

She jammed the belt into the pocket of her pink robe to resist that temptation. Murdering her mother would hardly get her what she wanted. She doubted she'd be able to care for her son from prison.

Pausing just outside the door, she took a breath, trying to calm herself. She knew it would be useless to rant and rave. She'd only upset her son. And she suspected nothing, short of murder, would get through to her mom.

Her murderous thoughts dissolved as soon as she walked through the door and took one look at her son. His cereal smeared mouth turned up into a huge smile when he saw her enter the room.

The other two faces at the table were wearing equally wide grins. Her father and Ryan were sitting on opposite sides of Mikie. Her mother wasn't even there.

Ryan! She grabbed the sides of her robe to cover the sheer baby doll pajamas she'd taken to wearing after a week of unseasonably hot weather had hit the area. She thought of running back to her room and getting dressed, then decided it didn't matter, he'd already seen her disarray. Vanity did force her to run her hand briefly over her wild honey-gold curls.

"I. . .I. . ." She stopped, realizing it was Ryan feeding her son and not her father. "I overslept."

"Not to worry, everything is under control," her father said. "And I confess, it was I who kidnapped Mikie this morning."

"Where's Mom?" She opened the oven and found the usual tin of oat bran muffins lightly browning.

"Certainly not in there." Her father laughed. "She got up early and started baking. Then she realized she had run out of flour."

"Good heavens, no flour on baking day," Lacy teased, glancing around the room at the empty pastry shells. She reached into the cabinet and pulled out a mug, then went to the refrigerator and took out the jug of milk.

"There's muffins already made, over here if you want," her father suggested.

She poured her milk, then returned the jug to the refrigerator before joining the two men. "I can take over there."

"I don't mind," Ryan said, smiling up at her. It was the first thing he'd said, he'd been so engrossed in his task.

She shrugged. "Watch it, he spits."

"I know," Ryan laughed. She glanced at his light blue tee-shirt and saw the slightly smeared cereal stains he must have tried to wipe off.

"That stuff's like glue," she said. "When you're finished you can borrow one of Dad's shirts while I wash yours."

"No need. I'm on my way home. Arlen asked me to drop off some information."

"You're out early. Did you have a call?"

"Another grass fire. It's too early in the season for this," he commented, his jaw tightening.

"It's been hot and dry."

Ryan shook his head, his green eyes grim. "It's not that. Though it doesn't help."

"We've got a fire bug." It wasn't a questions, it was a statement. It all added up. It was a Saturday morning. She knew they had other similar calls recently during the week, but they were later in the day. After school.

Ryan nodded, rubbing a hand on the back of his neck. "I'm afraid so. Arlen wanted me to give Carl the details.

"As usual, no one saw anything. Right?" Lacy asked.

"Actually, this time it was in the park. There were a few joggers out. They said a couple of kids passed them on bicycles. They thought they were racing. It was shortly after that they saw the smoke and reported the fire."

"Think they can identify any of the kids?" Even as she said it, she knew the odds of that were slim.

"The joggers were too busy talking about the latest drop in the Dow Jones averages."

"Oh, the yuppy brigade," she said sarcastically. She'd never understood the attitudes of the young professionals from town. They didn't seem the least bit interested in volunteerism. "All they're worried about is their profits while running in two-hundred dollar jogging shoes or driving their over-priced BMWs."

"Hey, don't knock it," Ryan looked offended. "I used to own one of them."

Lacy wrinkled up her freckled nose. "I thought you were a vintage Toyota man."

"I am now."

"Why such a drastic change?"

"I totalled the BMW." He shrugged, his expression veiled by hooded eyes. It was a time he'd rather forget. He wished he hadn't started the train of conversation.

Lacy suspected it was best to let the subject drop. From the look in Ryan's green eyes as he concentrated on feeding her son, she could tell he was uncomfortable.

Just then her mother came in the door with a large brown bag of groceries. "You could help me," she scolded her husband.

"We didn't hear you," Carl defended as he got up from his chair. "Besides, I thought you only went for flour."

"I remembered a few other things we needed. There's three more bags in the car."

"A few?" Carl laughed with good humor.

"Let me help," Ryan offered, scraping the last of the cereal out of the bowl and putting it into Mikie's mouth.

"No, you just sit there," Carl ordered, with a wink. "I left you handle the dirty work. I'll do this."

Lacy laughed, remembering Ryan's tee shirt. "Are you sure you won't let me wash that for you? I've got to go up and get dressed, I can easily throw down a clean shirt of Dad's for you to borrow."

Ryan stood. "Like I said, I'm on my way home." He carried the empty cereal bowl to the sink and rinsed it.

She watched him closely, his solid male frame not showing an extra ounce of flesh. She imagined him in one of her father's extra-large tee shirts, and smiled at the picture.

"What's so funny?" her mother asked.

Lacy decided not to lie. "I think Ryan only refused one of Dad's tee shirts because he's afraid it would look like Omar the Tent Maker struck."

"That's not nice," Lois scolded.

"What's not nice?" Carl asked as he came in carrying two of the brown bags.

Ryan's green eyes were sparked with humor as he looked back at Lacy, as though saying, 'Get yourself out of this one.'

"Lacy's suggesting you need to lose weight."

"Two of you now. They're ganging up on me!" Carl groaned. "If you wait Ryan, I might just come along with you. – Did you ever get that fitness center put up? I may want to use it."

Ryan joined in the laughter. "It's right downstairs in the basement."

In the basement, Lacy thought. Not in the nursery, or what had been the nursery while she was living there.

Before she moved she asked him if he ever worked out. When he said he used to belong to a fitness club, and that he intended to someday join one again, she decided to leave the equipment rather than return it. She figured it was easier than what she'd have to go through to return it. She was having enough trouble getting Mike's credit cards changed to her name.

"Isn't it too damp?" She asked, remembering Mike telling her it was.

"I've put in a dehumidifier. I also thought I might put some sealer on the walls, if you don't mind. And some screens in the windows.

"Hey, we've got some old screens up in the garage," Carl suggested. "Suppose we check if any of them will fit."

"You're really going over then." Lacy turned to her father.

"Certainly. I intend to put Omar out of business."

Lacy blushed, realizing her father had heard what she'd said. "Dad, you're perfect the way you are."

"I know." The jovial man laughed, then sucked in his stomach to prove that point. "I really only wanted to finish the conversation you interrupted."

Lacy watched as the two men left, feeling strangely left out. There had been a time her father wouldn't have hesitated discussing department business in front of her.

"Mom, suppose after I clean up Mikie and get dressed myself, I help you finish your baking?"

Lois couldn't hide her surprise. But she remained silent. Deep down she knew it was not what her daughter really wanted to do.

#

The shrill sound of a pager woke Lacy. She jumped from the bed and was at the door of her bedroom before she remembered it wasn't her own. She watched as her father came tumbling out of his bedroom, still buttoning his shirt as he raced toward the stairs.

"What'cha got, Dad?" she asked, following. She knew her father's pager only went off if the call was something serious. Otherwise each company fire chief handled his own call.

"An abandoned building," he said, stomping down the stairs.

She knew the fact that it was supposed to be abandoned didn't alleviate any of the hurry to get there as fast as they could. Nothing was cut and dry. You never knew when something unexpected happened. There could be someone inside. Something explosive could be stored there. The fire could even spread to adjacent buildings.

After her father was gone she went to the kitchen and poured herself a glass of milk. She no longer felt like sleeping. In fact, she felt strangely rejuvenated.

Looking at the clock above the sink she saw it was only one in the morning. She felt like she'd slept through the night.

She went into the living room and turned on the portable scanner her father kept on a shelf. She took it with her back into the kitchen.

"What are you doing up?" her mother asked as she, too, came into the room.

"Same thing as you. The pager woke me."

Lois looked at the scanner sitting on the table and frowned. "I guess you'll be up for awhile."

Lacy nodded. "A little while."

"Well . . . I'll see you in the morning." Without another word Lois left the room.

While she listened to the activity on the scanner, Lacy thought about her mother. She hadn't remembered her mother ever getting up before when her father went out on a call. Had she merely heard her downstairs and come down to check if there was a problem?

Familiar voices on the scanner pushed those thoughts aside, as Lacy returned her attention to what she heard going on over the scanner. She closed her eyes trying to imagine what was happening, almost able to visualize each person doing their job. Oh how she wished she could be there.

"Lois, Honey," she awakened to her father's voice. "Oh, Lacy," he said, stepping further into the kitchen. "With your head down like that I almost thought you were your mother."

"Oh, Dad. How did it go?" She yawned, glancing at the clock and seeing it was now four in the morning.

"I've got to go back in daylight, but I already suspect what I'll find," Carl replied, frowning. "We've got ourselves a fire bug."

"You mean they've graduated from vacant lots and parks to structures?"

"Not necessarily. There was a large patch of grass burning when we got there. It extended to the house. We figure that's how it started."

"Maybe you should call Aunt Rainy," Lacy suggested. "She could start working on some programs about juvenile firesetting."

Carl nodded. "That's what I was talking to Ryan about this morning. – Correction. Yesterday morning. – And you, young lady, ought to be in bed."

Again Lacy felt curiously shut out as she left her father. She wondered if he was avoiding sharing things with her because of the way her mother felt.

Lacy found it impossible to fall asleep again. It was so hot she felt like the room was closing in on her. Sometimes she felt it was that way with her life. She knew it was no longer all because of losing Mike and everything that happened since.

No, she had felt that way before. While she was pregnant. After she stopped responding to calls. Or, on those times she did respond out of pure nosiness, how useless she felt standing around just watching.

She got up and went to the window, feeling a faint breeze drifting in. With it came the scent of her mother's roses, just starting to bloom.

Tears filled her eyes as she thought of her son. She loved Mikie so much. She had hoped having him would take away all these feelings. But it didn't happen. She still longed to be in the forefront of the activity. Out there with the others during an emergency.

Oh God, What kind of mother am I? Am I terrible for wanting to do these things when I have a baby to care for? A son who depends on me?

Other mothers have jobs, she told herself. But she knew with her it was more than a job. It was a part of her. Her accomplishment. Something she knew she did well. Something she took pride in.

She couldn't go out and fight fires like she once had done. She couldn't just up and leave her son. Even with her mother. She knew the risks of the job. Knew them too well.

He'd already lost a father. She couldn't let him lose a mother too. She couldn't take that risk.

But she could return to the ambulance squad. Why should all that paramedic training go to waste?

Her decision made, Lacy returned to bed, finally able to sleep.

#

"You're what?" Her mother's blue eyes pierced at her in disbelief.

"I'm going to start running with the ambulance again," she repeated, putting another spoon of cereal into her son's mouth. She broke a piece off her muffin and popped it into her mouth.

"I just don't understand why?" Lois shook her head.

"Maybe it's time you try," Lacy said, wishing she could take the bitterness out of her voice. But she had suffered too many years of disapproval from her mother to hide the way she felt. "I'm not you, Mom."

"I never expected you to be me," Lois defended. "I just. . . well. . .I never thought you'd be. . ."

"So unfeminine," Lacy finished for her.

"No," Lois said firmly, coming to join her at the table. "Don't put words into my mouth Lacy."

"They aren't words you've never said."

"Maybe so, but you still aren't a mind reader. You don't know what I'm going to say. I could have changed how I feel."

"Have you?" Two pairs of blue eyes locked. They held each other's gaze.

"Not how I feel. I've had too may years getting this way," her mother admitted. "But I'm not so sure you know how you feel right now."

Lacy saw a new look in her mother's eyes. Something she had never seen before. Understanding.

"I love Mikie. But. . . I've got to . . .to – I don't know. I can't put it into words," Lacy struggled. "Mom, I can't dedicate every part of myself to him. I wish I could. Then I could be like you. But, I don't want to be like you."

She felt tears sting her eyes as she watched her mother flinch.

"I know you never thought I was a good mother. . ."

"Mom, it's just the opposite. You were a great mother. It's me who's probably being selfish. But I don't want to be like you because I saw what it cost you. – I'm explaining this all wrong."

"No. Go on."

Lacy took a breath. "Mom, when I went to school the first day, what did you do?"

"I cried," Lois replied, smiling at the memory.

"I knew that Mom. I thought I was doing something awful to you because I was growing up. And the worst was that I wanted to grow up."

"I never knew you felt that way."

"No one did. That's just it. I could no more admit that to you, than you could tell me you wanted me to stay a baby."

"I didn't!" Lois denied. "Not really."

"So, what did you do the second day I went to school."

Lois frowned. "I cried again. And the third day too, if that's what you're going to ask next."

"Mom, you met Dad in high school Married right after," Lacy said. "I'll bet you doted on him till I came along. Which as I recall, wasn't long. You were practically honeymooners."

"That's one way of putting it." Lois blushed. "It's not exactly something you talk to your children about."

"Mom, I'm not a child anymore," Lacy laughed.

"How well I know."

"And that about sums it up," Lacy continued. "You devoted your entire life to a husband and a child. You should have had a dozen kids, then you wouldn't have doted so much on one."

"We tried, Dear. We couldn't." Her mother's lip trembled.

Lacy took her mother's hand. "You hurt so bad because I was doing the one thing you couldn't stop me from doing. Growing up."

"Growing away."

"Not away Mom. Never away."

"We haven't exactly been close."

"Because you haven't been able to accept me for the person I am. The person I've grown up to be."

"And you haven't been able to accept me for the person I am, Lacy. I've had a lot more years being who I am."

Lacy thought about that, seeing her mother's point-of-view for the first time. "Why don't we both try harder?"

Lois smiled. "I'm still going to dote on my family."

"I know." Lacy nodded, smiling. "Just not so much that when we do what we have to do, we aren't hurting you."

"Tall order, but I'll try."

"That's all I can ask."

By this time Mikie gurgled loudly letting them know his breakfast should not be forgotten. Lacy gave her mother a kiss then obliged him with another spoon of cereal.

#

Lacy pushed the stroller down the street. It probably hadn't been a good idea walking into town, but she had so much nervous energy, she felt the walk would help release it. Now, as she looked at the threatening thunder clouds she frowned and stepped up her pace.

Mikie layed in the stroller, contently playing with the new rattle he'd just discovered.

She smiled, thinking how wonderful it was to watch her tiny son as he discovered so many new things. Each new item bringing him such delight.

She thought about all the things ahead as he grew. When he learned to sit up. When he crawled. His first step. Saying his first words. Nursery school, Kindergarten then first grade.

God, she missed him already. But she wouldn't end up forever crying because she missed him, she thought. She'd have something else to do.

With determination she saw her destination just a block away. Main Street Station. The single story brick building housed the Schuylkill Valley Fire Department's specialty units: ambulance, rescue, fire police, and their dispatch center.

The first drops of rain were just starting to fall as she pushed the stroller through the double glass doors. She heard the voices of several people talking, laughing. She'd known Saturday was a good day to find several people around the station. There were always more people around on weekends, when many of the volunteers were off work.

She saw Drew Arthur putting some money into the Coke machine. He was about to bend down to retrieve his can of soda when he spotted her. "Hey stranger!" the dusty-haired ambulance Chief called good-naturedly "It's good to see you."

"Thought it was about time I stopped by for a visit," she said. "And to introduce you to my son."

Drew stooped down and touched the dark-haired baby, laughing as Mikie grabbed his finger and tried to stick it in his mouth. "At that stage."

"Everything goes in his mouth."

Annie Baxter, a volunteer driver joined them, smiling down at the little boy. "He's so sweet. The last time I saw him he was in the nursery at the hospital."

Lacy cocked her head to the side looking at the other woman. She remembered Annie had been on duty the night of the fire. Had she been the one driving the ambulance that had taken her to the hospital. She didn't really remember.

"Were you there the night I nearly delivered in the ambulance."

Annie nodded, giving Lacy a grim smile. "I was driving. Brody was in the back with you."

"I remember that part." Lacy shook her head. She knew the driver had been the brunt of some pretty harsh words from Brody that night as he ordered her to driver faster. There wasn't a paramedic in town better than he. She had known she was in good hands. Yet, he was determined they were going to make it to the hospital before her child arrived. The few minutes drive must have seemed like an hour to him. Even longer to poor Annie.

"And you stopped by to see him."

"Both of you, but you were asleep."

Lacy was touched by the young woman's kindness. She'd been a member of the ambulance squad only a short while before Lacy had taken maternity leave. They'd hardly had time to get to know one another. The only thing Lacy really remembered about the girl were all the questions she asked about the paramedic training Lacy had recently completed. She'd said she wanted to be a paramedic too.

"So did you ever start paramedic training?"

"I'm going now," Annie replied with a widening smile. "I've only got a few months to go."

"That's great," Lacy said with sincerity. "Maybe we'll get to work together. That's why I'm here." She turned back to the Ambulance Chief. "I wanted to tell you I'd like to start running with the ambulance again."

143

"Are you sure you're ready?" Drew asked, glancing down at the child in the stroller.

"I'm ready," she assured him knowing there was no need to explain more.

"Okay, I'll get you a pager," Drew replied, heading toward the office. "You're still on the books. So, you can start responding whenever we need an extra crew. You know the routine."

She nodded. Yes, she knew. She'd respond from home whenever she was available. At other times, on days when they were short of personnel, she'd be expected to stand by at the station.

There were eleven full-time paramedics and EMTs on the ambulance squad. The rest of the unit was comprised of nearly thirty volunteers who helped fill the gap of service during peak periods when they received more calls than the full-time employees could handle alone. Still, those they assisted received care equal to that of the others; because, like Lacy, most of these volunteers were as highly trained as their paid counterparts.

"I admire you, Lacy," Annie said when Lacy turned back to her. Then, as though realizing her words could be taken wrong, the young woman blushed and started to stammer. "I didn't mean. . .Well. . . You know. . ."

Lacy smiled, putting a hand on the girl's forearm and giving it a squeeze. "I know what you didn't mean."

Annie relaxed. "What I did mean, was I admire the way you seem to be able to handle it all. Everyone knows what a great firefighter you were. You had a full time job. You took care of your home. Then to top it off you took classes to become a paramedic." The younger woman sighed. "I have enough trouble juggling a job and classes."

"Annie, I didn't do it all at one time. In fact, I wasn't at all very good at juggling." She remembered the arguments she and Mike had when she'd leave housework undone on the nights she went to school. His pet peeve had been when she didn't do the laundry and there was something in it he wanted to wear. "I'm afraid, you had the wrong idea if you thought that I was coping so well."

"Sometimes I feel the pressure. My Mom's not well, and it's tough to leave her when Dad's not home. I feel so guilty when I do. Sometimes, on her really bad days . . ." Annie stopped, shrugging her plump shoulders. "That's beside the point. I can't imagine what it would be like having a baby to care for."

Lacy remembered that Annie's desire to respond with the emergency medical unit had been inspired by her mother's medical problem. An accident had left the woman paralyzed from the waist down. Annie had once said if it weren't for the emergency units who'd responded her mother would have been dead.

144

"Not much different than what you're going through," Lacy said softly. "Trust me, I'm no luckier than you. I just have a plan."

"A plan?"

Lacy laughed, tossing back her long blonde curls. "That's what I call it. You see, I hated my job as secretary, and I wasn't very good at it either. On the other hand, I enjoyed being a firefighter, and I was good at that. So I figured, if I have to work – and I do – it better be at something I like and I'm good at. Well, they don't pay firefighters in this town. They do pay paramedics. At least I'd still be in the emergency service."

Annie's bright eyes clouded, but she gave Lacy a weak smile. "Looks like we have a lot in common. I'm hoping to get hired too."

Lacy knew it wasn't going to be easy for the other woman. It was more than just a regular job. There were pressures involved. A great deal of stress. At least she had her mother to help with her son. Lacy suspected Annie's father wasn't as eager to tend to his wife.

Perhaps that would change after she got a paid position on the squad. A position she, too, was after.

"Once your classes are over it will be a little easier," she said, watching the girl's expression turn grim, and wondered if they were thinking the same thing. They both wanted the same job for similar reasons. Would that create a competition between then? Lacy hoped not.

Lacy realized that Annie's eyes weren't on her, rather looking beyond her, in the direction Drew had gone. But from the obvious tension she sensed in Annie as she fidgeted with her own fingers she suspected she wasn't watching Drew return.

"Lacy!" She heard the Rescue Chief's familiar voice and turned her head with a smile.

"Yes, it's me, Brody," she said as he approached. From the corner of her eye she saw Annie leaving. *So that's what's wrong.* She knew Brody had that effect on people. He intimidated them. Funny, she'd always gotten along with him fine. But then, she hadn't really worked with him long. Who knew what laid ahead?

CHAPTER ELEVEN

"I think you should spend some time with Dad," Lacy ordered, placing a clean filter in the drip coffee maker before adding fresh decaffeinated grounds. "I'll bring you some coffee as soon as it's made. You can relax and watch some TV together. The national news should be on."

"What about the dishes?" her mother frowned at the table full of dirty dinner dishes, and then at the pots and pans on the stove.

"You cooked. I'll clean up," Lacy replied. She hated the way her mother still did all the work. When she'd first moved in with her parents, a little over two months ago, she had been exhausted, both mentally and physically. It had been nice to have her mother there to care for her.

Now she was feeling better and that kindness was getting down right smothering. Besides that, she felt guilty letting her mother do so much. Yet at the same time, she was afraid she'd hurt her feelings if she told her. It was much easier to let her do as she pleased.

"If you insist." Her mother glanced at her grandson contentedly playing in his wooden high chair. The dark-haired boy, was propped between two pillows so he wouldn't slide to either side. He still wasn't quite able to sit on his own, though he loved being on an equal level with the rest of them while they ate dinner. "I'll take Mikie in with me."

"He's fine in here, Mom," Lacy said. Especially since she'd tied a ribbon to his rattle and secured one end to the cuff of his shirt to keep him from dropping it on the floor.

Taking care of Mikie was a different story. Lacy insisted on doing as much with him as possible. She didn't want her mother to take over completely, and she knew that her mother easily could if she'd let her. It was enough having her there to babysit when she responded to emergency calls.

"Yes, but his Grandpa didn't have much time with him today," Lois argued, ignoring Lacy's wishes as she started to undo the strap that was acting like a seat belt on the chair.

Lacy sighed, turned toward the sink and filled the pot with some cold water to run through the coffee maker. It seemed useless to try getting through to her Mom. She had hoped after the talk they'd had just before she returned to the ambulance squad, that her mother would find other interests outside of her family. That she wouldn't devote all her time to them.

She supposed the temptation of having a baby in the house was just too much for her to resist.

She poured the cold water into the well and plugged in the coffee maker, then turned it on. Like all their appliances, it was only plugged in when in use. A fire safety measure her father had insisted upon ever since investigating a late night fire that started because of a toaster that had been always plugged in. Worse yet, was the fact that the owners of that home still had the old-style fuses instead of the more modern circuit breakers, and they had replaced those fuses with pennies – an old trick, that unfortunately some people still used. A deadly trick too, as the family very nearly found out when that toaster short-circuited and current kept feeding through the lines. They very nearly didn't make it out with their lives. As it was, they lost everything in their home.

Lacy watched as her mother carried her son from the room, knowing she better hurry to get the dishes done before her mother also decided to give Mikie his bath and get him ready for bed. It was something her mother did often now that Lacy had stopped nursing and was bottle-feeding her son.

She put the last dish away then quickly poured three cups of coffee and put them on a tray. She carried them into the living room, but found that her mother and Mikie weren't there. Her father's eyes were closed, his mouth gaping open as his chin rested on his broad, heaving chest. A loud snore told her he was asleep.

So much for a nice family evening, she thought, as she set the tray on the coffee table and picked up one of the cups. Absently she thought of her mother upstairs getting her son ready for bed, and her father sound asleep in his chair.

"What's wrong with this picture?" she whispered, taking a sip from her mug and burning her tongue. She winched and set the mug down, no longer in the mood for coffee.

Shoulders stooped, she was about to head up the stairs when the pager on her hip sounded. There was a need for a paramedic and an ambulance for an emergency call. "Suspected heart attack," the disembodied voice informed her.

Her father had wakened instantly at the pagers first beep. "It's for me, Dad," she said. He nodded, already focusing his attention to the coffee she had left on the table.

Her mother came to the top of the stairs. "I have everything under control up here," she said, turning so she could see the pajama-clad boy in her mother's arms. "Wave bye-bye to MaMa," she said, lifting his tiny, plump hand to make it wave.

"Bye-bye," Lacy replied, pasting a false smile on her lips, knowing it made no difference if she stayed or if she'd go. Her mother had everything under control. "I'll be back as soon as I can."

It was over an hour later when Rick Marlowe backed the Advanced Life Support ambulance through the giant bay doors at the station. She sat silently beside him, lost in her own thoughts.

Brody opened the door to her side, frowning when he saw her face. "Lacy, we can't save them all," he said grimly after seeing her somber expression.

"The family said it wasn't her first attack," Rick said when he, too, turned toward Lacy. "We did everything we could."

Lacy sighed, knowing that in her mind, but it didn't make losing someone any easier. She'd felt this way before. Each time they'd lost a victim in a fire. It just didn't happen as often as it did when responding with the ambulance. She wondered if it really ever did get any easier.

"Hey you guys, I appreciate the concern, but I'm okay." She forced a smile, knowing she was acting foolish.

"Okay, Lacy. If that's what you say," Rick said, looking at his watch and making a face. "I've gotta make a phone call. Can we do the paperwork after?"

Lacy nodded. She knew Rick was having problems of his own, though he didn't let them interfere with his performance on the job. He just worried twice as much afterwards. She suspected this time he had stood someone up and he was about to call and attempt an apology. It was tough dating when you were involved in the emergency service. Especially if the person you were dating was not involved. They didn't understand the demands.

"Come on, I'll buy you a soda," Brody suggested as she slid from her seat to stand in front of him. He reached into his pocket for some change. "What'll it be?"

"Anything with caffeine," she replied, not wanting to sleep till she worked everything through in her mind.

"It's pretty stuffy in here," Brody said as he handed her a can of soda. He pressed his own cool can against his forehead. "Suppose we go outside and sit on the back step."

She smiled, suspecting he was giving her the opportunity to talk about what was bothering her. She knew it was rare for the hard-edged rescue chief to allowed his softer side to show through. She wondered why he didn't do it more often. He was actually quite personable when he did.

"So, want to talk it out?" he asked as soon as they were seated on the concrete steps behind the station.

She shrugged, popping open her can and taking a long cool sip, before turning back to see his gray eyes staring down at her. She felt her cheeks burn. "Like you said, we can't save them all. I knew that when I was fighting fires."

"So what's the problem tonight?"

She frowned, looking away, but Brody wouldn't let her. He took his hand and gently turned her face back to his. He searched her eyes. "Is it something more than this call?"

She nodded.

"Did . . .did losing someone. . ." his eyes darkened, probing deeper. "remind you of losing your husband?"

"No, Brody," she stated through her frown. "I've come to terms with that."

His grey eyes seemed to soften, his body relaxed. "Whatever it is, I'd like to help."

"It's . . .well, I'm not adjusting well to motherhood," she confessed. "I thought I had it all figured out. I needed more than being a Mom. So I came back here."

"You'd go crazy if you stayed cooped up at home all the time with your son," Brody said with a crooked smile. "You need a life."

"That's not it." She sighed in frustration. The way he said it made her feel more selfish than she had before.

"Lacy, you're a very attractive woman." Brody leaned closer as he spoke. "Not just a Mom."

"But I am a Mom."

"You need more than that to make you happy." His voice was a husky whisper.

"Happy," she repeated, shaking her head. "I never looked at things in terms of happy or unhappy." For years she had thought in terms of success or failure. The things at which she was most successful, were the things she pursued the most.

"Maybe it's time you did." He smiled down at her, putting his arm across her shoulder and pulling her close.

A warning went off inside her head.

"You ready to do that report now, Lacy?" Rick called as he partially opened the door.

"Be right there," she replied, practically jumping up from beside Brody.

"I guess at least his love life is back in order," Brody said as he raked his fingers through his closely cut blond hair.

"Well, the job's not finished till the report's filed," she said, trying to hide her embarrassment. She realized Brody was offering her more than just someone to talk to. He was her friend, but maybe he wanted to be more.

She escaped inside, certain of only one thing – she wasn't certain of anything anymore.

Ryan read the fire service magazine, paying particular interest to an ad about several awards given at their state firemen's convention. One of those was the one Rainy had said they were entering. She thought winning an award in recognition of their work may increase the interest of the other members. He knew she was desperately trying to get more help.

They were to meet at her house later that evening to put together a notebook for their entry. He wondered who else would show up to help. He doubted very many. Less and less of the volunteers from the four borough fire companies were giving up their time for fire safety programs.

Before closing the magazine he glanced at the rules for each of the competition. The award he knew Rainy was entering had a first through sixth place plaque and cash award for fire companies the committee deemed had conducted, not only the most, but the finest, fire safety education in their communities.

Then he read about another award in the fire safety category. It was given to an individual member of the firemen's association who showed an outstanding dedication toward fire safety. He thought of Rainy and her dedication.

He knew much more about the special safety program she had been working on. It was a good program. More important, it was needed. She often showed him letters from public fire safety educators throughout the United States, and some even beyond, requesting more information about that program. Mark said she often worked late into the night trying to fulfill all those requests.

He suspected many others would have given up when facing the resistance of their peers. But not her. If anything, she was more determined than ever. Rainy went far beyond the call of duty when it was something she beleived in. And she definitely beleived in fire safety, especially the program designed to help people with disabilities.

He also thought about the extensive juvenile firesetter program she had begun in the school. How it had resulted in finding the two young boys who had been setting a string of grass fires in the community.

Then how she had convined Carl and Arlen the boys needed serious counseling more than they needed prosecution. In the end the two men worked with the courts to see that the boys did get the proper couseling. And since that time the boys seemed to have turned their lives around.

He tore out the page listing the awards, folded it and slipped it into his shirt pocket. Maybe it was time Rainy received the recognition she deserved. From the way she talked, he knew Lacy felt the same way. If she was at the meeting that night, he'd take some time to talk to her about his idea. That was if they could manage to get a private moment away from Rainy's range of hearing.

He was just starting out the door when the tones of his pager went off. Unfortunately he'd be late for the meeting. Very late, from the sound of what the dispatcher was saying. There was an accident. A serious one. Chances were, he wouldn't be the only one late for the meeting.

#

Bright lights from the emergency apparatus shined through the darkness, lighting up the scene where emergency crews worked.

Fire crews sprayed water on the over-turned vehicle to insure there would be no fire, while Brody, in charge of the rescue crew, knelt by the window trying to reach the victim of the terrible automobile crash.

Lacy, who had arrived in the ambulance, stood close at hand, waiting to help in any way she could. Brody had already attempted to get the women's vitals, but reaching her twisted frame without getting inside the particlly crushed vehicle made it nearly impossible.

"I want SkyCare put on stand-by," he said over his radio, to the faceless doctor monitoring the situation from the Schuylkill Valley Emergency Center. It was he who would make the final decision on whether or not the patient needed to be air-lifted to one of the area's trauma centers, basing his decision on the information provided by the medical team at the scene.

Still it was rare anyone questioned Brody's judgement. Brody was the best Paramedic in Schuylkill Valley. The doctor knew it, and so did everyone else. Including Brody; for if there was anything Brody was not, it was modest about his skills.

"I hate these compacts," Brody grumbled as he squeezed his broad shoulders inside.

"Let me go inside," Lacy said, feeling the need to do more than watch. "I'm smaller than you."

"She needs more than a novice can provide if there's any hope of saving her," Brody said sharply as he pulled back out of the narrow space. He started to remove his heavy bunker coat.

"You're not going in there without protection," Lacy argued, knowing immediately it had been the wrong thing to say. It could be considered insubordination to have phrased her statement like an order. Judging by the widening of Brody's gray eyes it was exactly what he considered it to be.

"Just stay here and wait for orders!" he spat abruptly. "Instead of giving them."

151

With great strength Lacy bit back any retort she may have left slip. This was not the time or place for a battle of authority. Besides, there was no question over who had the authority. Brody was Rescue Chief. This was a rescue.

His words were gospel. Perhaps that was why behind his back many people referred to him as 'god'. But Lacy knew that no matter what their skills, no one was above harms way. Including Brody.

Unfortunately by the time Brody realized that, it could be too late. Lacy hated taking unnecessary chances. And this was unnecessary. The unconscious woman inside that car could already be dead. From the look of it she was. Anything Brody could do for her inside that tiny space, she could do with his supervision.

Lacy wondered if it was more than her being a novice. If Brody was trying to protect her. He was showing more interest in her lately than that of an officer to someone who worked with him. Sure, he was in charge of rescue, and she was with the ambulance squad, but the two always worked side by side in a rescue. They had a professional understanding. Only sometimes she feared his feelings were going beyond professional to personal.

But there wasn't time to consider that now as Brody's command shattered her momentary lapse from the situation. "Call in and tell them I want SkyCare in the air! Her pulse is weak and thready, but she's alive. Barely!"

Lacy keyed the microphone of the radio and forwarded Brody's request. The doctor didn't ask for more information. He trusted Brody. It wasn't a matter of hospitals competing for patients, as had been the case many years ago when helicopter air-lifts, and trauma centers were few and far between. Today everyone knew the value of saving that *Golden Hour*, the time that could mean the difference between life and death. Brody would be basing his decision on what was best for the patient.

Like a well tuned engine others around them began to hustle in reaction to his command. She caught a glimpse of Ryan giving orders to his men to set up a landing zone for the helicopter. They knew what to do. They had done it before, both in drills and in reality. Another message was transmitted to fire police in the area to be prepared for crowd control, as there inevitably was for a helicopter landing. No matter what time of night, nor how remote the area where the landing would be, a crowd of spectators showed up at the scene.

Brody let out a curse, regaining Lacy's attention. "She's got a baby in here. It's pinned under her."

Lacy felt her adrenaline rush as she poked her head into the tiny space. "Can you get it out?"

152

"Give me the neck brace," he shouted. "Then slide the end of the backboard in here so we can try lifting her enough to slide the baby out from under her."

Lacy did as ordered while an EMT and the ambulance driver knelt close behind her waiting to assist in any way they could. It took only a moment for Brody to get the baby out from beneath its mother's unmoving body. She practically crawled in beside Brody to take the child from his hands.

Quickly she slid back outside again. It's lips were already blue from lack of oxygen, but miraculously it had a slight pulse. Though it was extremely weak. Lacy leaned forward and covered the baby's mouth and nose with her mouth and gave two short quick breaths of air.

She placed the baby on a pediatric board before giving two more quick breaths. Getting up from the ground they raced toward the waiting stretcher. She gave the child two more breaths, then watched as its tiny chest started to rise and fall as it began breathing on its own. Suddenly it left out a loud cry. Lacy looked at her companion with tears in her eyes and smiled.

"Someone get over here and help me!" Brody shouted, sticking his head out of the car's window. "I've gotta get her out of here so I have some room to work."

The EMT quickly rushed back to the car. Lacy looked up at Annie, the driver of her ambulance. "You better see what you can do to help." As soon as the young woman left she started immobilizing the child on the backboard, quickly glancing at the child for any visible injuries. Just then she heard shouting.

She glanced outside the ambulance and saw a team of firefighters helping lift the woman on the backboard and carrying her a safe distance from the over-turned car. Annie was stooping down to pick the med-case off the ground.

"Next time keep the thing out of the way!" Brody shouted at her. "Or stay out of the way yourself if you don't know what you're doing."

Lacy could see the young woman's face flush with embarrassment as she stood again, but she quickly followed the others carrying the bag. Checking the baby's vitals she was surprised it was doing so well after everything it had gone through.

"How's the baby?" Annie asked as she returned to her side. Her voice was trembling slightly.

"Vitals are good. Now as long as there's nothing internal, she may be okay," Lacy looked at Annie, then frowned seeing her dejected expression. "Are you okay?"

"Don't you think we should get the baby to the hospital?" the driver said, ignoring Lacy's question.

153

Lacy nodded, suspecting the woman was suffering from an attack of the Brody. Everyone had to endure it at least once during their time working with the hot-headed Rescue Chief. Some people remained and endured, others couldn't. No one had to volunteer to take his abuse. Many moved on to other units in other towns. Those who were hired as part of the paid crew seemed to take it in stride, as though they had to take the good with the bad. The good far out-weighted the bad. Brody wasn't always in one of his abrasive moods. Besides, even he wasn't in service all the time.

Lacy left the driver to watch over the baby while she went to find out if Brody wanted her to remain with him or go with the baby to the hospital. It seemed as though he and the EMT were working quite well together.

Her question was practically drowned by the drone of an engine and whirl of blades chopping the air as the helicopter circled above them before heading to the landing zone set up a few hundred feet away.

"Just go with the kid," Brody ordered. "We won't be long behind you."

Lacy hurried back to the ambulance and jumped into the back, relieving Annie beside the baby. She looked at the infant girl's tiny tear-stained face and thought of her own son. She wanted to pick her up and comfort her, but knew that wasn't possible. To move the child any more than they already did would be risking further damage should she have sustained any injury to her neck or spine.

"Shhhh. It's okay, Sweetheart," Lacy said in a soothing voice as she felt the ambulance pull away. She took hold of the child's small hand, leaning closer, and started singing her own son's favorite lullaby.

The soothing tones of her voice helped calm the child. By the time they reached the hospital the baby girl's eyes had closed. She had checked her vitals once again and was relieved they were still strong. Now if only her mother will be as lucky, she thought with a frown.

She and the driver were waiting just outside the emergency room for word about the child when the Rescue Seven truck turned into the driveway with Brody, the EMT and two other members of the rescue team inside.

"I'll go check the progress of the little girl," the other woman said with a growing frown, as soon as she saw the truck.

Lacy suspected she was trying to avoid Brody. It was understandable after his sharp words to her at the scene. She was probably afraid she was in store for a bigger reaming now that the emergency was under control.

Brody got out first and came toward her. "How's the girl?"

"Annie is checking again," Lacy replied.

"Good, she can finally make herself useful."

"Brody, that's not fair. Annie is usually very competent." Lacy defended the young woman, unable to remain silent any longer. "Did you have to be so hard on her back there?"

"Setting the bag where she did was a stupid mistake. We very nearly tripped over it carrying that woman out."

"And I'm sure she'll never let it happen again."

"She does and I'll have to go to Drew about her," Brody promised, his gray eyes narrowed as he watched the object of their conversation approaching the double glass doors.

Lacy glanced over her shoulder at the other woman. "But you're not going to jump all over her about it anymore tonight."

"Look, one thing you girls better learn to understand. . ." Brody said, lowering his voice, the effect being more dramatic than had he shouted. "I call'um as I see'um. If I have to reprimand someone, I'll do it. Once done, the subject is dropped, until there's a reason to bring it up again. If she, or you, intend to let everything someone says bother you so much that you're afraid to face them again, you may as well get out of this business, cause there's going to be a lot of things said you may not like to hear."

"Thank you Brody," Lacy said through clenched teeth, hoping not to sound too sarcastic. "I believe I've been in the emergency service long enough to know that. But thank you for reminding me."

"Then maybe you should inform her," he replied as the young woman slowly approached, followed by the police officer who had been inside. Ignoring Annie, Brody turned to the officer. "What's the word on the girl?"

"Lucky kid. No serious injuries," the officer replied. "It's the father I pity. They got hold of him at work. Poor guy's torn between coming here to be with his daughter or heading to Brandywine Hospital to be with his wife. He ended up giving consent to treat his daughter over the phone and is on his way to be with his wife."

"Tough choice," Brody agreed. "The kid's probably so scared she could use a familiar face, while the wife's so bad she'll probably be in surgery by the time he gets there, and then, if she makes it through that, she probably won't even know he's there for quite some time."

"You might be surprised," Lacy said, remembering hearing about cases of comatose people being touched, talked to, sometimes even sung to by loved ones, and remembering it after they returned to consciousness. "Maybe he'll be just what she needs."

"Love knows no bounds," Brody said sarcastically, turning to smile at the officer and wink. "I believe we have a romantic among us."

Lacy felt her face flush, but refused to let him goad her. "The world could use a few more of us." She turned to Annie. "Shall we go back to the station?"

A smiling Annie agreed and they headed toward the ambulance to return to the station.

She was just about to go out the door when Rescue Seven backed into the garage. "Wait up," Brody called as he stepped down from the cab of the truck.

Lacy sighed, not in the mood for more of Brody's sarcasm.

"It's still early. You feel up to some coffee and donuts at Dunkin Donuts?" He asked when he came around the vehicle to face her.

"Not tonight, Brody," she said, trying to keep the coolness out of her voice.

Still he sensed her change. "Lacy, you need to realize that what happens when we're on duty remains on duty. We can't take it home with us, or let it effect our personal lives."

"I agree, we shouldn't, Brody," she replied. "But some of us are human, and it's a little harder for us to divide ourselves in half."

Brody's eyes narrowed at her comment. He took hold of her arm and pulled her through the door so the others couldn't hear. "You don't have to be inhuman to be able to separate the professional and personal parts of your life. I thought you, of all people, would understand what I meant."

She did. She knew exactly what he meant. Things hadn't always been rosy between her and Mike at the station. Yet, somehow their marriage had withstood those times. But how long would it have had she not made the changes necessary to avoid some of their confrontations? It wasn't the first time she'd wondered that very thing.

She hated it, but there were times since Mike died that she felt a sense of freedom to do what she wanted to do. And that very thought angered her. It also frightened her that she could even think such a thing. In spite of everything she had learned about her husband since his death, that thought still made her feel as though she were being disloyal to him.

Her shoulder's slumped as she took a breath, looking up at Brody with pain-filled eyes. "It's late, and I'm tired," she nearly whispered. "Let's just call it a night before we both say something we'll regret later."

"Lacy, if I said something to hurt you, I'm sorry," Brody said softly as he lifted his fingers and gently touched her cheek. "I'd never intentionally hurt you." His gray eyes shining like polished silver held her gaze, he leaned forward, brushing his lips against her's.

Just as he did, they heard voices from behind the door and they knew someone was about to intrude on their moment. He dropped his hand, stepping back, but he didn't break eye contact.

"Soon Lacy," he said with assurance. "Very, very soon, you're going to stop running away." Then without another word he reentered the building just as the others were leaving.

Lacy quickly turned and walked to her car, more certain than ever, Brody Langford wanted more in a relationship from her than she was ready to give. Yet, somehow she sensed even if she were ready Brody wouldn't be the one. And she didn't want to analyze the reason why.

She was almost home when she remembered the meeting at her Aunt's. She hadn't seen Rainy back at the station and suspected she'd gone straight home after the accident. If she knew her aunt, it was because she was still planning to have the meeting.

Lacy doubted there would be many others there. Some would jump at the excuse of the accident preventing them from coming. Others never made meetings anyway. She knew her father was at a County Chief's meeting so he couldn't attend. It could very easily be just herself and her aunt and uncle.

And probably Ryan, she thought, remembering he was now helping on her aunt's committee. She had seen him at the accident call too, though she doubted that would prevent him from making the meeting. Somehow she didn't picture him as the type to make excuses once he said there was something he was going to do.

As she rounded the corner she spotted a familiar black Toyota just pulling into her aunt's driveway. He waited as she pulled her car in beside him.

"How's the baby doing?" he asked with genuine concern.

She gave him the details and noticed his taut features relax slightly as he got the news. "Hope the mother makes out as well," he said.

She did too, but from the way Brody talked, it was far less likely.

"Before we go inside there's something I wanted to show you," Ryan said as he pulled the folded page out of his pocket. He opened it, then handed it to Lacy, pointing out the award that had earlier caught his attention. "I couldn't help but think it would be nice to nominate Rainy for this."

Lacy read the information, nodding. "I agree. . .but," she looked up at him with a smile. "Some might say I'm biased because we're related. It would be the same, if not worse, if Dad suggested nominating her."

"It only says the person must be a member of the state association and nominated by a Chief," Ryan refolded the page. "I'd say we have several in the borough who would go along with nominating her. I'd at least like to talk to a couple of them and see what they think."

"I'm sure Arlen would go along with it," she said, feeling her earlier tension dissolving. "As for the others," she shrugged. "Maybe Friendship's chief. She's been doing a lot of programs in his section of the borough. He seems pretty keen on fire safety, but like most officers, he's often too busy to do much himself." Except officers like you, she thought, knowing Ryan was busy too, yet he made time to help on the committee.

"I'll talk to Arlen first and we'll go from there," Ryan said enthusiastically.

Lacy smiled feeling much better than when she had arrived. He seemed to have a way of making bad things good and wrong things right.

CHAPTER TWELVE

The fourth arose as a warm, muggy morning, after a long night filled with thunderstorms. Everyone involved with the Fourth of July celebration had been on pins and needles, hoping the weather would be fit enough for the weekend of events to go as planned.

Thankfully the storm had remained in the distance the previous night, just long enough so the Schuylkill Valley Symphony Orchestra could play its last strain. Drum beats blended with the approaching thunder adding a certain intensity to the music. The first drops of rain finally fell just as everyone was leaving their seats.

Fortunately spirits were high. No one seemed to mind the impending storm. It would mean a break in the heat and humidity. Even if it were only a temporary reprieve.

Now, as the sun rose high in the sky, the moisture from the previous night's storm turned to steam rising from the grassy field where most of the day's events would be held. But first, there would be a huge parade. Every piece of fire apparatus, rescue truck and ambulance in town, and several from the outlying township fire companies would join in the long procession, marking the beginning of the holiday celebrations.

Lacy felt the anticipation of the day as she fed Mikie his breakfast. It was their special time, and she enjoyed it, laughing at the funny faces her four month old son made as he tasted the new flavors and textures of foods she put into his mouth. His tiny pink tongue seemed to curl around the soft food, always pushing more outward than what went in.

Her mother came into the kitchen carrying a large box for the cakes and pies they'd baked for the Ladies Auxiliary bake sale that day. It was the first time her mother had ever helped with anything associated with the fire company, but then Lacy supposed she had little choice in the matter.

It had been Lacy who'd begun the baking early the previous morning. She'd helped Lois bake before, but she'd never been as accomplished at it as her mother. By the time Lois came into the kitchen to see how she was doing, she had already covered every bit of counter space with freshly rolled pastry crusts.

"My Goodness, Lacy, are you going to fill all these pie shells?" her mother asked, her blue eyes bright with disbelief. "You'll be baking till midnight tonight."

Lacy tensed at her mother's disapproving tone. For months she had felt useless. Finally when she started doing something worthwhile, her mother was finding fault in it. Or, was it just the building tension between them.

"Then I'll be here till midnight," Lacy snapped, wiping perspiration from her brow. The temperatures and humidity, not to mention the hot oven, only added to her irritation. "At least I'm doing something on my own."

"Well you've certainly gone to an extreme this time," her mother chided. "How will you manage to take care of the baby with all this work?"

"You're here, Mom," Lacy replied as her spine stiffened and she took a breath. *What more does he need?*

"Of course I'll take care of him for you."

You always do, even when I'm not busy baking a zillion pastries. Lacy bit back her angry retort, feeling tears sting her sapphire eyes. The last thing she wanted to do was start crying. What was wrong with her lately?

"I could take Mikie with me," her father offered.

Lacy turned, surprised that she hadn't heard him enter the room. Then again, she had been focusing all her energies on not picking a fight with her mother.

"I don't have to be in the office today. I was just going to go check on some of the preparations for the weekend."

Lacy turned and smiled at her dad. She suspected he had picked up on the tension. Then again, why shouldn't he? The house had been filled with it lately.

"That might be a good idea," her mother replied, glancing again at the counter covered with pie shells. "Then I'd be able to chip in here and help Lacy." She looked up at her daughter.

Lacy met her gaze. "You don't have to help me, Mom," she said sarcastically. "After all, these are for the fire company."

Lois frowned. "All the more reason I should help. From the number of pie shells you've got here, it should make up for all the years I didn't bake."

"If you're sure you want to," Lacy replied, pushing a wisp of damp, honey-gold hair out of her face.

Lois smiled grimly. "If you're sure you want me to."

"Whatever you decide," Carl said as he looked from his wife to his daughter. "Just remember to save one of those for me."

"The whole thing?" Lacy laughed.

"What about your cholesterol?" His wife chided.

He looked contrite, then shrugged and sighed. "Okay, I'll share it."

They all ended up laughing at his begrudging reply. In that instant the tension dissolved and the rest of the day Lacy and her mother had worked in harmony. In fact, by the time they were finished, Lois had even suggested they bake a few extra things.

Now, Lacy smiled, watching her mother packing the two types of pastries they had baked; gooey molasses, wet-bottomed shoo-fly pies and chocolate-bottomed funny cakes topped with moist yellow cake.

Yesterday, had been a nice day. The kind of day she'd always wanted to spend with her mother.

She sighed, wishing it didn't have to be strictly on her mother's terms. It didn't have to be Lacy fitting into her mother's mold.

She spooned the last of Mikie's rice cereal with bananas into his mouth then cleaned his chubby cheeks with the wash cloth she always kept at close hand when feeding him. "Well, young man, you did very good this morning. You ate every bit."

The tiny dark-haired child cooed his pleasure, as though knowing his mother had just given him a compliment. Before she could take off his messy bib he grabbed it and pulled it toward his cherub face, once again smearing the sticky cereal onto his chin.

"I think I did this backward." Lacy laughed. "I should have taken your bib off first."

Again the child cooed his pleasure, laughing along with his mother.

"I'm one very lucky mother to have you," Lacy spoke to her son as she removed his bib then again cleaned his face. "Even if you are a messy eater."

"All babies are messy eaters," her mother informed her. "You should have seen yourself when you were his age."

"I can imagine, goo from head to toe."

Her mother nodded. "That's about it. You grabbed at everything. The spoon, then your clothing, your hair. I even had to wrap a towel around myself to keep you from getting me all full of your food."

Lacy turned to her son. "Don't you get any ideas."

"Was I a good eater?" Lacy asked. "In spite of the mess, did I eat a lot of different foods."

"Nearly everything. The way you ate, I was afraid you had a tape worm."

"Mom!"

"Really," her mother continued, her eyes sparkling bright from the memory. "We even took you to the doctor to find out if something was wrong. I was really afraid of over-feeding you. So I cut down, then you always seemed hungry."

"So what was wrong?"

"Nothing. The doctor said as long as you were active and didn't gain more weight than was considered normal, I didn't have to worry. He

161

suggested I just be careful not to give you foods with too many empty calories."

"So you gave me a lot of vegetables?"

Her mother nodded as she put another pastry in the box. "You loved them."

"Hear that," Lacy turned to her son. "You're supposed to like your vegetables."

It had only been a a week since she'd started feeding him jarred vegetables. He liked carrots the best, green beans he barely tolerated, and he spit out every spoon of spinach she gave him, eventually refusing to open his mouth at all. It was a trait he must have inherited from his father, she had thought. The greener the vegetable, the less Mike had liked it.

Mikie picked that moment to stick out his tiny pink tongue. Both Lacy and her mother broke into laughter.

"I guess he told you," her mother said.

"Yeah, body language," Lacy agreed, then wrinkled up her lightly freckled nose. "I think he's sending me another message that it's time to change his diaper." She lifted her son from his high chair. "I'll get him changed and dressed for the parade, then I'll be down and help you with those before we leave for the station."

"I told you, you didn't have to take him with you," Lois said. "I'm more than happy to watch him for you."

"I thought he'd like the parade."

"You're not actually taking him along in the parade, are you?"

Lacy ignored the tension that had again entered her mother's voice. "No, Mom. I'm not going in the parade. I'm going to watch. Then after the parade we'll go to the park for the rest of the festivities."

"Don't you think that will be a bit too much for him in one day?"

Lacy sighed. "I'm taking him in his stroller. If he gets tired I'll put the seat back and let him nap."

"But he'd rest much better here in his own bed."

Lacy silently counted to ten, something she'd started doing a lot lately with the growing tension between herself and her mother. "If he seems uncomfortable, I'll bring him home." Without waiting to see if her mother accepted her decision she left the room and went into the hallway.

"Be patient with her," her father said as she passed him. "She means well."

Realizing he must have heard their exchange, Lacy nodded, forcing a grim smile. "I know, Dad. But that doesn't make it any easier."

Silently she turned and hurried up the stairs. She had been looking forward to spending the day with Mikie. By evening she'd be on call in the event they needed an extra ambulance crew, and it was almost certain they would. There was always an increase in emergency calls over a holiday.

She'd also agreed to join Brody and two others on duty at the park the following day. This way the members of the volunteer crew who worked today would have time to enjoy some of the festivities too. They kept an ambulance on stand-by at the park both days in the event of an emergency there.

"Today is our day, kiddo," she said to her son as she placed him on his dressing table. "We're going to have a great time."

#

They had made their way through most of the park, looking at the exhibits, watching the shows. Just after lunch, she had found a shady willow tree near the bank of the Manatawny Creek, and stopped for a rest. Mikie was growing restless and she knew it was time for him to settle down for a brief nap.

As he slept she leaned back against the tree, closing her eyes too. She hadn't really dozed. She had been more in a state of total relaxation, yet completely aware of things going on around her. It was at this point she sensed the presence of someone close by.

Forcing her eyes open she saw Ryan standing a few feet away, looking down at her son. His eyes were hidden behind dark glasses, yet she had the strangest feeling his expression was sad. Was he remembering that night four months ago? she wondered. Was he sorry he hadn't been able to go back inside and save Mike?

She hoped he wasn't blaming himself. She had never thought of that before.

He turned to her. Seeing she was awake he came closer. "I'm sorry, I didn't mean to disturb you."

She smiled without hesitation. "With all the activity going on you were hardly disturbing me."

"I think you found the most quiet spot," Ryan acknowledged. "It's peaceful here."

"Care to join me?" She patted the ground beside her. "This was my father's favorite fishing spot when I was a child."

"You were reminiscing." He sat down in the shade, slipping the sunglasses into the breast pocket of his shirt.

She shook her head. "A little. Mostly I was giving Mikie a chance to nap. He was getting tired. I was afraid I'd have to take him home."

"And miss our program."

163

Lacy thought a moment, then remembered. Aunt Rainy had told her she was having a couple of fire safety demonstrations later that afternoon. Knowing there wouldn't be many from her committee available that day, she'd asked her to help.

Lacy pulled a face. "I'm glad you reminded me. I had so much on my mind, I nearly forgot."

"I think she's getting used to people forgetting to show up when she has a program scheduled."

"It's one thing when the others forget. It's another thing entirely when family forgets," Lacy replied.

"I'm sure your Aunt would have understood."

"She would. But I'd be angry with myself if I missed it. I've acquired a healthy respect for what she does since . . ." She shrugged. "Once it hits home you look at it a little differently."

"I got the impression you were always supportive of her work."

"I was supportive because I love my Aunt. I did it for her. Like when she had surgery and couldn't do any programs. I chipped in and helped because we're family. Now, I really believe in what she's doing. Too bad I had to be hit on the head with a tragedy to realize a fire prevented could mean a life saved."

"You're not alone. Sometimes that's what it takes," Ryan replied grimly.

"You're talking about yourself, aren't you?" Lacy turned to face him squarely. "I never thought of how difficult it must have been for you the night Mike was killed."

"What?" Ryan had wondered how she had guessed his secret, then was surprised when he realized she meant the fire that had killed her husband.

"You started helping Aunt Rainy right after that fire."

"Let's just say her timing was good," Ryan replied. "But I guess, it was one of the reasons I decided to help her."

"She didn't have to twist your arm very hard," Lacy continued. "She says you've been great. Most of the others aren't as willing to help her."

Ryan frowned. "So I've heard. . . Tell me, is it true someone actually confronted her once and told her she shouldn't be doing fire prevention. . . That it's not part of our job."

Lacy rolled her blue eyes skyward, remembering the occasion. "That someone was Woody Brown. And his exact words were that it wasn't our job to prevent fires, only to put them out."

Ryan shook his head in disgust.

"Oh, it got worse." Lacy remembered. "How she kept her cool I'll never know. Especially after he said she should be spending more time helping her fire company rather than running around the community putting on shows, trying to make a name for herself."

Ryan whistled. "Knowing your Aunt, as I do now, I find it hard to believe she didn't let into him."

Lacy burst out laughing, remembering that day. "No, Uncle Mark had a hold of her arm so she couldn't do anything drastic. I was a bigger problem."

"You? What happened?" Rainy hadn't told him about that. His curiosity grew.

Lacy frowned. "I was suspended for a month."

"Why?"

She sighed. "I told him my aunt had more intelligence than he did and all those like him wrapped into one. That she went out and really did something for the community, rather than sit around doing nothing."

"That doesn't sound so bad to be suspended."

She looked up blushing. "That was the edited version. I'm not very proud of what I actually said."

Ryan had difficulty keeping from laughing. "I see, so you were suspended."

Now Lacy's frown deepened, as more of the unpleasant memory returned. Barry Carlisle had been there during the exchange. He had suspended her on the spot for unacceptable behavior for a member. She'd been so furious it took every last strength to maintain some semblance of control.

She had known she still had one recourse. She could file a grievance with the fire company and request a hearing. She could win based on the fact that she had justifiable cause to lose her temper. Woody's statements had been uncalled for.

But the worst part of all had been that her own husband had agreed she was wrong. At that time he was a Trustee of the company and would be sitting on the grievance committee. He could decline to vote because of conflict of interest. That would be in order if he were going to vote in favor of his wife. But he made it clear that wouldn't be the case.

Lacy turned away from Ryan. Picking up a stone she tossed it into the water, watching the tiny circles of water start out small where the stone had disappeared beneath the water, and grow as they moved away. Like the effect of that incident had grown between her and Mike.

"If it's any consolation, Lacy," Ryan said softly, breaking into her deep thought. "I'd say you were right in what you said. Just wrong in the way you said it."

She turned to him with a forced smile. "Tact was never one of my strong suits."

165

His smile grew, reaching his eyes and making them shine like emeralds. "I'm beginning to realize that."

She glanced toward her son. "I'm trying to do better, though. You know . . . to set a good example for my son." She shrugged. "It's just hard sometimes."

"Woody has a way tripping people's triggers," Ryan acknowledged. "You aren't the first. Probably won't be the last."

"Yeah, too bad for you he's worming his way back at the station." Lacy again rolled her blue eyes skyward, a sign of disgust she showed so often when regarding Woody Brown. "At least I saw him riding the pumper in this morning's parade."

"He's been around a lot lately."

"Friendship is probably counting their blessings. – Ooops." Lacy pressed her hand to her lips, looking contrite as she lowered it again. "I did say something about trying harder to use tact."

"Well, I don't think you have to worry about setting a bad example this time." Ryan looked at the tiny, dark-haired child sound asleep in his stroller. "He's down for the count."

"Probably all this fresh air and sunshine."

"I guess I'll see you later," Ryan said as he slowly rose from his seat beside her. He didn't want to leave. It had felt good sharing these past moments with Lacy. And that was all the more reason he should leave.

Mikie slept for another half hour, awaking abruptly, startled by a loud popping sound near by. A small child started to cry, probably from disappointment at losing her colorful balloon. Her son joined in the sad refrain, more from fright than commiseration.

After calming him down and changing him into a fresh diaper, Lacy glanced at her watch and saw that it was nearly two o'clock. If she didn't hurry she'd be late to help her aunt with the fire safety program.

When she arrived at the area sectioned off for their use, she saw Aunt Rainy and Ryan already at work. She watched as Ryan sat on the ground surrounded by several young children as he talked about what to do if their clothing caught fire. She smiled, as she saw him actually demonstrate Stop, Drop and Roll for his audience.

Not for the first time she noted he had a real rapport with children. They all seemed to be listening intently as he spoke, laughing at the right times, serious at others.

She was happy to see Colin Smith standing in front of a group of people showing them several varieties of fire extinguishers. It was always good to have the support of a local chief.

Quickly she turned her attention to her Aunt. From what she remembered, she was scheduled to present a new program for parents of infants and toddlers. "Baby Bag," she had called it.

Lacy wished she could have paid more attention. From what she saw it looked quite interesting, not to mention humorous. Her aunt was in the process of putting on a tiny red baseball cap and a child's pair of bright blue sun glasses.

She knew she had better get on with her own assignment. She was to help Uncle Mark and her younger cousin, Brad, with a demonstration about crawling under smoke. The two were already opening the dark blanket they would use to represent smoke. It had been decided she would do the crawling. At the same time she'd use Mikie to demonstrate how a child could save a younger brother or sister's life by helping get them to safety.

Since neither of the males preferred doing the talking, she explained how when there is a fire, smoke rises high toward the ceiling, filling the room from the top to the bottom. The blanket was raised and slowly lowered as she spoke.

She then explained how smoke is black preventing someone from seeing where they were going. At this point the two dropped the blanket over her head completely. She took a few awkward steps, reaching around her as though trying to find her direction.

Then she showed them how if they crawled they had less smoke to choke and blind them.

"Smoke kills more people than fire," she explained. "Does anyone know why?"

A few older children raised their hands. She pointed to a little flaxen-haired girl in a pink polka-dot sun suit.

"Cause you can't breath," the child responded.

Lacy smiled. "Very good. Now does anyone know why you can't breath?"

A few less hands raised this time. Lacy chose an energetic young boy who's bright red hair had been shaved on the sides, spiked on the top and long in the back.

"The smoke chokes ya," he replied.

"It sure does," she continued. "You're really a smart group."

The kids were all smiles at the compliment, the boy who responded puffed his chest out with pride.

"I've got a tougher question this time," she replied. "Why does the smoke choke you?"

A second boy, who could have been a twin to the first except his hair was black, raised his hand. Lacy pointed to him.

"The smoke's got all kinds of poison and junk in it."

"I can't pull anything over on you guys today," Lacy continued. "How about one more question, then we'll all try crawling under our pretend smoke. . . How many of you think you'd smell the smoke before it got too bad?"

Nearly all the children raised their hand.

Lacy smiled. "I got you there. . .The fact is, there are invisible gasses in the air that travel even faster than the smoke. Those gases actually deaden your sense of smell, so when the smoke gets to you, you can't smell it, and it doesn't wake you up." Lacy reached into a box. "But, there is something that can sense those invisible gases. I'll bet you all know what this is." She held up a smoke detector.

Most of the children yelled the answer.

"And what do you have to do to make sure your smoke detector is working?"

"Change your batteries," they chanted in near-unison.

"How many of you have one of these at home?" After most of the children raised their hand she asked how many were sure their smoke detector was working. A few hands went down. "Before you leave today, I have a little booklet that tells you everything you need to know to make sure your smoke detector is working properly. I hope you'll all take one with you and give it to your parents."

After that the children each took turns crawling beneath the slowly lowering blanket, trying to get to the area marked exit before it completely covered them. Lacy even allowed two girls to place Mikie on a blanket, as she had done, and carefully drag him with them, as though they were saving a younger sibling.

By the time she was finished Lacy brushed off her jeans and looked around at a new group of children forming. They had seen the ones before them and were draw over out of curiosity. It always happened like that. There were the ones who saw that the program was listed and made certain they were there. Then others followed, drawn by the activity.

Among the group of spectators she caught a glimpse of her father and mother. She was surprised to find her mother listening so intently to Aunt Rainy's presentation. She was even laughing as her aunt got down on the ground, struggling into a crouched position, then pulled something else from inside a giant diaper bag. Her "Baby Bag", Lacy assumed.

Lacy was more curious than ever about her Aunt's new program. After all, she too was a parent of a young baby. There could be something she didn't know. Well, she decided, she'd just have to ask her mother about it later.

She smiled, liking that thought. It wasn't often she'd be able to go to her mother for something related to fire. Perhaps, this time, it wouldn't be such a sore subject.

#

"I guess I should have expected as much, knowing Rainy," her mother enthusiastically explained that evening after Lacy had put Mikie down for the night. "I couldn't believe it when she put on that hat and those sunglasses."

"I saw that part." Lacy joined her mother's laughter. "I wondered what she was doing."

"Reminding parents that small children should wear something to protect their heads and eyes when they're out in the sun for prolonged periods."

"Mikie hates his hat, but fortunately he doesn't know how to untie it," Lacy said, thinking of the way her son had first tried to pull off his hat that day, and his irritation at being unsuccessful. "I'd probably have a terrible time keeping sunglasses on him."

"That's what another mother said," Lois explained. "But Rainy said a baby's eyes are very sensitive to the sun. Imagine what it's like for us, then imagine it being worse for them."

Lacy frowned, wishing she had thought of that. "You don't think I hurt Mikie's eyes do you?"

Her mother smiled, shaking her head. "Honey, you had a hat with a wide brim on Mikie, as well as a stroller with a canopy."

"Yeah, thanks to the Mulholland's." Lacy remembered. "That was their gift at my baby shower."

"Yes, and you were smart enough to leave the canopy on," her mother continued. "A lot of the parents out there today either took them off their strollers or didn't have any in the first place."

"Remember that one baby we saw," Carl said as he entered the room and picked up on the conversation.

"Oh, yes. That poor thing." Lois winced, shaking her head.

"They were at the ambulance for medical attention," Carl explained. "That little gal who drives the ambulance hardly knew how to touch the kid."

Lacy thought of Annie, who had been on duty that day. "Brody said we should expect that sunburn would be the majority of what we get at the first aid station."

"Hope you don't end up with any more like that." Carl frowned. "They took that one to the hospital."

"That bad!" Lacy sat up stiffly in her chair. "I guess I was lucky having Mikie out there all day. Maybe I should have listened to you, Mom."

169

Lois briefly glanced toward her husband and back to Lacy again, her blue eyes narrowing hesitantly. "I don't think you have anything to worry about. During the hottest part of the day you stayed in the shade."

"Yeah, I sat down by the river while Mikie napped. If you saw me, why didn't you stop?" *To check up on how Mikie was doing.* She didn't add, not wanted to ruin the harmony of their conversation.

The corners of Carl's mouth curled into a slight smile of approval. "Didn't want to interrupt. You were pretty deep in conversation."

"Oh, with Ryan," Lacy said, watching her mother sit forward slightly, as though anxious to hear more. For the strangest reason she felt her cheeks grow warm and it irritated her. She had no reason to be embarrassed because she had talked to a man. My goodness, at the station she'd been with men all the time. They were all like brothers. "We talked about Aunt Rainy and fire prevention."

"You better not let her hear you say that," Carl teased. "It's fire safety education."

"Pub-Ed." Lacy laughed, pointing her finger to accent her words. "To those of us who work in the field."

Her mother watched the exchange and shrugged. "I guess I've missed out on a lot. I haven't the foggiest idea what you're talking about. Fire prevention, fire safety education, pub-ed. What's the difference?"

Lacy explained. "You see, for years we called what we did fire prevention. But then we started to learn, we're not really preventing fires. Hopefully the people we teach are preventing fires by practicing good safety habits."

"The department sent Rainy to school a couple of years back. To the National Fire Academy in Maryland," Carl explained. "Right after I became Fire Chief and she approached me about a joint fire prevention committee."

"Fire Safety Education Committee," Lois corrected, showing more interest than she'd ever had before.

"No, it was still fire prevention then." Her husband laughed. "It became fire safety education after she returned from her course two weeks later. After that prevention became my job, getting new codes and enforcement of those codes through more inspections. She took charge of the education end of things."

"I remember when she was away." Lois nodded. "I watched the boys after school until Mark came home from work."

"Yes, and you said they were such monsters, you were happy you never had a son." Lacy reminded her, laughing at the vision of her mother's bedraggled appearance when she returned each night after caring for her nephews.

It was her mother's turn to laugh. "I think it was a case of while the cat's away," she said. "They had never acted that wild when Rainy was with them. I used to tell Carl we had more of a problem raising a Tom-boy than his sister and her husband had raising the actual thing."

"I wasn't that bad?" Lacy's mouth dropped open.

"Exactly. . ." Lois made a face. "After that, I realized you weren't nearly as bad as they were. I decided you weren't so bad after all."

"By then I should have outgrown my rowdiness. Besides I had an outlet for my energies."

Lois's smile faded at the reminder of her daughter membership in the fire company. She had wanted to forbid her to do it, but knew it wouldn't do any good. It was Carl who convinced her that it was better to have Lacy learn how to do things the right way than to hang around the station and eventually get into a situation she didn't know how to handle.

They both knew that was a possibility. The girl had on more than one occasion attempted some type of minor rescue. Fortunately it was usually rescuing a neighborhood pet from some form of disaster, each attempt getting more daring. Then there had been her last good deed before being allowed to join.

Lacy had been on her way home from school when she'd heard a woman cry out for help. She looked up to the window of the old house and saw that a baby had crawled out onto a dilapidated porch roof. One of the baby boy's tiny legs had gone through a hole in the roof and it looked like it wouldn't take much for him to fall the rest of the way through.

The mother, who looked to be at least three-hundred pounds, was about to crawl out the window after her child. Lacy knew beyond a doubt that the roof would not withstand such weight. She had yelled for the woman to wait, falsely identified herself as a firefighter and told the woman she would get the child.

Lying flat, she slid out on the porch to the child, dislodged its leg and brought him safely back inside to the mother. It was then she realized what trouble she'd be in if anyone found out she had falsely impersonated a firefighter.

Her solution was to boldly tell the woman she would forget the entire incident happened if the woman saw to it that her porch was properly stabilized and repaired. She said she didn't like people making a big deal out of it when she saved someone's life. So, if the woman remained silent, she'd do the same and not report the condition of the roof to the building inspector.

Lacy hadn't counted on the fact that a neighbor would call the newspaper to report her heroics. By the time they got there, Lacy had gone, and the mother stuck to her agreement and didn't admit a thing. Unfortunately, the reporter wasn't about to give up his story so easily. He questioned other neighbors and learned that one of them thought he had recognized the blonde-haired girl who had made the rescue as one who was often at the neighborhood fire station.

From there he'd gone to the Fire Chief of the closest fire station – her father – to obtain information on the girl who had made the daring rescue. Needless to say it took some fast talking and a few owed favors to get the newspaperman to forget about writing his story.

Yes, after that, Carl was more certain than ever it would be far better to have his daughter join the department's junior firefighter program than to have her daring things on her own without the proper training.

That was what had finally convinced Lois. She never agreed that she should join. But she knew her husband was right. Her Tom-boy daughter would have a better chance of surviving till she out-grew this difficult phase, if she had the proper training and supervision to do it.

Lois sighed, wishing she could forget the many frightening times she'd waited to make certain her daughter arrived home safely from an emergency call. It had been bad enough worrying about her husband. But to have her daughter do the same, was almost more than she could bare.

"Thank goodness you've now got a better outlet for those energies, right upstairs," Lois acknowledged.

Lacy frowned, unable to look her mother in the face. She hated what she always saw there. The disapproval. The disappointment. It would be worse if she knew how much Lacy missed being active with the fire company. She would never understand.

"In fact, I don't see why you even bother running around with the ambulance," Lois continued. "Seeing all those people suffering. All that blood and gore."

Lacy got up from her chair, knowing now was the time to leave, before she and her mother got into another disagreement. "Well, with Mikie to keep me busy, I don't have much time for that either," she said stiffly, trying to keep the bitterness out of her voice. She turned and started to leave the room.

"You make it sound like he's a burden standing in your way."

Lacy squeezed her eyes closed, fighting the threatening tears. She refused to look back at her mother. "You misunderstood, Mom. I love my son, and for him, I'd give up the emergency service completely if I had to." *But I don't have to.* "As it is, my time away is no different than any other working mother."

"Yes, but most of them get paid for what they do," Lois added.

Lacy started to turn stiffly back to her mother, her hands clenched into fists at her sides. It was on the tip of her tongue to tell her mother she didn't want to turn into her. Devoting so much of herself to her child that when that child no longer depended on her so completely, she was left with nothing. As though her only worth was through her family.

Then Lacy saw her father's brown eyes pleading with her not to lose her temper. She swallowed her anger, and forced a smile.

"Maybe if I'm lucky. . ." Or, unlucky, she thought. "I'll get the next paid opening with the ambulance squad. For now, I better get some sleep. I'll be on duty tomorrow."

"Yes, you don't have to remind us," Lois said after her. "All right, Carl. . . I know. . . I did it again." Lacy heard her mother's faint acknowledgment as she headed up the stairs. "I can't help it if I worry."

Lacy sighed. Wishing for the millionth time her mother wouldn't worry so much, yet knowing someday she'd do the same for her child. She only hoped she wouldn't be so verbal about it, making him wish he were something he didn't want to be, just to keep her happy.

She wondered, as she did so often why she had such difficulty being the person other people wanted her to be. The sweet, well-mannered, feminine, June Cleaver-type, her mother wanted her to be. Or, the super, bring home the bacon, fry it up in the pan, always let him know he's your man – as long as you don't do any of it better than me – type of woman Mike had wanted.

As always, she had no answer.

CHAPTER THIRTEEN

Lacy dressed in a pair of old well-worn jeans and an extra-large tee shirt that had once been solid red, but now was speckled with white paint. The giant shirt had been a favorite during her pregnancy. The speckles of white were from the last time she'd worn it, when she painted what was to be Mikie's nursery.

She thought of that room, wondering what it looked like now. After he offered to rent the house, she had told Ryan to make any changes he wanted to make. She wanted him to think of the house as his home not her's.

Besides, today she had plenty to do to get ready for the company picnic. After her baking adventure for the ladies' auxiliary's Fourth of July bake sale, she'd been encouraged to attempt something more challenging. Of course, she was hoping that once again her mother would chip in and lend a hand as she did three weeks earlier.

As if on cue her mother came into the kitchen, smiling as she took in the assortment of mixing bowls and other utensils. "So, what's on the menu today?"

"About the best thing I know how to make is veal parmesan," Lacy said, remembering the last time she had made the dish. "I haven't had much success with anything else."

Her mother's eyes rounded. "That's a pretty costly dish for a large picnic."

Lacy laughed. "I know, I tried calculating the cost and gave up around astronomical. I decided to improvise and make egg plant parmesan. What do you think?"

"I think the men will adore you," Carl said as he entered the room carrying Mikie. "Look who just woke up."

Lacy smiled, reaching out to her son. He spread out his arms to go to her.

"Looks like he's already wearing a dry diaper," she acknowledge after checking. "Thanks Dad."

"Figured I couldn't cause any punture wounds with those plastic stickies they have on those throw-away diapers." Carl went to the pot and poured himself a cup of coffee. "You really going to make egg plant for the picnic?" He wrinkled up his nose as he turned back to her.

"Of course she is, and a lot of people will love it," Lois replied to her husband. "Not everyone is as finicky an eater as some people we know."

"Do you think I'd be better off making something else?" Lacy asked, as she settled her son in his high chair. She thought about the three large purple-colored egg plants in the bottom of the refrigerator.

"They probably won't even know what they're eating," Lois said. "I'd suspect they'll all be too busy drinking and telling dirty jokes."

Carl shook his head and frowned. "Might even be too busy molesting small children," he added sarcastically. "Better keep a close eye on Mikie."

His wife turned back to her husband, her face burning as she sighed. "I did it again. I'm sorry." There was no doubting the sincerity in her voice.

Lacy watched the exchange while she mixed her son's cereal. In recent weeks her mother had been making an attempt to be more open toward the fire company. In fact, this would be the first fire company picnic she'd willingly agreed to attend, though she had insisted it was only to help keep an eye on her grandson, and not because she thought he'd be molested.

"What were you going to make, Mom?" Lacy said, hoping to change the subject and reduce the tension. In all the years she could remember, the fire company seemed to be the only thing her mother and father had ever argued over.

She used to feel sorry for her father. But now, looking at her mother, she thought she understood. It must have been difficult for her thinking she played second fiddle to a fire. All those years feeling she couldn't compete. When, in reality, she didn't have to.

It had been worse when her father was a volunteer. Now, at least, he was only doing his job. The job that paid the mortgage and put food in their mouths.

But perhaps part of her understanding had come from several of the long talks she and Lacy had had. Times when Lacy tried to explain how she felt.

"Dealing in life and death makes you treasure what you have all the more," she'd said, and her mother had considered her statement a long time before admitting she'd never thought of it that way.

"I thought a garden salad would be nice," her mother drew her attention back to the subject at hand. "Can't quite go against my principals." She laughed, relaxing again. "There will probably be enough cholesterol dished up today."

Carl groaned, but when Lacy looked at him there were golden flecks in his brown eyes, belying his return to good humor. "Egg plant. . . Garden salad. . ." he grumbled. "With you two around I'll be lucky if I can sneak something that has a little good-ol'-fashioned grease."

"Today you're on your own, Mister," Lois replied, her sapphire eyes sparkling with good-humor. "I'm going to be busy enough with the baby."

"Wait a minute, Mom," Lacy paused as she was about to put the first spoonful of cereal into her son's mouth. "I thought we agreed, we'd take turns with Mikie. Besides . . ." She looked lovingly down at her son as he waited impatiently for his breakfast. "There's no one I'd rather spend my day with."

"Well, you two hash it out between you," Carl said, making a quick escape to the door. "I've promised to help take some chairs and tables out to the park this morning. I'll be back in time to shower and change."

"Mom, you really don't have to spend the entire day with Mikie and me," Lacy said as soon as her father left. "I think it would be nice to let Dad show you around. You might be surprised to find some of the members aren't as bad as you think."

"You act like I don't know any of them," Lois reminded her as she stuck her head in the refrigerator and came out again with a bag full of onions. "I've been around long enough to have gotten to know quite a few."

Lacy wasn't going to ask what she thought of them. She knew her mother had never been overly fond of Barry Carlisle, even though he had been Mike's best friend. Whenever he stopped by to visit Mike while her mother was at their house, she'd find an excuse to do something in another room.

In truth, it had been all she could do to stand her husband's boasting friend. Or, to bare his constant jibes about women in the fire service. Lacy had to bit her tongue more than once.

Lacy suspected her mother's feelings hadn't mellowed in light of recent events. As for herself, Barry probably would never be one of her favorite people either, but she did have to give him credit for one thing – he'd been man enough to thank her for getting him off the hook with Rose.

The thought of the other woman caused mixed emotions, ranging from empathy to hatred, though she knew that was wrong. In spite of her feelings, she did feel sorry for the life Rose must have lived. It was the only life she'd ever really known. Her mother had been even more laxed in her morals, even while her husband had been alive. Rose had had a terrible role model.

Lacy looked at her mother and knew it was just the opposite for her. She'd had an excellent role model in her mother. If only she'd been as successful as Rose living up to her mother's example.

"Honey, you suddenly look so glum," her mother said, rousing her from her thoughts. There were tears in her eyes, but Lacy suspected they were from the onions she was peeling. "I promise I'm going to be on good behavior today. I won't pick on any of your father's and your friends."

Lacy forced a smile, hoping that was true. More for her father's sake than her own. "You know there's going to be music there later this evening," she said. "A few of the juniors belong to a local band. They promise to play lots of oldies but goodies. If I remember, you and Dad used to cut a pretty mean rug."

Lois's threw back her head and laughed. Her eyes bright with humor and tears. It had been a long time since she and her husband had danced. The last time had been at Lacy's wedding.

Lacy must have been thinking the same thing, for suddenly her smile was gone.

"I never understood how you got Dad to be so uninhibited on the dance floor," Lacy said, trying to break the solemnness of the memory. "You and he danced more than Mike and I that day."

"He had no choice but to learn to dance," Lois admitted, with no false modesty. "There were a lot of young men, before I married your father, who were willing to wait in line for a dance with me. And I certainly did enjoy dancing."

"I remember when I was – actually, I don't know how old I was, just that I was small – but I remember the way you'd turn the radio up and dance me around the room."

Lois laughed. "I'd dance with you. I'd dance with the vacuum cleaner. Sometimes with a mop. But it was with your father, I enjoyed dancing with most."

"Well today you might just have to wait in line," Lacy teased. "Dad's dance card fills up faster every year."

Her mother turned to her with surprise. "What have I been missing by not coming to these picnics?"

Lacy laughed, enjoying the look of shock on her mother's face. She wondered if she should tell her that it was she who danced most often with her father every year, since Mike hadn't liked to dance. And that when she wasn't dancing with him, several un-attached, widowed ladies from the auxiliary used to enjoy getting the Borough Fire Chief up to dance.

"Let's just say you may have a tough time keeping up," Lacy replied, trying to remember what one of those ladies had said to her the year before. "Mrs. Arthur says, there may be a little rust on her fenders, her engine has a miss, and her headlights are dim; but as long as she's running, she'll stay on the road."

"Now don't tell me," Lois said as she started chopping the onions she'd just peeled. "This Mrs. Arthur is the same one who's husband used to have the garage in town. The one who once did all the mechanical work on the fire trucks."

Lacy nodded, trying to hide her smile.

"Then she has to be at least. . ." Lois glanced at her daughter from over her shoulder. "eighty if she's a day."

"So you can stop crying, Mom," Lacy teased. "You have nothing to fear."

"That's easy for you to say." She sniffled, as tears streamed down her face.

#

"I'll bet that's Mrs. Arthur," Lois whispered to Lacy later that day. They had finished eating and were sitting at the picnic table just a few feet away from where her husband and Ryan had teamed up with two other men to play a game of quoits. The elderly woman had just shuffled over to get a closer look.

"How did you know?" Lacy asked.

"She has a hungry look in her eyes," her mother teased.

"Mom, you're bad," Lacy scolded. "I never knew you had it in you."

"There's a lot of things you don't know, young lady."

"Hey Lacy," Brody said as he came by their table, he nodded to her mother. "Mrs. MacDonald."

"Did you just get here?" Lacy asked.

"I took the early shift at the station so some of the others could come early with their families," he explained.

"Well there's plenty of food left," Lois said politely. "Why don't you get some, then you can come back and join us.

Lacy almost wished her mother hadn't been so polite. She didn't want to offer Brody any encouragement that may cause him to think of her as anything more than a friend. She feared he already did.

They had spent such a nice day, she didn't want it spoiled with tension. She looked over to her father and Ryan. If only they'd finish playing their game so they could help occupy some of Brody's attention.

Her father cheered, then she saw Ryan pat the man heartily on the back, before both of them extended their hands to their opponents.

"Great, why couldn't you lose?" she mumbled.

"What was that, Dear?" her mother asked.

Lacy's cheeks burned as she bit her lip. "I said, isn't that great. Dad and Ryan just won." Trying not to draw much attention she reached for Ryan's glass of birch beer and got up from her seat. "Here, give me Dad's glass. I'll bet they're both hot and thirsty."

Lois's eyes narrowed slightly as she handed her the glass. "What was that you said earlier about my acting like Daddy's maid when I got up and fetched him some salad?"

"I'll be right back." Lacy ignored her mother's statement.

She stood holding the two men's empty glasses as they started their second match. Silently she willed them not to win again. Glancing over her

178

shoulder she saw that Brody had taken the seat right next to her's. The one where Ryan had previously been sitting. If she had just left the glass there, he might have known the seat was taken.

Frowning she realized she wasn't acting at all like herself. She had always preferred the direct approach. Unfortunately the local emergency services picnic was not the place for that.

Turning she returned to the table, determined she wasn't going to ruin anyone's day. At that moment she spotted Woody Brown staring at her with a dark, evil glare. She wished she could say the same about her day not being ruined, she thought with a sudden chill.

"You a two-fisted drinker these days," Brody asked as she returned to her seat beside him, tightly clutching a plastic cup in each hand.

She forced a smile, placing her father's empty cup across from Brody, then placed Ryan's beside it. "No, I'm practicing being a waitress."

"Not nearly as fulfilling a profession as paramedic," Brody's gray eyes were teasing as he gave her an assessing gaze. His eyes narrowed ever so slightly. "You having second thoughts?"

"No," she lied, knowing that she was. "I'm joking."

He relaxed, returning his attention to his food. "So, tell me, what did you bring?"

"None of it's on your plate," she acknowledged after giving his platter a quick glance. "I brought the egg plant parmesan."

Brody made a face similar to the one her father had made that morning. "Oh, I saw the sign and thought I'd pass. I'm not much of an egg plant eater."

Lacy had decided to put a sign by her large dish after seeing Ryan's surprised look when he bit into his portion of the vegetarian version of the veal parmesan she'd served him once before. He had loved that, she remembered. It was probably why he'd taken such a large portion of this.

She had really begun to regret her choice of dishes to make that day when his shock had turned to a look of surprise. "Whoever made this, it's almost as good as the veal you make, Lacy," Ryan had said after he swallowed that first bite. "Wonder what's in it."

"Egg plant," she had told him, then laughed when she again saw his expression change. It was obvious he, too, did not prefer the vegetable.

"Never thought I'd see the day," he said, looking back down at his plate, then back at Lacy. "It's pretty good."

"Looks like you're not much of a vegetable eater at all," Lois scolded Brody, shaking her head. "I don't know about you men."

Lacy returned her attention to her companions, smiling as her mother gave Brody the same lecture about cholesterol as she had Ryan earlier that day and her father many times in the past.

"I'd say you better eat something green," Lacy whispered, when her mother turned her attention to Mikie as he started squirming in his stroller. She was hardly able to keep from laughing out loud.

"Is she always this way?" Brody asked, making a face. "My grandmother gave up telling me to eat my veggies when I was ten."

Lacy darted him a warning glance, refusing to answer while her mother was there.

"Mikie's getting restless. I'm going to take him for a walk," Lois said as she stood up from the table. She turned back to Brody with a smile and a twinkle in her blue eyes. "I'd say she shouldn't have given up so easily."

Lacy laughed at Brody's expression. "How did she hear that?" he asked.

"Brody, you wouldn't understand this, but it comes with being a parent. Right along with having eyes behind the head."

Brody's eyes narrowed as he glanced back at Lacy. "And mother's intuition."

"You got it."

He nodded. "In that case, I'll have to be extremely careful what I say, do, and think while your mother's around."

"You're forgetting, I'm a mother too," Lacy reminded him.

He pulled a face. "Then I really am in trouble."

There were cheers from the on-going game of quoits. Lacy turned to see the opposition raising their hands in the air. Obviously they had won.

Her father and Ryan laughed good-naturedly as they congratulated the two men from East End Station who had won that game. They turned and headed back to the table.

"Hello there, Brody," her father said with a beaming smile as he held out his right hand to the Rescue Chief.

"Hello, Sir." Brody took his hand, then turned to her father's companion and nodded. "Simon."

"You just get off duty?" Ryan asked as he, too, extended his hand to the Rescue Chief.

Brody nodded. "Yes, I was filling in so some of the others could come here earlier with their families."

"Which reminds me," Lacy started, happy for the perfect opening. "I'll go find Mom. She kidnapped Mikie."

"Yeah, tell her to get back here before the music starts," her father said, looking toward the corner of the pavilion where the young players of the band were busy setting up their equipment. "Looks like it won't be long."

"Okay, I'll tell her," Lacy said, then smiled impishly, her blue eyes alight with humor. "But I think she figured you wanted to save the first dance for Mrs. Arthur."

Her father held up his index finger and shook it at her in a scolding fashion. "You, young lady, better behave."

"Oh, I don't know about that." Ryan laughed as he locked eyes with her. "I kind of like her this way."

"Sure, the only one who can pick on the Big Chief and get away with it," she teased.

"I didn't say that," Ryan defended mischievously.

"What's this Big Chief stuff?" Carl bellowed, sucking in his gut. "I'll have you know, I've lost several pounds."

"Thanks to Mom making sure you get the right diet and exercise," Lacy responded. "Which is why I'm going to go and find her so you can work off a few more pounds on the dance floor." Without another word she turned and started to walk away.

"Speak for yourself young lady," her father called after her.

Lacy's mouth dropped open, but when she turned to retort, she saw that the two men with her father had their eyes glued to her backside. Suddenly her cheeks burned as she turned again and hurried on her way. She had put on a few pounds since she'd had Mikie but she didn't think that it showed.

She found her mother talking to several other women, one she recognized as Arlen's wife, was holding Mikie on her lap. She was quick to note that Woody Brown's pregnant wife was among them too.

Forcing a smile she joined them. They were talking about the money they made at the Fourth of July bake sale and making plans for another before Christmas. She was glad to see her mother joining in, offering to donate some of her baked goods to the sale.

Then the discussion changed to what they thought usually sold best. From there it went to their favorite recipes.

It didn't take long for Lacy to begin feeling out of place. Her culinary skills were rarely put to the test. And when they were, sometimes they didn't have the desired effect.

She thought of the pan of egg plant parmesan that, on last check, had still been half full. If only all the men were as easy to feed as Ryan, she thought, reminded of how much he seemed to enjoy their meals together the few times she'd cooked for him.

Mikie's patience at being held grew thin, and he started to squirm. Lacy politely took him from the other woman and placed him back in his stroller.

"I think I'd better go to the car and change him," she said.

Karla caught up with her as she walked away. "Hey, you did a great job on the egg plant parmesan," she said.

"You could have fooled me," she replied.

"What do you mean? It's all gone."

"All of it?" Lacy's eyes darted to the side of the table where all the hot foods had been kept.

"Yeah, I saw Ryan up there polishing it off."

Lacy smiled, allowing her gaze to go toward the table where her father and Ryan were still seated. Brody was still there too.

"Where are you sitting?" Lacy asked.

"Back there," Karla pointed to a table near where the band was setting up. "Paula thinks it's great she'll be close enough to hear the band. – You might think she's deaf. – Jack and I will probably be moving just about the time the band starts tuning up their instruments."

"Why not join us?" Lacy suggested, knowing she enjoyed Karla's company. Besides that, she hoped the other woman and her husband would help act as buffers between her and Brody.

"Okay, we'll do that," Karla replied with a grin. "I see Ryan's with you."

"He's with my whole family," Lacy said, not wanting her friend to get the wrong impression. "So is Brody."

"Mr. Fun himself," Karla said sarcastically, making a face. "He's not your date, is he? I mean, if he is, I'm sorry. Not sorry for you. . .well, I am – but I'm sorry I said it. . .Sorry I opened my big mouth at all."

Lacy laughed, taking no offense. She knew Brody had that effect on people. Somehow she felt more sorry for him than ever. "No, he's not with me, really." Though she was certain he wanted to be. "He's with all of us. Like Ryan."

"Well, count us in too," Karla said. "I'll find my husband and let him know, then get our stuff and meet you over there."

"Okay, right after I change this little guy." Lacy was certain that the evening would be more relaxed with a larger group of friends at their table. At least it would be for her.

#

Lacy threw back her head, laughing at the antics of her father as he swung her mother around on the floor to the swinging jitter-bug beat. Even Mikie sat in his stroller, eyes wide as he gazed at his grandparents spinning around before him.

She wondered what he was thinking.

"Did you ever wonder what goes through their minds?" Ryan asked, as he slid into the seat closest to the child.

"All the time," Lacy admitted. "I can't wait till he can tell me."

"Don't hurry him. They grow up fast enough," Karla said as she, too, slid a little closer. "Before you know it, you have this," she motioned toward her daughter and a gangly teen Lacy had never met before.

"New boyfriend?" she asked.

Karla made a face. "I prefer to say a new junior member."

Ryan laughed at his friend, putting his arm around Karla's shoulder as if to console her. "Hate to tell you, Mom, but he's both. I think he only joined so he could be closer to your daughter."

"Not a very good reason," Brody put in his opinion. "If he's busy making goo-goo eyes at her, he's liable to do something stupid someday. That's how accidents happen."

"Now's the time to find out if that's all it is," Lacy turned to Brody with a smile. "If he's still making goo-goo eyes by the time he's eighteen and ready to be a senior member, we just don't recommend him to become one."

"The station's not the place for young love," Brody continued.

"It's not the place for any love," Lacy replied, thinking of the tension that had often resulted from Mike and her working together.

Brody's body tensed, his gray eyes narrowing as though something unpleasant just went through his mind.

"Actually, he's turning out to be pretty good," Ryan said, breaking the tension. "I think he's not easily distracted from the job, he has good concentration and he's a fast learner."

"So I see," Karla added, looking at the couple who were now in an embrace as the music slowed and the couples still on the dance floor drew closer together. "Come on, they're playing one you'll dance to," she said as she got up from the table, grabbed her husband's hand and gave him a tug. "Maybe we can intimidate them."

"Is she always like this?" Brody asked.

Lacy laughed shaking her head. "Sometimes worse – but she's only kidding around. She knows she doesn't have to worry about Paula. She's a good kid."

"Maybe she is. But what about him?"

"I'll vouch for him," Ryan interjected, smiling. Keeping it light. "He's got a healthy male appreciation for an attractive female."

Brody laughed at that, then turned to Lacy. "That's something I can understand." His smile remained, but his eyes darkened as he searched her face. "Dance with me, Lacy?" he nearly whispered his request, making it sound more like a plea than an order.

Lacy nervously pushed a honey-gold curl behind her ear, looking down at her son. "I really shouldn't. . ."

"I'll stay with him, if you want," Ryan interrupted.

"Thanks," she replied, but the sapphire ice that met his eyes told him she'd wished he hadn't offered. He watched as she got up onto the floor, wondering about the relationship that seemed to be growing between Lacy and the rescue chief.

Ryan watched the two, noting the way Brody pulled her close within the circle of his arms. The way his large hands spread possessively across her back. Caught off guard he was possessed with the strangest feeling.

Mikie suddenly started squirming, twisting his little body as far as it could go, as though straining to see where everyone had gone. Ryan lifted him out of the stroller and held him on his lap.

"Are you looking for your Mama," he said close against the boy's ear. He pointed as the couple turned slightly, and Lacy could be seen within Brody's arms. "There she is, see her?"

Lacy spotted them, lifting her head slightly and smiling. She raised one hand from Brody's shoulder and waved to her son.

Ryan watched as Mikie made the strangest face, as though trying to decide what he made of the situation his mother was in. The child didn't look pleased as he jutted out his lip.

"Yeah, I know how you feel," Ryan said.

Mikie twisted around for a better look at the man holding him, and when he did, Ryan smiled. "Good idea, we'll ignore them," Ryan said.

The baby seemed to like that and laughed. A pleasant sound vibrating through his tiny body. Soon he threw back his dark head, giving Ryan a toothless smile.

Ryan hardly noticed the music change to a more upbeat tempo, nor the couples returning to the table. He was far more interested in the child in his arms.

"Looks like Mikie's showing off again," Lois said as she first approached the table.

The child turned and gave her a smile, bouncing with his arms in the air. Ryan felt tears sting his eyes as he relinquished the baby to his grandmother.

"Hey Ryan, this old fuddy-duddy won't dance a fast one with me," Karla said as she returned to the table. "How about you dance with me?"

Ryan laughed as Karla grabbed his hand and gave him a tug as she had done earlier with her husband. "You really ought to stop feeding this woman raw meat. She's turning into an animal," Ryan teased Jack, as Karla practically drug him to the dance floor.

"Quit complaining and thank me," Karla spat, as she swayed her hips to the music.

"Thank you. What for?"

"For keeping everyone from seeing you wear your heart in your eyes," she replied, leaning in closer so no one else would hear. Not that they would through all the loud music.

"You imagine things," Ryan replied, but he couldn't meet her eyes as he said it.

"Whatever you say," she spun a little closer. "But I don't believe a word of it."

He smiled grimly. "You're reading a blank page."

"No, actually I think I'm reading the first chapter of the book."

"Thought you wanted to dance, not play analyst."

"Okay, okay." Karla threw back her auburn hair, darting Ryan one last knowing look. "I'll wait till we're further into the book to comment."

A few moments later the music stopped and they returned to the table. Lacy was again holding her son.

"Some kids would be scared by the loud music," Ryan acknowledged before he sat down again. "It doesn't seem to phase him."

"There's always a radio going at home," Lacy replied.

"He's certainly a good kid," Brody put in. "A couple of others over there were really getting to be a pain. Weren't you glad when their parent's took them home?"

"Actually, he'll be the same very soon, I'm afraid," Lacy commended, looking down as her son gave a big yawn. "He had a long nap today, but I think it's still finally catching up to him."

"It is getting late," Lois agreed. "Your father and I were heading home, why don't we take Mikie."

"I'll come along," Lacy replied, putting her son into his stroller.

"No, you stay with your friends," her mother replied. "It's time for babies and grandparents to get some rest."

"Yeah, someone wore me out." Carl glanced at his wife and winked.

"Oh, was Mrs. Arthur too much for you, Dear?" Lois turned back to him with a smile.

Everyone at the table jeered in good nature.

"We'll see who's too much for whom when we get home?" Carl threatened suggestively.

Up until then her mother had been holding her own. Fitting in. Had her father just gone a step too far? Lacy watched her mother blush, then saw her turn back to her father and flash him a beguiling smile.

"Lacy," she turned back to her. "Don't be early."

"I'll be delighted to see to that," she heard Brody reply.

She was happy her mother was accepting the banter and even dishing out some of her own. But what had she just gotten her into?

185

"We'll all see to it that she stays out late and that she has a good time," Karla added, giving Lacy a knowing smile. "And don't worry, Jack and I will see that she gets home safe and sound."

Out of the corner of her eye Lacy saw Brody's smile fade slightly.

"Maybe," he whispered, then patted her hand.

She took a breath feeling panic set in. More than ever she felt certain Brody's intentions were far more serious than she wanted. More than she was ready for. Maybe more than she'd ever be ready for.

Somehow she had to get that point across to him. She twisted her wedding band around nervously, trying to decide how.

The music started. She listened to the sound, hoping it would be something fast. Brody had told her he didn't dance unless it was slow.

She smiled recognizing the sixties tune, 'Wipe-out'. "Hey Karla, want to give this one a try?" she asked.

Always game, her friend joined her on the dance floor.

"Is that panic I detected a moment ago?" Karla asked as they moved to the lively beat.

"Thanks for noticing," Lacy replied.

"It's rather obvious."

A shadow passed over Lacy's blue eyes. "Yes, I guess it's been getting worse."

"You're going to have to tell him if you're not interested."

"Yeah, but not here. You know Brody."

Karla rolled her brown eyes. "By reputation, everyone knows him. I don't envy you."

"Yeah, but Karla, he has a side most people don't see," Lacy said almost desperately. "I don't want to hurt him."

"You don't want to lead him on either. Not if there isn't any hope."

Lacy glanced toward the table and frowned. "I'm not interested in anything serious right now."

"Brody should understand that."

But would he understand that she just wasn't interested in a serious relationship with him, period. All she wanted was his friendship. Did it have to be an either-or situation?

They were both getting breathless.

"Least I won't have to worry about dancing with him for this one," Lacy said as the music stopped and the band immediately switched to something slow. "I'm too exhausted. I've got to sit down."

"After that, you can always ask Jack. . . or Ryan?" Karla said. "He'll dance fast or slow."

Lacy looked toward the man who had become a close friend. There wouldn't be any reason why she shouldn't dance with him.

"I just might," she said then they both changed the subject as they returned to the table.

A little later a fast song again was immediately followed by a slow one. Lacy looked up at Ryan, who had been her partner and smiled. Wordlessly he reached out and took her right hand, putting his right around her, pulling her close.

"I hope you're having a good time tonight," Ryan whispered, his breath warm against her ear.

She thought about it a moment, then smiled. "You know. I really am." If not for the shadow of Brody hanging over her. She wished he, like Ryan, could be just friends.

Well, maybe not exactly like Ryan, she thought. They were two very different men. It was understandable they'd be different kinds of friends. Ryan was far less demanding. Not at all intimidating.

"You might have an even better time if you'd relax." He squeezed her hand, gently tucking it closer against his chest.

She realized he had sensed the tension her thoughts were creating. He seemed to know her so well. She allowed herself to relax against him, drawing comfort from his strength.

"That's better." His lips brushed against her temple as he spoke.

Oh yes, it was better, she thought, her eyes closing as she allowed herself to sink further into the luxury of his embrace. His hand absently stroked her back, soothing her more. Making her feel. . .

She opened her eyes with a start, pulling away, her eyes bright as she looked up at him.

"You're not going get your message across like that," Ryan said softly, his green eyes grim as he pulled her back against him.

She felt her cheeks burn as she realized Ryan thought she was using him to get to Brody. "It's not what you think."

"What do I think?"

"That I. . .I'm trying to make Brody. . .notice me."

Ryan pulled away and looked into her bright blue eyes. "Wrong. Anyone can see he's already done that."

"Then. . .then what do you think?"

Ryan sighed, pulling her back against him. "I think you're afraid. Afraid to get involved."

"Looks like you're wrong," she whispered. "I just don't feel that way about Brody. I don't think I ever will."

"I see."

"Do you?" She looked up at him again, hoping he did understand. Suddenly it meant a lot to her.

He gave her a smile without humor. "The direct approach is more your style, Lacy. Now I understand why tonight you've decided to go against nature."

"I don't want to hurt Brody. But, I'm afraid that's what might happen."

Ryan could see why a man would be easily hurt by her. Lacy was a very special woman. He doubted she had the faintest idea how special.

"So you thought if he saw you showing interest in other men, he'd realize you don't want a singular relationship."

She nodded.

"It didn't occur to you he'd see it as competition and step up the chase."

Her panicked sapphire eyes darted to Ryan's face just as the music stopped. "Oh no," she groaned. "I should have stuck with the direct approach."

"One more dance. . .or. . .back to the table?"

"Back to the table," she replied softly, turning in time to see the dark expression on Brody's face. "Why do I feel like I'm being sent into a den of lions."

"Only one lion," Ryan replied as he propelled her froward. "I'd say you're up to the challenge."

She looked back and darted him a grim look. "Thanks for the vote of confidence."

They were just about at the table when the sound of pagers pierced through the air, followed only seconds after by several more. Two companies were being dispatched.

Lacy immediately looked at Brody, recognizing the sound of the rescue unit's tones. The second set had been to dispatch Friendship Hook and Ladder.

Brody stood, silently listening to the location and nature of the call, while several others were racing by. "I better go," he said, glancing at Lacy. "I think I'm needed a little more there than I am here." He looked up at Ryan through narrowed gray eyes. "Besides, I doubt all these characters were drinking birch beer today. I don't want them anywhere near the scene unless they were."

Lacy knew the township fire companies were put on stand-by to assist at any calls within the borough that evening. It was standard procedure whenever they had their department picnic or any other event that might put a large number of members out of service.

She knew drinking was about as far out of service as you could get. Her narrowed eyes followed the back of Woody Brown as he hurried toward his car.

"That's one who shouldn't be out there," Jack Mulholland said, his gaze following her's. "I saw him holding up a corner post a few minutes ago."

Ryan frowned. "Probably shouldn't be driving."

They all watched, as if on cue, Barry Carlisle ran after his friend, stopping him as he was about to get into his car. He pushed the car door closed and tried to take Woody's keys.

Woody swung a wild fist at Barry and missed.

"So much for a nice peaceful picnic," Lacy said with a frown, shaking her head.

Several other men joined Barry as he restrained the drunken man. Finally Woody handed him his keys, then got into the passenger side of the car, slamming the door behind him.

Woody's wife rushed over to the scene, obviously upset. She said something to Barry, then got into the back seat, while he got in to drive.

"You look beat," Ryan said as he turned his attention back to Lacy. He knew seeing Barry and Woody must have brought back some unpleasant memories. That on top of the situation with Brody.

"I am tired," she admitted as they heard the music starting again. She looked at Karla who was once again pulling her less-than enthusiastic husband out onto the dance floor. She was tempted to walk home, but she suddenly felt too tired for that. Instead she sat.

Ryan looked over her shoulder and saw Rose Sinclair glancing in their direction. He had managed to escape her earlier when she'd cornered him. But not before she insisted she was going to get him to dance with her at least once during the evening.

"I can give you a lift home," Ryan said to Lacy, knowing the last thing she needed was to have Rose stop by their table.

"Thanks Ryan, but Karla and Jack said they'd drop me."

"It's no problem. I was leaving," he persisted, seeing that Rose had ended her conversation with several wives who's husbands had gone to the call. She stood staring in their direction. "Really, Lacy. I'm leaving right now." He got up waving to Karla and Jack. "See you two later. Don't worry about Lacy. I'll drop her off on my way home."

Having been given little choice, Lacy stood, waving good-bye to her friends. Her smiled faded when she caught a glimpse of Rose out of the corner of her eye.

She looked up at Ryan and saw him purposely looking the other way. "She sees you," Lacy teased.

Ryan grabbed her hand and pulled her close beside him. He looked down at her with a mischievous grin placing his arm across her shoulder as they walked toward the parking lot.

"Do you think she's following?" Lacy asked, unable to resist the urge to tease some more. Ryan had looked downright frightened at the other woman's approach.

"Just in case. . ." he started, turning her till they faced each other. Before she knew what was happening Ryan cupped her face in his hands, leaned forward and gave her a kiss. For a moment he stared down into her face, seeing her shocked expression.

"You owe me that," he whispered huskily, sighing as he pulled away. "So, I'm not going to apologize."

A rose colored hue blended with the freckles on Lacy's face as she realized what he had been doing. The same thing she had done hoping to deter Brody's attention. Then she remembered him saying something about Brody stepping up the chase if he knew there was competition.

She wondered if Rose would do the same thing, and for some reason that thought bothered her.

CHAPTER FOURTEEN

"This is the part of our job I hate," Annie said as she drove the ambulance slowly down the highway, looking for any sign of the one car accident to which they had been dispatched. "Not knowing what to expect when, and if, we find something."

"It's beginning to look more like if." Lacy sighed, rubbing her hand across the back of her neck. Though false alarms were less frequent with the ambulance, in the two months since Lacy returned to service there had been a few. "If they only realized while we're out on a wild goose chase, if there is a real emergency, it could take longer to get help to respond."

"Yes, and on something like this there's a lot of personnel tied up," Annie agreed.

They both knew fire apparatus were also on the road, beaming their spotlights down the steep embankment looking for the car.

The dispatcher had said the vehicle had jumped the rail and gone over the side. Whoever had called it in must have decided they had done their duty by calling. They had hung up and hadn't even given their name, too often a sign that the call was someone's idea of a joke. But they still had to respond. They couldn't afford to make that assumption when someone's life could be at stake.

Besides, too often people were afraid to get involved at all. Looking at it from their point of view it was hard to blame them. It seemed no one was immune to lawsuits, even for doing something good. Even though a person is protected by the Good Samaritan Act, a law protecting citizens who stop to render aid, it did not prevent another person from suing them. Even though those lawsuits would inevitably be thrown out of court, it created an inconvenience many people wanted to avoid.

"Stop!" Lacy shouted, pointing to where the spotlight pierced the darkness, picking up the shadowy figure of a person moving between two trees.

Over the radio they heard others had seen him, too. She jumped out of the ambulance and walked toward the rail, noting the steepness of the incline.

"Are you injured?" she shouted to the man who seemed to be struggling to climb in their direction.

"Ha'elp!" the man shouted in reply, slurring his words. He seemed to slump to the ground.

191

Firefighters were already climbing over the side and rushing down toward the man. "I've got the bag," Annie said as she too climbed out of the ambulance.

"Here, I'll go down to him, you wait up here. There's no sense both of us spraining our ankles."

"It is steep. Lucky he even got out," Annie said as Lacy took the bag and quickly climbed over the guard rail.

"I wanna go home," the man was saying to the firefighters just as she carefully picked her way down the hill to join them. "Mildred's gonna. . .kill me. . .for dentin' her new car."

"Was anyone else in the car with you?" Chief Maxwell asked the man.

"Wh-at?" The man hiccuped.

"Was anyone else in the car?" the Chief asked once again, shaking his head as he looked over his shoulder at his men.

"Mildred's car," the man replied.

"Whew," Arlen fanned his face as he stood up from beside the man and turned to the police officer who had joined them. "I think this one'll be for you, once Lacy's through with him."

"Simon, you better go check the car. It must have ended up down there somewhere." He pointed further down the steep hill. "A couple of you other guys follow him with your line and hose down this whole area. Judging by the smell of gas, I'm betting he split open his gas tank on a rock or something. Probably lost gas all the way down."

Lacy pressed a bandage to a cut on the man's hand, then went about checking him for further injuries while the officer waited patiently to ask him a few questions. Not that he expected to get many answers. Judging by the man's state he probably didn't know who he was. And she suspected that once his wife found out what happened, he'd wish he were someone else.

"We'll be taking you to the hospital to make sure you're all right," she told the man, feeling pretty sure he was fine, but knowing he had probably consumed enough alcohol to mask symptoms and that there could be something internally wrong.

"Noooo," the man groaned. "No, hospital. . .Gotta get out of town."

She laughed, turning to the officer. "Would you care to be the one to inform him otherwise?"

The officer knelt down. "Sir, you don't have to go to the hospital. But I suggest you do."

Suddenly there was a loud cry, and commotion coming from below them. Lacy grabbed her flashlight and aimed the beam, but couldn't make out what was going on. She was certain she had recognized Ryan's voice as the one that had cried out.

She looked up at the officer. "Here, hold this on his hand," she ordered. "He's just bleeding a little. Annie, you better come down here and help. I'm going to see what happened down there."

She grabbed the medical bag and started down the hill, sliding part of the way as she got closer to some of the crew. She landed on her backside and would have slid further had someone not taken hold of her arm.

"Easy, girl," it was Arlen who had grabbed her. "You ain't helpin' no one if you get yourself hurt too."

"What happened?" she asked, standing. She stood sideways, planting one foot above the other to keep her balance.

"Ryan fell. Looks like he's hurt."

Lacy felt her breathing quicken. A comrade – a brother in the emergency service was injured. But Lacy knew it was more than that. Ryan was also a special friend. He had proven that many times since their first tragic meeting. Now, she had to do whatever she could to help him.

"How far down is he?" she asked.

"Far enough that you aren't going down," the Chief informed her. "I've called for the rescue truck."

"Arlen, how do you know there's time? We're miles out of town," she argued. "You know I'm trained to repel."

"I expected you to say that," Arlen said, shaking his head. "I've got the guys aiming every light we've got down here. Now you go get into some descent gear before you try any climbing."

Lacy hurried back up the hill, nearly falling in her haste. She had to get herself in hand. She would not help anyone if she ended up hurt herself. She slowed her pace, thinking each action through.

She knew there'd be two of them going down the side. When she got to the top. she saw Jack Mulholland pulling heavy, yellow, nylon ropes out of the back of the equipment truck. She assumed that meant he'd be the one making the descent with her. She was glad. He was the best man they had for that job.

"As soon as we saw it was you, we figured you'd want to go down," Jack said with a wink.

Beside him was his daughter, Paula. She turned when she saw Lacy, removing her own junior firefighter helmet and handing it to her. "You'll be needing this," the girl said.

Lacy smiled as she took the girl's hard hat and put it on her head, strapping it securely beneath the chin. "Perfect fit."

"How about my bunker pants?" the girl said, already lowering the suspenders on her own heavily padded and insulated pants. "I know you ambulance jockeys don't carry any."

Lacy was about to refuse, knowing it was more awkward to move in the heavy pants, then remembered the time she'd practically scolded Brody for removing his protective gear. With the rough terrain, the padded bunker pants were in order. She accepted the girl's gloves, but the jacket she declined, knowing it would hamper her agility too much.

Together she and Jack returned back down the hill. "Is he conscious?" she asked Arlen.

"I'd say so," the Chief informed her. "Sounds like he's in a lot of pain. Says he thinks his leg is broken."

Lacy nodded, feeling her heartbeat accelerate. "Have someone tell Annie. She'll know what other equipment I'll need. You can lower it with the stokes basket."

They tied the ends of their ropes securely around two nearby trees then started their descent, each on opposite sides of Ryan.

Lacy slowly lowered herself, using her right hand in front of her to guide her descent, her left out to her side to stop. The rope was secured through a metal clip on a harness around her waist. At one point, the embankment was so steep she had to press her feet against the sides, bend her knees and repel herself out, lowering herself as she did.

About a hundred feet down, they were level with Ryan. At that point they started a horizontal trail until they met their victim in the middle.

"'Bout time you got here," Ryan complained with a groan.

"Nice to see you're in such good spirits," Lacy said, trying to make light in spite of the quivering of her voice. "I hope that helmet came off after you landed not during your fall." She flashed her light on Ryan's face. There was plenty of dirt, but she was thankful to see no blood.

"Do you think I'd be sitting here patiently waiting for you to help me if it had?"

"You'd probably be a lot more patient," she retorted, checking his leg as she spoke. "Unconscious victims are usually far less argumentative."

He winced in reply as she reached the point where his leg bent at an awkward angle. She turned back to Jack. "You gotta bullet you can lend him to bite on?"

Within moments the stokes was lowered with the splints and bandages they would need for a broken leg, and the medical bag for anything else that could be wrong with him.

"No, but shall I check and see what I can find in here?" Jack lifted the medical bag from the basket and set it between them.

"How about a shot of whiskey instead?" Ryan groaned. "Oh yeah, I almost forgot, I don't drink. What else do you have?"

194

"Sorry, paramedics aren't allowed to administer painkillers." Lacy said, as she reached for the surgical scissors to cut up the leg of his bunker pants.

"Geez, they don't stop you from administering pain though," he said as he tensed, gritting his teeth.

Lacy turned to look up at him, her bright blue eyes showing her concern in spite of her humorous way of handling him. "Trust me, I'm doing my best not to."

"I know, Lacy, just do what you have to," Ryan said as he squeezed his eyes tightly closed, as though to squeeze away the pain.

To her relief, there was no sign of blood on Ryan's jeans. That eliminated the possibility of a compound fracture, where the bone was broken through the skin. Without that to worry about, she could check for other injuries before splinting his leg.

"Now what are you doing?" Ryan moaned as she started opening his bunker coat.

"I'm making sure you're okay to move."

"I've been moving everything but my leg," he argued.

"Especially your mouth," she spat, reaching for the neck brace. "And before you ask, yes, you do need this."

"May as well let the lady do her job," Jack said with unhidden humor in his voice.

"That's right," she snapped. "I didn't risk life and limb climbing down here to have someone give me a hard time. Not to mention getting back up again."

"Care to ride with me," Ryan asked.

"Yeah, sure," she said doubtfully. "Sorry, we don't have a stokes for two."

"Too bad," Ryan replied. "I'd have loved to see their faces when we got back up there."

"Shut up, Ryan," she snapped, then stopped as she heard the sound of sirens in the distance. "I think it's best we get him packaged and start up."

"Brody's not going to like you stealing his glory," Ryan said knowingly, but Lacy didn't reply as she went about her task. She knew this would just be icing on the cake as far as Brody was concerned. He'd been irritable enough with her ever since the night of the picnic. So irritable she'd begun to think she didn't need to tell him she didn't reciprocate his feelings toward her.

They had Ryan loaded in the stokes and were just helping guide it up the bank when they heard the sound of the rescue truck arriving. The sirens stopped. She could just make out the sound of doors slamming, but they had no difficulty hearing the sound of Brody cursing as he joined the other members of the crew who were helping pull the basket to the top.

"If the thought of retiring from the ambulance squad comes to mind tonight. . ." Jack said, huffing heavily as he balanced the foot end of the basket. "just remember. . . there's always a place for you back at the firehouse. Right, Ryan?"

Ryan looked up at Lacy's face, now lit clearly by the lights from above. "Any time she's ready."

Grasping her own rope with one hand, and helping guide the stokes with the other, Lacy pretended concentration on her work. But in her mind, she wondered about the possibility. She'd had a taste of action that evening she'd missed. Not that she'd enjoy making a habit out of rescuing friends.

Once they were at the top, firefighters and rescue personnel grabbed the sides of the stokes basket and carried it toward the waiting ambulance. Lacy started disconnecting her rope.

"We'll take care of everything here," Jack said softly, aiming his chin toward the confrontation now taking place between the Fire and the Rescue Chiefs. "You just take care of Ryan."

She sighed, knowing she wasn't going to escape Brody's wrath for long. She only hoped Arlen wasn't taking too much abuse. When Brody was in one of his moods there was no telling what he'd do. And lately his moods had been getting progressively worse and she knew she had a great deal to do with it.

She had almost made it to the back of the ambulance when Brody caught up with her. "Lacy! What did you think you were doing back there?" he asked sharply when she turned to face him.

"Taking care of my patient the best I could," she replied, ignoring the fact that she had to go to the patient, rather than waiting to have him brought to her.

"You know very well ambulance crews wait for trained personnel to bring the victim to them," he spat, puffing his chest out and stabbing his finger in the air.

"I am trained personnel," she replied in growing anger.

"That's not the point here! If anything happened to you back there, who'd have taken care of the injured then? That dingbat driver?"

"What's going on out there?" Ryan asked, propping himself up the best he could considering the neck brace and the other restraints Lacy had put on him.

"They didn't delay Chief Langford long enough for Lacy to get away," Annie answered him.

Ryan frowned, feeling helpless. "Do me a favor Annie. Go start the ambulance and give the siren a long blast."

"Gladly," the young woman said with a smile. She couldn't help but hear Brody's statement concerning her, and it would be a delight to retaliate. "Try

196

and yell louder than this, Chief High and Mighty," she said to herself as she pushed the button and the shrill siren's cry cut through the air.

"Look Brody, catch me later," Lacy said, trying to hide her relief that his tirade had been interrupted. "I have a patient to take care of, and he should be on his way to the hospital."

"We will talk about this later. In Drew's office." Without another word, Brody turned and stormed back toward the rescue truck.

Lacy climbed into the back of the ambulance. She looked up and saw Annie flash her a satisfied grin before she turned to close the back doors. "You may as well wipe that smug look off your face, if Brody thinks you did that on purpose, you'll be on the hot seat with me."

"I told her to do it," Ryan said as she came to sit beside the stretcher.

"For your information, patients don't give orders," she snapped, pushing him back against the stretcher.

"Obviously, because if I had known it was you coming over the side, I'd have ordered otherwise. I don't know what got into Arlen, letting you pull a stunt like that."

"Don't you start, too," she threatened, picking up surgical scissors and waving them in the air.

"Hey, get those away from me, you did enough damage to my gear as it is!"

"I'll do a whole lot more if I decide I need to cut your sleeve to take your blood pressure."

"You can take off my bunker coat."

"What? And break procedure. You know victims of falls must remain strapped to a backboard."

"I'm not strapped to a backboard," Ryan said smugly.

"I can remedy that."

"You know I don't need one," Ryan continued. "In fact, I'd be able to move a whole lot better if I weren't strapped down so tight on here."

"Procedure," she replied. "We can't have patients falling off their stretchers. How would that look?"

"Okay, you win," Ryan said, his face showing signs of strain. "You were wrong to do what you did, but I was never so happy to see someone's face as I was to see yours when you came down there for me." He reached out, took her hand and gave it a squeeze. "Thanks."

"Just doing my job," she said, swallowing the lump in her throat that was belying the truth of her words. When she had realized someone she knew – someone she cared about – had fallen down the side of that slope, she knew she had to break any rules to get to them. "And you would have done the same thing had you been in my shoes."

Ryan couldn't tell her just how right she was. He knew she meant if he had the ability to save any of his personnel, he'd have broken every rule to do so. But there was truth in her words that went beyond that.

Within moments, they were at the hospital. Lacy and Annie each took a side as they pushed the stretcher through the double doors of the emergency entrance. A young, attractive nurse met them inside, getting all the details from Lacy about their patient.

"Haven't we met before?" the woman asked, flirting openly with Ryan. "Several months ago when you were injured at a fire."

Who could ever forget that fire? Ryan thought, as he glanced toward Lacy seeing her bow her head, looking away. *Certainly neither of us ever will. But for very different reasons.*

Lacy had lost someone she loved that night. Ryan had gained a special friend. No, more than that, even if he was only willing to admit that to himself.

In the months since that fateful night he had tried to help Lacy learn that pain did lessen over time, that wounds did have a way of healing. And without even knowing it, Lacy had proven to him that the void left empty, could be filled. That part of his life hadn't died with his wife and child.

He sometimes hated himself for feeling that way. It was as though he was being disloyal for allowing Lacy to fill parts of his mind that once only Norma had filled. To allow Mikie to fill the spaces that had been reserved for only Michelle.

Especially the times when he'd close his eyes and think of his wife and child, but the vision in his mind's eye was of a blonde-haired, blue-eyed Madonna, holding her infant son close against her breast, whispering sweet words as he nursed. The face of that Madonna was Lacy.

He realized the nurse was still talking and had to force himself to listen.

"Did he sustain any head injury?" She was looking again at Lacy, who was also looking at him strangely.

"I didn't hit my head," he replied, forcing a smile. "It's the other end that's damaged."

The nurse lifted the sheet then wrinkled her nose distastefully when she saw his dirty bunker pants. "We'll have to cut him out of these," she said.

"Might as well," Ryan groaned. "She already rendered them useless. . .But the coat remains intact."

Lacy shook her head and smiled at the woman. "He's very touchy about his gear." Then turned to Ryan. "I'll see it gets back to the station. Intact. Though I doubt you'll be needing it for awhile."

The nurse joined them as they pushed Ryan's stretcher into one of the little rooms where the doctor on duty would give him a preliminary examination. As carefully as possible, they helped Ryan slide onto the examination table, but Lacy could see the movement was taking its toll. She saw the dull look in his usually bright green eyes, and the lines of stress on his face, and knew Ryan's pain was increasing. The initial numbness of the nerves after an injury was wearing off.

She stood back as the nurse helped remove Ryan's bunker coat then handed it to her. "You said you'd take this with you."

Lacy knew she was being dismissed and obediently pulled her stretcher back out the door, glancing over her shoulder for one last look at her friend.

When she returned in the direction of the waiting room she saw a familiar figure waiting. With two long strides, her father approached, then stopped as the hefty, gray-haired receptionist flashed him a warning look.

"Their guard dog wouldn't let me in," he said gruffly when Lacy reached his side. "Your partner said it was Ryan who was hurt. How bad is he?"

"Broken leg, a lot of bumps and bruises. But I think that's all," Lacy replied with a sigh. "He was lucky."

"You look pretty bad yourself," her father said with concern as he took hold of the stretcher and helped her pull it through the door toward the waiting ambulance. "What did you do, fall down with him?"

"I went down after him," Lacy corrected, watching his dark eyes widen. "And don't you start, too! I've gotten enough flack for one night. You know I'm as skilled as anyone at rope rescue."

"Did I say anything?" He shook his head. "That was Arlen's call. What did he say about it?"

"I didn't give him much choice," Lacy replied. "Anyway, he knew I was right."

"You're the most stubborn woman I know."

"Daddy that's sexist," she scolded, with a wide grin.

"Okay, then, the most stubborn person I know," he corrected. "I don't know where you get it. No, I do know. It's gotta be from your mother. . .And that's not sexist. It's fact."

Lacy laughed, knowing she got a fair amount of stubbornness from both sides of her family. But, she'd have to agree, her mother always had shown the most strength of will. In all the years of marrying into a firefighting family, she had stubbornly refused to like the job they did. Oh, she had accepted it, but she still voiced her fears whenever they gave her an opening to do so, which they did their best not to.

In spite of her mother's recent attempt to be more understanding, Lacy had a feeling that once her mother found out she had joined in the rescue that night she'd be in for a long list of objections – worse than any she'd heard so far, including Brody's.

"I'm going back inside and see if I can't get past that line backer to find out how Ryan is," her father said gruffly. "You gonna stick around or do you want me to call you at the station?"

"I'll be back," she replied, glancing at her watch. "I was only filling in for Jen tonight. It was her husband's birthday and she wanted to have one entire, uninterrupted evening with him. Next shift was due in at midnight. That means we're done for tonight," she turned to Annie. "Ready to go?"

"Sure am. I've got class tomorrow. My big test," Annie replied. "Then I'll be right in line after you for a paid opening."

Though Annie was a quiet girl, Lacy knew she loved her work with the ambulance squad. She had struggled to become an EMT while working at her regular job, then worked still harder to finish her paramedic's training. All that, on top of caring for her ailing mother.

No one ever said Lacy had to be the first choice. It had just been assumed. She knew if anyone deserved a paid position on the squad Annie did. She had joined out of real desire to do the job. A job she loved. Lacy had joined as a solution to a problem. And though running with the ambulance had its moments, to her, it never quite gave her the personal satisfaction that being a firefighter had.

Brody was waiting when they got back to the station. Drew had come on duty and she knew without a doubt that Brody had already spoken to him. The last thing she wanted, or needed was another confrontation. Right now, she just wanted to go back to the hospital and see how Ryan was.

"I'll save you the time, Brody," she said walking right past him to face Drew. "I think I should be given a thirty day suspension for what I did tonight. If I had been injured, Annie would have been the only other person able to care for us, and though I know she's every bit as qualified as I am, she still is not certified as a paramedic.

"I acted on impulse, going over everyone's head. I should have considered the fact that Rescue Seven had already been dispatched. Had something happened to me, it would have taken at least fifteen minutes to have gotten another ambulance on the road and to the scene. I took a needless risk."

Brody's jaw practically dropped open as he listened to her speech. She knew he had probably nothing more than a reprimand in mind. She was suggesting far more.

"Hold on a minute." Drew raised the palm of his hand to silence her before she could go on. "We don't have to be that drastic. I think you realize the chance you took. We don't have to over-react." He glanced briefly at Brody, then back at Lacy.

"No, Drew, I insist," she said firmly. "I deserve the time off. . . I need the time off. . ." she continued more softly, certain he would understand. They had discussed some of her doubts before in private. "to think."

Drew nodded, a grim expression on his face. "Okay. But it's not an official suspension. You can come back any time you feel you've worked things out. You're still a member. Just like you're still a member of the Vigilantes." He smiled and she knew he truly did understand how she felt.

Without a word to Brody, she turned and went to the back of the ambulance to help Annie finish cleaning from their call. Lacy knew by the look in Annie's eyes that she had heard the conversation.

"If an opening comes up, Annie, don't wait for me," she said. "Go for it!"

"What are you going to do?"

Lacy shrugged. "I wish I knew. I know what I'd like to do. I know what I don't want to do. The problem is, they're both the same thing. I guess no one said life had to be easy."

Annie reached over and gave Lacy a hug. "But you're never alone when you have friends. I hope I'll be yours no matter what you decide to do. Even if it means you getting that paid spot."

Lacy shook her head. "I'm confused. But I'm almost certain that isn't the solution for me."

"Why don't I finish up here?" Annie offered. "I know you wanted to go back and check on Assistant Chief Simon."

As she got into her car Lacy looked down at the dirt smudges on the front of her blue uniform shirt, and made sour expression. She suspected her face was just as bad. And her hair was probably a mess.

She thought of going home and for a quick shower and change into fresh clothes, then wondered why it should matter so much. She was simply going to stop by the hospital and find out how Ryan was. Whether they were going to keep him for observation, or send him home.

Home, she thought. Her home. The one he was renting from her. Unlike his previous accommodations, he wouldn't need to go upstairs. Still, she wondered how he would manage on his own.

Continuing her thoughts, she pulled out of the parking lot and onto the main street, her mind still filled with concerns for Ryan.

Perhaps her father would stay with him.

No. Caring as he was, her father's bedside manner was terrible. Besides that, he was a terrible cook. Ryan would certainly suffer gastral problems if Carl MacDonald acted as his nurse.

What he needed was a woman's touch. "Now who's being sexist?" she said to her reflection in the rearview mirror. Then seeing the dark streak of dirt across the bridge of her nose, she gasped. She reached into the glove compartment to search for a tissue. There were none.

Pulling to the side of the street, she reached into the back seat, thankful she had forgotten to remove her son's diaper bag. She unzipped the bag and pulled out a container of baby wipes. She removed one, inhaling the baby oil scent as she used it to clean her face. Another glance in the mirror showed a definite improvement so she returned to the road.

"They're checking his X-rays now," Carl explained when she arrived. "If nothing else is wrong, they're letting him go home. Or maybe I should say he's intimidated them into letting him go home. Something about refusing to wear their hospital gowns again."

Lacy felt her cheeks burn at the memory of night she and Ryan had met in the hospital stairwell. He had some legitimate objections that night, in spite of the fact he was supposed to be safe beneath warm covers, not sneaking around in drafty stairways.

"They want him to go to an orthopedic specialist tomorrow for a cast," her father explained. Until then, he's got to be careful. It's pretty painful for him, I gather. He looked worn out when I saw him. Barely enough spunk left to argue with them about going home.

"So how did he intend to get there? Not to mention care for himself once he was there."

Carl shrugged. "If you ask me, he probably didn't admit he lived alone. Besides, they've got him so doped up, he probably didn't think beyond going home to bed."

"We could tell them he's alone," she said, hesitating, as she looked up into her father's concerned brown eyes. "Or one of us could stay with him."

"I guess I could stay till morning," Carl replied.

"Actually, Dad," she hedged, glancing nervously around a moment before meeting his eyes again. "I said one of us, but I meant more like. . . me."

"Think you can handle him?" Carl asked, a knowing glint lighting his dark, brown eyes. "I suspect he's a stubborn one."

"Funny, he said the same thing about me," she laughed, then sobered slightly as she watched them wheeling the subject of their conversation into the corridor. "He does look kind of out of it, Dad. I doubt he'll be much trouble tonight. But do you think Mom would mind keeping an eye out for Mikie till morning?" she turned back to her father.

"He's going to need help tomorrow, too. You think I should contact Arlen and see if any of the others will come out and help?"

"Not yet. . .I mean, why bother them, when I've got time? I probably could duck out sometime in the morning and check on Mikie in case Mom has anything she wants to do."

"I told. . . her," Ryan said casting a dark glance back at the nurse pushing his wheelchair. "that I won't be alone. Just because I'm living alone, doesn't mean I don't have anyone to care for me."

"He has a lot of people who care . . .who will care for him," Lacy said, meeting his pleading green gaze. "He won't be alone."

"Okay," the nurse replied suspiciously, glancing between her ward and the two people who had come to claim him. "Milly, this one is being discharged," she said to the linebacker who was hovering close at hand, as though ready to block any attempt Carl may have made of entering the restricted area.

"He'll have to sign here, before he can go." With one hand, the receptionist pushed a clip board onto his lap, with the other she held a pen under his nose.

Lacy could barely keep from laughing. She glanced at her father.

"Gotta be twins," he mumbled for her ears only. That was her undoing. Lacy had to turn toward the door. "I'll go get my car," she said. "Dad, you bring him out."

Once they had Ryan situated in the back seat, Lacy turned around and smiled. "No hospital gowns tonight. But it looks like I'll have to cut the leg of your p.j.'s."

"Sorry to disappoint you Edwina Scissorhands, I don't wear pajamas."

Lacy turned back and started the car, feeling her cheeks burning once again. It irritated her that this man could so easily embarrass her. She didn't understand it at all. She had grown up around the firehouse and had heard everything coming out of the mouths of some of the men. She had thought nothing could make her blush. Yet practically from the first moment they met, Ryan did just that.

"By the way, Lacy, thanks," he said from behind her. "I appreciate you lying for me. I hate hospitals." *Too many bad memories.*

"Who lied?"

"You did." He yawned, not bothering to disguise how tired he was.

"Hope you're going to make it in with those crutches they gave you," she said. "I'd hate to have to use the firefighter's drag on you."

"I'll make it," he promised. "Wouldn't want you showing off your skills twice in one night."

"Be glad I had the skills you needed tonight, or it may have been Brody who had to come down to get you. I get the feeling you two aren't exactly best friends."

Ryan laughed. Though they had worked together often, the few times he and Brody had actually spoken, the encounters had been cool. "Somehow I doubt he'd have been as gentle about my ascent as you were."

"Like I said. Be happy it was me and not him."

"So did Brody have any more to say when you got back to the station?" Ryan asked, letting a huge yawn escape his lips once again.

"Nothing. I didn't give him the chance," Lacy replied, glancing in the mirror again. "Why don't you rest till I get you home."

"If I rest, that'll be it for the night," Ryan said. "You will have to drag me into the house."

"In that case, hang in there a little longer. We only have a about a mile to go." She accelerated slightly to hurry their trip.

It was strange pulling into the driveway of the place that had once been her home. Sure she still owned it. But it was no longer her home. She wondered how it was going to feel stepping inside again for the first time since she moved.

She had loved the house from the first moment she and Mike had seen it. She had pushed so hard for them to buy it, in spite of the fact he wasn't as sure it was the right time for them to move. He had loved living in town. Apartment life appealed to him. She wanted a single family home, with a yard for their children to play.

She wondered how much the inside of the house had changed. The outside was exactly as she'd left it. She had given Ryan a free hand to do anything he wanted to make the house his own.

"Lacy," Ryan said softly, breaking into her thoughts. "Are you okay?" He could not see her expression in the darkness, but he sensed her unease at returning to her home. He had heard the faint sigh escaping her lips.

"Time to get you inside."

"The fun part will be getting out of the back seat," he replied. "Once that's done, we're in the home stretch."

Lacy put her left arm around Ryan's waist, allowing him to put his right across her shoulder, and helped balance him as he slid his broken leg off the back seat of the car. She saw him wince, and wished she could take away his pain. But knew he'd be hurting much more if not for the pain-killers he had already been given.

"They said I should take another pill when I get home," he said as though reading her thoughts. "Then guaranteed sleep. All you need to do is see that I'm snug in bed, then you can go. I've really appreciated your help."

She wondered if she should tell him she was staying, or just let him think she was going home. She knew he hated feeling like a burden. He'd probably waste what little energy he had left arguing that she should go home.

What you don't know, may help you. She decided if they entered through the garage because it was level with the rest of the house and he wouldn't have to climb the front steps.

She smiled at Ryan trying to balance himself on one of his crutches, fumbling in his pocket for his key.

"Got it," he said, dangling the set of keys in front of him. For a minute, I thought the nurse lost them when she took off my pants. I wouldn't let her cut them off." He slipped the key into the lock.

"I got the feeling she'd have enjoyed doing that," Lacy teased.

"She was friendly, wasn't she?" He smiled. "Unfortunately after I went to X-ray, they turned me over to Conan the Barbarian."

Lacy started laughing, imagining his disappointment. She had never seen him with a woman at the few social events they both attended. She remembered the company picnic. Her cheeks burned from that memory.

There had also been a couple of area fire company housings, open houses held in honor of a fire company's purchase of a new truck. He'd often danced with some of the women, as he did with her, but he didn't seem to have anyone special.

She wondered what she'd find as they entered his house. Would there be a photograph of some long lost love? Would there be a little black book filled with numbers of the women he dated socially? Of course, none of them were from the emergency service. At least not in this county. Word would spread too fast. Everyone would know.

Perhaps he didn't like women who were involved in the fire service or EMS. Maybe he preferred a different type of woman.

She caught her train of thought and wondered why it should matter. Ryan was just a friend. Perhaps her best friend, if she were willing to be honest. He'd never shown the least bit of interest in their relationship becoming something more. Oh, sure, he teased – like most of the guys did – but it was nothing she'd ever take serious.

Like earlier that night, when, in spite of his pain, he suggested she climb into the stokes basket beside him.

Again her cheeks burned as she tensed. *What's wrong with me?* She wondered if she had made a mistake coming here to care for Ryan. Being so close to him was having a strange effect on her. She was feeling things she hadn't felt in a long time.

Ryan felt her change as they stepped through the doorway, and looked down at Lacy's face, seeing the confusion written there. Coming back to her home must be hard on her. He understood that. It had been so hard to return to his home, or what was left of his home after Norma and Michelle had died. It had brought back so many memories.

But he had done it. Because he had to. He had no where else to go. He couldn't afford a hotel indefinitely when he could just as easily live in his office until he decided what to do.

Living there had been so painful. Memories of the horrors of that night. The helplessness. The fear. Each time he looked at the charred remains, he relived those memories. Even drinking hadn't helped drown those memories. And the guilt. Such terrible guilt. Wondering if there had been more he could have done.

Then there had been the accident. Luckily, no one had been hurt, though it had been close. He'd been too drunk to drive. Too drunk to know it. But he had. And when the little blond-haired girl had run out in front of him and he heard the thump, he'd been sure he'd hit her. He'd jumped out – rather fallen out – and crawled away from his car, looking for the body of the child he had just killed.

Then miraculously, he heard the faint voice of a child mixed among others. But he'd been too far gone to know anything but relief. Relief the child had been alive.

One lesson was all it had taken. After that night, he'd never drunk again. He knew he could just as easily have killed that child, instead of just thinking he had. Instead, he'd been reminded there was a higher power looking out for him. Very likely trying to teach him a lesson.

He spent a lot of time in prayer after that, realizing just how little he'd turned to God after the fire. Realizing that distance had been wrong.

He'd also realized something else. He needed to do something positive with his life. He had to turn tragedy into something good.

It was then he started following the fire trucks to whatever emergency they were responding. Whenever he heard their sirens sound, he'd follow. He didn't know if it was some kind of personal torture he had to inflict upon himself, or if it was a way of reaching out to someone else who may be suffering the same pain he had suffered.

What he did know was what he learned from watching those firefighters in action.

He had seen their dedication. How they struggled to save lives and property, just as they had tried to save his own. He saw the difficulties they faced, often with shortages of personnel, as had also been the case the night of his fire. He wondered what, if anything, he could do to help them.

It was then he realized there was something he could do. He could become one of them. He could volunteer to be a firefighter. He could try to prevent a repeat of what happened to his family.

But even that wasn't enough to chase away the demons inside him. The memories still brought so much pain. He knew only time would help him heal. And distance, he had thought.

So he sold what was left of his home and got in his car and drove. He had no particular direction. He just sensed that when he found the right place, he'd know it. In his heart, he suspected God would give him a sign so he'd know when he got there.

There were several small towns before Schuylkill Valley. But it was there his car decided to break down. It was in Schuylkill Valley he had to get a hotel room while they fixed the old Toyota he had driven since totaling his BMW the night he thought he'd hit the child.

Then one night, there was a fire right across from his hotel.

It was from his vantage point, at the hotel window, he watched the first to arrive, a feisty, golden-haired firefighter. She slipped into her air pack, put the hat back on her head, grabbed the hose off the back of the pumper and started into the building, uncaring that she had no one to back her up as she went inside.

It was in Schuylkill Valley he decided to settle down. That fire had to be a sign.

Lacy reached for the switch and turned on the light, surprised to find the living room had changed little from the way she had left it. She turned back to her companion and caught him staring at her strangely.

"Do you need help into the room?" she asked.

"Not the room I'm going to," he said, watching as understanding lit her blue eyes. She smiled.

He loved it when she smiled. The way the corners of her mouth turned up forcing dimples to her cheeks. Her eyes flashed like sapphires. She made you feel joyous just looking at her.   She'd pass for a little girl when she smiled like that, he thought, hoping she did that often. It would make being alone with her, even for a short time, so much easier.

Sometimes she looked so vulnerable. It aroused his desire to hold her. To make her life right again. Yet when her eyes darkened to a deep ocean blue, he felt his the stirrings of a different feeling.

For a moment he forgot his leg. But only for a moment. As he put pressure on it, pain shot all the way up his thigh.

"You better take your pill while you're in there," Lacy ordered as she followed him down he hall, ready in case he lost his balance and needed her help. "I'll turn down your bed while you're in there."

"Yes, the pill," he stated. "I'll definitely take it while I'm in there." *Perhaps it will help erase more than the pain.* Like his thoughts, that were suddenly taking a new direction.

CHAPTER FIFTEEN

Lacy didn't think she'd fall asleep so easily, but she did – practically the moment her head hit the pillow she had stolen from the sofa in the living room.

At first, she had just stood there, glancing around the room that had, for such a brief time, been her son's nursery. She'd been surprised to find Ryan hadn't changed a thing. Even the stenciled drawings were still on the wall. The same brightly painted, red, white and blue shutters still hung from the room's single window. It was a cheerful room. Still that way, in spite of the fact it was empty of the nursery furniture she had so carefully chosen – furniture that was now squeezed into the tiny room next to her bedroom in her parents' home, looking out of place against the flowery papered walls of a room that had been her mother's sewing room.

She was certain she would suffer the same restless, interrupted sleep she had during those first exhaustive nights following Mike's funeral. But within seconds she was sound asleep.

Several hours later she was awakened to the sound of Ryan calling out. She raised herself from the floor and rushed to his room, hearing the desperation in his raspy voice as he begged someone to help him.

She supposed it was understandable after all he'd been through.

As she approached she saw he was sitting upright in his bed. "Please save them!" he pleaded.

Strange, she thought, realizing he had said "Save them", not "Save me". She could see by the glazed, horrified look in his emerald eyes he was having a nightmare. A bad one, judging by the feel of his cold damp skin as she pushed him back against his pillow.

"Shhh, Ryan," she whispered soothingly. "It's alright. It's a bad dream."

He grasped her arm, clinging to her almost desperately. "Norma?" Then his eyes began to clear, he relaxed against his pillow as if in defeat. A long sigh escaped his lips as he dropped his hand back to his side. "Lacy, it's you."

"Yes, it's me," she said as she reached out, gently brushing his dark, wavy hair out of his face with the tips of her fingers, feeling the dampness of perspiration, and of tears. "Everything is okay. You can go back to sleep now."

But was it? she wondered, curious about his nightmare. Who was Norma?

"My mouth is so parched," he said in a gravelly voice, still drugged from sleep, and probably his medication.

"I'll get you some water," she said, quickly turning to leave.

"You're still here," he said in the same thick voice.

She turned back to make certain whether he was really speaking to her, or the unknown woman who had entered his dreams. His eyes looked clear.

"I was too tried to drive home," she lied. "I decided to spend the night."

"Thanks," he replied simply, then smiled before closing his eyes.

When she returned with the water, his breathing was deep and regular. She stood looking down at him wondering what haunted him so that it caused such a nightmare. She was more certain than ever he had once loved and lost. Whoever Norma was, Lacy knew she had been very special to him.

She placed the glass on the nightstand in case he awoke and wanted it later then returned to the nursery floor. But this time it wasn't as easy to return to sleep as she thought about the man in the next room.

She felt she knew him so well, yet really, she knew so little about him. She felt so close to him, as though they were kindred spirits. He always seemed so open, yet she realized, not for the first time, there was a part of himself he didn't share.

It was that part she wondered about, realizing she wanted to know everything there was to know about him. As he had come to know everything about her, getting her to open up to him about her many doubts and her fears.

They hadn't known one another long, but they had developed an understanding of each other. Even more than the understanding she had shared with her husband. And it was that very thought that plagued her most as she lay, praying for sleep, so she wouldn't have to analyze the reasons.

#

Except to run home to shower, change, and pick up her son, Lacy stayed with Ryan the entire next day. He hadn't minded the fact that she had brought her son along. Rather, he seemed to enjoy having the boy there that day.

But a couple of times, she'd wondered if bringing Mikie along had been a mistake. He hadn't been content to just sit in his stroller, and when she put him on the floor he wanted to explore. He'd just begun crawling and his curiosity kept her from getting a moment's peace.

"I suggest tomorrow when you come, you bring his play pen along," Ryan stated when she chased Mikie for what seemed like the hundredth time. "That is, if you'll be coming again tomorrow. I do have my appointment with the orthopedic surgeon. I'll need someone to take me."

Lacy smiled, finally sitting on the floor between her son and the archway separating the kitchen and living room. "I'll take you. But I have my doubts about taking Mikie along. I'll have my hands full with you."

"We can stop and pick him up afterward," Ryan said, laughing as the child tried to crawl around his mother. Finally, she grabbed the boy and lifted him into the air.

She was lying on her back with her aims outstretched, laughing at her son. "Now what are you going to do?" she teased. The baby's return giggle had a bell-like ring.

Ryan smiled at the exchange, feeling more contented than he had in years. At least, until he moved, and stiffness from the unaccustomed inactivity made him grunt with discomfort.

"Are you okay?" Lacy quickly asked, lowering her son back to the floor. She sat up looking at Ryan more closely.

"Actually, I could use a change in position," he said, then spotted the baby quickly making his escape. "But you better catch him first."

Lacy made another dash for her son, scooping him up and putting him back in his stroller. She then turned her attention back to Ryan.

"How about you just help me up till I get my balance, then I'll move over to the chair," he said. "I'd like to sit up for awhile."

"Okay. What about something to eat? Is it still too early for you?"

He nodded. "Besides there's not much here."

"So I saw when I raided your refrigerator to make lunch. I probably should do some shopping for you."

"I don't want you to become my maid, Lacy."

She shrugged. "I haven't got much else to do. Mom can't stand me helping her with much at home. And I can take care of Mikie whether I'm here or there. Of course, I do have to admit, he is much less troublesome at home. I think I will bring his play pen tomorrow."

About that time, Mikie started to cry. She could tell he was tired. He had napped very little that day. He was probably thirsty, too. "I better go get his bottle out of the refrigerator."

Ryan smiled. "Why not sit him over here next to me?"

She pushed the stroller beside his chair. "Maybe I should take him home."

"Let me give him his bottle first. Then if you think it's best, you can take him home."

She agreed, silently watching as Ryan held Mikie as he drank his bottle. It was the most peaceful time she had had all day.

So peaceful she started to doze. But the doorbell awakened her with a start.

It had also jarred Mikie who she assumed had been almost asleep. Now he started to cry. "That, is his sleepy cry," she told Ryan. "I really am going to have to take him home."

She opened the door as she spoke, frowning as she turned to see it was Rose Sinclair on the doorstep. The other woman looked surprised to see her, then she remembered she had parked her car in the garage to keep it out of the heat of the mid-day sun.

"Oh, Lacy," Rose stammered. "I. . .I ahh. . . didn't know someone was here taking care of Ryan. When I heard about his accident, I thought. . . I thought maybe I could help out."

Lacy forced herself to smile, knowing it was no longer in her place to decide who entered this house. "Ryan, you have company," she said, stepping aside.

Ryan looked up. Seeing Rose, he forced a smile. "Excuse me if I don't get up." He knew it was stupid, but it was all he could think to say. He couldn't imagine what she wanted. Well, he could imagine, but he didn't want to think about that.

"I didn't know you had someone to take care of you," Rose started nervously. "So I thought I'd stop by."

"Actually, Lacy's been here all day."

"Then she must be due for a break." Rose said as she came further into the room, glancing at the squirming, crying child. "Looks like she has enough to do."

"Yeah, I do have to take Mikie home." Lacy rushed over and took her son out of Ryan's hands.

Ryan looked up at her pleadingly. Mikie still sobbed. He felt like joining him. "You will be back with that dinner you promised me."

"I can make something for you," Rose offered.

"Actually there's nothing here to make, is there Lacy?" Ryan quickly added with a smile.

"I could call for something." The auburn-haired woman persisted.

"If you'd like that Ryan, it's okay with me," Lacy said, seeing his green eyes look at her beseechingly. "I'm sure my mother won't be too disappointed."

"No! I don't want to disappoint her," Ryan grasped at her words, not knowing what they meant, but he was happy she had said them.

"My Mom made extra for dinner tonight," Lacy didn't feel she was lying. In reality, she had expected her mother to call before now and make the offer. "She's expecting me to pick it up when I take Mikie home for the night."

"Your mother's so thoughtful," Rose said with sincerity.

So much sincerity, Lacy almost felt guilty for making up the excuse – almost.

With a promise to return after getting Mikie fed and into bed, Lacy left. She was almost home when she realized Mikie didn't have his favorite stuffed toy. She pulled off the road and looked in the back seat, but it wasn't there. She must have left it back at the house.

Turning around she headed back, knowing Mikie wouldn't go to sleep without it.

The door was open, but she still knocked before stepping back inside. Her eyes froze when they reached the chair where she had left Ryan seated. He was leaning forward and Rose was giving him a massage. Their position awkward as Rose stood beside the chair, leaned over to reach the top of his shoulders. She didn't even stop when Lacy entered. She only flashed her a big, too-innocent smile.

Innocent! Ha! Lacy thought feeling her cheeks burn.

"I, ah. . .I forgot something," she explained. "I'll be right out of here."

"Lacy!" Ryan called after her, his green eyes bright with panic as he waited for her to turn back to him.

"I can't stay, I have Mikie in the car," she said impatiently.

"You will be back, right?" he asked quickly.

She frowned, not certain now that she would return. That she should return.

"Please," he said, holding her gaze with pleading eyes. "I'm really hungry."

Lacy looked at Ryan's panicked expression. If ever there was a man in a compromising predicament, it was he. Well, he was a big boy. He'd have to get out of it on his own.

"I'll be back," she replied. "But it won't be for a while."

Rose smiled, looking something like a cat with a catnip toy. Ryan winced and hung his head forward.

She was almost to the door when she looked back at Rose and her next victim. An unwilling one, she knew without a doubt. And that pleased her.

"On second thought," she said. "Since I know how hungry you are, I'll be right back. Mom won't mind putting Mikie to bed."

CHAPTER SIXTEEN

On the second day after Ryan's accident, he finally had his leg in a cast. The doctor's appointment had been exhausting for Ryan, yet he had insisted they stop and pick up Mikie on their way home.

Home.

Lacy thought about that to a great extent later that afternoon while Ryan and Mikie rested. This had been her home for several months before she moved. It had been the home she'd dreamed about. The home she'd taken great care in planning. The home she decorated with all the little things that labeled it as her's.

Now it was Ryan's and funny as it felt, strange as it seemed, it felt more like Ryan's home than it had ever felt like hers.

There were few physical changes in the house. Yet, there were many small things. It seemed strange to her that in such a short time, Ryan had put his subtle brand in every room.

On the refrigerator there was an awkwardly sketched picture of a firefighter in his full bunker gear. At the bottom was written. *Thank You, from Mrs. Smith's First Grade. We love you.* She suspected he had earned that affection by working with her aunt in one of her programs at the elementary school. And it had meant enough to him to keep the memento hanging long after the school year closed.

In the bathroom she noted the brands of toothpaste and mouthwash he used were different than what she used. His shaving cream, the kind that smelled like citrus. His razor, the double-edged kind. Towels were neatly hung from the shower curtain rod to dry. The hamper was filled with his dirty clothes.

Enough dirty cloths that she gathered it all together, deciding to fill her time by doing some of his laundry.

Downstairs she found another change. The fitness equipment was set up in a corner near the laundry. She suspected it had been well-used since he'd installed it there. He didn't maintain his firm-muscled torso from sitting all day behind a desk. He was a man who enjoyed physical activity.

She was glad she hadn't returned the equipment. It was nice to know someone was getting good use of it. She decided to take advantage of it, too, while she waited for the first load to go through its wash cycle. After all, she had put on a few pounds, as her father reminded her the day of the picnic.

She didn't start with too much weight, afraid her unused muscles would tighten from the unaccustomed activity. She knew she hadn't exactly left herself go, but then neither had she stayed in as good shape as she'd been while she was a firefighter. She'd often thought that was why she had had such an easy pregnancy.

She decided to stop when she started to work up a sweat. Maybe she'd bring extra clothes next time. Something old to work out in, or her sweats. Then she could shower and change after she was through.

That is, if there is a next time, she thought, wondering how long Ryan would need someone there to take care of him. She suspected it was more a case of how long he'd allow someone to care for him.

She felt good as she returned upstairs to check on the two sleeping males. Mikie was busy sucking his thumb. Ryan was gently snoring. She smiled as she went to the kitchen to begin planning dinner, feeling content.

When she heard the familiar squeaky brakes of the mail truck, she decided to go outside and check the box for Ryan's mail. It was still too early to begin making dinner, and she was restless, in need of more activity. Her light workout had left her wanting more.

She pulled several envelopes from the box, a long brown one with the picture of a familiar celebrity on it, and the message that Ryan could be their next big winner. The various-sized white ones she supposed were bills. She glanced at them only briefly, more out of habit than curiosity.

The return address on one in particular drew her attention. It was from the State Firemen's Association. She suspected it contained information about the award they had nominated Aunt Rainy to receive. Ryan had said the award committee made their choice in early August.

He'd told her he and several of the other chiefs had all written separate letters submitting her name; though she had suspected he had written them all, and the others had only signed them. But the important thing was they had agreed her aunt deserved the award.

She rushed back to the house, anxious to find out what the letter contained. Fortunately, she wouldn't have to wait long. She could hear Ryan stirring. She stood in front of the recliner where he had taken his nap, waiting for him to open his eyes.

When he did, his long-lashed lids fluttered open slowly, then closed again, as a contented smile crossed his face. She realized he wasn't fully awake. She ruffled through the letters, making more noise than was necessary, hoping the sound would wake him. Then she felt guilty knowing he needed his rest.

Patience had never been her strong suit.

214

She bit her lip as she looked down at his still figure. Humming, she walked to the opposite side of the chair, stooping to pick up the magazine he had dropped when he dozed.

As she raised her head, she found clear emerald eyes staring into her own.

"I'm sorry, did I wake you?" she lied, and knew the warmth she felt rising in her cheeks was revealing that she wasn't really sorry at all.

"I could be awakened like this every day," he said huskily, still obviously drugged from sleep. He stretched, giving her a smile that made her body heat rise still more. More than even her earlier exercise had.

She stood, about to step away, but Ryan's hand grasped her's stopping her escape. "Of course, I can think of a few other ways that might be even more enjoyable."

Lacy eyes widened as the suggestive nature of his words registered to her. Ryan's teasing around everyone else was one thing. But alone, it was more than she could handle.

"Does that mean you'd like a cup of coffee with your mail?" she said, nervously thrusting the mail she was still holding into his lap.

"No, it doesn't mean that." He laughed, letting go of her hand. "But I suppose that's what I'll have to settle for."

"You don't have to," Lacy retorted, more in control now that he wasn't touching her. She didn't like the way his touch had such an effect on her senses, making her feel less in control. "I could always call Rose to . . . give you another back massage."

"Coffee's fine." He gave her a sobering look. "Perfect, in fact. Just stay away from the telephone."

Lacy laughed, then remembered the reason she had been so anxious for him to wake. "By the way, you'll find a letter in there from the State Firemen's Association."

"Then hurry up with that coffee and I'll read you the news," he ordered.

"You're a very bossy man, Ryan Simon." She darted him an icy look.

"Please," he added with a curl to his lips as he watched her head for the kitchen.

"That's more like it."

"If I'd known saying please was all it took, I'd have added that with my first request," he called after her, laughing as she picked up the pillow from the sofa and threw it at his head.

When she returned carrying two cups of steaming coffee, Ryan was sitting with the open letter in hand, a wide grin on his face. "She's got it!"

"Was there ever any doubt? You went out of your way to see that she did."

He took the mug she offered him. "Only because your aunt taught me a lesson I really needed."

Lacy took her coffee to the sofa, curling her feet beneath her as she sat, waiting patiently for Ryan to explain what he meant. She detected a serious note to his voice. His eyes darkening to near black, a faraway expression on his face.

"For the first time I've felt like I'm really doing something. Really making a difference," he continued, searching for the words to explain to Lacy. He wanted her to understand what drove him. More than anyone, he realized, he wanted her to understand. "Some people say that we can't save them all. . . But. . .we've got to save more."

"Ryan, we do the best we can do," she said, thinking she understood what was going through his mind. Many times she'd sensed Ryan felt driven by his inabilities, rather than his abilities. Fighting what he couldn't do. Perhaps in part because of that night when he'd lost his partner. The helplessness he must have felt then.

"Your aunt says for every fire that doesn't start, there is a life saved. She really believes that. It's that belief that keeps her going."

"That's why she deserves the award." Pride showed in Lacy's deep blue eyes as she looked back at Ryan. Her expression softened. "Thanks to you, she'll get it."

Ryan looked away, lost in his thoughts. He'd wanted to tell her all about himself. Share the good and the bad. But somehow he couldn't find the right words to begin. Maybe there weren't any right words.

He was about to open his mouth when the other occupant of the room beat him too it. Mikie let out a cry that told them he was awake and he wanted out of his prison.

"Look!" Lacy jumped to her feet, her excitement showing in her beaming smile. "He's pulled himself up. He's standing!"

Ryan warmed at the sight. As much the sight of the mother as the child. She cherished all those special moments. Each new thing her son learned as he grew. He'd known that feeling once.

He knew it again, he thought, sharing her enthusiasm.

"Don't scare him by racing over," Ryan warned her, remembering doing much the same thing the first time his daughter stood. "He'll think he did something wrong and. . ."

Too late, the boy's startled, blue eyes opened wide, his hands letting go of the upper rail of his playpen. He tumbled backward with a thump on his behind, his smile disappearing, replaced by the shock of his fall.

Mikie started to wail. Ryan laughed. Lacy comforted, adding words of praise for her son's accomplishment.

"He'll stand up again," Ryan assured her as he lowered the footrest of the recliner and reached for the crutches close beside his chair. "Probably better than I do."

His moment of truth was lost as he watched Lacy busying herself with her son. It was the child's turn for some attention. He'd have plenty of time to share his thoughts with Lacy later.

But later, they had an unexpected guest. Rainy came to visit.

He'd slowly returned from the bathroom having heard the doorbell. When he entered the living room, Rainy was holding her grand-nephew while Lacy held a large casserole dish.

"Look what my aunt brought for dinner," Lacy said when he entered the room. "Now you don't have to suffer though one of my meals."

"I wouldn't call it suffering through," he said as he hobbled over for a closer look. "You're a good cook."

"You've only ever eaten two things I've made," Lacy reminded him. "And they were different versions of the same recipe."

"What about breakfast?"

"Breakfast is hard to ruin," Lacy replied, shaking her head of honey-gold curls.

"You could burn the bacon."

"You don't eat bacon." Her blue eyes were bright with humor as she turned back to her aunt. "He insists on toast or Grapenuts. How can I ruin those?"

"Same way I did the first time I made breakfast for Mark," Rainy replied. "I started the curtains on fire after burning his toast."

"You're kidding." Ryan turned to her with surprise. "Bet you never lived that down."

"Wouldn't have, if anyone knew," she admitted. "I hope you'll keep the secret. I mean. . .there's a few who would love rubbing that one in. Ms. Fire Prevention nearly burns down house."

"It couldn't have been that bad. I don't remember it," Lacy put in.

Rainy shook her head. "No, I managed to use the hose over the sink to spray water on the curtains to douse the flames."

"But the toaster!" Ryan said aghast.

"I didn't say I was smart back then," Rainy confessed. "Luckily Mark came into the room just before I started squirting water and managed to pull the plug."

Ryan shook his head. "Ms. Fire Prevention nearly burns down house," he teased good-naturedly. "then nearly electrocutes husband."

"Shut up or I'll take my offerings home," Rainy scolded.

"Wait! I want to check to make sure they're not burnt offerings," Ryan continued, leaning heavily on one crutch, propping the other one under his arm while he lifted the lid of the casserole. "Doesn't smell burnt."

"You're pushing your luck, Buddy," Rainy warned. "So, do I get invited in, or do I just stand here and get verbally abused?"

"Come right in," Ryan waved his hand palm up before him, motioning toward the living room.

"Ah. . .Maybe I should clean up a little," Lacy said quickly, remembering the letter Ryan had just been reading.

"Doesn't matter to me," Rainy replied. "I'm here to visit. Not to inspect the house."

"Yes, but Ryan's made quite a mess."

"I'd have never suspected you for a slob," Rainy teased Ryan as Lacy hurried ahead of them into the room.

"Oh, she exaggerates." Ryan hobbled along behind. "She has no compassion for a cripple."

"No compassion!" Lacy turned back to him, her eyes flashing like sapphires as she tried to act put out. "Why am I here if I have no compassion?" She raised her chin in challenge.

"Because you enjoy giving me a bath."

Lacy's jaw dropped open, her cheeks on fire. He'd caught her off guard with that comment. Quickly, she grabbed the mail from beside the chair and started back across the room. She knew Ryan had been teasing.

"Look out, she'll use ice water next time," Rainy teased.

"I'll have you know, the only baths I give are to that little guy in your arms!" Lacy said indignantly as she escaped the room, hearing their laughter following. Her aunt knew her well enough to know that was the truth.

When she returned to the room she saw Ryan with a letter in his hand. She thought she'd just disposed of them all safely beneath the dish towels in a drawer in the kitchen.

"Listen to this, Lacy," Ryan said, meeting her hesitant, blue eyes with smiling, green ones. "Rainy just got a letter today from the State Firemen's Association. Says our department fire safety team is going to receive an award at their convention."

"Congratulations." Lacy turned to her aunt, her face alive with pleasure.

"We all share in that," Rainy said with pride, turning back to Ryan. "You helped with most of the work."

"Some of it," Ryan corrected. "Most of it was done by you."

Rainy's modesty was admirable. She never failed to share credit for any project they did. No matter how small the role a person played she made it seem as though their help had been indispensable. It would be nice seeing when Rainy, too, received her just reward. Lacy knew no one worked harder than she.

"I thought it would be nice if some of my committee were there with me to receive the award at the convention," Rainy added to the conversation. "I'm going to drive out the night before so I can be there for the whole day. I'm game to take passengers. I hate driving alone."

"What about Uncle Mark?" Lacy asked, knowing he had been pre-warned about Rainy's nomination for the award. He'd said he'd think about joining them if his wife won.

"He's got to work," her aunt replied, her brown eyes sadly mellow, almost wistful. "It would have made a nice second honeymoon."

Lacy glanced at Ryan and saw him smile. She knew he was thinking the same thing as she. Rainy was going to get her wish.

"Looks like you won't have anything better to do for awhile," Rainy added, looking across the room at her host. "I figured you might agree to go along."

Ryan stroked his chin as though thinking about it. "I don't know. . .I might not be up to a trip with you. I hear Lacy gets her wild-woman ways from you."

Lacy darted him another icy glance.

Rainy's red locks bounced as she threw back her head and laughed. "I promise you'll be safe. Besides, I was assuming you'd provide your own room since rooms aren't exactly in our budget." She turned to her niece. "Now you, Lacy, if you decide to come along, I can offer to share my room."

"Talk about special treatment."

"Nepotism," Rainy responded with a smile.

Lacy had every intention of being there, but she doubted she could spend the night. Perhaps she could ride in with her uncle if he joined them. There would be room even if her nephews came too, though they hadn't been told about the award for fear they'd let something slip.

"I doubt I can make it," Lacy lied. "I know Mom would keep Mikie, but I hate leaving him overnight." At least that was true.

"Guess that leaves just you and me." Ryan frowned at the cast covering his right leg. "Unfortunately, you'll be in the driver's seat."

"That's no problem, as long as you keep talking so I stay awake," Rainy replied with a relieved smile. "Mark's afraid I'll fall asleep at the wheel, knowing how sleepy I get whenever I drive. But I told him not to worry, it's only a three hour drive. Of course, I plan to leave right after work that Thursday."

"I'll not only talk, I'll keep you full of coffee," Ryan replied. "I'll make sure my Thermos is filled before we leave."

"It's too bad you can't join us," Rainy turned back to her niece. "I know Lois won't mind keeping little Mikie."

"I didn't say she'd mind. It's me who'll mind," she replied as she looked at her son squirming to get down from her aunt's lap. "I can't imagine being away from him for an entire night."

Rainy laughed, heartier now than before. "Being a mother is still too new. Give yourself a year or two and you'll be begging for a night to yourself."

Lacy wondered if that really would be true. It hadn't happened with her mother. She had never tired of having someone to care for. It had been the focus of her entire life.

"Boy, is she in for a surprise!" Lacy exclaimed after her aunt had gone. "I know I'll be there for sure. I can't imagine Uncle Mark won't go. And I suppose the boys would have no complaints about taking a day off from school."

"No, they probably won't," Ryan absently replied, lost in his own thoughts. Finally, he smiled. "We could make this an extra nice surprise for Rainy."

"Whatcha got going through your mind?" Lacy asked as she raced after her son as he crawled toward the kitchen. Scooping him up, she carried him back to his playpen.

"She mentioned making it a second honeymoon if Mark could come along. Unbeknownst to her, we can make the reservations for a second night so she and Mark can stay over and celebrate."

Lacy suspected there was a great deal of a romantic inside Ryan. She smiled, liking his idea. "What about you and me? And the boys if they come?"

"Well, chauffeur, it would hardly be a romantic evening if we stayed and tagged along. Besides, I figure you meant that part about leaving Mikie for a entire night."

Lacy forced a smile. "When I have to, I will."

"You already did. Two nights, in fact," Ryan commented, his green eyes locking with hers. "I want to thank you."

Lacy tried to shrug his words aside. What could she say? To brush it aside like nothing would be a lie. Yet, she wasn't ready to admit how much being there to help him had meant to her. Instead she settled for a simple, "You're welcome."

"And tonight, Lacy, you're going home," Ryan added with authority. "I think now that I have the regular cast on this leg, I'll be able to get around much better."

That was it. The shoe had dropped. Ryan was telling her he no longer needed her. She tried to force a smile.

"But I would like it. . .if you could sometimes. . .still come by during the day – whenever you're not too busy." Ryan quickly added. "There's still a few things I'll need help doing. And I'm not too proud to admit it."

"Of course I'll come." *No man is an island.* She smiled, remembering his very words. She was pleased he practiced what he preached.

"And bring Squirt along," Ryan said, using the nickname he had tagged on her son. "I kind of like having him around."

"He'll be around all right," Lacy laughed, watching as her son again pulled himself up in his playpen. "Before long he'll be around and around and around, everything."

Ryan laughed with her, relishing the feel of having a family again. He almost hoped his leg wouldn't heal, so it wouldn't have to end.

\#

The day of the State Firemen's Association convention award ceremony finally came. Rainy's surprise was total when she saw Lacy, Mark and her sons come into the huge convention center auditorium where the ceremony was to be held.

"What in the world are you doing here?" she asked.

"You made me feel so guilty for not coming, I called Lacy last night and asked her if she'd ride along," Mark effectively lied, his expression casual, not giving away one thing. He shrugged. "Then I figured, why not go all out and bring the boys. They've helped you one or two times with some of your fire prevention stuff."

He's a great actor, Lacy thought, noting that his sons weren't quite as ready for the stage. She nudged them when they looked about to burst at the seams, ready to spill the beans.

Ryan leaned on his crutches, smiling at them. "She was trying to talk me into going up on stage with her to accept the department's award," he said. "I told her it would take me too long with these crutches. Now maybe the rest of you can."

"No way!" Brad, the youngest said, wrinkling up his nose. "Look at all these people."

"It would be worse than giving a verbal report in front of the class," his older brother added.

Mark didn't look any more keen on the idea than his sons, so Rainy turned to Lacy.

"Wait a minute!" She held out her hands palms up. "You're not going to steamroll me, Aunt Rainy. I agreed to come. But you're not going to get me up there in the hot seat. That's what committee chairs are for."

"It's lonely at the top, Rainy," Ryan teased, motioning to the rest of the group. "If we hurry we can still get some good seats. Preferably with one along the right isle for me."

Ryan led them toward the front of the room. There would be no hiding in the back pews that day. He wanted to make certain they all had a good view.

Rainy waited as they started giving out the special awards to individuals.

The man at the microphone announced several awards. The next was Rainy's. He started listing the many accomplishments Ryan had written in his letter.

"In particular, this member, has worked diligently to develop a program that will help ensure the safety of people with disabilities," the announcer concluded. "The program has become a much needed program to also train the emergency service. Because of her work we have chosen Lorraine Shelby as this year's recipient of the Fire Safety Educator of the Year Award."

Rainy was so anxious for the final group awards that she barely realized they were speaking about her until they mentioned the special program. Then she looked stunned with disbelief, even after they gave her name.

"That's you, Aunt Rainy," Lacy said as she turned to her baffled aunt, giving her a wide smile. "That list of endorsements just read was for you."

Rainy looked at the members of her group, tears sparkling in her brown eyes. "You didn't. . . "

"Yes, we did," Ryan said with a grin so wide it lifted the corners of his mouth. "Now get up there and accept your award!"

Rainy still seemed in shock as she went onto the stage. Her voice trembled as she thanked the award's committee and the association, then she looked directly at her family and friends. "And special thanks to all of you," she added. "For believing, not in me, but in fire safety education. This isn't for me. This is for all of you."

"How did she do it?" Ryan whispered to Lacy. "She managed to again turn around and give the credit back to everyone else."

"That's our Aunt Rainy," Lacy said with a smile, watching as the woman in question came back to join them.

"You know what they say about paybacks," Rainy whispered, tears still filling her bright eyes. "But in this case. . .I don't know how I could ever pay you back."

"Hey, we weren't in on this alone," Ryan said. "You should have read your letters of endorsement."

Lacy looked at Ryan, seeing him as the wonderful man that he was. She knew he was a lot like her aunt. He, too, was managing to turn things around and share the credit with others.

"Hey, Dad said to give this to you. He's sorry he couldn't come." Lacy handed her aunt a card from her father.

Rainy opened it slowly so as not to disturb the next part of the ceremony. Lacy glanced over as she opened it. Inside was a simple congratulations card, with a note, written in Lois's familiar scrawl. *It's time to give you a night to remember. The boys will stay with us tonight. So don't worry. They'll be fed and in bed by ten.*

Lacy smiled at her aunt, handing her a tissue to catch the tears that were now beginning to overflow. "Better dab those away. They're about to give the group awards."

#

It was a long drive home, so after a bit of coaxing from her sixteen-year-old cousin, Lacy let Kevin drive. But only after they had gotten out of city traffic and onto the turnpike. After all, she thought, he had dozed during part of the drive that morning. Maybe she could get a little rest in the back seat with Brad.

But she quickly learned, adults don't rest when younger drivers are at the wheel. She found herself craning her neck to watch the road, not that she knew what she could do to prevent an accident from the back seat.

Once or twice she caught Ryan's smile as he glanced back and shook his head. He seemed totally at ease with a teen at the wheel, chatting away about the upcoming football season. She knew her cousin was a tight-end with Schuylkill Valley High School's football team.

Mike had played football, she remembered. But he had never noticed her in high school. Nor, she him, other than by reputation. Their worlds had been miles apart. She was three years younger than he was, and all her extra time had been spent at the fire station.

Then again, she remembered, he had never seemed to pay much attention to her after he joined the fire company. Except when their paths had to cross as part of their job. And even then, it had been obvious he didn't approve of her.

That only made her try all the harder to be good at her job. No, that wasn't true, she admitted. She had to be the best. She had to be better than everyone else. And she knew she wasn't alone in those feelings. Many women, who worked in what had traditionally been a male job, said the same. It was the only way to survive.

And she had survived. Of course, it had cost her a lot. She learned along the way she was never going to win over those who were hard core sexists. She would always be a threat. A thorn in their sides.

223

Her frown deepened as she remembered how much that had bothered her back then. As a teen she had struggled to fit in, and never really had. She never seemed to be what other people thought she should be. She wasn't the daughter her mother wanted. Nor, the son her father wanted. Not even the wife Mike had wanted.

She closed her eyes at that thought, remembering how she had been so overwhelmed by Mike's sudden attention. Infatuated by his charm. So willing to try to be the kind of wife he wanted. Yet, she never could be that. And now, she knew why. Mike had never really loved her. She was just a means of getting out of a difficult situation. For him, in the end, it must have been like jumping from the frying pan to the fire.

She sighed, not realizing exactly how much that sound had revealed – until she opened her eyes again to meet Ryan's emerald gaze, concern clearly etched on his face.

She broke away from that gaze afraid he'd read her mind. That he'd know her thoughts were still often plagued with doubts. Afraid he'd feel sorry for her. She didn't want his sympathy.

Turning back to the carrot-topped boy beside her, she wished he had continued the incessant conversation he had during the morning trip. But almost as soon as he got into the car, he'd dozed, his nervous energy exhausted from the big day. He'd been so excited for his mother.

She heard Kevin yawn, then looked front again as the boy stretched one long arm, rolling his dark head as though he had a kink. She glanced back at Ryan, watching the accelerated beat of the pulse in his neck, the only sign that he wasn't as relaxed as she first thought him to be.

"I'm about ready for some coffee," he said, glancing toward the young driver. "How about you, Kev? There's a rest stop up ahead."

"Yeah, coffee," the boy replied. "Or, maybe a coke."

Lacy hid her smile, knowing her cousin didn't like coffee. She suspected he was grasping at something that would give him a break without having to admit he was tired. She looked in the mirror and saw his weary, narrowed gaze.

Aunt Rainy would kill her it anything happened to her boys. And driving when exhausted was an accident waiting to happen.

As soon as the car stopped, Brian woke – though awake wasn't exactly what she would have called it. Lacy guided the zombie-like boy into the turnpike facility.

"I don't know about the rest of you, but I need a bathroom," she said, leaving their side and taking the direction toward the restrooms.

"We've still got a long ways ahead of us," Ryan acknowledged. "Maybe we should all make a pit stop."

Lacy glanced back over her shoulder and nearly laughed at the picture they made. Ryan hobbling on his crutches with two tired young men behind him: one making a noble effort not to show his fatigue, the other, she suspected, possibly sleepwalking.

She laughed to herself, knowing beyond any doubt, it was her turn to drive.

They had traveled only a few miles when Ryan turned around to check the silent occupants of the backseat.

"Exhaustion is, having a Coke and still being able to sleep," he said when he turned back to her. "That caffeine and sugar jolt isn't keeping Kevin awake."

Lacy laughed, turning back to Ryan with a smile. "And the worst part of it is, if either of those two were with a bunch of their friends right now, sleep would probably be as far away as home."

"Undoubtedly," Ryan agreed. "That's not saying much for our company, is it? Maybe that's why Kevin jumped at the chance to let you drive."

"I thought it was more because I suggested we sing a few songs because I was bored sitting in the back with Sleeping Beauty."

Ryan joined in her laughter, loving the way it tingled from her lips. "That could have had something to do with it."

"It had everything to do with it," Lacy confirmed. "You haven't heard me sing."

"Oh yes, I have," Ryan informed her. "And I enjoyed it just as much as Squirt did."

"Anyone can sing lullabies. And believe me, I wasn't exactly suggesting we sing them. I was trying to keep our driver awake, not put him to sleep."

"Now I guess it's up to me to keep our driver awake," Ryan acknowledged. "We've still got about two hours drive. What do you suggest?"

"Singing is out of the question," Lacy teased. "I've also heard you sing."

"When?" He gave her a mortified look.

"When you were putting Mikie's nursery furniture together."

"It didn't stop you from sleeping."

"That's exactly my point," she smiled, remembering his deep baritone voice, softly singing an old Elvis tune, *I've Got To Be Me*. She remembered thinking, just before she'd drifted off to sleep, how much those words seemed to hold a message.

"Do you ever miss it?"

"Your singing?"

"No," Ryan laughed. "The house. Your home."

She thought a moment before replying. It had seemed strange returning there, but not in the ways she had thought. How could she explain?

"Actually, my memories are more what I wanted our home to be. We hadn't lived there long. And we weren't home very much. It hardly gave us time to make memories."

Ryan wanted to ask her more, but he wasn't quite certain he wanted to hear the answers. Earlier he had glimpsed something on her face. A weary, sad expression. He didn't want to see her look that way again.

"We lived in an apartment in town for a year before we moved there," she explained, surprised to realize she had few memories from there either. "Mike preferred the apartment." Now why did she add that? she wondered.

"Because it was closer to the station?"

"That was one of the reasons," she replied vaguely.

"I wondered why neither of you ever joined the township station."

Lacy laughed, her eyes bright with good humor. "At a fleeting moment, it may have occurred to us. But they have the reputation of going through members like Imelda Marcos goes through shoes. They get some new ones, use them, then get them out of the way. We've gotten a lot of their previous discards in out stations and many of them have turned out to be good people."

She turned to glance at Ryan. "Maybe I should learn to shut my mouth. Were you thinking of joining them?"

"No. I suspected much the same thing. After all, when you have so many township residents belonging to the Borough fire companies, it makes you wonder why they don't volunteer in their own community."

"In defense of the Incredible Hulk and his crew, there are some who go for the action. There's definitely more of that in town than in the township. There's also a matter of roots. People hang on to what's familiar, like dedication to the community where they were raised or where they lived for a long time. It takes a long time to build new roots somewhere else."

"Yeah, I understand that," Ryan said, thinking how long it had taken him to adjust to the different life he lived here from the one in New York.

"It must have been difficult for you to adjust to the slower pace of small town life, rather than the city," Lacy stated, as though reading his thoughts. "The change between being a C.P.A. and the accounting department at the factory."

"The fire company was the common denominator for me," he said. "I guess that helped me make the adjustment." *Along with my fascination with a honey-blonde beauty who's made me realize I not only can have a new life, but that I want one.*

"And if you didn't live so far away from New York, you'd probably still be responding to calls there."

He doubted that. He hadn't been responding to fight fires. He'd been fighting memories. Fighting the feeling of helplessness. Fighting pain and suffering. As much his, as anyone else's.

But that had changed, too. He wasn't fighting anymore. Least not the memories. He could face those now.

And as far as the helplessness, he finally felt like he had that conquered, too. He was making a difference.

"You know, today was really an experience," he said, speaking aloud what was suddenly on his mind.

"Seeing Aunt Rainy get her award?"

"That, too. But, also seeing so many people who share her beliefs about fire safety," he added. "Maybe once she gets home with that award more people will get the point. Maybe they'll jump on the bandwagon."

"I sure hope so." Lacy sighed, nagged by a doubt that she had tried to dismiss. "It would mean a lot to her."

"It could mean a lot to everyone." Ryan mused. "Especially if we could cut down on the number of fires."

"That's exactly what I was thinking," Lacy replied, trying to hide her frown, knowing there were those who would prefer the opposite effect. But why dampen Ryan's spirits. Not after he had worked so hard to see that her aunt received the recognition she deserved.

CHAPTER SEVENTEEN

It was unusually hot for the last week of September. Ryan tried to ignore the way his leg itched beneath his cast, and decided if he had to break his leg, it would have been far better to have done it in the middle of winter. But then, itching wasn't his only problem. He was also plagued with a feeling of uselessness.

Lacy had come again to run the vacuum through the house. The noise was irritating. Or, perhaps it was just that everything was getting to him these days. He had escaped outside to the patio to get away from it.

He looked down at the child sleeping so peacefully in his stroller and wondered how it was the noise didn't bother him. He thought of another child who had been just the opposite at the same age, crying desperately each time she heard the roar of the vacuum.

He remembered the way Norma would always plan the task of running the cleaner for a time when he'd be there to distract their daughter – sometimes taking her outside for a walk, when weather permitted.

Something he couldn't do now without the help of his crutches. But Mikie certainly didn't need the distraction of a walk. He slept well. Through everything.

As that thought occurred to him the portable telephone rang, proving him wrong. The boy's blue eyes opened wide with a start, his tiny lower lip quivering as though he were about to cry.

"Hey, it's okay, Squirt," Ryan said as he pushed the button to answer on the second ring. "Hold on, please," he said into the phone, not even bothering to find out who it was.

He laid the phone back down, then reached for Mikie and sat him on his lap. "Can tell you've got firefighting in your blood," he said to the boy, watching as his surprised expression changed to a smile. "Sleep soundly through all the other noise, but let anything that sounds remotely like a pager go off and you're instantly awake."

Ryan again reached for the telephone, pulling it away as the baby on his lap made a grab for it. "Hey, I promise I'll let you have it if it's for you." He laughed.

"Thanks for waiting," he said into the phone, listening as the female on the other end introduced herself as Mrs. Jenkins, Administrator of his mother's nursing home in New York. He recalled the slender woman with her graying brown hair pulled back in a severe style that added to her business-like

228

appearance. It was her quick and friendly smile and sparkling green eyes that told of the warmth beneath the surface.

He hadn't spoken to the woman since calling several weeks earlier to tell her about his accident and his inability to make it to visit his mother. As kindly as possible the woman had assured him not to worry, not adding why. She didn't have to. He already knew the reason.

His mother's mental state had regressed to the point she failed to recognize him on his more recent visits. In fact, his visits had been more for himself than for her. It was to ease the guilt he sometimes felt for putting her into the home almost immediately following the fire she had started that fateful night.

Sure, he hadn't known what else he could do. She needed care. More care than she would get living with him in a hotel room. More care than he could give her with all the funeral arrangements that needed to be made.

No, he hadn't done it out of any feelings of animosity toward her for having started that fire. He had reassured her of that during one of her more lucid moments, when realizing what she had done, she'd asked him if he hated her.

Tears had choked him as he told her he would never hate her. Tears he could no longer hold back when she replied that she could, and that she did hate herself.

If there was anything to be thankful about from the disease that threatened her mental state, it was the fact that those moments of tragic memory for her were few before they finally became non-existent, along with so many other things.

He squeezed the phone as he waited for what the woman was about to say. In his heart he already knew it was one of two things. He had known for years that his mother was dying. Either the final moment was close, or it had already come.

"I'm sorry, Mr. Simon," the woman consoled. "Your mother passed away early this morning. We've contacted the funeral home you specified, and unless there's a change in any of your requests, the director of that home should be here shortly."

Ryan left out the breath he hadn't realized he'd been holding and told the woman there would be no changes. "Thank you, Mrs. Jenkins. Please thank all your people . . .for . . .for making my mother's last years as comfortable as you did," he said, in a voice choked from pain and relief.

He had known the day was coming, yet hadn't know how he would feel when it did. Yes, it hurt, but the pain was tendered by the knowledge that there was an end to his mother's suffering. But perhaps suffering wasn't the right word. That had ended some time ago when the disease had eaten away at enough of her mind to give her relief from the helplessness she had felt during her coherent times, knowing something was wrong, yet unable to change it.

Ryan looked down at the small child in his arms, his tiny face focused so intently on his own, as though trying to read his thoughts. He lifted the boy to face him, smiling when Mikie's tiny fingers reached out and grabbed his nose. The child served as a reminder of what is now, rather than what had passed.

"You are today," Ryan whispered. He pulled the boy closer and gave him a long hug, picturing the faces of those people he had loved, and were now gone. His beautiful wife, Norma. His adorable little girl, Michelle. His strong, proud father, Andrew. And now, his loving and devoted mother.

"And maybe tomorrow, too," he said as he pulled back and again looked into the little boy's face, realizing how much he hoped that would be true.

He put the baby into his stroller and turned back toward the door to find Lacy standing there watching. She wore a half-smile, that disappeared when she looked up into his face.

"Ryan, what is it?" she asked, perceptively, stepping through the door and onto the patio with him.

"I have to go to New York. My mother just passed away," Ryan said grimly. "Do you suppose you could. . ." He paused realizing how much he hoped that she could. "Could you drive me?"

More than anyone, he wanted her with him. But did he dare ask her to do more than give him a ride?

"When do you want to leave?" Lacy said softly as she came to stand in front of him. "And how long will we stay?"

"Tomorrow will be soon enough," he replied. "The plans were made a long time ago. It'll be a small, private service. Probably a day or two after. But, you won't have to stay . . ." He looked down at her, trying not to let his feelings show. Hoping she wouldn't guess how much he wanted her – needed her – to be there with him. If she stayed, she would do it on her own.

She smiled her Madonna-smile. "I'll ask Mom if she minds keeping Mikie for a couple of days."

"He's welcome along," Ryan said, glancing down at the little boy as he squeezed his favorite rubber toy making it squeak loudly.

"Babies can be distracting," Lacy replied, making a face.

"That's my general idea," Ryan laughed, pleased he still could in the face of everything. "Besides, Mom loved kids." He thought of his mother with one particular child, sometimes not even remembering she was her granddaughter – not caring – just loving her for the child that she was.

"What about the others who will be there?"

Ryan smiled grimly. "Mom once had a lot of friends. Some have died, others are also in nursing homes, or have moved to warmer climates. Some she lost touch with after . . ." He frowned.

"She was sick a long time." Lacy remembered him telling her about his mother's disease during one of the long talks they'd had since his accident. She reached out and gently touched his sleeve, feeling his tension hidden beneath the light-green cotton shirt.

"There's no immediate family left," Ryan said with a sigh. "Cousins, maybe. I doubt they'd even remember Mom."

"We'll be there," Lacy said softly, including herself among those who would mourn the woman she had never met. She didn't have to meet her to know her. She suspected knowing her son revealed a lot about the woman. It took a special woman to raise such a remarkable man.

Ryan covered her hand with his, his darkening eyes meeting hers, then breaking away to glance at the boy as he squeaked his rubber toy once again. "He's going to grow up to be very special," Ryan said, looking back at her again and holding her blue gaze. "Because he's being raised by a very remarkable lady."

Lacy was warmed by his words. Words that mirrored the very thoughts she had just had about him.

Another squeak from below and the mood was broken as Lacy turned her attention back to her son. "It's about time I check your diaper. Then, if you like, Ryan, I'll put something together for dinner."

"Actually, I'm not very hungry," he replied honestly, though he hoped that wouldn't chase her away. He was glad she was here with him today. He didn't relish the thought of being alone. He had been that way too long.

Funny, since Norma's death he had never thought of being anything but alone. He had been certain he'd go through the rest of his life that way. He had been satisfied that way. No, satisfied wasn't the word. It was more like he had accepted that as a fact fate had willed.

Now, he felt different. Now, he wondered if it had to be that way. He wondered if he wanted it that way.

Everything had changed since he'd met and grown to know Lacy Boyce, he mused. But would she ever feel the same toward him?

#

It had been a long night. One with very little sleep. Ryan found himself tossing and turning. Or more accurately, considering the awkward weight of the cast on his right leg, he did a good imitation of tossing and turning.

He ached physically and mentally by the time he finally gave up all thought of sleeping. It wasn't even light. Four o'clock, the lighted dial of his clock told him. He still had five hours before Lacy arrived to drive him to New York.

There had been so many thoughts going through his mind as he lay staring into the darkness. Thoughts of his mother had mingled with thoughts of the other people he had loved and lost.

He had also thought of Lacy and her son. He hadn't wanted them to leave the night before. He hadn't wanted to be alone with his thoughts. Some thoughts he had expected. Others had surprised him.

His feelings for Lacy and Mikie had grown beyond fondness. His frozen heart had thawed. Who'd have thought he could love someone so different than Norma? Yet, experts say you should never try to find someone who was exactly like the person you lost. You would always end up comparing the two.

He still couldn't help but do just that. He had tried not to, making a feeble attempt to push all thoughts from his mind. Still, two faces kept returning. One fading into shadows. One vivid and clear.

Finally, he had given up and allowed his determined mind to take its course. Until then he had only realized the differences between the two women. As visions, like pictures on a movie screen, surrounded him, he realized there were also a lot of similarities between Norma and Lacy.

They both looked very much the same. They could have passed for sisters. It was uncanny he should love two women who looked so much alike. But, in honesty he had never even realized that until his nighttime appraisal.

No, he had noticed the way they both carried themselves.

Norma's ballerina-like way of almost gliding into the room with so much grace. So very feminine. Her dresses always flowing lines, in pastel colors that only added to her softness. Her movements sometimes like those of a kitten, whose closeness never failed to receive attention.

She was used to using her femininity to get her what she wanted. She had been a model when they'd met. An expert at attraction. An attraction that hadn't passed on him. His firm had been hired to do the financial records for a popular designer and he had been assigned the job. A job that was made more difficult since they wanted him to come to their location to do the work.

It had been difficult to keep his attention on the columns of figures in the books when so many lovely columns of figures were attracting him through the glass enclosed office where he was supposed to be working. In particular, one lovely figure who had a habit of quickly looking shyly away every time their eyes met. It had been such a contrast to the other models' boldness.

It hadn't taken him long to realize the reason was one they had in common. Her Christian background set her apart from many of the other models. It was a job she only did until she met the right man to take her away from all that. She wanted a four bedroom house, with a white picket fence around it. She wanted two children, a girl and a boy, and a husband who adored her. She wanted what for many was the American Dream. And he wanted nothing more than to give it to her.

His mind flashed to Lacy.

Her firm, determined steps. Her natural, yet attractive swing to her hips. She wore jeans and tee shirts, or tailored cut shirts. He had never seen her in a dress. Not even at her husband's funeral where she had shocked some while gaining the respect of others, by wearing the fire company dress uniform.

Lacy took great pains to keep any sensuality she possessed concealed with actions that were precise and no-nonsense. The name of the game was that it was no game. It was life and death. And no one could doubt Lacy took that seriously.

For many who had watched Lacy growing up, she was a comrade in the fire service. They probably never even thought of the woman beneath the surface. There were others who never forgot she was a woman. Their bruised egos wouldn't let them accept that she could do the same job they did, sometimes better. Fortunately there were few of them.

Lacy had earned her right to be among the members. She hadn't forced it like many women had done. He'd heard talk about them. Their attitudes 'I'm equal and you have to treat me that way when I want you to. The rest of the time I'm different. And you better never forget that either.'

With Lacy, you knew she was equal, because her hard work and dedication had proven it that way. Being different was just a fact. She didn't flaunt it. Nor did she use it as a convenience or an excuse if there was a job she found she couldn't do.

Again, there were those things the two women had in common. Both were caring mothers to their children, yet each in different ways. Norma had doted and protected, focusing so much attention on Michelle. Instilling so much of herself on the child.

He had never had a doubt that Lacy loved her tiny son, but she had confessed to him once, she feared she wasn't good mother material. She knew she hadn't been cut from the same pattern as her mother, and it was her mother she both wanted and didn't want to emulate.

He had seen how torn Lacy was between staying home with her son, and remaining active in the emergency service. He had learned her plan had been to switch over to ambulance work, hoping to get a paid position as a paramedic. Only there had been no guarantee when one would open and he doubted her enthusiasm was really in that direction.

He knew he had helped take some of the stress off Lacy when he'd offered to rent her house after she decided to move in with her parents again. That eliminated her need for the secretarial job she had hated. But it hadn't eliminated the deep-seeded love she had for the fire service.

He had seen her restlessness since his accident. The taste of his rescue had left her wanting more. She had taken her suspension from the ambulance squad without the bat of an eye, yet each time the tones went off, signaling an emergency to which their fire company would respond, she'd grow alert, and get a longing look in her eyes.

Still she was torn between how she could be both a good mother and respond to emergencies. The way he saw it, it was more how she could fail to do both? The fire service was part of who she was. Her son would grow up knowing, and understanding that. Certainly she couldn't respond every time there was a call, most volunteers couldn't do that. But she could remain active and still be a good mother. The obvious love she had for her son would insure that.

Could it be worse then giving him too much attention? Ryan wondered, remembering the concerns he'd had that Norma was doing just that with their daughter. His fear that his child might not grow up to have a mind of her own. Might have her own personality smothered beneath the one his wife would create for her. The few arguments he and Norma ever had, were over just that.

He felt a momentary guilt at remembering those fears. . . Memories he had squashed after the night they both died. Memories that no longer had any relevance. Except that they gave him a different perspective to look at Lacy's situation.

Lacy's situation.

Lacy's life.

They both filled a large part of his mind. He realized he also wanted them to fill his life. His future.

Well, he hadn't been looking for someone to love. He had never intended to replace his wife.

Yet, there it was so obvious – there was room for both. Norma would always have a place in his heart, as would his daughter. Still there was a place for Lacy and her son, too.

But was it too soon for her? It was only months since Mike had died. Would it take her years, like him, to reach the point of being able to love another person? Perhaps not. Not if he had anything to do about it. Then he reminded himself, he had to be careful not to rush her. Not to overwhelm her with his own desires.

With his goal in mind, he was finally able to sleep.

#

Lacy rang the bell, then slowly turned the knob, still, after all these months, feeling awkward entering her own home. Not my home, she reminded herself. I'm owner of this house. But it is not my home.

Still, as she stepped inside, she felt the same warmth she felt so often lately drawing her in. *Contentment. Peace.* They were the words that came to her. Words describing the feelings she had.

Yet she knew it was not just the house, but also the man living there. He'd made her feel welcome. Beyond the fact that she was there to help him after his accident. He could just as easily turned to someone else.

In her mind she pictured Rose Sinclair, and she quickly dismissed it, uneasy with the turbulent emotions it aroused in her. Even the mention of the other woman's name triggered pangs of jealousy. Jealousy from the past. And from the present.

"I thought I heard you come in," Ryan said, interrupting her thoughts as he hobbled into the living room, his shirt open and untucked from his pants. "I was laying a few things out for the trip." Seeing her expression, he sobered. "Are you okay?"

She eyed his tousled hair, unshaven face, and down to the dark sprinkling of curly hairs covering his torso.

"Lacy." Ryan said her name twice before she finally broke her gaze. Cheeks burning, she quickly looked away. "Are you okay?" he asked again.

"Sure," she croaked, wishing her voice wouldn't betray her. She never was much good at lying.

"Where's Mikie?" Ryan knew she wouldn't have left him in the car, yet she had been going to bring him along.

"He was so irritable this morning, when Mom suggested I leave him home, I took her up on it. I think he's cutting a tooth," Lacy replied, wondering now if she had made the right decision. Mikie had always served as a distraction between them.

"Are you having second thoughts about the trip?" Ryan asked, astutely reading her doubts, yet misunderstanding their reasons. "If so, I can still take the train. If you'll drive me to the station."

"No," she replied too quickly. "I want to be there for you. . . For me, too," she added. "I need the time away. I have a lot to think about."

Ryan nodded, understanding. He knew she was still like a sailboat adrift without the wind. Sometimes feeling helpless against the current. Other times paddling violently to keep from getting caught up in it. Often losing sight of her direction.

"I know," he replied softly. "I've been doing a lot of thinking myself." But he didn't elaborate. Not yet. It was still too soon.

"Need any help?" she asked, her eyes darting quickly to his exposed chest, then up again to his face.

"If you want to put everything I have on the bed in my suitcase, it would help. It's in the back of the closet," he replied, reaching up and stroking his day's growth. "I'll go and shave awhile, then bring that stuff in to pack." He turned back toward the hallway. "Sorry I'm running late. I spent most the night awake, then when I finally did sleep, I ended up sleeping late."

"I understand," she replied from behind him.

No, I don't think you do. He stared straight ahead, still seeing that look on her face when he entered the room. Though she denied having many fond memories of living here, he felt certain it was difficult for her returning to the house where she had once lived with her husband.

He'd hoped it would grow easier as time passed. But he saw it was still taking its toll. Just one more thing that would take time. *It's a good thing I'm a patient man.*

#

The trip to Long Island passed by pleasantly. As they drove they talked little about the reason for their trip, but it was always just beneath the surface as Ryan told her many stories about his life growing up in a big city. Memories. All of them fond.

In the weeks since his accident, Lacy had shared many stories from her own small-town childhood. Most of them somehow related to the fire service that had been such a major part of her life.

Rarely during that time had Ryan shared much information about himself. He had hinted that his own interest in the fire service was far more recent, but had never given her any specifics. That had only served to raise her curiosity, so that now, as he spoke she drank up his stories like August flowers drink up the rain.

Once on the island they stopped at a small local restaurant for lunch. The place had a tropical effect, with lush, green plants adorning every conceivable corner. Fans buzzed above the wicker chairs and tables that were filled with a lunchtime crowd.

Lacy knew without asking that this was a place Ryan had frequented often when he'd lived here. The way his eyes seemed to search the room, glancing at the faces as though looking for someone he might know.

236

Adding to her certainty was the smile of familiarity their waiter flashed them as he approached their table. "Long time no see," the man said in a heavy Jamaican accent, surprising Lacy when he included her in the welcome. "Would you care for a cocktail?" the young, dark-skinned man asked, again eyeing them both. "It's been so long, I'm not sure I remember . . ."

"Nothing for me," Ryan replied a bit too quickly. His smile was forced as he looked across the table at Lacy. "How about you?"

"I'll be happy with just coffee."

"Make it two coffees, Bobby," Ryan ordered, relaxing slightly. "And tell me, do you still have the best seafood between Maine and the Caribbean?"

The black man smiled. "Of course. It's all still flown in fresh every day. We have lobster fresh from the traps off the coast of Maine, shrimp from the Gulf of Mexico, and salmon from the Pacific coastal regions of Canada."

"And everything in between, though some of it may have to be ordered a day or two ahead." Ryan pointed to where the menu read that they would fly in any type fish known to the continental United States.

He laughed, remembering the times he would try to pick something the specialty restaurant could not provide. It had become a challenge, though he would inevitably fail, since they went out of their way to please their customer's palates, as long as they also had pocketbooks large enough to accommodate their tastes.

"I'd like some fresh Manatawny catfish," Lacy said, picking up the challenge.

The waiter's dark eyes sparkled as he leaned his head to the side as though thinking. "Catfish is quite popular, Ma'am," he replied. "Though, I have to admit I, myself, haven't heard of Manatawny catfish. Is it a different variety? We'd have to bring that in on special order."

"It's more like catfish from the Manatawny," she explained.

Suddenly, she caught the mischievous look in Ryan's eye. "Order it for tomorrow. Dinner," he said. "We'll come back again then."

Lacy hesitated, wondering if Ryan would feel up to going out again the following evening. The next few days would be hard on him. Then she nodded, deciding it would be good to help keep his mind off all his heartache. She wanted to do anything to erase the lines of pain from his face.

"Manatawny catfish, batter-dipped and fried to a golden brown," she specified.

The waiter wrote her order. "And for today, may I suggest our house special, deluxe seafood salad."

"Actually, I'm not overly hungry," she lied. "I'll take a garden salad." She waited as Ryan ordered the special.

"You've been here before," she said after the waiter left their table. "Many times, it seems."

For a moment when the waiter recognized him, and obviously mistook Lacy for Norma, he had almost regretted choosing this place to have lunch. Now he knew it was right that she knew. He took a breath, searching for words to tell her about the past. But he stopped, knowing it was not the place for such a disclosure. Once he started opening up the floodgates, he'd have to tell her all. Every detail. Because it was all part of who he is today. The man he's become.

After lunch, they went straight to the funeral home where Ryan met with the director to make the final plans for his mother's service. That complete, Lacy waited as the director escorted Ryan to the private room where he could see his mother.

He was understandably quiet when they finally returned to the car. He leaned back in the seat, resting his head against the backrest with his eyes closed.

"Do you want to go get a room now?" Lacy asked softly, seeing the lines of strain on his face had deepened.

"Not yet," he sighed. "I may as well get it all over with." He opened his eyes and turned slightly to look at her. "Have I told you how much it means to me, having you with me?"

Have I told you how much it means to me, being needed by you? She smiled, knowing this was neither the time nor the place for that confession. Instead, she replied, "That's what friends are for," and knew as soon as she said it, it sounded too trite.

Their next stop was at a large, rambling, single story building with beautifully landscaped lawns. Judging by the number of senior citizens scattered about the grounds, she guessed this was the nursing home where Ryan's mother had spent her last years.

She again joined him as they went inside, heading straight for the Administrator's office. A thin, gaunt-looking woman looked up from her paperwork, warmth generating from her eyes as she looked at Ryan. She greeted him, getting up from her seat and coming around her desk, right hand outstretched.

Lacy found she immediately liked the woman. She was a professional, but she also had compassion, a combination that went too rarely together.

The visit turned out to be another difficult one for Ryan as he asked the woman to give him every detail of his mother's last days. It was as though he was searching for reassurance that his being there really wouldn't have made any difference.

The hardest part was just before they left, when the woman turned over all of his mother's belongings. Two boxes contained everything she had owned, except for the few house dresses he had asked the administrator to give to someone who may need them.

He stood staring a long time at the boxes before finally reaching inside and lifting out a china doll. It had been a gift to his mother, from his father on their first Christmas together. He had told her it reminded him of her. Beautiful and fragile.

She had told Ryan the story so many times. How his father had given his carefully rehearsed speech. "Beauty I will bask in the rest of my days. And fragility I will care for and protect till my last dying breath, and beyond."

Ryan sighed, the sadness of the moment abated by the fact that he knew his mother and father were both in a better place.

He looked back at the doll, knowing it would have gone to his daughter, had she lived. But now. . .

Tears made his eyes a brighter green as he looked back at Lacy, holding the doll out to her. "Will you accept this, please?"

With trembling fingers Lacy reached out and took the doll, knowing it was meant as his way of saying thank you, yet to her receiving it meant so much more.

They said little else as Lacy pushed the cart holding the two boxes out to the car. She carefully placed the doll in the back seat after putting the rest of the things in the trunk. Then she returned the cart while Ryan got silently back into the car.

There was a small motel down the street where Ryan suggested they spend the night. It was several hours since they'd eaten, but neither one cared much about food. Right now, what the both needed was rest.

Lacy followed Ryan into the office, momentarily silent as he requested two rooms. But the manager told them they only had one room left that night.

"There's another motel a couple of blocks away," he commented, turning back to Lacy.

"Ryan, we can share, it's no problem with me," she suggested, watching as the desk clerk gave them an impatient appraisal. *Let him think what he wants,* she decided, waiting for Ryan's decision.

"Are you sure?" he hesitated, not sure himself. There was a part of him that definitely wanted her with him that night. Yet, he knew having her that close could be pushing the limits of his resistence. It would take a lot of prayer to give him restraint.

She smiled. "You know me by now. I wouldn't have offered if I wasn't." Besides, he looked so forlorn. Like the last thing he needed was to be alone. He had hinted as much the night before. But then she had gone anyway.

More because she was afraid of what she might do if she stayed. It felt so good to be needed.

"If you're sure," Ryan said, then turned back and booked the room.

They drove around to the back part of the motel, where they had a room on the ground floor. Lacy carried their bags from the car while Ryan slipped the plastic card inside to unlock the door. He stepped inside first, then held the door for her.

"This is what I hate most about having a broken leg," he grumbled. "Having to let people wait on me hand and foot."

"Who's waiting on you?" she asked. "Fair is fair. I carried the bags in, you can hang up your own clothes."

He laughed, relaxing some of the lines of tension from his face. She was good for him. He knew that. She always made him feel better.

He obediently opened his suitcase while she pretended to relax on the bed nearest the door. She'd allow him the one closest to the bathroom, she decided. Then he wouldn't have to walk as far. Of course, in spite of his cast, she knew he was anything but helpless.

She hadn't realized he had opened her suitcase too until she saw him putting her own black dress on a hanger. It was the one her mother had bought for her to wear to Mike's funeral. He glanced at the dress, then at Lacy.

"Yes, I do wear them sometimes," she replied, reading what she was certain was on his mind. "And you don't have to hang up my things."

"Just stay there and relax," He ordered, laughing, as he turned and hung the dress beside his own suit and white shirt. He returned to the suitcase and pulled out a giant pink tee shirt with a picture of Garfield on the front, saying 'Hold Me, Kiss Me.'

Ryan looked back at her again and saw her faint blush.

"That's what I sleep in," she said quickly. "Before you get the wrong idea, turn it around and read the rest."

His laughter filled the room as he read, 'Make Me Eat Chocolate.'

"Aunt Rainy got that for me a couple years ago," she said. "She said it was the perfect gift for a chocoholic."

"So I learned two new things about you today," he acknowledged as he laid the tee shirt on her bed.

"Two things?"

"Your love for chocolate, and comfortable sleepware," he replied throwing the tee shirt across the bed to her.

"I'll have you know, you should be glad I've chosen such modest apparel," she retorted.

"Oh, why?" He raised his eyes to meet hers.

"I have to protect your reputation," she teased.

"My reputation?" he returned to his work. "You think it needs protecting?"

"According to the department grapevine, I've been doing more than nursing you back to health," she replied, biting her tongue as he quickly looked back at her in surprise. "You didn't think my spending so much time with you would go unnoticed."

"How do you know about this?" he asked, looking genuinely concerned.

"I hear a lot," she replied, breaking his gaze. "Some of the guys must think I'm either half deaf, or they don't care. I catch bits and pieces of what they say."

"Doesn't it bother you?"

She smiled. "There was a time it might have," she tried to explain. "But I've been around a long enough time to know complaining about it, or getting angry doesn't change it. Besides, the ones who do the most talking and speculating, have the least to talk about. What they think doesn't matter to me."

Ryan didn't look convinced.

"Ryan, what do you honestly think of my Dad?" she asked, as though changing the subject.

"I respect him. He seems like a fair man."

"How do you think he got where he did?"

"Hard work and dedication," Ryan replied instantly.

She smiled. "There are those who once said, and some who still say, he brown-nosed Borough Council to get the job. There was even one rumor, though short-lived, that he paid off someone to make Fire Chief. Through the years it's been said he's overlooked code violations for favors, and even accepted bribes."

"Not your father," Ryan said with assurance.

"That's right. We all know that. So it doesn't matter what the others say."

"I see your point." Ryan nodded, but still wasn't smiling. "It doesn't matter, because the people who matter know it isn't true."

"'Guilty people scream innocence the loudest,' is what Dad always says."

"I'm going to get some ice and a soda, want one?" She got up from the opposite side of the bed and walked toward the dresser.

"Sure," he replied, reaching into his pocket for some change.

"This one's on me." She picked up the plastic ice bucket and turned for the door.

It had been a long day, and it came as no surprise when she returned to find Ryan had dozed on his bed.

But it was a restless sleep, as Lacy realized when she heard Ryan's incoherent mumbling.

She lay listening, wondering if he was dreaming about the death of his mother. Or if he was again dreaming about the mysterious Norma as he had the night of his accident.

As if her thoughts had invoked that very thing, Ryan began thrashing on his bed. His mumbling growing louder. "No! God, no!" he practically shouted.

Lacy quickly jumped up from her bed and went to his side. Sitting on the edge of his bed she reached out to stroke his brow. "It's okay, Ryan," she whispered, soothingly as she had the last time he'd had a nightmare.

He sat up with a start, reaching out and grabbing her by the shoulders. There was a wild look in his emerald gaze, so bright, she knew he still wasn't fully conscious.

"Ryan, everything is okay," she said a little louder, feeling the tension finally draining from his body. But he didn't let her go. Instead he pulled her close against his chest. She could hear the thudding of his heart, feel his swift rise and fall of his chest. She would have almost thought he was running rather than lying in his bed.

Slowly his heartbeat slowed, his breathing returned to normal. He lay back, pulling her with him. She decided for a moment she wouldn't move. It wouldn't hurt. He was once again asleep.

"I'm sorry if I frightened you," he whispered, surprising her that she was wrong. He was definitely still awake. He didn't let her go.

"Are you okay?" she asked, shifting to look up at him, her cheek rubbing against the stubble on his chin.

"Fine now," he whispered, turning his head to look down at her. He brushed his lips against her forehead, then shifted his arms so that he held her more securely against him.

After what seemed like an eternity in heaven ended too soon, he pulled away. His breathing was heavy, but this time not from fear.

"I'm sorry, this is something I shouldn't have started," he whispered, loosening his hold.

She felt her cheeks burn as she got up from his bed, realizing with embarrassment, she had enjoyed those moments in his arms. Moments she suspected he hadn't really spent with her. Rather with the unknown Norma.

She suspected his regrets were because he suddenly realized who she really was.

CHAPTER EIGHTEEN

Ryan lay awake listening to Lacy's breathing. He had awakened at first thinking she was Norma. But only for a moment. It didn't take him long to realize the woman beside him was not his wife.

They had had a wonderful life. A happy marriage. Their relationship had been good. He suspected it could be that way with Lacy.

But it's was still too soon for Lacy.

He had had years to come to terms with the loss of his wife. She had only months. He needed to give her time. Yet, he'd very nearly forgot those good intentions.

God, thank you for bringing me to my senses before I did something that I know goes against your rules of how we should live. Something that would dishonor you, and Lacy. But, I have to admit it, I do want Lacy. In my life, not just in my bed. I think you mean for us to be together. I just have to give her the time. I have to wait till she is ready. Please, Lord, help me to know when that is.

As if in answer to his prayer, a thought came to him.

A flower only survives when it's allowed to grow. Cut it and bring it inside, and no matter how much loving care you give, it will wither and die.

He knew he had to allow Lacy to grow. To blossom. He knew when she was finally in full bloom, it would be time to harvest her heart.

He also knew he had to tell Lacy everything about his past. She needed to understand him. Because the past is what molds a person into what they are today. And in turn, both yesterday and today determine what we will be tomorrow. Norma was his yesterday. Lacy is his today. Did he dare hope she would be his tomorrow, too?

When she awoke, Lacy automatically glanced at the clock between the two beds. She realized it was well beyond morning. Quarter past twelve to be exact. Lacy slipped from her bed then stood a moment looking at the man sleeping in the next bed.

Something had nearly happened the night before. She was glad Ryan had come to his senses and stopped them.

I couldn't have stood being wanted by someone who mistakenly thinks I'm someone else.

A tear rolled down her cheek as she turned and headed to the bathroom.

Just once, I want to be loved for who I am. And I thought maybe Ryan was that person.

"You realize we slept through breakfast and lunch," Ryan said, when she returned to the room fully dressed.

"I've been intending to take off a few pounds."

"You're perfect the way you are," he replied. "Besides, we have a dinner date this evening, or have you forgotten?"

"Ahhh. . . fresh Manatawny catfish. Do you think they'll actually get some."

"I know they will. They're one of the few places left that believes in honest advertising. They say they'll order any kind of fish from within the continental U.S., or surrounding waters, fresh and made to order."

"Then I suppose I have a problem," she confessed. "I hate catfish."

First, Ryan looked surprised, then his lips turned up at the corners. Suddenly he burst into laughter. "You hate catfish."

She wrinkled up her freckled nose. "Always have, since the first time Dad took me fishing along the banks of the Manatawny. His rule was we eat what we catch."

"And?"

"Well . . ." She shrugged. "I was only little. When he told me I caught a catfish, I thought it was part cat and part fish. It wasn't the fish part I minded eating. But, my kitten had disappeared only a few days before – the reason for the fishing trip – a way to distract me. Anyway, I was convinced my kitten had fallen into the river and by some miracle, before he could drown, he had been miraculously turned into a fish."

By the time she finished explaining, Ryan shook with laughter. "And you never grew out of it," he said between bouts of shaking.

"Would you have?" She flashed her sapphire gaze at him indignantly. "Were you ever forced to taste something you formerly cuddled, caressed and adored."

"Can't say I have," Ryan replied, laughing even harder at the picture she presented. "I'm surprised it didn't leave you emotionally scarred for life."

"It did," she replied, happy they could return to the comfortable banter between them. "To this day I can't come face to face with a catfish without breaking out into a sweat."

"In that case, I have a better idea for dinner," Ryan suggested. "Let's go get some pizza."

#

He took a bite, chewing slowly, thinking of how he could put into words all that he was feeling. He didn't know if he wanted to. There were so many things on his mind. Some would have to wait till Lacy was ready. Others couldn't.

He swallowed, putting the slice of pizza back into his plate.

"I've been sitting here trying to think of the right words to tell you how much having you here with me means. I don't know what I'd have done without you. . . Last night and today. . ." He turned to look into her deep, blue eyes.

"You'd have gotten through, and will get through," she said, understanding what it is to lose someone you care about.

"Yeah, I understand that." *This was the opening. But was it the place, in a crowded pizza shop.*

"You were close to your mother, weren't you?" Lacy asked, suspecting that even with the distance between them, Ryan had remained in constant touch with his mother.

"We were. . ." He thought of the guilt he had felt at putting his mother into that nursing home. He had thought it was the only thing he could do under the circumstances. Yet, it didn't diminish his fear that she'd take it as a punishment for what had happened.

"Before her disease," Lacy finished for him.

"And other things happened," he replied, suddenly realizing he didn't want to think about those times. Rather the happy times. "She used to spoil me rotten, you know."

"You, spoiled?" Lacy looked up at him with sparkling, blue eyes and smiled, trying to picture him as a little boy. Even as the vision of a boy with tussled, dark hair, and mischievous green eyes came into focus, she couldn't quite picture him as spoiled. "You're a very giving, caring person. I don't associate those qualities with someone who was spoiled."

"Maybe doted on, is a better description. Like any only child, I guess. You know how that is."

She nodded. "Did you want brothers and sisters?"

"I always wanted something I didn't have," he reminisced. "Mom tried to teach me to be satisfied with what God gave me. 'Good or bad, take fates as they've been dealt and make the very best of them you can,' she would say, 'God will judge you, not on what you have, but on what you accomplish with your life.'"

"Your mother was a wise woman," Lacy smiled, thinking of her own mother. "Did she try to change you?"

Ryan watched Lacy tense as she waited for his answer. He knew about the strained relations between her and her mother. He had suspected Lacy's independent nature hung by a thin thread. What most people looked upon as rebellion was more a young woman's attempt to remain true to herself. But a lot of what people saw was a ruse – the outward image Lacy presented to others. It was only in recent months he was able to see beyond the surface to the woman beneath. A woman filled with doubts and insecurities.

"Tell me more about your mother," she asked. "Unless it bothers you to talk about her right now?"

"Trying to push her out of my mind would bother me more. Not the bad times. Those are the ones I need to forget." He smiled down at her. "You've helped me forget those. Let's go for a walk," he suggested.

Once outside they walked in the opposite direction of the motel. As she walked, and he hobbled, he told Lacy about his mother, and about their life as he was growing up.

It was growing dark before they finally got back to their room. Ryan knew he still hadn't told Lacy many things about his life. Things he would have to tell her eventually. But for now, he much preferred the night to end on this peaceful note.

Before he, too, fell asleep, Ryan glanced at the woman asleep in the bed beside his. Tomorrow would be a time for farewells. A time to write the final words in one chapter of his life. And hopefully a time to continue with the one he had just begun.

#

Lacy stood beside Ryan in front of the open grave. A minister spoke words she heard, but didn't absorb. Her mind kept returning to the last such service she had attended. The one for her husband.

There was such a difference between the two services, she reflected. One for someone cut down in his prime, whose best years were still ahead. Someone whose death was swift and shocking. The service had been attended by hundreds of mourners, some out of respect for a brother in the fire service who died in the line of duty, while others to say their final farewell to someone they had known and loved.

Then there was this service, for someone who'd lived through wonderful times, trying times, happy times, sad times. Most of all, someone who had lived a full life. Lacy had learned all this from Ryan's reflections about his mother the previous night.

Yet, as Ryan suspected, there were few there to share in his grief. A half dozen people who had been friends of the family. People, she sensed, Ryan hardly knew.

But then he had her. She wondered if her presence was making a difference. He had told her she didn't have to come. He seemed worried that it would bring back those haunting memories of a less pleasant time in her life. But being here, made her realize how far she had come.

Being here was part of her present. The memories were finally safely tucked in the past. She could begin thinking about a future.

She glanced up to the man standing beside her, catching his gaze as it strayed from the sight of the pewter-colored casket before them. The lines at the corners of his bright green eyes deepened as his narrowed gaze settled on the ground only a few feet from where they stood. A nerve twitched slightly as his jaw tensed.

She realized he was no more listening to what the minister was saying than she had been. There was a blankness to his stare, and she knew he was lost in his thoughts.

What thoughts? she wondered. She reached for his hand, instinctively knowing his pain. It was comfort he needed now.

His palm was cool to the touch, yet damp, belying his inner turmoil. She gave it a squeeze, then felt his fingers wrap firmly around her own, as though seeking and giving strength. He turned slightly to look down into her face, the blank look gone now, replaced by concern.

"Amen," they heard the others saying and quickly returned their attention to the man at the head of the casket as he gave the final benediction, then turned his attention to Ryan.

Ryan held her beside him as he accepted the man's condolences. Then as the minister came to her, she had to pull free to accept his firm handshake. Ryan, too, was now occupied as two elderly women claimed his attention.

"I'm pleased to see there is someone here for Ryan," the older man said with genuine warmth in his sable-colored eyes. His left hand joined his right, cupping her hand. A gesture of sincerity. "He's had more than enough sadness for one man," the minister continued, his gaze wavering slightly in the direction Ryan had earlier stared. "More than enough."

"It's the least I could do," she said with honesty. "He's been there for me during some difficult times."

"Yes, that would be our Ryan." There was respect, even pride in the minister's words. "He would understand hard times."

Yes, his mother's lengthy illness, Lacy thought, yet suspected there was more meaning to the man's words.

"When we first got here, I thought I was seeing a ghost," one of the older women was saying to the other in the way someone hard of hearing would call whispering, yet others around them would call loud.

The minister's greying brows raised only a fraction, showing that he'd heard what the woman had said. He dropped Lacy's hand and placed an arm across her shoulder almost protectively, leading her away from the others.

"Tell me what our Ryan has been doing with himself," the minister continued talking. "We've lost touch since he moved away. I'd stop in to visit his mother from time to time and she'd talk about him. . ." The minister shrugged. "but, it was often difficult to tell if she was talking about something that happened recently or some fond memories from the past. I often suspected it was the latter."

"Ryan visited her as often as he could," she defended. "At least until his accident."

The minister smiled down at her, gold flecks entering his sable eyes. "You're a loyal friend indeed. But I never doubted that Ryan visited her often. I guess it was more a matter of concern for how he was doing. When he left we knew he was doing what he had to do, but that didn't stop us from worrying.

"I've known Ryan since he was a lad," the minister continued. "I had him for confirmation. Oh, he was quite a character. Good thing he settled down as he got older. In fact, by the time I presided over his wedding, Ryan had turned into quite a responsible young man." He shook his balding head as he reflected.

Lacy was stunned by the minister's revelations. Yet, plenty of people were married and divorced. It shouldn't have mattered either way. It just stung that he hadn't confided in her. She'd thought they'd been so close.

"Looks like he has done a complete turnaround once again," the minister was saying, recapturing Lacy's attention.

"How did he manage to break his leg?" the man asked.

"He'd say it's all part of the job." She smiled. "He just happened to fall doing it."

"His job?" The minister sighed. "I suppose I can safely assume you don't mean a C.P.A."

"Firefighter," she said.

"I see, he's still on his crusade," the minister said with a sigh, the humored look in his eyes was replaced by one of concern.

She remembered her father once saying something much the same.

"At least he has good friends looking after him."

The man again smiled, the golden flecks returning to his eyes. "I'll pray that he's found peace where he now is . . .And that he never gets worse than that broken leg."

"In our line, we can always use a prayer," she replied.

The minister turned to her, a look of undisguised surprise on his face. "We? You mean, you . . .?"

"Yes, Reverend. Her too," Ryan said as he came up behind them, having heard their last exchange.

Lacy looked up and saw that although he was smiling now, Ryan still looked tried and drained. The paleness of his complexion made the dark rings beneath his eyes all the more prominent. She suspected he'd had very little sleep the night before. She knew he had very little the night before that after his nightmare. After they almost. . .

She felt her cheeks burn, and was thankful their companion could not read her thoughts.

"Don't be embarrassed, My dear girl," the minister said with a wide smile. "I'm very aware times have changed. It just takes some getting used to."

"Don't feel alone there," she replied. "There's still people who've worked with me for years who have difficulty getting used to the fact that I'm a woman."

The minister's brows drew together as he shook his head. "Yes, times are changing."

Lacy looked up at Ryan and caught his smile. She was happy he had that moment's distraction. She, too, was happy for it. It kept her from wondering about other things. Things she had just learned about Ryan.

As Ryan spoke with the minister a few moments, Lacy stepped away to give them the chance to talk alone. She wandered slowly back toward the site of the grave, then turned slightly, toward the unknown place that had drawn Ryan's gaze. Curiosity drew her closer.

As she drew closer to the brass plaque that marked the head of the plot, a gasp caught in her throat as she read the names.

Norma June Simon and Michelle Allison Simon. Loved forever, nere forgotten.

A dark shadow cast over her, warning Lacy she was no longer alone. She swallowed hard, waiting for what Ryan would say. Would he be sorry he hadn't told her sooner? Or angry for her intruding on his past?

His touch was gentle as he placed his hands on her shoulders, drawing her back against him. A sigh escaped his lips. She sensed his regret. But was it regret that she now knew?

She read the dates, realizing both had died on the same date. One, she realized would have been his wife, Norma. The name he had called out in his sleep. The other had to have been his daughter. What tragedy had taken them?

Suddenly, she knew. She understood Ryan's crusade.

"They were killed in a fire," Ryan said what she had already suspected.

Why didn't you tell me? She wanted to ask, but didn't. It was all too clear. He hadn't felt close enough – hadn't trusted her enough – to tell her.

He sighed again. "It's been a long morning, Lacy. What do you say we head home? There's nothing else for me here."

Did she understand what he was saying? he wondered. Yet, somehow he couldn't put it into words. Not here. Not now. Not while standing in front of his dead wife's grave.

Lacy turned and saw him staring at the ground before them. The pain was in his eyes again. He looked back at her, his expression grim.

"We need to talk," he nearly whispered.

"No, Ryan." She forced a smile. "You don't have to talk about it. I understand."

"Do you?" *I wonder.*

"I'll be at the car." She started walking toward the car ahead of him.

He stood a few more moments staring down, looking for answers. *Loved forever, nere forgotten.* His eyes focused again on the words. They were still true, and always would be. But could Lacy understand. After everything she'd been through herself, he'd thought she would. But perhaps he'd waited too long, rather than not long enough to tell her the way he felt.

"How do I make her understand?" he asked, closing his eyes.

The vision of a smiling, blonde-haired woman seemed to be looking at him. Shaking her head. "You can't make her do anything. You forget she's a female, too. Haven't I taught you anything. You can't force her to bend to your will. You can only guide her until she sees for herself that you are right."

Norma had been talking about their daughter then. He had been trying to teach her not to chew on his slippers like a puppy dog.

He laughed at the memory.

Now you understand. The face faded, leaving only darkness until he opened his eyes.

"Yes, now I understand," he whispered, giving one last look at the plot where his wife and daughter were buried. "Thanks."

Lacy was in the car waiting when he got into the passenger side. "Ready to go home now?" she asked with forced cheerfulness.

He reached over and took her hand. "I'd like to make one stop, if you don't mind."

She wondered what he had in mind now, but remained silent, following his directions. They drove for several blocks before he finally told her to pull over to the curb. He didn't get out. He just sat looking out his window.

She followed his gaze to the beautiful house surrounded by a white picket fence. A man was in the front yard, mowing. A woman was kneeling by her garden of beautiful, bright-colored flowers, still untouched by frost. From the angle they were parked, she could see children playing in the back yard.

Ryan turned to her and smiled. "This is how it's supposed to be."

She knew he was speaking about more than the family. "This was your house."

He nodded. "Yes, it was. After the fire, I didn't have the heart to fix it up again. I sold it as it was."

"You wouldn't even know there had been a fire," she acknowledged, not knowing what else she was supposed to say. Only afraid to say what she really wanted.

"They've done wonders with it," he reflected, glancing back at the house again. "I'm not surprised."

"Is this . . .the first time you've been here . . .? Since the fire."

"No." He shook his head. "I lived in my office above the garage for awhile. Till I couldn't stand it any more."

She remained silent, waiting to see what was next. She decided silence was better than the questions. Questions she was afraid to ask. Or maybe it was the answers she was more afraid of.

#

They spoke little on their long drive home. Each were lost in their own thoughts. When they pulled into his driveway at home, Ryan could bear the silence no longer.

"Lacy, will you come inside so we can talk."

"It's really kind of late," she hedged. She was more uncertain than ever about her future. All the way home she was plagued by one thought. Why hadn't Ryan confided in her about his wife and daughter?

She suspected she understood why. It wasn't easy to talk about someone you loved and lost. Especially when you loved them still. Hadn't that been what the brass plaque had said? *Loved Forever, Nere Forgotten.*

He'd never forget the woman who still haunted his dreams. Nor his child, born of that woman.

Was it any wonder he regretted what nearly had happened with Lacy during his moment of weakness? She had overheard the woman at the cemetery saying she looked just like his dead wife. Had he been reaching out to her because she was the closest thing to having his wife's comfort? That thought stung.

She thought of the days since his accident as they grew to know one another better. Had they really?

Worse, his closeness to her son. Was Ryan using Mikie as a substitute for the child he lost?

Could lightening strike the same place twice? She was in the fire service. She knew very well it could.

She was again falling in love with someone who wanted her for totally different reasons.

251

"We need to talk." Ryan said with determination, interrupting her thoughts. "There's things I need to tell you."

"No. Not now." She bit back her tears. "I want to go home."

"Lacy, I love you," he blurted, watching her flinch. Not the reaction he had hoped for.

Don't force her to see it your way. Guide her.

"Don't say that to me!" she shouted, turning away. "I don't want to hear it."

"Lacy, Honey, I can't take it back," he whispered, reaching out to touch her arm. "All I can say is what I really feel."

"You don't love me!" She turned to face him with unconcealed anger mixed with regret. "You love Norma!"

This time it was Ryan who flinched. Yes, he had loved his wife. He always would. But he knew, now, he could love two women equally, but differently, because they were different. He had hoped Lacy would understand. It was a disappointment that she didn't. Especially when he had been so certain she would.

"I've never asked you to stop loving Mike," he said desperately.

Her eyes turned icy blue. "That's not even comparable."

Ryan could have been slapped. He had never expected to replace the other man. But he had hoped he meant more to Lacy than what it now seemed he did.

"So, you've got to be first or nothing," he said bitterly. "Like everything you do, Lacy. It's number one, or nothing."

Tears froze in her eyes. "Get out!" she ordered, her trembling words tinged with anger and pain.

"Not until we hash this out."

"Suit yourself. You can sit here as long as you like," She turned to open the door of the Toyota. "It's your car."

He grabbed her arm to prevent her escape. "Running away, Lacy? I can tell you from experience, it doesn't work. Neither one of us are going to run from this.

"We have nothing!" she spat as she pulled her arm from his grasp and slipped out the seat and slammed the door. "Not even friendship," she added as the tears finally started to fall.

"Lacy, don't!" Ryan slammed his fist against the dash as he watched Lacy rushing to her car. He felt helpless to stop her. He didn't know if he should.

Guide her. The words entered his thoughts again. But he knew, some things were far easier said than done.

CHAPTER NINETEEN

It had been two weeks since Fire Prevention Week. The last time Ryan had seen Lacy. Though his cast limited how much he could do, he'd agreed to join Rainy in a special program at one of the schools. If he admitted it, he'd gone mostly because he knew Lacy would be there.

Though they had spoken little, their words had been polite. Cool and polite, he remembered. But coolness wasn't what he had seen in her sapphire eyes. It was a spark of something more. Something that once again made him hope.

Hope. And faith, that if this was what God wanted, his prayers would be answered. They were the only things that kept him going long after his anger had faded. He was in love with Lacy. And that wasn't something he could easily change. He didn't know if he wanted to.

But he had two weeks to think about what he had seen that day. Not just the warmth in her deep, blue eyes, but the passion he'd seen there too. Passion for her job.

He had watched her slip into a set of bunker gear, showing the children what firefighters looked like when dressed to do their job. Then after donning an air pack, he'd watched Lacy crawl around the floor, giving the children a chance to see what a firefighter looked like in action.

All the while Rainy explained to the children what Lacy was doing and why. The usual routine had been to first chose a child from the audience to act as a victim trapped in a fire. And show how difficult it would be for a firefighter to find them if they were to hide from a fire.

But that day Rainy had asked him to play that role. Her brown eyes had dared him to refuse in front of the children. What choice did he had? He'd seemed so useless just standing their in his cast while his two companions did all the work. He suspected that was exactly how Rainy had it planned.

He took her challenge and had lain on the floor, pretending to hide beneath their makeshift bed. Lacy came into the area they had designated as a room, through the area marked as a door. She was crawling, her hand outstretched, waving all around in front of her.

Rainy reminded the children firefighters could not see through the darkness of smoke. They depended on feeling their way instead of their eyesight.

Finally, Lacy had found him. And pulled him out from under the bed. He heard the children laughing, suspecting this little bit of a woman certainly wouldn't be able to move this giant of a man. But he knew different. This little bit of a woman was good at her job.

He looked into the big, blue eyes behind the face mask and saw she was intent on her task. She worked with confidence gained from years of experience. Slowly she drug him to the pretend door.

Rainy had then told the children that because he had hidden, and had not know how to escape from fire, he would probably be overcome by smoke. At that point one of the children had shouted to Lacy to give him mouth-to-mouth resuscitation.

He had been unable to hide his smile as he feigned continued unconsciousness. Lacy had pretended not to hear as she started taking off her gear. Rainy took the situation in hand, and returned to the original topic.

Ryan knew it was also time for him to return to the topic at hand. He had been allowing himself too much time for daydreaming. But it was going to stop. His cast was finally removed and he was ready to go back to work at the station.

He slowly went upstairs to the office, happy to find Arlen in there alone. He had something on his mind and he didn't want anyone else to hear it until he had the chance to see what the Chief had to say.

#

Lacy frowned as she hung up the phone. "That was Arlen," she said to her father. "He wants me to come by his office at the station."

"Something wrong?" Carl asked, knowing already that there wasn't. Arlen stopped by his office earlier that day to tell him what he was going to do. But he wouldn't let on.

As Fire Chief, he had fully agreed with the other man's decision. As a husband, he knew he was going to have his hands full. As a father he knew whatever happened, it would be totally up to his daughter.

But he suspected he already knew what Lacy would say when Arlen offered her the position as company training officer. He knew she hadn't been content since returning to work after her suspension from the ambulance. If fact, she'd been downright miserable the last few weeks. Though he suspected that had less to do with the fire service than one of its members.

"Since Mikie's asleep, do you mind if I go?" she asked her mother.

He watched his wife force a smile. Perhaps she wouldn't be as difficult to handle as he'd thought. He'd detected a change in his wife lately. She'd shown less hostility toward the fire department.

"Don't worry, he'll be fine," Lois said with a sigh.

Yes, perhaps she already suspected, Carl thought.

Lacy got her jacket and started for the door. She looked back at her parents and wondered about the strange look passing between them. There was something in the wind. And she suspected she was on her way to find out about it.

Upstairs at the station she knocked on the door before opening it and stepping inside. First she saw Arlen seated at his desk, then she noticed his two assistants seated in chairs nearby. One with a faint frown turning down the corner of his lips, the other's emerald gaze belying his inner tension.

"So, what did you want to see me about?" she asked, trying to act less like a sacrificial lamb than she felt.

"Sit down, Lacy," Arlen ordered, motioning to a vacant third chair in front of his desk.

She did, waiting. Wondering what was going on.

"I'll get right to the point." Arlen finally ended her suspense. "We want you to come back. It's up to you how active you want to be. But we need a good training officer."

From the corner of her eye she caught a glimpse of Barry's discomfort as he stared down at the floor. She suspected the "we" in Arlen's sentence didn't include him. And she felt pretty certain Ryan didn't want her around, though for very different reasons.

"Why?" she blurted, feeling her cheeks redden. The question could easily be misunderstood. She wasn't fishing for a complement. But she did want to know what was suddenly going on.

Arlen leaned back in his chair wearing a grim smile. "You know as well as I do, there's too much around here to do and too few to do it. This is pure and simple delegation of duties."

"I don't think it's as pure and simple as you want to make it out," she said, directing her attention to the Chief first, then to his assistants. "I've been gone a long time. But one thing hasn't changed. I know a snow job when I see one. Now, what's really going on?"

Barry practically jumped from his chair, turning to her. "Lacy, can't you just accept something for what it's worth. Do you have to have it analyzed."

She flashed him a look through angry, blue eyes. "How can I, when I get the feeling I'm not being told the whole story?"

Ryan turned to her, meeting her eyes for the first time. His smile didn't match the sadness in his eyes. "Has it gotten so bad, Lacy, that you can no longer trust your friends?"

Her eyes grew wide in astonishment. Ryan was not pulling any punches. "I'd say I have my reasons." She looked back at the First Assistant Chief. "You haven't exactly been a fan of women in the fire service. Why the change?"

"Lacy, maybe it's time you got that chip off your shoulder," Ryan responded instead of the other man.

She flinched at his hardness.

"No, I'll answer her," Barry turned from Ryan to her again. "I'll admit, I don't think women belong in the fire service. But I'm not sure if it's because I'm prejudice or 'cause I'm scared you may be able to do the job as well as a man. Better than me. . .or, bitter because, like Ryan says, you've already proven you can."

Without another word, jaw clenched, he stormed out of the room. The admission had definitely taken its toll. She knew it couldn't have been easy for Barry.

Lacy was silent as she sat staring at her hands in her lap, nervously twisting the gold band on her left hand. She knew it took a lot for Barry to admit that. Worse, she knew Ryan was right. She did have a chip on her shoulder. Possibly even a boulder.

She looked up at Arlen, watching him leaning back in his chair, waiting. "Well, whatcha going to do, Lacy?" he asked gruffly. "Seems everyone's said their piece. Now it's up to you."

She swallowed hard.

"There is one thing you didn't tell her," Ryan said to the other man.

"Oh, yeah," Arlen sat forward again leaning his elbows on the desk in front of him. "Well, since it was your idea, why don't you tell her."

Lacy waited, wondering if she was going to like what was coming.

"It's like this, Lacy," Ryan started, getting up and leaning casually on Arlen's desk as he looked down at her. "If we're going to have a training officer, we feel it's time we have someone who's qualified to do the job."

Qualified! Her eyes darted up to meet his ready to remind him just how qualified she was. But that wasn't her style. Nothing she did tonight seemed to be her style. She wasn't certain she knew what had gotten into her.

"You'd be expected to take classes on instruction," Ryan continued.

"Why me?" She looked up and met Ryan's gaze.

"We need you, that's why," Ryan said as his emerald eyes locked with hers in a silent message. "You'd be able to make sure our personnel are trained properly."

He leaned forward. "I realize, Lacy, it's not that paid paramedic position you've been waiting for." His voice grew softer. "I also realize, you're not happy doing that kind of work. It's not just saving lives for you, Lacy. It's also the physical challenge and the feeling you get when you meet that challenge."

She licked her lips, tasting the temptation. The desire to return. Ryan knew her so well. He was giving her the chance to do a job she loved. A job she knew she did well.

And yet, how little he really understood her? Did he still think it was a matter of being number one. First above all others?

Well, that doesn't matter now, she tried to tell herself, knowing all along it really did. What Ryan thought meant very much to her.

"Okay." The dryness in her throat made her croak as she accepted. "You've got yourself a training officer."

#

Lacy opened the door to the classroom and stepped inside. She was early, no one else was there, not even the man scheduled to teach this class. For a moment, she thought about going home and forgetting the idea of being an instructor. But she chalked that up to nerves.

Funny, a new challenge had never bothered her before. In fact, she had enjoyed one, welcomed it. But for some reason this time it was different. She felt in over her head. Floundering. If she failed at this, what would she do? Go back to running with the ambulance? Quit the emergency service completely? Go back to being a secretary?

None of those choices was very enticing. She needed a steady job, and the way Brody was acting lately it didn't look like being a paramedic was going to be that job. Besides, she missed the fire end of the department. It had been a part of her life for too many years.

It hadn't taken much convincing when they asked her to be the company training officer. She knew it would be a good way to remain involved during a time when she couldn't make emergency calls.

Much to her mother's displeasure, she had even taken Mikie with her on a few occasions. He was such a good baby and adapted well to the firehouse environment. He didn't even seem to mind when his mother was wearing gear and a face mask. But then he was probably still too young to know that kind of fear. And with any luck, by the time he reached that stage he would be used to bunker coats and SCBAs.

Going on to become a county and state instructor had been Ryan's suggestion. Since becoming assistant chief he had been far more open about his feelings. And his feelings were that their firefighters should get as much of the best training as possible, and that it should be from an instructor with the highest credentials.

"You're a natural instructor. One of the best I've seen," Ryan had said. "Why don't you make it official? Apply with the county and the state academies."

"I've never thought about it before," she had replied, which was not entirely true. At one time she had mentioned something similar to Mike. He had replied that the men would receive the same training from her whether she was simply a company training officer, or a county or state instructor so what difference did it make? Unless she felt she needed to prove how good she was at one more thing, he had added with just a touch of animosity.

After that, she decided it was best to keep her view on the subject to herself, though she still felt strongly that the day was fast approaching that it would be a mandatory requirement for firefighters to have state academy training before they could do their job. She also knew the firefighter certification program was growing at a fast pace and that before long all fighters would be required to go through this type of competency based testing. Good training all through their careers would help them when the time came for them to pass the ultimate test.

Lacy dismissed her thoughts as her classmates started entering the room.

First was a tall, large framed man with curly dark hair and a quick smile that lit his equally dark eyes. He greeted her immediately upon entering as though they had been friends for years. But if the navy blue sweatshirt with the Cheltenham insignia was any indication of his home fire department, she knew it was doubtful they'd ever worked together at a fire.

"Don't I know you from someplace?" the man asked. "Did you take the Vehicle Rescue Course here last month?"

Lacy forced a smile, knowing that he probably didn't remember her from a course. No, more than likely he was among the crew of firefighters from Cheltenham who had attended her husband's funeral.

"No, I couldn't make that course," she replied, for some reason preferring that he didn't remember where it was he had probably seen her. "Must have been a different one."

"In any case, I'm Lou Mills," the man smiled and extended his right hand.

As he walked away, several more people entered the room. Two, a man and woman with matching jackets saying Monarch Fire Company, also looked familiar, though in their case she knew it was entirely possible they had worked together. Monarch was fairly close to Schuylkill Valley Ambulance and covered on a lot of their calls.

Behind them several more people entered, some talking among themselves, others obviously alone, glancing around the room for any familiar faces in the group.

Lacy said hello to quite a few people before her eyes strayed back to the man from Cheltenham. He was seated beside a man from Norristown and judging by the way they glanced her way, she guessed they had said something about her. A look of recognition crossed Lou's face, and she suspected he just realized where it was he had seen her.

Just then, the instructor entered the room and everyone's attention turned to him.

Tonight was a new beginning. Lacy smiled, relaxing as the instructor made his introduction.

#

Lacy's first homework assignment caused her several sleepless nights. It hadn't been as much the assignment as the many other thoughts and emotions going through her mind. Most of them about Ryan.

She had faced the fact that she was in love with him. But that didn't make him love her. Sure he said he loved her. But was it for her similarity to his wife?

She couldn't accept being a clone of his dead wife.

She just wanted to be herself. To have people accept her the way she is. Not try to change her.

But the more she thought about it, the more she realized that was something Ryan never had done.

All he had ever done was be her friend.

Her first assignment finally seemed easier.

#

Lacy wiped the perspiration from the palms of her hands as she stepped up in front of the group. The moment of truth had arrived. If she couldn't give a five minute speech on a topic of her choice, she certainly couldn't teach a lesson.

"My name is Lacy Boyce," she started. "And my topic for tonight is what I've found out about friendship." She looked up and gave a sad grin.

"Sometimes it takes a real tragedy to find out who your friends really are. In my case, it was the death of my husband eight months ago. And since that time, I've had a great deal of time to find out a lot about friendship.

"There are those people who give you so much sympathy they smother you. They may love you and only have your best interest at heart. They may want to make everything better for you – to make everything right – but they think the only way to do that is to try and shelter you. To try and prevent you

259

from doing anything that could possibly hurt you again. They only manage to stifle you, and in the end the are hurting you more.

"Then there are those other well-meaning people who tell you things you already know, like 'Life goes on.' Or, 'The best thing you can do is keep busy. Be strong. Don't let it get you down.' They don't know what else to say. Maybe they are afraid to say anything original so they stick to the safe stand-by phrases.

"There are also those people who don't know what to say. Those people who don't seem to know how to act around you. The ones who, rather than take the chance of saying or doing the wrong thing, avoid you completely.

"And then there are those people who give true meaning to the word friend. Those people who express themselves, not in words, but in actions." She felt her tension draining as she took a long breath, feeling stronger, more confident as she continued.

"People who listen if you need to talk. Offer you a shoulder if you need to cry. Share their strength when you are feeling weak. They offer these without strings or conditions, expecting nothing in return. And they do this for as long as you need them. Both during your time of grief and thereafter. Because they are not just your friend for the moment, but for all time.

"That, to me, is the true meaning of friendship."

Some of her fellow students smiled, a few even applauded. Most just looked thoughtful. She got a good grade from her instructor. She left class that night feeling better. About herself and her future.

She may have ruined any future she and Ryan might have had together. But she felt that they, at least, could still be friends.

With the fire company election fast approaching, she could start by offering Ryan her moral support. Nominations would be in only a few days. She would nominate Ryan to keep his position as second assistant chief. She could think of no one better who could do that job.

CHAPTER TWENTY

Lacy felt Woody's dark eyes follow her across the engine room as she climbed into the back of the utility truck. The fine blonde hairs on the back of her neck seemed to stand straight on end, warning her of impending danger. She wondered why he had lagged behind after all the other members had gone home, in a hurry to see the afternoon football game.

Maybe he isn't a football fan, she thought, but knew instinctively that wasn't the case. Woody had often bragged about winning money by betting in the company's football pool. He'd be watching the game if for no other reason than to see whether his wallet was going to be thicker or thinner the following day.

Yes, he liked to gamble, she remembered. But he couldn't take losing – at anything.

She double checked that the air bottles they had filled after practice were properly closed. She was just about to climb out of the back of the truck when she heard the soft tread of footsteps coming around to the back of the vehicle.

Woody's solid frame stood below the doorway, filling the frame, making it impossible for Lacy to step down from the truck without getting closer to him than she'd like. He flashed her a wicked grin, reaching up with one hand as though to help her down.

Lacy quickly took a step back, forcing herself to sound more casual than she felt. The last thing she wanted was a confrontation with Woody. The earlier tension between them had been bad enough. It was always that way. It was as though he went out of his way to disagree. He couldn't accept that she had been appointed training officer.

He had returned to their station only months before thinking he'd be greeted like the Prodigal Son. He learned quickly that wasn't going to happen.

Quite a blow, after his self-imposed eight month alienation. But not a surprise. Most people didn't like quitters. And Woody had been that after Mike had been elected to second assistant and again after the Chief had chosen Ryan over him for that same position.

Neither was it a surprise to her when he lost his bid for that position when he ran against Ryan in last week's election. But when they read the votes, everyone could tell it had been a surprise to him. Woody could not disguise his disbelief or his anger.

Lacy stooped down, opening the tool box, pretending to check something inside. She felt the truck shift as Woody silently climbed inside. She was tempted to take out a hammer in case she needed it to fend off her unwanted companion, but she knew that wasn't her style. She had learned years ago it didn't pay to argue with him.

Besides he could have a legitimate reason for staying behind. He probably wanted to prove he was right about the air bottles not being closed correctly after they were filled. He had insisted Stan Walters, the newly appointed equipment engineer, wasn't doing his job. She suspected the bottles had been tampered with. That was why she had stayed to double check each bottle herself.

Suddenly a frightening thought occurred to her. If she was right about the tampering, it could be the reason Woody had remained behind. He could be the one doing the tampering.

Somehow that wouldn't surprise her. He didn't have too many friends left in the company. His bitter rivalry during the election campaign had alienated him from many of the members who were tired of the bickering and fighting.

She picked up the tire pressure gauge, as good an excuse as any. She was about to stand, but Woody had again come to stand so close she couldn't do it without rubbing against him.

"Excuse me," she said, as she stood, forcing herself not to flinch as their bodies touched. She knew he was trying to intimidate her, and she wasn't about to bite onto his bait. "I only have one more thing to do before I can head home."

"Checking tires is the Chief Engineer's job." He didn't move. She could smell the foul mixture of beer and bad breath on his breath. "I saw Art doing it Thursday night after he took that new guy out for driver training."

"It's everyone's job to chip in and help if they think something needs to be done."

"I'd say it looks like you don't have faith in your officers." He still wasn't stepping aside. "Of course, if you have to check up on them, maybe they shouldn't be in the position they're in."

Lacy swallowed her retort, reminding herself it was best to ignore Woody. She had done that twice already that day and it was getting more difficult each time.

"We had the truck out today. It's only fair to make sure we return it in exactly the same condition it was when we took it out. Especially since Art couldn't be here to do it himself. Lucky dog, actually had tickets to the game." She changed the subject, hoping to break the tension.

Woody finally moved just enough to allow her to pass. She was thankful he didn't follow again, but her feelings were short-lived when she realized she'd have to go back inside the truck to return the tire gauge.

She thought about leaving it out and just going straight home, but neither was that her style. She always preached returning things to their proper place so the next person could find them. She knew she had to do the same.

She went to the back of the truck and saw Woody still standing there, his hip pressed nonchalantly against the shelves, his piercing gaze directed on the doorway.

"Here, would you mind putting this back for me?" she asked, preferring asking a favor over joining him once again in the back of the truck.

He slowly walked to the back of the truck, reaching for the tire gauge, but passing it and grasping her wrist instead.

"You got it out, you should put it away." His words were laced with sarcasm as he tightened his hold, ignoring her resistance. "Isn't that what you always say?"

She allowed him to help her up, but yanked her hand out of his grasp as soon as she was inside the truck.

"What's with you today, Woody?" she snapped as she went toward the tool box to return the gauge. "Don't you think it's about time you tried to get along with me?"

He laughed dryly as he closed the back doors of the truck, then turned back to face her. "Funny, that's just what I was going to ask you." His eyes looked venomous as he took the three determined steps till he stood right in front of her.

She stood slowly, taking a deep steadying breath, unwilling to let him intimidate her. That was all he was trying to do. She was certain of it.

Her chin jutted out stubbornly as she raised her head to meet his ominous gaze. She placed her left hand on her hip, and her right hand palm up between them.

"That's close enough, Woody. It's time to stop playing games."

"Oh, I'm not playing any games," he said coarsely, his dark eyes narrowing. "I'm going to teach you a lesson."

"Woody, I'm warning you!" She pressed her hand against the solidness of his chest as he stepped still closer.

"I'm gonna show you your real place, woman," he spat. "Something that wimp of a husband of yours wasn't man enough to do. Though he wanted to. He just didn't have it in him."

Lacy felt a cross between anger and fear as she raised her left hand to join her right, trying to push the repulsive man away. She sensed the dangerous determination in him and knew she had to defuse the situation quickly.

"Woody, that's enough! Stop it now, please. If you're trying to prove you macho men are stronger than us weak women, you're right, I'll admit it."

She knew physically that was true. She'd admit that. She'd say anything, for that matter, if it would prevent him from doing what she suspected he was about to do.

"Don't pacify me, Lacy," he ground out the words through gritted teeth. "You think you're better than the rest of us. Well, I'm going to show you there's only one thing you're good for. And maybe not even that. I'll just have to find out."

She took a step backward, but he grabbed her, pulling her against him, trapping her within his arms. He turned her slightly and she could feel the metal shelves digging against her back as he used his body weight to press her against them more firmly.

She knew the only desire he felt was a desire meant to punish and hurt. If only she could get away, but he held her so tightly she couldn't even move her legs. Her arms were pinned firmly to her sides.

He lowered his face toward hers, but she turned her head before he captured her lips. His rough beard scratched the side of her face. His sickening breath gagged her.

He merely laughed, a menacing laugh as he his lips charted a new direction, pressing against the hollow of her neck.

She was so repulsed she was certain she would vomit, and wondered if that would be one way of deterring him. But she suspected even that drastic measure wouldn't work. He'd relish seeing her suffer that further humiliation.

Her mind sought a means of escape, but could find none.

"I thought that Brody would be the one to teach you your place. Maybe he did and you couldn't take it. So you ran back to us rather than let him be boss. He should'a made you stay. We didn't need you back here flaunting how great you think you are.

"Sure got Simon wrapped around your finger, don't ya," Woody whispered as he bit into her ear, actually causing pain. "He's worse than the whole lot of fools you've strung along."

"Woody, you don't know what you're doing," she pleaded. "You hate me so much you're only trying to hurt me. But don't you see, you'll only hurt yourself. This is rape."

But no amount of reasoning would get through to him. He was too filled with hatred-driven insanity. He wanted to destroy her self-respect. And more.

She had been careful to never allow herself to send any messages to the men that could have been taken as sexual. Never allowing her relationships with them to cross that invisible line. Even her courtship with Mike had been conducted with great discretion so she wouldn't lose the respect of the other men.

It was that respect Woody was hoping to destroy. If he could take that away from her she'd lose everything she'd worked so hard to accomplish. In the fire service a woman never slept her way to the top, only out the door.

Only hard work helped her achieve anything. Hard work that gained her the respect of her peers. But Woody wouldn't see that. He didn't think on those terms.

Her mind suddenly grasped the answer. She had to think on his terms. He wanted her total submission.

Perhaps he'd get exactly what he expected, only sooner.

She relaxed slightly in his arms. "Please, don't do this," she pleaded, but her words were purposely said with little veracity, so he'd think she was weakening. "I don't want the others to think less of me."

"When I'm finished you won't care what they think," he said, sliding his one hand up to her head, grasping a handful of blonde curls till she gasped.

She seductively licked her lips, seeing his near-black eyes suddenly blaze as though on fire as he watched her.

"Please, I don't want anyone to know," she whispered, biting her lip. "Maybe . . .Maybe we could just once. If . . .if you'd promise to keep it a secret."

His breathing was so rapid she thought his chest should explode. But her words caused his drunken mind a moment's hesitation. That was all she needed.

She sensed his guard was finally down. It was time to act.

With her left hand she grasped his beard and yanked. He left out a howl of pain, automatically pulling back his head to resist. At that moment she released him, giving him a push away, his own resistance accelerated by her push, throwing him off balance.

He was still blocking the way to the back of the truck, so she headed for the front, climbing over the driver's seat since it was closest to the outside door. But before she made it out of the truck, she felt strong arms grasping her around the waist.

She grasped the wheel, but felt her hold slipping as Woody pulled her back. In a last ditch effort, she reached for the tiny knob that turned on the siren. One more inch and she'd have it, but Woody was too strong.

Again she used the technique she had once learned in a class on self-defense. She jerked forward, in the same direction Woody was pulling, the unexpected motion again sending him off unbalance.

She had to act fast, knowing it was only going to take him a moment to recover. But a moment was all she needed to turn the tiny knob.

The siren blasted. She then grabbed the radio transmitter, but Woody was back and yanked it from her hands.

"You could have made this easy!" he shouted as he grabbed her hair to pull her aside so he could reach across her sprawled body to turn off the siren.

"Woody, think about it! You'll not only get kicked out of the fire company for this," she reasoned. "You'll probably end up in jail."

"You gotta prove it first," he said bitterly as he practically threw her into the back of the truck and onto the hard floor.

Lacy saw the hatred in his eyes and knew he no longer cared about his position in the fire company. Nor did he probably care that he could go to prison for his deed.

No, all he cared about was reaping his revenge on her for not conforming to what he thought she should be. He saw her as a threat that had to be thwarted.

As Woody learned over her, Lacy tried to crawl away, but Woody grabbed her again, catching the back of her blouse. She heard it tearing, but didn't care. She had to get away. But whether he threw himself on top of her, or simply lost his balance, Woody now had her pinned.

Suddenly she was filled with more fear than she had ever known before. Even within the smoky darkness of a burning building, with temperatures so high that if you stood up it would melt your helmet, she had felt more in control than she did just then. She hated this helplessness even more than she hated the man above her.

Through her fear she saw light, and felt movement, then just as quickly she felt Woody's weight lifted off of her. She didn't hesitate a moment to quickly crawl toward the back of the truck to attempt another escape. But this time she realized Woody wasn't after her. He had problems of his own.

She turned and watched in horror as the two men struggled. Woody was a big man, but the other one, whose face she could not see, was a worthy opponent. He slammed the fist of his left hand into Woody's face, then his right one into his stomach.

She heard Woody grunt, then watched him double over. The man turned slightly, reaching for Woody and slammed him against the metal shelves. She saw his face and immediately recognized her rescuer.

"Ryan!" She called out wanting to stop him. This was a side of him she had never seen before. Ryan had such a peaceful, easygoing manner. Such a gentle touch whenever he held her son. So different than the violence he now was inflicting on his adversary.

"Ryan!" she shouted again, this time jumping up and grabbing his arm. "As much as I'd like to see him beaten to a pulp, I'd like it even less to see you end up involved in the mess it'll stir up."

"My God, Lacy, what he was trying to do to you . . ." Ryan turned to her, letting Woody slide to a heap on the floor. Concern was clearly etched in his emerald eyes.

"Almost did," she corrected, holding her torn blouse closed in front of her. "But if you hadn't . . ." reality hit her like a missile hitting its target. Tears filled her eyes as she started to tremble.

"Come on," Ryan ordered, putting his arm around her and guiding her over the figure crouched on the floor, through the back doors of the truck. "Let's get you someplace where you can sit down."

They started through the doorway leading to the stairs, turning when they heard the heavy footsteps of Woody as he hurried in the opposite direction.

"There's nowhere for him to run after this," Ryan said through gritted teeth.

"Don't go after him," Lacy pleaded. "Vengeance will only turn you into the same kind of monster he is. That's what he was after. Vengeance. . .I had no idea he hated me to that extent."

"He can't get away with this," Ryan cupped her face in his hands, looking down into her face with eyes bright with anger.

She looked up and saw a red line running down from his lip. "You're bleeding," she gasped, reaching up to gently touch the wound.

"Yeah, he got a punch in," Ryan said, covering her hand with his own. "I'll be okay. But what about you?" He looked down to where she had released her blouse when she reached for his face. He saw that the buttons were torn off.

Seeing the focus of his examination Lacy felt her cheeks burn and quickly grasped the edges of her blouse closed in front of her.

"Here," Ryan said as he pulled his sweatshirt off over his head and handed it to Lacy. "Put this on while I go call the police." He started up the stairs to the office, taking two at a time.

"Wait!" she called, quickly following.

"Hey, it's okay. I doubt he'll be back."

"It wasn't that," she said, knowing Ryan thought she was afraid. And she was. But not that Woody would return. No, she figured he'd be long gone, looking for someplace to hide while he came up with a story to tell everyone. "Wait before you call the police."

"Lacy, we have to call the police after what he almost did to you," Ryan said softly. "I know what they say about what the victim is put through. But I was a witness."

"Ryan, you keep misunderstanding," she said, somehow comforted by his eagerness to stand by her. "I was going to suggest you call Chief Maxwell first. Arlen should be made aware of what happened first."

Ryan nodded. "Then we'll call the police."

They called the chief then the police. After that they waited until both would arrive. The police got there first. Lacy had just finished telling what happened when the door to the office opened and Chief Maxwell stepped inside.

"You okay, Lacy?" he asked, then when she nodded, he turned to Ryan, taking off the baseball style cap that had "Fire Chief" on the front. In spite of the cold December weather, he took a red handkerchief and wiped the perspiration from his nearly bald head. "We need to talk."

Lacy and the police officer watched as Arlen took Ryan outside the door. Then the officer turned back to Lacy.

"I suppose he's worried about this getting into the papers," she said. "It's never good for a fire company to get this kind of publicity."

The officer nodded. "We know how that can be. We go through our share of bad press every time a cop somewhere gets charged, rightfully or not, with brutality."

"People seem to think if you have one bad member, we're all bad."

"Exactly."

Ryan clenched and unclenched his fists as the chief told him the turn of events. When Woody left the station he headed straight for the chief's home just three blocks away. He arrived there just after they called, with a slightly different version of what they said had happened.

"He said that when he interrupted you and Lacy, you told him to get out so you could be alone."

"And you believe that?"

The Chief frowned. "I didn't say I believed it. I'm just telling you what he said."

"What else did he say?" Ryan asked, certain there was more to Woody's underhanded scheme.

"Said he told you the firehouse wasn't the place for that sort of thing and that you told him to mind his own business. . . Then, when he said it was his business you hit him."

"He's lying."

"Sure, I know that. You know that. But will everyone else know that?" Arlen sighed, again wiping sweat from his head, not quite meeting the other man's eyes. "It's common knowledge Lacy spent a lot of time with you while you were recovering from that broken leg."

Ryan's eyes narrowed to dark slits. "And you believe everything you hear?"

"No, I don't! I'm saying we nail Woody. I just didn't want to upset Lacy till I found out if you have a way to substantiate your story."

Ryan nodded. "As a matter of fact, I do. I left practice with the rest of the guys. I was supposed to go over to the Shelby's to watch the game. I was almost there when I remembered I was supposed to pick up the pizza. I stopped to order, then figured while I had a minute I'd come back here and check the air bottles."

Ryan looked up. "You know the problems we've had lately with bottles being only part full when we go to use them. Some have been quick to blame Stan. I was going to double check they were full and closed when we left them today."

"Okay, so the pizza place can put you there when you ordered the pizzas. Anything else?"

"When I pulled up to the station there were a couple of kids outside the bay door trying to look in. I asked them what was up and they said they heard a siren coming from inside. They were curious where it was coming from, and were busy trying to assure me they hadn't touched anything."

"Neighborhood kids?"

Ryan nodded. "Yeah, a couple of the ones who play basketball over in the church parking lot. I'm sure we can find them if we have to."

The Chief smiled. "Then we can go back in there and tell the police."

They agreed and stepped back into the office.

When Lacy heard Woody's tale she was furious. The police officer assured her that with the information Ryan had provided it would be easy to refute Woody's version of what happened. Their biggest concern would be the scandal if his story hit the newspaper.

By the time the ordeal was over, Lacy wasn't sure she was more upset over Woody's attack or the possibility that the fire company would receive adverse publicity. Then suddenly she realized the most upsetting thing of all. Sometime her mother would undoubtedly find out about what happened.

She had been totally against Lacy returning to the fire company, even as training officer, rarely responding to emergency calls. If she found out what happened today, she'd be able to add one more reason to her list of reasons why Lacy shouldn't be a firefighter.

"You look like you could use some rest," Ryan said as he walked her to her car. "It's been a tough day for you."

"And the worst is yet to come," she said. "I never thought I was a coward but I don't want to face my mother."

Ryan smiled, suspecting he understood. For a long time he'd known Lacy's mother had not approved of her life. "You could postpone it till later. After you have the chance to talk to your father."

"They're together on Sunday so I won't have a chance to get him alone today."

"So, why not just avoid them both. Go get Mikie ready and I'll be by as soon as I pick up the pizzas. You can come along over to your Aunt's and watch the game."

"Your pizzas are probably cold already."

"So," he shrugged. "A few more minutes won't make any difference then, will it?"

"I guess not," Lacy replied, smiling for the first time since she had found herself alone with Woody. "Thanks, Ryan. For everything."

#

When she pulled up at her house, they spotted a familiar black Bronco parked in her parents' driveway. Barry was on the porch talking to her father.

"I wonder what he's doing here?" She hesitated, seeing her father's thunderous expression. She had a fair idea she knew why.

Getting out of the car, she walked toward the porch.

"Are you okay, Lacy?" her father asked in concern.

"Yeah, Dad. I'm fine. I see, as usual, bad news travels fast." He flashed Barry an icy look.

"Lacy, can we talk?" Barry asked as he glanced toward her father.

"I'll leave you two alone." He looked back at Lacy. "We'll talk when you're ready."

"It takes a lot of nerve for you to come here and tell my father what happened!" she spat. "Besides how did you find out so quickly?"

Barry shook his head, his expression weary as he glanced toward the door. "Let's walk."

Yes, Lacy thought, I don't want my mother hearing this. Least not yet.

While they walked, Barry told her that Woody had stopped by his apartment right after he left Arlen.

"He tried to feed me the same cock-n-bull story he must have given the chief," Barry said, surprising her. "I told him right out I didn't believe him."

Lacy was puzzled, but she waited as her companion took a breath and continued.

"Woody and I and Mike had once been friends, Lacy. Drinking buddies. Only somewhere along the way our friendship got totally confused. I don't know. We were more drinkers than buddies."

"What does that have to do with what happened today?"

"Woody's a drunk, Lacy. He's not thinking straight."

"Should that excuse him?"

"No, he should have the book thrown at him. That doesn't mean I don't understand. I haven't always been the sober fellow you see today."

270

Lacy looked up at her companion, realizing he was trying to tell her something.

"I quit drinking a short time after Mike's accident. I wasn't given a whole lot of choice. Ryan cornered me one day. Said he was going to be the next first assistant if I didn't get my act together. He said a lot of other things, too. And most of them made sense. But I'll admit, most of all I didn't want to lose the rank."

That was something that didn't surprise Lacy. Losing rank rarely came easy to any of them. It was a matter of ego. They'd give it up before they let someone take if from them.

"Becoming assistant chief was the only thing I did first. . ." he continued. "Before Mike. It was tough living in his shadow. I guess deep down, I resented him. When he started dating you, I saw my chance. All his attention was on you."

Lacy didn't want to hear this. It was all over. A dead issue. All it did was dredge up unhappy memories.

"Why don't you just get to the point? I don't need a trip down memory lane."

He flinched at her bitter words.

"I'm sorry," she said as tears filled her blue eyes. "I just don't need to remember how Mike started dating me. Now that I know the truth it's really irrelevant."

"Listen, Lacy. I know you've been through enough pain over all that. But maybe what I'm saying will help you understand. When I became assistant and Mike didn't, it was because he didn't try. He even told me so."

"He was too concerned with putting up a smoke screen so no one would think he was the father of Rose's child."

"Sure, Lacy, that's exactly what he did. And you know what? It backfired."

"You got assistant chief and he couldn't stand that."

Barry laughed. "Right. And then one day he thanked me. When he asked me to be his best man. He said if he'd have known what I was up to instead of spending all his time chasing after you, he'd have probably taken his chances with Rose, rather than see me get assistant before him."

"He wasn't a very nice man, was he, Barry?" She acknowledged grimly.

"And you have a very bad habit of interrupting. One thing I still find hard to take about you. But you're starting to win me over."

She looked stunned with disbelief, unable to believe his words. Nor his next statement.

"Lacy, Mike told me he was glad he never found out. Said he might never have gotten to see the part of you that he fell in love with. Might never have asked you to marry him. And he said, that would have been his loss. Then he said the way he had it figured, he was still ahead."

Tears filled Lacy's eyes. She knew her marriage may never have stood the test of time. But she now knew her husband had loved her. And if Mike could, just maybe someone else could love her, too.

"Thank you, Barry."

"Anytime. Now, about Woody. . ." He stared into her face. "The lousy bum's got a problem. He needs help, Lacy. But if you let him off the hook, he'll never get that help."

"Well, Barry, I should tell you then. He's not getting off the hook. The police are looking for him now."

"Then I guess my coming here didn't make a difference after all."

"Oh, you're wrong there. It made a big difference."

CHAPTER TWENTY-ONE

Lacy sat with Mikie on her lap, Ryan at her side, all their concentration centered on the barrel-chested man in the center of the room wearing a red suit trimmed in white fur. He reached into his giant bag of goodies for yet another prize for one of the many children scattered around him.

Ryan smiled down at the child on Lacy's lap as he clutched the soft furry stuffed dalmatian, a toy they knew had been chosen with great care. It had been only a week earlier that the Mulhollands had purchased a Dalmatian pup and the picture of puppy and child on the floor playing was still fresh in their minds.

The man's attention turned to the woman beside him. He'd been happier in the last two weeks than he remembered being in a very long time. They had finally come to terms with their problems, in no small part due to hours of talking. Of finally opening up to each other about so many of the things that had happened in their past. The good memories and the unhappiness that sometimes still haunted them.

And now, new memories. Like those when they had been decorating the Christmas tree together in Ryan's living room, using a hodgepodge of decorations her mother had passed down to her, that she'd insisted they use on his tree. Ryan had suddenly pulled out some mistletoe and held it above her head. His emerald eyes looked mischievous at first, then hesitant as he slowly leaned closer, giving her the opportunity to refuse.

But she hadn't. Instead, she'd taken him by the front of his shirt and pulled him closer, speeding up the process. The kiss was sweet, but all too short as he pulled away, looking intently down into her beautiful, upturned face.

"Some things shouldn't be rushed," he whispered.

"And some things have taken long enough," she replied with an impish smile lighting her blue eyes. "You once admitted you love me, Ryan. I'd like to make certain it's still true."

He smiled. "Why?"

"Because I hate rejection."

"Did that kiss give the impression you'd be rejected?"

"I'm not sure," she teased, taking the mistletoe from his hand and holding it above his head this time. "Maybe we should try again and find out."

When there was only a fraction of distance between their lips she whispered the words Ryan had longed to hear.

"I love you."

"Thank you God," he whispered in reply, then closed the gap between them.

During the weeks that followed they'd shared even more. Ryan spoke with her of his deep faith in God. A faith she had once shared, but admittedly had drifted from after the death of her husband. At first it had felt awkward, but they had even prayed together, asking God for a new beginning. They had asked God for a second chance with Him and with their own relationship.

Lacy looked over and met his gaze, her smiling, blue eyes warm with the promise of tomorrow. A world of hopes and dreams had finally opened up to them.

"Look at that," Lacy whispered as she broke his gaze, spotting a scene just beyond them.

Barry Carlisle had just sat in the vacant chair beside a silent dark-haired girl. The child had looked so forlorn sitting there all alone, but her eyes seemed to light as he leaned close and said something to her.

"What do you think?" Lacy asked.

Ryan smiled, taking her hand. "I think we're not the only ones who have been doing a lot of soul-searching lately. I even invited Barry to church on Sunday and he didn't say no. It's a start."

She nodded, hoping he would go. Since that awful day Woody had attacked her, she and Barry had more than one chance to speak. He'd been more open than ever about some of his feelings.

She remembered one thing in particular he said. "Sometimes your actions have to be based, not on what you know is, but on what you know might be." At the time, she thought he had been trying to pass along some hidden message about women in the fire service.

Now she suspected it was much more. There was just as much a chance that Amy was his child as there was she'd been fathered by Mike or Woody. Barry was basing his actions on what might be.

"Do you think we'll ever find out for sure?" Lacy asked, knowing the knowledge no longer had the ability to hurt her.

Ryan shook his head. "I doubt that it matters to him. She's a child who needs a father figure. One who'll stick around. Someone who's interested in having her around, not getting her out of the picture so they can be alone with her mother."

Lacy frowned, her eyes turning to Rose as she stood extremely close to the man with whom she was talking. Would she ever change? she mused. "From what my mother says, Rose was just like Amy once. Her mother had men around all the time. And their visits weren't exactly meant to include children."

"It's a vicious cycle, like so many things," Ryan said. "But cycles can be broken."

His words were shattered as pagers throughout the room went off simultaneously. Then for a second all was quiet, except for the voice that seemed to fill the room from every conceivable corner.

Not on Christmas Eve, Lacy thought. *Please let it be a false alarm, at worst maybe a dumpster or a trash fire.*

But the worst of their fears was quickly confirmed as the dispatcher advised them it was a structure fire and gave them the address.

Lacy watched as Ryan hurried to the door, her own heart pounding, her breathing quickening. She clutched her son tightly, loving him, but her thoughts were somewhere else.

"I'll take over here if you like," her mother said, breaking into her thoughts as she lifted Mikie out of her lap.

Lacy looked up at her mother in puzzlement.

"It's Christmas Eve, and someone's house is on fire. They could be losing everything they own," her mother said. "We've got everything under control here."

Licking her lips, Lacy looked into her mother's bright blue eyes, knowing what she was saying, and knowing what it cost her to say it. Then she looked at her son.

"He's not likely to be emotionally scarred because his parent is a firefighter." Lois said softly. "His mother turned out just fine. And Lord knows how many holidays and other occasions her father rushed off to fight a fire."

At mention of her father, they both turned to the man in red. He had stood when the tones went off, but now was standing frozen in his spot as over thirty-five sets of eyes stared up at him.

"Tell Chief Maxwell, I said good luck," Santa said, giving Lacy a thumbs-up as she headed toward the door. "I'll see him later. . .If he was a good boy this year."

"Will do," she shouted as she hurried to join the other members slipping into their gear. The engines of the trucks were already roaring to life, exhaust fumes filling the room. Adrenaline filling their bodies.

Lacy wasted no time slipping into the bunker pants, with boots already attached for ease and speed in dressing. She slipped an arm into her heavy coat, then grabbed her helmet almost simultaneously, racing toward the last truck as she slipped in her other arm.

She jumped into the equipment truck just as it was about to pull out of the station.

"Glad to have you on board," Jack said, glancing back to her, just before he shifted the gears of the old truck and pulled out onto the street.

Her gear was securely in place when they arrived. She had donned one of the air packs mounted in the truck as they made their way toward the scene. When she jumped out of the truck she was ready for her orders.

Familiar voices issued orders to those already starting their attack, the loud speakers making them heard above the din of truck engines and shouting spectators. Heavy smoke billowed from the front windows of the lower floor, but the fire was moving fast. They had to be faster.

A figure in a white helmet approached them giving more orders. Lacy saw it was Ryan. He tapped each on the shoulder then told them what they were to do.

"Take the two and a half off Engine Six and enter in the rear," he said to two other men who had ridden with them in the equipment truck.

He paused only a fraction of a second as his frown met Lacy's. "There are victims inside – kids."

She nodded, knowing he was giving her the chance to refuse. It was her first time at a serious call since returning. But she had a job to do. "I'm packed and ready to go. Just give me a partner?"

"You got him," Ryan replied, radioing to tell the Chief that all personnel were accounted for and given orders, adding that a second team was ready to go inside on search and rescue. He was part of that team.

As Lacy followed Ryan to Ladder Thirteen, she wondered if going inside with her had been his original intention, or if he was trying to look after her. As they ascended the ladder, she dismissed the thought. This wasn't the time for idle curiosity. All concentration had to be focused on the job at hand.

They entered through an upstairs window, making their way on their hands and knees through the a mist of smoke and intense heat. Ryan led, she followed, he took the right side of the room, she the left. It was a matter of teamwork now. They were not two people in love with one another. They weren't even friends. They were partners. In the truest sense of the word. Because they depended on each other for their life.

The roar of the fire below them was deafening as they made their way to the closed door, carefully opening it and entering the hall where the smoke was thicker, the heat more intense. Lacy followed to the left, because that was the way they had it planned, not because she could see him turn. A person couldn't see their hand in front of their face in the dense smoke. They could only depend on the fact their partner would not make a change in direction without letting them know, and that they would do the same.

There was a voice coming over Ryan's radio. He stopped and she almost bumped into him. He turned giving her the thumbs-up. "They've got the kids," he shouted, his voice muffled through mask covering his face.

She turned around heading back the way they had come, this time Ryan following. It would be easy to lose their way. She had to judge the distance of how far they had come since entering the hall through the bedroom door. She ran her gloved hand along the edge of the wall until she felt a slight indentation to the right. The door.

She turned, tapping Ryan on the shoulder then motioning she was making a change in direction. They went right, back into the room, heading straight to where they saw faint light coming through the window.

Once outside, they saw the Snorkel just lowering two firefighters and two children to the ground. Though they were hugging the children close, it seemed the kids were alive.

When she and Ryan made it to the ground, they heard excitement coming from the small group who had gathered a short distance away from the children.

"They're okay," the message passed from one firefighter to the next.

As she removed her face mask, Lacy turned to Ryan and smiled. "I'd say they're a lucky pair."

Ryan sighed, nodding his head in agreement.

They heard Barry's voice over the speaker telling them the fire had been knocked down in the living room. All that was left now was finding hot spots, then using giant fans to get the heavy smoke out of the building.

"Tell me something, Chief," she turned to ask what had previously been on her mind. "You have any special reason for being my partner in there?"

"Two very special reasons," he replied, looking down at her, his eyes serious. "One, Arlen wanted another team inside for search and rescue. Since you and I were the only two people left who weren't occupied with another job, not to mention already in packs and ready to go, it was us."

"You said two reasons," she noted when he didn't say more.

This time he smiled. "If you insist – but don't let it go to your pretty little head – because I couldn't think of anyone I'd rather have had inside there watching my backside."

Her smile grew wider as she leaned back for a closer look at his backside. "What about now that we're outside?"

He threw back his head and laughed. "That is hardly professional behavior for a firefighter," he scolded. "What would your students think about that?"

"A few might agree with me," she winked. "We had over a dozen females in our last Firefighter One class."

"No problem with me. I'll work with them anytime. Especially since I know they're being trained by the best."

"Maybe someday everyone will feel like you." Lacy sighed easing her air pack off her shoulders.

"Give it time, Lacy," he replied. "If those women in your class turn out to be anything like you, it won't be too long before some of the hard core cases change their mind."

"Thanks, Chief," she replied with a wink. "I'll team up with you again any day."

"I hope you mean that," he whispered. "I really do."

Just then they saw the familiar red beacon atop her father's Chief's car as he rounded the corner and pulled in behind the equipment truck. They smiled when they saw him get out of the car still wearing his red Santa suit.

"Everything under control here?" he asked. "I heard they got everyone out."

Ryan nodded. "Looks like things are wrapping up. We were lucky this time. It could have been worse."

"Sure could have," Rainy said as she approached from behind them. She was wearing her fire police hat, orange vest and badge, and a smile wide enough to light the entire town.

"So what's on your mind?" Carl looked suspiciously at his sister. "I know that look."

Rainy's chin raised as she practically danced in front of them. "I just found out the kids who were trapped inside were taking a nap when the smoke detector woke them. They were sleeping with their door closed because they learned that from the fire safety program we put on in school. And they knew what else to do because of what we taught them!"

Lacy thought her aunt looked even happier than when she received her award. She suspected she was.

"Their parents were resting, too, since they were planning on having some relatives in tonight for Christmas Eve." Rainy's smile turned to a frown. "They got out because their bedroom was in the back and their window opened onto a porch roof. They were able to climb out. They've already said they think they'll change the sleeping arrangements after they're able to move in again."

"Any ideas what started it?" Carl asked.

Again Rainy frowned. "They think the tree. Unfortunately the parents said they were too busy getting ready for Christmas to read the newsletter we put out with Holiday safety tips on how to prevent a fire."

"It's because of you the kids are alive," Lacy said giving her aunt a hug.

"Because of us all." Rainy acknowledged modestly. "But we have to start working twice as hard to reach people. If they aren't going to read the information we give them, we'll have to see about another way of reaching them." They could see that already the red-haired fire safety officer's mind was at work. "Maybe it's time to talk to you about the fire escape trailer I saw at the convention," Rainy added. "You won't believe all the fire safety lessons we could teach with a trailer like that. Now, if we can approach the Borough Council to come up with the money. . .And, of course, there's no time like the present to begin selling the council on a residential sprinkler code. I know, I know," she continued. "Good things don't happen over night. But we have to strike while it's on everyone's minds."

Carl shook his head. "Well, looks like we're going to have our work cut out for us."

"By the way, big brother." Rainy turned back to him. "Since you're already in character, why not get your beard and give this family a little cheer. I think they need it, all things considered. Got any presents left?"

"That reminds me." Carl turned back to Lacy. "We did have some presents left. One in particular, marked for you." He reached inside the front seat of his car and pulled out a package along with his beard. The package he handed to Lacy before following his sister in the direction of the family who had just had the fire.

Lacy looked at the large square box wrapped in brightly colored paper. She then turned to Ryan, suspecting he had something to do with the gift.

"Open it."

The card had instructions to be opened first. She did and tears made her eyes bright as she read.

I feel sorry for those in this world who have never loved. Who have been unable to open their hearts to another. I feel lucky knowing I have been able to love, not once, but twice in my life. Twice blessed with the fortune those people may never have.

I want to have a permanent place in your life and you in mine. Because life is what we both still have. And as long as we have that, there is still room to love.

I want to be your husband. I want to be a father to your son. Not to replace Mike, but to do what he no longer can do.

I will never expect you to forget him, nor will I allow Mikie to forget him. Mike is a part of both of you. As Norma and Michelle are part of me. I know you understand that now. And it is no longer a threat to our happiness. To our future.

What happened in the past has made us the people we are today. What we do today, will make us into the people we will be tomorrow. Let me be a part of each today that will mold our tomorrow.

With soot-covered fingers Ryan wiped a tear that was slowly rolling down Lacy's cheek, smiling when he saw the dark smudges left by his fingerprints. His brand, as he wanted his ring to brand her as his own. But before he could do that, he had to be sure she really did understand that the past was no longer a threat between them.

She slowly tore the colored paper from the package already knowing what she was going to say. She bit her lip when she saw the familiar china doll. Then she saw the small locket hanging around the dolls neck. There were words engraved on the tiny gold locket. Looking closer she read, *'Forever Loved, Nere Forgotten.'*

More tears flowed as she read the words, remembering how much pain they had once caused her. But now she suspected Ryan meant them to have new meaning. She opened the locket and saw a large wedding band laying on a bed of black velvet, too large to fit a woman's finger.

Lifting her left hand she understood the meaning of his gift. It was a gift for him as much as for her. Slipping the gold wedding band from her finger she laid in on the velvet bed with his larger one then closed the locket.

"I have another gift for you," he whispered, pulling her gently against him. "It's at home under the tree."

The tree she had helped him decorate. The one they had chosen together, having spent hours at the local tree farm trying to find just the right one. Then after decorating they had stood in front of it and professed their love.

"Do I have to wait until tomorrow?"

"No, Lacy, we don't have to wait another day."

"Wait!" She pushed out of his arms, then looked up to see worry enter his green eyes. "Look at me! I'm a sorry sight. And the man I love has just proposed to me."

Relief filled Ryan's eyes as he laughed at her. "It's fitting you look like this. The way you did the very first time I saw you. The day I decided my future was going to be in this town."

"Put like that, I don't feel so unattractive," she teased.

"Anything but." His head lowered until their lips touched, their kiss deepening.

"Good grief, Howard." They heard a woman's loud voice and realized they had an audience. "Look at those two firefighters. That's disgusting."

Lacy felt her cheeks burn as Ryan stepped back and turned to face the older couple who had been watching their display.

"The most beautiful firefighter here tonight has just agreed to be my bride," he shouted. "I don't call that at all disgusting."

The woman shook her head and smiled. While her husband took off his knit hat and scratched his head. "What's this world coming to, Milly? Women firefighters."

The woman flashed her husband a stern look. "Looks to me like it's becoming a right nice place, you old coot. Back to what it used to be when a woman stood beside her man during feast and famine, during war and peace. . ." the woman's voice faded as she continued chatting as they strolled along, leaving Lacy and Ryan smiling after them.

EPILOGUE

Lacy waited as Ryan put the last of her belongings into the back of her car. His Toyota was already full. As was her father's pick-up truck. They were ready to go. Ready to go home. Their new home.

Shortly after they became engaged, they'd decided it would be nice to make a fresh start and build a house of their own. For weeks after that they searched for just the right location, finding a beautifully wooded lot just a few miles on the other side of town.

They looked at pictures and decided which style house they wanted, a two-story colonial with plenty of room for children, because they both knew they wanted more children. They didn't want Mikie to be an only child as they both had been.

It was Rainy who insisted they remember residential sprinklers, so they had been included when they drew up their plans. The perfect opportunity to practice what they preached and in the end they didn't cost any more than the carpeting.

Yes, they were ready to go.

Almost ready, Lacy thought.

"Do you mind going ahead with Mikie?" She handed the squirming child in her arms to her new husband. "I'll follow soon."

Without waiting for his reply, she turned and headed back into the house. To the kitchen where Mikie and her mother had moments before said their goodbyes.

She opened the door, preparing herself for what she expected to find. The reason her mother had chosen not to watch them as they drove away.

"Mom, I. . ." She stepped into the room, pausing as she saw her mother sitting at the table hunched over a notebook.

"Oh, you haven't gone," Lois said, her face turning a rosy hue. "I guess you missed this after all."

Lacy realized the notebook her mother had been reading was hers. "My instructor's training notebook," she said as she came further into the room, looking more closely at the chapter's heading. *Instructional Methodology.*

Lois smiled. "I gave Rainy a call the other day."

Lacy's eyebrows raised as she waited for her mother to continue.

"I wanted to find out if she needed any help with her fire safety programs," Lois continued. "She said she certainly did. Especially after getting that award."

Lacy's expression turned grim as she thought about the aftereffects of her aunt receiving her award. Perhaps she should have thought of that when Ryan suggested they submit her name. There would always be those members who couldn't accept it when someone else received recognition. Even when it was deserved.

"It's the nature of the beast," Lacy said grimly. "There's a lot of egos in the emergency service."

"And a little of the green-eyed monster thrown in for good measure," her mother stated. "Well, I thought she deserved that award. After I watched what she did, I realized my sister-in-law's got the right idea."

"And you want to help," Lacy said proudly, so happy to see her mother showing an interest in what they did. Though it was in a different direction than firefighting, she'd still be saving lives.

"It seems I'm going to be having a little more time on my hands," Lois said, her sapphire eyes sparkling with unshed tears. "And I can certainly put it to better use than. . ." She sniffled, lifting up her chin. "than sitting here and crying."

Lacy felt her own eyes filling with tears. She'd expected to find her mother crying as she'd done at so many other turning points in her life. Her first day at school. Her first week at camp. Her first date. Her wedding. Crying not because she was happy, but because of what she thought she was losing.

Her mother finally realized she wasn't losing anything.

"You sure you're not going to be too busy to watch your grandson sometimes?"

"I'll have plenty of time for everything."

Carl entered as if on cue. "Hope you have some left for me." he asked, a giant smile lighting his round face.

Lacy watched her mother turn back to her father. "Always for you."

"Any time, any place?" he asked, suggestively.

If possible her mother's eyes were brighter than before. Her cheeks were definitely redder. But she was indeed smiling.

"I guess I'll be going," Lacy said, feeling like the proverbial fifth wheel.

"Yes, you do that," her father said, winking at her. "I'll be along with the rest of your things later. . .Much later."

"Carl," her mother scolded. "What are you up to now?"

"Something nice, I promise," he replied as Lacy escaped through the door.

She was smiling as she headed through the hall. Her parents were definitely not acting as they normally did, she thought. Or, perhaps it's just they never acted that way with her around. In fact, she suspected she wouldn't have to worry so much about her mother adjusting to her leaving this time.

Just then, she heard hearty laughter coming from the kitchen.

No, I won't have to worry this time.

There was a bounce to her step as she went out the door. Everything was going to be all right. With a wide smile she saw that her husband and son had waited for her. Yes, everything *was* going to be all right. They were going home. Home together.

Dear Friends,

I want to take a moment to thank you for purchasing my novel *Into the Flames*. I hope you enjoyed reading it as much as I enjoyed writing it. It certainly was a labor of love. If you haven't guessed by now, I have a special place in my heart for the emergency service. In particular, for those people who stubbornly persist in their quest to teach as many people as possible to live safer lives.

However, no matter how hard we try, some burns and injuries still happen. That is why I am donating 50% of my profits from this book to SafeKids.org, an international organization dedicated to child safety. I have known the organization for many years and can promise that the money raised from the sale of this book will be put to good use.

I also wanted to let you know some of the characters of this novel will live on in future novels. In fact, I'm in the process of starting Annie's story. It should be ready for a Christmas release so add it to your wish list. The title will be *Rescued Hearts*. And that is the only clue I can give you about it.

Once again, thank you for choosing my book. May your life be filled with God's blessings.

Pam Garlick